'Why Are You Marrying Her, Nick?'

Conscious of his sustained stare she made to turn away, but he moved at the same time—unintentionally, she felt sure—and they collided. His hands went out to steady her and she felt herself quivering at the contact, realising with a little shock of disbelief that the past seven years had dissolved into nothing. They stared into one another's eyes for a long, electric moment before, bending his dark head, he kissed her hard on the lips. She twisted away, color flooding into her face, anger in her eyes.

'How could you!' she cried. 'You're engaged to be married! Supposing she had walked in?'

ANNE HAMPSON
currently makes her home in England, but this top romance author has traveled and lived all over the world. This variety of experience is reflected in her books, which present the ever-changing face of romance as it is found wherever people fall in love.

Dear Reader:

I'd like to take this opportunity to thank you for all your support and encouragement of Silhouette Romances.

Many of you write in regularly, telling us what you like best about Silhouette, which authors are your favorites. This is a tremendous help to us as we strive to publish the best contemporary romances possible.

All the romances from Silhouette Books are for you, so enjoy this book and the many stories to come. I hope you'll continue to share your thoughts with us, and invite you to write to us at the address below:

Karen Solem
Editor-in-Chief
Silhouette Books
P.O. Box 769
New York, N.Y. 10019

ANNE HAMPSON
There Must Be Showers

Silhouette *Romance*

Published by Silhouette Books New York

America's Publisher of Contemporary Romance

SILHOUETTE BOOKS, a Division of Simon & Schuster, Inc.
1230 Avenue of the Americas, New York, N.Y. 10020

ISBN: 0-671-57250-4

First Silhouette Books printing October, 1983

10 9 8 7 6 5 4 3 2 1

Map by Ray Lundgren

America's Publisher of Contemporary Romance

Printed in the U.S.A.

BC91

GLOUCESTER,
WORCESTER
AND WARWICK

Places in *italics* are fictitious.

Chapter One

Shelley Scott drew a satisfied breath and decided this was about the best thing she had ever done in her four years as an interior designer.

'It's perfection, Miss Scott!'

'You're pleased?'

'Pleased! I'm enthralled with my new home!' Sarah Weston turned to smile at her fiancé. 'David, darling, I'm so glad you engaged Miss Scott's firm to make a lovely home for us.'

David turned to the girl who was by now used to praise of this kind. His eyes focussed on her face and he thought it was even more beautiful than that of his fiancée. The smooth alabaster skin, the high cheekbones and widely spaced eyes, the high forehead portraying intelligence and the golden-bronze hair above it, waving slightly so that there was a quiff at the front which seemed to match the up-curling ends that reached almost to her delicately-sloping shoulders. Shame she was not married, he mused, for some man was missing out all right.

'We're inviting you to our wedding,' said Sarah. 'You'll come, won't you?'

Shelley nodded at once. From the first she had taken to this young couple and she was delighted at the idea of being a guest at their wedding. She would never have attended a wedding at one time—for it would remind her too poignantly of her own. But it was six years ago now—no, almost seven! How time did fly! She had recovered totally, she assured herself even while the image of her handsome husband would rise before her, and she would see that smile, the warmth in his eyes, the tenderness, the love. . . .

So dark, he was, but then his mother was Greek, a lovely looking woman who had married into the English nobility, hence the perfection of her son's aristocratic features; he had all the good breeding of his father plus the classical background of the Greeks . . . and he was also possessed of their ardent nature.

'Well, we must be getting along, Miss Scott.' David's quiet voice brought Shelley from her musings and she nodded her head.

'I must be off, too,' she said and it seemed that David just had to ask, 'You have a date?'

'Yes, with my boss.'

'Oh . . . you and he are—'

'Just good friends,' broke in Shelley with a laugh. 'We often discuss business over a pleasant dinner.'

'He's married already?' from Sarah curiously and Shelley shook her head.

'A confirmed bachelor,' she returned and picked up her handbag from the deep armchair where she had dropped it on entering the luxury London flat twenty minutes earlier. She had had this final appointment with the engaged couple, just to see if all was to their liking. 'Stephen and I are fortunate in that we haven't had any complications in our relationship.' She spoke in a quiet yet clear voice which held a musical quality which added to her attractions.

'You mean—you're able to maintain a platonic relationship?'

She smiled. David had recently become rather concerned about her, she thought.

'That's right. We couldn't have worked together like we do if we'd allowed emotion to rear its—head.'

'You were going to say its "ugly" head,' cut in Sarah with a sudden frown. 'Have you never been in love, Miss Scott?'

'Once . . . or perhaps twice,' she mused and she was now thinking of someone other than the man she had married. Paul, her very first boyfriend who had later been the cause of the divorce. . . .

'Twice? But you haven't yet met the right one, obviously.'

Shelley said nothing. She often told herself that she had not yet met the right one. But then, once again, Nick's face would appear before her mental vision.

'Goodbye, Miss Scott.' David was at the door, a hand resting on his fiancée's shoulder. 'We'll see you at the wedding.'

Shelley let herself into the hall of the attractive mews house which nestled in a little backwater, away from the hustle and bustle of the city and yet was so very convenient for Shelley's office. Not that she spent much of her time there; she was more often on the site of her activities, planning, drawing numerous sketches and then supervising the various people who were working from those sketches.

Somehow, she was feeling depressed today, and was glad, therefore, that she and Stephen were to dine out—at the Ritz. Stephen knew all the details of the breakup of her marriage; he was the only one—apart from those personally involved—who was in possession of the facts. The facts . . . Stephen knew the *real* facts whereas Nickolas and his mother and sister knew only what *appeared* to be the facts.

'Oh well,' she was saying to Stephen a few hours later, 'it's all in the past. And if Nick had really loved me he'd have listened to my explanation.'

She didn't know just how or why the conversation had drifted from business to the very private affair of her divorce.

'You ought to look around for someone else.' Stephen, thirty-five and good-looking in a rugged sort of way, had mixed feelings about his Number One assistant as he called her. For although he felt she deserved happiness with a charming partner, he knew that if she did marry then she would most likely give up her job and raise a family.

He did not like to think how he would get along without her uncanny flair for colour-combinations, her instinctive knowledge of what particular type of furniture would suit a particular type and shape of room. Stephen reckoned that half the business that came to him was on account of the reputation which Shelley had built for herself since she had come to him, a green girl, just over four years ago. She had been floundering before then, getting over the traumatic experience of her divorce and at the same time trying vainly to settle into a job. Nothing seemed to be just what she wanted—and, thought Stephen, the decision of her mother and her new husband to go and live in Spain did not help.

'You do not look around,' she said at length. 'The right one comes—or he doesn't. It's fate and nothing more nor less.'

'You're very philosophical about it all.' A small pause and then, 'You never hear anything about your ex-husband?'

'No, nothing. I don't even know if he's still in England. I know he had expectations in Greece in the form of a large estate on the island of Corfu. His mother's sister had always said that her property was to go to Nick.'

'But Nick was very English, you said.'

'He was, yes. . . .' Her voice trailed to silence as she recalled her husband's passionate nature . . . inherited from his mother, of course. And his temper! Shelley would never ever forget the terror of that last scene when he had threatened to strangle her.

'His mother's still here?'

Shelley nodded her head.

'She lives in the ancestral home left to her by her husband—Nick's father—for life. On her death it comes to both Nick and Anna, so it might have to be sold.'

'You never think of visiting his mother?' Stephen lifted his wineglass to his lips and studied Shelley from above the rim. The candlelight was in her hair, and it also accentuated the alabaster skin, lending it a peach bloom sheen that was very alluring. Not for the first time Stephen wondered if the time would come when he would suddenly find himself in love with her.

'No, never. She didn't say much at the time, and I don't think she hates me, but she never tried to bring Nick and me together again.'

He looked at her strangely.

'You believe that was possible?'

She paused in thought before shaking her head.

'No,' she admitted and with an unconscious little sigh. 'No, there wasn't any hope after—after that awful scene.'

'Don't think about it,' advised Stephen in soothing tones. 'He was a brute—'

'He had some sort of an excuse,' she broke in, but weakly.

'No excuse! You were his young bride and he should have known you'd never be unfaithful!'

Shelley shrugged her shoulders. It was marvellous, she thought, how one managed to get over these things. 'Time heals' was a truism indeed.

'It's all water under the bridge now,' she returned indifferently. 'It was fate that Nick and I weren't meant to end our days together.'

'You scarcely began from what you've told me.'

'We had seven months together.'

He observed her with a keen look.

'And you were happy?'

'Deliriously so.'

'Did he not show this jealousy before—before the business with your former boyfriend, I mean?'

'He was always jealous, but of course he had no real cause to be . . . until. . . .'

'Do you ever see this Paul— But no, or you'd have told me, wouldn't you?' Stephen picked up the basket containing crusty rolls and offered it to her. Absently she took one and then realised there were nicer things to eat than bread. She put it on her plate and looked across at her companion.

'I hope I never set eyes on Paul again as long as I live,' was her fervent reply at last. 'I wish I'd never met him in the first place.' She took butter, again absently, and broke the roll.

'Let's change the subject,' suggested Stephen, glancing around and mentally counting the celebrities—two titled men, a film star and her latest boyfriend and a publisher entertaining a couple of his authors. He transferred his attention to Shelley, who had never used her married name —in fact, Stephen didn't even know what it was. He had never asked her and she had never vouchsafed the information. She smiled at him across the candlelit table and he responded. Her face was pale and her eyes a little sad; her hair in the subdued light seemed to become the warm colour of tawny brown highlighted with pure gold.

'Yes, let's,' she agreed and then asked, 'What shall we talk about?'

'I've had two potential clients in today.'

'You have?' Shelley was interested. 'Anyone famous?'

'Not that I know of. The first lady seemed to be wanting to get the house she's just bought ready for the return of her husband from Nigeria where he is at present working for an oil company.'

'It's a house, then, not a flat?'

'Both are houses. The second was a man who's bought a manor house in the Cotswolds and he wants it completely renovated inside. He's having work done outside, I believe, but of course that's not in our line.' He paused a moment and then, 'I want you to take it over completely because it sounds just your particular mark—'

'A manor house in the Cotswolds?' she broke in and her companion noticed a strange expression cross her face. 'Whereabouts?'

'A place called Allswick—a real beauty spot; I know it well. The house is called Allswick Manor and it's Tudor. . . .' His voice trailed and he was frowning slightly now. 'Is something wrong?'

She shook her head, a mechanical gesture rather than a negative one. Allswick Manor. . . . The home which she and Nick had planned to buy when the owner eventually decided to sell. Mr. Hawks, it was who owned it, and he had fallen into conversation with the young couple at a party and the next thing he was inviting them to his home. But he was intending to sell up and settle in Canada with his married daughter, for his wife had died a few months before he met Shelley and Nick. They were so thrilled when he showed them over that they at once begged to be given the first chance to buy the property, surrounded as it was by acres of wooded land and with a delightful stream dancing through these grounds. It wanted a great deal doing to it but the young couple had the money—at least; Nick had for he was a millionaire, while Shelley even then had her flair for interior design, although she had never had the chance to try it out for they were living at Ravenscroft Hall, the stately home of the Montpelier family. Alida Montpelier, though Greek, had seemed over the years to have acquired all the arrogance and nobility of that ancient line, and Shelley had at first gone in awe of her. But they had managed to get along together . . . until the incident with Paul. . . .

'You're miles away, Shelley.' Her boss's voice slid into her mind-wanderings and she glanced up to meet his eyes. 'Where were you, for heaven's sake?'

Should she tell him? She decided against it because she felt he would want to spare her feelings and, therefore, give the task of renovating Allswick Manor to someone else.

And despite the fact that it might hurt a little, Shelley very much wanted to have the task . . . the task of putting that lovely house into the sort of order she had envisaged.

Stupid, really, she mused after a space. Far better to fight shy of going anywhere near that particular property. And yet she said, 'I was thinking of this manor house; it sounds intriguing—and as you say, it's just up my street.'

'It's for a couple who are getting married. The man's name is Longford—' He stopped suddenly as if trying to recollect. 'Yes,' he went on, face clearing; 'that's the name.'

'Mr. Longford. When does he want to see me?'

'I said you'd meet him at the property on Wednesday afternoon at three o'clock.' Stephen took a drink of his wine. 'I'll give you the address when you come into the office tomorrow.'

Later he drove her home and she was still thinking of Allswick Manor and the plans she and Nick had made for its renovation. New bathrooms . . . a nursery . . . a study for Nick, using a room which Mr. Hawks had been using for the storage of unused furniture. . . . The gardens landscaped to include fountains and terraces and rustic bridges over the stream.

'The children'll love to play on them,' Nick had said tenderly.

A sigh escaped Shelley as she entered her sitting

room and threw off her coat. So many plans . . . at only seventeen. Nick was just twenty-four but seemed so mature that he could have been several years older. And now she was almost twenty-four and he thirty-one.

Although it was almost midnight Shelley was wide awake—and of course she knew the reason. Allswick. Impatiently she chided herself for the memories, and decided all at once that she wouldn't do the renovations after all. She would take on the other house, for the woman whose husband was returning from Nigeria. What was her name? Did Stephen give it to her? No, she did not recall his doing so.

She had been in bed for an hour before sleep claimed her. Memories again had kept her wide awake, memories of that fateful episode when Paul had called at Ravenscroft Hall to return some records and books he had borrowed from Shelley over a year ago. And she was alone in the sitting room, her husband being out and her mother-in-law resting. Anna, Nick's sister, was in the village, shopping. For some reason Paul suddenly became sentimental, then declared the marriage to have been a mistake.

'You and I, Shelley, were meant—'

'Paul,' she had interrupted swiftly, 'please don't say such things as my marriage being a mistake. I adore Nick and he adores me.'

'It all happened far too quickly,' he protested. 'Why, you never gave yourself time to get to know him properly.'

'I just knew I loved him the moment I set eyes on him, Paul,' she replied seriously. She had been so very young, gloriously, madly in love and she had no wish to have any other man's company, and this was more than obvious to Paul who, becoming angry and jealous, seized her and crushed her protesting body to his in the most intimate way.

'Your mother didn't approve of him—a foreigner!' he reminded her.

'Let me go! My mother let me marry him, didn't she?'

'Reluctantly. She told me she was terrified that, being a Greek, Nickolas would seduce you—'

'Don't—stop it!' Wrenching herself away Shelley, breathless and with her cheeks burning with anger, pointed to the door. 'Please go, Paul. I'm married and our little affair is forgotten.'

'Not by me! I ought not to have let you go! I love you, Shelley—' He leapt close and grasped her wrist, jerking her slender body to his. It was clear that he was in the throes of some deep emotion and she began to twist and writhe, actions which only served to increase what she realised was Paul's swiftly rising passion. She was soon helpless and exhausted, clinging to him for support, allowing him to kiss her because she had not the strength to fight him. Every vestige of strength had left her.

And it was at this moment that Nick came into the room, to jerk his tall lean body to a halt as he stared disbelievingly at the scene before him.

'What the hell—!' Galvanized into life, he tore across the room, took Paul by the scruff of the neck and threw him so violently that Shelley winced as his head hit the door.

'Nick,' breathlessly and with a fervent relief which her husband in his anger failed utterly to notice. 'Oh, Nick—'

'Who is this man?' he thundered, face like an evil mask. 'Who, I said! Answer me!'

'Paul . . . we went out together—once—'

'You took her from me!' almost screamed Paul suddenly, gaining courage. 'We're in love—surely you can see that!'

Nick's eyes were fiery as a tiger's as he turned on him.

'You're in love!' His teeth ground together. 'Explain yourself before I—'

'Nick—don't!' cried Shelley in terror lest her husband should hit the other man. 'Let him go—and—and I'll explain in—in a minute. . . .' She was weak and drained, her eyes filling with tears. 'I can't think what made him—him—'

'Kiss you, and fondle you!' Fire blazed in her husband's dark satanic eyes as he turned to her. 'I'll strangle you—' He broke off as the door opened and his mother stood there; just behind her was Anna, eyes almost popping out of her head as they took in the scene, for it was plain that something dramatic was happening. It was her mother who broke the short silence as she asked, in a mild sort of tone that seemed ludicrous in the situation, 'Is something the matter, Nick?'

For a moment he seemed unable to speak for the fury that consumed him, and Shelley recalled how she had seized the moment to make her escape, gathering the strength to cross the room and brush past the two in the doorway.

Nick had come to her within minutes and she did not ask what had happened downstairs. She really had no chance anyway, for Nick in his unbridled fury shook her till her teeth rattled, demanding an explanation which he never afforded her the opportunity to give. He was plainly beside himself and Shelley, outraged by his rough handling of her, and by his readiness to condemn without a hearing, began to pack a bag the moment he had stalked from their bedroom. That he would cool and eventually ask for an explanation did hover at the back of her mind, but her one resolve at the moment was to leave him, to go home to her mother.

Mrs. Scott was all too ready to take her daughter's side, reminding her that she had warned her about marrying a foreigner.

'He's half English,' began Shelley, already regretting her hasty action in leaving Ravenscroft Hall.

'And half Greek. The Greeks are notorious for their ruthlessness towards their wives; they regard them as chattels, and ill-treat them. What awful marks he's left on your arms, my darling! I could go over there and kill him! Oh, why didn't you marry Paul?'

Shelley had said nothing; she was weak and listless and wondering how long it would be before her husband came for her, as he must have guessed where she was.

'I think I'll go and lie down,' she said in a voice edged with tears. 'If Nick comes—'

'I'll send him packing!'

'No, Mother—please. He'll be ready to say he's sorry, and to listen, so call me, won't you?'

How sure she had been that Nick would come and take her home! But she had reckoned without his Greek characteristics of arrogance and pride, and she had not taken in to account his youth. Angry and hot-headed, feeling in every way humiliated, degraded even, he had waited for Shelley to make the first move. So time elapsed, with each beginning to believe that the other did not care. Neither mother made any attempt to close the rift, and in fact Mrs. Scott was instrumental in widening it, although her daughter never knew of this. Never knew that it was her mother and her alone who had engineered the divorce.

Shelley awoke with a headache, frowning as she remembered lying awake, tossing and turning as memories flitted about in her head. She remembered having decided not to take on the manor house at Allswick, but now, as she went into the neat little kitchen to make some tea, she changed her mind. What quirk of fate caused this she would never know . . . but it was to have momentous consequences which made her so unsettled that she reached the point where she could have almost thrown up her job.

Chapter Two

Shelley and Stephen had been looking through a wallpaper pattern book when, glancing at the clock on the office wall, Shelley gave a start and said swiftly, 'I must go, Stephen, or I'll be late for the appointment with Mr. Longford.'

'Good Lord—I forgot! Three o'clock you're to be there; you'll have to hurry. He struck me as a man who'd expect strict punctuality.'

Shelley merely gave an absent nod to that and walked briskly from the office towards the lift. As her car was not too far away she was soon on her way, leaving the traffic behind and driving towards the glorious county of Gloucestershire. She had mixed feelings now but knew there was no going back. Mr. Longford would expect her to be there, to go over the house with him on what at this stage would be but a preliminary examination of the property, although she would of course be making suggestions and noting his reactions to them.

She arrived at a quarter to three, parked her car in the drive and began to stroll around the house, strange sensations sending cold shivers along her spine. The house was even more neglected now than when Mr. Hawks lived here so his successors had obviously done little or nothing to it. To make it seem even more forlorn and lost it had plainly been empty for several months, or even perhaps a year. The garden was in a terrible mess, overgrown with weeds and tangled rose shoots with vicious-looking thorns. Only the dancing little stream was clear, its waters sparkling in the spring sunshine; she stopped, and bent to trail a hand in the water . . . and then she straightened swiftly and spun around on hearing the voice . . . *that* voice with its most attractive depth of tone.

'Miss Scott?' Nick's face was blank for a fleeting moment as she looked into it. 'Good Lord—you! I thought it was a strange coincidence, my having to meet a Miss Scott here. . . .' His voice trailed away but his eyes were alert, examining her as if he would take in every line, every contour, every tremulous movement of her lovely mouth. She was as white as her blouse, staring disbelievingly at him, telling herself that this could not be true. And foolishly she stammered, 'Mr. Longford— You ought to be—be Mr. Longford.' Of course she knew that Stephen had somehow mixed the names of the two new clients and yet she shook her head and muttered again, 'Mr. Longford— It was him I came here to meet.' Her hand was wet and unconsciously she slid it down her skirt.

'Mr. Longford—' He stopped abruptly. 'Who's he?'

'Another client—there's been a—a mix-up in the names. My employer's a bit absent-minded sometimes.' She felt foolish, inadequate, and she wanted to run away, into the mass of overgrown bushes that had once been a neat, well-cared for shrubbery. But of course she did no such thing; she just stood there wishing she had not obeyed the force that had led her to change her mind.

'You use your maiden name, then?' The harshness came through and she wondered at it. She nodded her head.

'I thought it best,' was all she answered to that.

Nick continued his scrutiny for a moment and then, with a sardonic inflection that had not been there in the old days, 'You're older, and you've filled out a bit.'

Her blue eyes glinted.

'So are you older, and so have you filled out a bit.'

He laughed then and said, 'So you took up interior designing for a living.'

Shelley did not answer that, but murmured instead, 'I believe you've bought this house . . . after all.' Why had she added those two last words, she wondered in vexation.

'For my future wife and myself, yes.' He paused a moment. 'It's rather ironical, don't you think that it happens to be you who are going to renovate it for us?'

She was still pale, but much more composed now as she lifted her face and looked straightly into his eyes.

'Ironical that we two should meet here like this,' she agreed, but went on to add, 'However, it'll be someone else who will be doing the job. I came merely as a sort of—consultant. If you tell me what you want I can pass it on to Miss Wandford.'

The dark steely eyes narrowed perceptively.

'Is it customary for your firm to work like this?' he wanted to know.

She paused, but quickly made up her mind.

'As a matter-of-fact, no. It's just that I have changed my mind, naturally, about doing the work for you.' The emphasis on the last word came through quite plainly and Nick's lips quirked.

'I take it that if it hadn't been for the mix-up in the names you'd not have come in the first place?'

'Your conclusion is correct; I'd have grasped the fact that it was you who had bought Allswick Manor.' Because his was not a common name, she could have added but felt it was unnecessary.

'Come,' he decided at length, 'and let us go over the house.'

Shelley hesitated.

'Perhaps,' she suggested with a frown, 'we ought to leave it—what I mean is, now that I'm not to be doing the work it seems a waste of time—'

'Not at all,' he broke in authoritatively. 'I haven't any intention of this being an abortive visit.' All arrogance and mastery! Shelley examined his face, noted the mature lines, the sprinklings of grey at his temples, the firmness of a mouth that was yet as sensuous as she had once known it. The flexed jawline, the dark, metallic eyes with their long lashes and straight black brows above . . . all these she remembered so well. He was perhaps rather more handsome in his maturity, and al-. though she had retaliated by declaring he had put on weight she now admitted to herself that he did not carry much excess weight at all on that lithe, athletic body.

She shrugged and led the way, but at the front door she stopped to look enquiringly at him.

'Yes, I have the key,' he reassured her. 'There is only one so I didn't give it to your Mr. Fanchot. I'll get another one made and give it to you.'

'To my employer.' Shelley followed him into the musty-smelling hall and left the heavy oaken door wide open behind her. What a strange situation! She and Nick so cool and collected, so casual with one another. She could not help recalling passionate nights, tenderness mingling with mastery, kisses as savage as they were gentle. Vibrations sent blood to her temples so that they seemed to ache for a fleeting moment. 'The house has been sadly neglected.' Her voice was faintly hoarse, the result of an inexplicable dryness in her throat. She wondered why he had come alone but was glad. She had no wish to come face-to-face with the future Mrs. Nickolas Montpelier.

'Even more neglected than before,' he agreed, head lifted as he examined the ceiling which was of the French rococo period. Much later than the original, it represented a style of decoration popular in the first half of the eighteenth century. Oaken beams had been removed in order that this lovely ceiling could be introduced. Shelley remembered it so well; she had liked it even while regretting the loss of the lovely beams.

She and Nick wandered from room to room, Shelley making notes in shorthand as Nick rattled off his requirements with what she felt was quite unnecessary speed. If she hadn't learnt shorthand she would not have been able to keep up with him. He seemed almost to be ignoring her; aloof and superior, the valued client looking on her almost as a servant.

No emotion, no mention of anything that had gone before. . . .

Shelley was piqued . . . and she was hurt, too, in a way she could not understand.

They were on the property for over an hour and the sun was slanting by the time they were leaving, Nick in a white Mercedes and Shelley in her Beetle, a ten-year-old car which she could easily have replaced if she wasn't so attached to it. But the contrast was starkly apparent—Nick, the wealthy owner of vineyards and hotels in Greece in addition to the fortune left him by his English father, and his ex-wife who had never tried to claim a penny from him because she was too proud. Nick had not offered anything because he obviously considered her to be the one to blame. He had never learnt the truth . . . and plainly he had never wanted to learn it.

'I'll get in touch with your boss,' he informed her casually as he slid into his car. 'While the interior's being done work will also be under way on the outside—and on the garden.'

'I shan't be interested,' she could not help retorting. 'It will be Miss Wandford who will be in charge here.'

In the act of closing the car door he looked hard at her, an unfathomable expression on his dark set face.

'We shall see,' was his quiet comment and the next moment the big car was purring almost noiselessly along the drive.

'But he knows I don't want to do it!' Shelley was speaking to herself after Stephen had left the office. 'It's spite! And I'd never have believed *that* of him!'

She was fuming as the aftermath of what Stephen had just said—that Mr. Montpelier was insistent that she and no one else should take charge at Allswick Manor.

Stephen was taking her out to dinner and so she left the office early in order to do some chores before she made herself ready for the evening out. He called for her and they took a taxi, Stephen leaving his car outside her front door because there were no parking facilities near the restaurant in Soho where they were intending to dine.

She said, as they sat with their aperitifs, 'I still don't want that job, Stephen.'

He sighed impatiently and frowned at her.

'You've said that already, several times, yet you won't give me any reason. It's crazy! You've never done this before.'

'I have given you a reason,' she argued. 'I don't like the man.'

'That's not a good enough reason. We've had dozens of clients you haven't liked.'

'None I dislike as much as this one.'

Another impatient sigh escaped her companion before he said, 'You must have some explanation for this dislike, Shelley. He seemed all right to me—a little haughty, perhaps, but we've had worse.'

She hesitated a moment, half inclined to tell Stephen who their new client really was, but after reflection she decided against it, although she could not have explained why, since Stephen already knew so much about her marriage and divorce. He was speaking, telling her that if she refused to do the job they'd probably lose the business.

'I can't believe that,' she frowned. 'Monica's as good as I am—'

'We both know very well that she isn't,' he interrupted quietly, his eyes fixed on her face as if he would probe until he had the answer to the question that was puzzling him. 'This man's heard of your reputation, your expertise—'

'I don't believe that,' she almost snapped, knowing as she did that it was spite and spite alone that was making Nick insist on having her. He was going to punish her by making her work on the house they had both wanted so badly, punish her by the knowledge that another woman was soon to be its mistress. Spite, and still she could not quite take it in. Nick had never been petty like that, yet he was certainly being petty now.

'You'll have to believe it, for he said so. I've already told you that,' he added with an edge of impatience to his voice.

She drew a breath and sipped her drink. It seemed that she would have to do the work or they would lose it to another firm.

Resignedly she said at last, 'All right, Stephen, but I shall be glad when it's finished.'

'It'll be up to you how long it takes. When you've done your costing I can let him have the estimate, and then it's no concern of his if we rush the job.'

Rush the job. Shelley frowned. She had always prided herself on taking the utmost care, on never rushing through anything no matter how urgent the client said it was. But with the Manor—well, she thought she would certainly waste no time, as the sooner she finished with her ex-husband the better.

She went over the following day, booking in at an hotel so that she needn't drive back to London that evening. With notebook and pen she went from room to room, painstakingly using her imagination in order to create something of real beauty.

But this was different from the beauty she had at first envisaged and anything suggested either by Nick or herself so long ago was—in the main—rejected in favour of something quite different. Many fixtures had to stay the same, of course, as for instance the beamed ceiling of the dining room, and the satin wall-covering in the drawing room. These needed a thorough cleaning but that was all. As to furnishings—well, Shelley knew she would have to consult Nick's fiancée in order to discover her preferences. Shelley sincerely hoped they were vastly different from what she herself and Nick had once planned.

It was growing dark when at last she slid into her car and drove to the Angel, a first class hotel where she had a bedroom with bathroom—very luxurious and paid for by the firm. Stephen never expected any of his staff to take anything but the best accommodations when they were away from home.

Shelley had booked dinner for eight o'clock but now thought she would rather have it in her room; she never cared much for dining alone, with everyone staring, as if they expected her to make an excuse for being there at all!

Funny, a man could dine alone and no one bothered.

She rang for room service and was informed apologetically that as three of the staff were off ill it could be half an hour before she was served, or perhaps an hour. She sighed into the receiver and told the person at the other end not to bother. She would dine in the restaurant.

Instantly she entered she saw him, sitting there

in a corner with a dimmed light above him and a candle flickering on to the cutlery and glass. There was a bottle of wine beside his table, in a cooler. Shelley was just about to turn and leave when the head waiter came to conduct her to her table. She had to pass where Nick was sitting and he looked up, dark eyes widening.

'Shelley.' Quiet the voice but compelling. 'You must join me—'

'No, thank you.'

'I'd like to discuss these renovations with you.' He glanced at the waiter. 'The lady will sit here,' he said imperiously. 'You will please lay another cover.'

Fuming, she sat down rather than cause a scene.

'You must know I have no wish to have a meal with you,' she seethed.

'Don't be childish,' he admonished. 'You know we have much to talk about.' He picked up the bottle and filled his wineglass then glanced around. Immediately another glass was placed unobtrusively before Shelley and Nick poured wine into it. She made no protest but said curiously, 'How do you come to be here—Mr. Montpelier?'

His fine lips twitched at the way she had addressed him. She expected him again to tell her not to be childish but instead he said matter-of-factly, 'I was at the house this morning, and this afternoon I've been to an exhibition of paintings. I've bought three—rather large ones which will be stored for me until they can be delivered to the house.'

'And you decided to stay here tonight?'

He nodded his dark head. 'There's a sale of antique furniture tomorrow in the Guildhall—'

'You intend having antique furniture—every where?'

'In most of the rooms. Some things will be brought from my home, of course, but I'm buying some as well.'

'*We* were going to have. . . .' She tailed off, colouring up.

'To have antique furniture? Of course we were; it's the only kind which will suit the house.' He paused, puzzled. 'Surely you were not contemplating putting in modern furniture?'

She looked at him across the table.

'I was intending to consult your—your—fiancée.'

'Of course, and that is to be expected. Delia will want to be consulted all the time.'

'But you haven't consulted her over the pictures,' she could not help reminding him, and when this was ignored she went on to add, 'Nor, apparently, are you intending to consult her about this antique furniture you're thinking of buying tomorrow.'

'She likes antique furniture,' was all Nick said to that and as the waiter was handing Shelley the menu there was silence between them until she had told him what she wanted. It came quickly and again there was a small silence until broken by Nick, who said curiously, eyes travelling from her face to her firm round breasts outlined by the neat fitting bodice of her dress, 'How is it that you've never remarried?'

'I haven't found the right one. . . .' She looked at him, at his dark, handsome face with its clear-cut features and dark metallic eyes. He had the straight classical nose of the Greeks, the firm aggressive chin. Time had added more arrogance, increased the air of superiority, made more obvious his high breeding. Her lashes fluttered beneath his searching stare and she felt colour drift into her cheeks.

'Haven't found the right one,' he murmured as if to himself. 'What is your ideal man like, Shelley? Obviously that one who caused all the trouble didn't come up to your high standards after all.'

She swallowed hard, amazed and angry to know that her eyes were moist.

'I think,' she managed in a voice amazingly steady, 'that we shall change the subject. I believe it was to discuss the house that made you ask me to join you. You've been there this morning, you said?'

He nodded but he did not seem to be all that interested in what she was saying; in fact, he appeared to be miles away . . . thinking about what . . . ?

'Yes, I have. I've some suggestions to give you.'

'Suggestions to give?' she repeated, emphasising the last word. 'Or do you mean orders to issue?'

His eyes glinted but there was a curve of sardonic amusement on his lips. 'The added years have given you a sting, it seems,' said Nick suavely.

She found herself smiling, but without humour. 'I'm very different from what I was then,' she said, aware of a strange sense of satisfaction that the past had been introduced. His complete evasion of any reference had piqued her. She realised that she wanted to be remembered even though he now loved someone else. She owned that it was a kind of dog-in-the-manger attitude, yet not by any means unnatural. It gave her a sense of inferiority to think she was of so little consequence that Nick had completely forgotten all that had gone before.

'A little different,' corrected Nick with an all examining glance. 'Certainly not *very* different.'

She lowered her lashes, conscious of fluttering along her spine, of a quickening of her heartbeats.

'Can we get back to the house?' she suggested and heard a low laugh escape him.

'I make you nervous,' he stated and she glanced at him with the light of swift denial in her lovely, widely-spaced eyes. 'Oh, yes, I do, Shelley,' he added with a hint of satire. 'But I suppose it must be a little disconcerting for a woman to come face-to-face with the man who once knew all about her, who had given her her first taste of what—er—love was all about!'

She coloured hotly, flashing him a wrathful glance.

'There was no need for that!' she seethed. 'Can we keep this conversation on business, please?'

'All right.' Nick helped himself to a bread roll. 'Delia will be at the house tomorrow afternoon, with me. She wants to plan the bedroom.'

More colour! Damn the man! He was doing it on purpose. Shelley said in a calm voice, 'There are six bedrooms, as you know.'

'It's the main one she's interested in mostly. We want, somehow, to make two en-suite bathrooms, and a dressing room. Also, there's the colour scheme to be worked out—but that'll be between you and Miss Unwin. I'm not interested so long as it's attractive.' His face was straight, but all the same, Shelley felt sure he was laughing at her, deriving amusement at her expense. He paused in thought. 'Maybe I *shall* be interested in the colour scheme after all.'

'What time will she be there?' Shelley's voice was curt.

'About three. She's driving down from Cheshire.'

'She lives in Cheshire?'

'That's right.'

How had they met? wondered Shelley, then tried to remove the wretched girl from her thoughts. Wretched? She might be very nice. . . . Shelley put down her knife and fork, aware that her appetite had gone. She felt depressed, wanting to go to her room and yet knowing she would not sleep for hours yet.

'What's wrong?' demanded Nick rather in the old familiar way. 'You look as if you'd lost a pound and found a penny.'

That brought a smile to her lips and, somehow, dissolved her depression.

'It was nothing.'

'But you've no appetite anymore.' Nick's glance had gone to her plate.

'It was too much; they always do give you too much in these restaurants.'

'You travel a lot, for your firm?'

'A fair bit, yes.'

'Tell me about it. How did you start, and when?'

To her surprise she found herself enlightening him; he listened for some time, interrupting only when she spoke of her mother's marrying again and going to live abroad. The dark eyes glinted strangely and unfathomably and for the very first time Shelley wondered if her mother had had any conversation with him after she, Shelley, had run from him. But she did not ask and Nick did not come forth with anything. She told him of her little home, of her interests other than her job.

'I collect antique snuff boxes,' she began and saw his eyes widen.

'That's an expensive hobby, surely?'

She nodded her head; the muted glow from above brought lights to the swaying hair and Nick seemed fleetingly to be fascinated by the changing colours—gold and bronze and honey-brown.

'It is expensive, and means I can't collect many. In any case, the boxes are hard to find.' Her voice was low and serious; her mind was on a particularly lovely box she had seen here, in the High Street, in an antique shop. She had toyed with the idea of buying it but common sense had prevailed. Two hundred pounds could be spent in a more useful way than that.

'We're straying even yet again from business,' was his observation after a moment had passed. 'About the drawing room—we shall want a polisher on that floor—'

'I had planned fitted carpet,' broke in Shelley hastily. The floor was beautiful—or at least it would be once it was polished. She and Nick had both been eager to have Persian rugs scattered about. . . . 'Everyone has fitted carpet these days,' she was quick to add as he opened his mouth.

'Nevertheless, Delia and I want a polished floor with rugs. We thought that Persian rugs would look rather good.' The merest pause and then, smoothly, 'Surely you can picture what I have in mind?'

Something hurt in her throat and she swallowed convulsively.

'Yes—I s-suppose so,' she murmured, feeling flat again. What on earth was the matter with her? True, it was rather trying, this task which had been given her, but why get emotional over it? Yet undoubtedly she *was* getting emotional, and even at this early stage, so what would she be like by the time the job was finished? Suddenly she knew she could not go on and said determinedly, 'You'll have to have one of the others to do this work for you. I'm not willing to carry on.'

Nick's knife and fork were suddenly idle in his hands; his eyes were riveted on her, narrowed and almost threatening.

'I've asked for you and it's you I want.' Curt the tone and just as determined as hers had been.

'You've done it on purpose,' she accused. 'If we hadn't met on that first day then you'd have been quite satisfied with someone else.'

'I agree, but we did meet—and I want you to do this work for me.'

'I'm refusing! You don't seem to understand.'

'If you refuse then I shall take my money elsewhere.'

She bit her lip till it hurt, aware of his unwavering stare.

'Does it give you any satisfaction to insist on my doing the work for you?' she questioned presently.

'I was told by your employer that you are the most gifted of his staff and so it was natural that I wanted you.'

She lifted her eyes to meet his.

'Did you suspect, on hearing the name: Scott, that it might be me?' He was shaking his head even before she finished speaking.

'No, because Scott is a fairly common name. In any case,' he added with a hint of harshness, 'I never expected you to resume your maiden name.'

'There seemed no point in my keeping your name.'

He frowned and said in a slightly more friendly tone of voice, 'Let us forget this argument and enjoy our meal. Tell me some more of what you've been doing.'

Chapter Three

Shelley was at the house by nine o'clock the following morning, and intended to stay all day, so she took some sandwiches from the hotel, and a flask of tea, as there was no electricity switched on at the house because the whole of the wiring had to be renewed.

The girl, Delia, came sauntering up to her when she was in the garden, taking a short break in the sunshine. Nick followed after taking a briefcase from the car.

'Miss Scott—meet Miss Unwin—my fiancée,' he called.

'How do you do,' coolly from Shelley, aware that the girl was looking her over from head to foot in the manner of a mistress to a kitchen skivvy, and her blood boiled. No 'nice' girl, this, but a bitch if ever there was one. And Shelley was just wondering what her appeal for Nick was when the most dramatic transformation took place as Delia turned to see Nick at her side. The big green eyes widened and softened, the mouth curved into a delicious smile and the perfectly-manicured hand that came to rest on Nick's sleeve seemed to have a tender touch.

'Darling, it's in an awful mess, as I remarked when you first brought me to see it. Are you sure this person can put it right for us? I mean—I feel a man would be more capable—' She turned a dazzling smile to Shelley. 'No offence, Miss Scott, but I'm afraid I am one of those women who believe that men can do certain jobs much better than women. No believer in Women's Lib,' she added, 'as you have now guessed.' She lifted doe-like eyes to her fiancé. 'If you are satisfied that Miss Scott can do this work for us, darling, then you know I shan't argue with you, don't you?'

Shelley's blue eyes met those of her former husband and on her lips was a faintly sardonic smile. She knew from experience that even at twenty-four Nick had never brooked argument from anyone. A mask slid over his eyes for a brief space before he looked down at the lovely girl who was standing very close to him, that hand still resting possessively on his arm.

'Yes, Delia,' he murmured in a very soft voice, 'I do know you won't argue with me.' For some reason the moment became tense and Shelley heard herself say briskly, 'We'd better go inside and begin planning; we haven't a lot of daylight left.'

'No; time passes so quickly.' Delia linked her arm through Nick's and they preceded Shelley into the house. Then Delia went ahead, leading the way to the main bedroom.

'Oh, dear, Nick, darling,' she pouted after a swift glance around, 'it seems to me that nothing can be done to this place—just nothing at all. I'm wondering if we ought to change our minds and go in for something more modern?'

'You'll not recognise it when it's finished,' submitted Shelley before Nick could speak. 'And now, perhaps you can give me some idea of what you want in here?'

Delia gave a sigh and walked further into the room.

'It has a lovely view,' she observed on staring out of the window.

'It will be better still when we've deepened the window.' Nick's quiet voice . . . gently reminding his former wife of what they had planned together. She felt some of the colour leave her face and turned from his half-amused stare.

'I don't think the window needs deepening,' objected Delia. 'After all, we're not going to be admiring the view all the time, are we?'

Again Shelley and Nick exchanged glances, and she suddenly couldn't help saying, 'But wouldn't you like to be able to see some of the view from the bed?'

Nick's lips twitched and Shelley thought: what a strange situation this is!

'From the bed?' with an uncomprehending frown. 'We couldn't see it at night, and I myself am far too sleepy in the morning.' Delia looked up lovingly at her fiancé . . . as if to remind him that they would be far too occupied when in bed, and the view would be forgotten.

About an hour and a half later Shelley found herself alone with Nick, Delia's having gone off to wander around the grounds.

'What made you buy this house, Nick?' she wanted to know. They were in the drawing room where the three of them had been discussing the renovations needed there. Delia had suggested green as the basic colour but Nick had said they would have crimson. He was definite about not changing the wall covering.

'I expected that question before now,' he said.

'I wondered, of course. I suppose you've had it in your mind all these years and so when it came on the market you were delighted?'

He nodded.

'I was, especially as I was contemplating marriage.'

'You'll marry as soon as the house is ready?'

'Yes, of course. It's all we're waiting for.' He moved away, to the window, to look out on the same view as was to be seen from the main bedroom. 'Did we settle on the colour of the bathroom suites?' he asked, turning his head. 'I can't remember.'

'Miss Unwin has chosen blue for hers and oyster for yours.' They had not planned two bathrooms before, she recalled. Nick had said it wasn't necessary, as she could take her bath while he shaved.

'She has? Well, change both colours. Lilac for hers and avocado for mine—'

'But—' Shelley set her mouth, recalling that it was she herself who, so long ago, had chosen lilac for the bathroom. 'Miss Unwin—'

'Those are the colours I want,' broke in Nick firmly and in that old familiar tone which recommended that she did not argue. She said quietly,

'What shall I tell your—fiancée?'

'There's no need to tell her anything. Just do as I say.'

Shelley looked puzzled, as well she might, and without having time to stop herself she was saying, 'You don't sound wildly in love, Nick?' And then she blushed with embarrassment and wished with all her heart she could withdraw the words. He turned his head slowly, to stare down into her face.

'Of course I'm in love,' he assured her. 'But that doesn't say that my word isn't law. You heard Delia say that she doesn't believe in Women's Lib. She's adorably feminine—but you must have noticed?'

Adorably feminine. . . . Shelley eyed her ex-husband with a look of deep suspicion. Was he serious—or merely having fun at her expense? Undoubtedly his was not altogether the casual, 'don't-care-less' attitude one would expect of a former husband who had totally lost interest in his ex-wife. Or perhaps he was being spiteful in more ways than one—not only as regards the renovations but also he seemed to enjoy praising his fiancée—not that there was anything wrong in that . . . if he were in love. But was he in love with the girl? True, he had just declared he was, but it seemed to Shelley that it was in a rather halfhearted way.

Conscious of his sustained stare she made to turn away but he moved at the same time—unintentionally she felt sure—and they collided. His hands went out to steady her and she felt herself quivering at the contact, realised with a little shock of disbelief that the past seven years had dissolved into nothing and his hands were gentle and possessive . . . but only in her imagination. She and he stared into one another's eyes for a long, electric moment before, bending his dark head, he kissed her hard on the lips. She twisted away, colour flooding into her face, anger in her eyes.

'How could you!' she cried. 'You—engaged to be married— Supposing she had walked in?'

'She didn't,' smoothly and bringing out a handkerchief because he suspected he'd have lip-rouge on his mouth. He was smiling faintly as he used the handkerchief, and his eyes with their half-veiled expression of amusement never left her face. 'No,' he murmured almost to himself, 'you haven't changed much at all.'

'I think,' said Stephen on looking through Shelley's report, 'that this is going to cost a great deal more than the sum I at first suggested to Mr. Montpelier.'

'You gave him a figure?'

Stephen nodded, his eyes fixed on the papers lying on his desk. Shelley was sitting opposite to him, her shapely legs crossed, one slender hand resting on the tooled leather, fingers tapping almost nervously. She had tried, during the past twenty-four hours, to convince herself that she was *not* affected by Nick, that she had managed to get over him a long time ago. But had she? The question was superfluous for she had at last to own that the reappearance of her husband had awakened all that she had first experienced. She was still in love with him—or perhaps it would be more appropriate to say she had fallen in love with him all over again, and with the swiftness of that first time, when she was a mere seventeen years of age. She and he were older now and she did wonder if, were that incident to have occurred now, they would act in the same stubborn way. She knew for sure that she wouldn't; she'd have gone back—no, she'd never have run off at all, but stayed and explained, forcing her husband to listen to her.

But what of Nick? Would he be reasonable and appreciate that the fault in no way lay with her? He seemed so mature and she had no great difficulty in accepting that he, too, would have acted very differently.

And they would still have been together. . . . Living in that lovely old manor house, perhaps with children playing on the lawn. But instead they had parted, driven by pride and obduracy and influenced ultimately by their youth so that they had gone the whole way . . . divorce.

'I've been speaking to you, Shelley!' Her employer's voice cut sharply into her reverie and she gave a start.

'I'm sorry; I was miles away.'

'Obviously,' he almost snapped. 'This darned job seems to be affecting you in the oddest way. I've just told you that I gave Mr. Montpelier a rough estimate, and it looks by your report as if the final figure will be twice as much.' He paused a moment. 'Can't you cut the cost down in any way?'

'I suppose I could, but wouldn't it be best to consult our client first? I rather think he'll not count the cost as long as he gets what he wants.'

'It's rarely we have a renovation costing this much.'

'There's a great deal to be done to that house—' Shelley broke off, frowning. 'Get Miss Wandford to take over, if you're not satisfied—'

'For heaven's sake, Shelley, stop all this! You're the one engaged on the job and it stays that way.' Something in his tone made Shelley say, 'Mr. Montpelier's been talking to you again?'

'To insist that you remain on the job.' He looked hard at her. 'There's something I don't understand about the whole thing. You never wanted the job in the first place, and now you still don't want it, yet it's right up your street. And our client—I feel sure you've hinted that you'd like to be taken off the job?' A question which she chose not to answer and Stephen went on, 'Why should he phone in early this morning and make sure that you were to remain on the job?'

Perhaps, mused Shelley, because Nick feared, after that kiss, that she would definitely make a demand to be released from the job of doing up Allswick Manor.

She said at length, 'I've no idea why he should phone early this morning.'

Stephen frowned heavily but let the matter drop, referring again to the question of cost.

'I think I'll come along with you—' He stopped to ponder. 'I'm engaged with a new client until about noon tomorrow but after that I'm free. We'll go off to Allswick immediately after lunch—say one o'clock?'

'Yes, all right. You feel you can suggest ways of cutting the cost?' He had never done anything like this before but then as he said, they had never had a renovation costing so much before.

'I hope you're not offended?'

She shrugged.

'Not at all. However, don't reckon without our client. He's a strong-willed man and what he wants he'll have.'

Stephen's glance was swift yet probing.

'You almost could know the man, the way you talk.'

'I've had several meetings with him, and find him a very forceful person. I do think you ought to see first whether or not he objects to the cost.'

'I've not finalised it yet,' he said unnecessarily. 'But as I've hinted, it'll be enormous.'

'I still don't think he'll mind.'

'Nevertheless, I'll come and see for myself.' Stephen's voice was firm and Shelley made no further attempt to convince him that his client would not be troubled about the cost.

Stephen was a fast driver and they arrived at the manor at a quarter to four despite the traffic delays on the way. Nick's car was at the front and another, smaller one. Shelley heard voices and realised that Nick was talking to at least one other man, at the back of the house.

'I expect he's wanting an estimate for the outside repairs,' explained Shelley in response to the enquiring look Stephen gave her.

'He could have had the place pulled down and rebuilt for little more than it's going to cost him when everything's put in order. Just look at this garden! It wants clearing completely and landscaping from scratch.'

'No, it doesn't. It wants careful handling as there are some rare bushes and trees among all that undergrowth.'

Stephen turned his head swiftly. 'You seem to know. Have you been exploring the grounds, then?'

She merely nodded and said she had taken a few breaks, getting out of the mustiness of the house

into the fresh air. What she did not tell him was
that Mr. Hawks had enthused over the garden,
though even in his day it was rather neglected. He
told them of the rare plants, some having been
brought from various parts of the world by a
previous owner who was a garden addict.

'Well, let us go inside. . . .' Stephen's voice
trailed as Nick and two other men came round the
corner to the front forecourt of the house. 'Oh,
hello, Mr. Montpelier. I thought I had better come
and take a look for myself.'

Nick's expression was unreadable as his eyes met
Shelley's. He said slowly, 'Miss Scott has everything in hand, and I find all her suggestions to be
satisfactory.'

'The cost is rather high and so I felt we might
economise,' began Stephen in his customary businesslike way. 'You see—'

'I don't believe I've had your estimate?' Nick's
voice was bland and his eyes interrogating. There
was an air of superiority about him that Shelley
found most disconcerting and she wondered if her
employer was similarly affected. If so he didn't
show it at this time.

'No, because it happens to be very high, Mr.
Montpelier.'

'You assume it will be beyond my means?' Nick's
voice was crisp now and edged with arrogance.
Stephen did then begin to look uncomfortable.

'Not anything like that,' he was swift to deny.
'It's just that we seldom have a renovation costing
this kind of money.'

'Until you submit your estimate I can't accept or
reject it, can I?'

'Well—no—'

'In that case, I suggest you let me have it as soon

as possible.' With that Nick turned to one of the men and suggested they go to the other side of the house where, he believed, the roof needed some repair.

'Stuck up so-and-so!' snapped Stephen when the three men were out of earshot. 'Is he always like that?'

'I warned you he had a forceful character.'

'Well, he'll get the estimate—and I hope he likes it!'

'You might as well take a look around now you're here,' suggested Shelley when it seemed he was ready to go again. 'I can explain just what will be happening to the place.'

Stephen was rather casual at first but became more and more interested as time went on and more rooms were entered and left. The galleried landing was beautiful but needed a great deal of money spending on it.

They were just coming downstairs when Nick entered the hall, having finished with the men outside.

He stood there, watching Shelley and her boss coming down, a strange expression on his dark countenance. How Greek he looked at this moment! thought Shelley, so forbidding with those strong classical lines, the outthrust jaw, the firm, determined mouth. His shoulders beneath a Saville Row jacket were broad and square; his long lean frame was reminiscent of an athlete at the very apex of his career. A sort of splendour in his movements as he stepped to one side as Shelley and Stephen neared the bottom of the stairs, and she caught her breath, vividly recalling how he had thrilled her in every way, so long ago.

And he thrilled her now. . . .

Suddenly she felt tense, and from the chaos of her mind bred by the apparent hopeless of her situation, she was conscious of rebellion against fate! Why not fight to win him back? There was still time and it wasn't as if Delia was a nice girl. In any case, decided Shelley with the hint of hardness entering her eyes, all was fair in love and war.

'And I did have him first,' she reminded herself, flushing a little as she saw his expression of amused satire. He was plainly trying to guess at her thoughts.

She smiled at him, noting his tiny start of surprise at this unexpected hint of friendliness.

'We've been taking a look,' began Stephen. 'This place is certainly going to be something special once it's renovated.'

'Renovated to my satisfaction,' said Nick. 'I don't want any alterations to what Miss Scott and I have arranged.'

'No—well, there won't be,' agreed Stephen and then, glancing at his watch, 'Would you care to join us for a drink before we drive back to London?'

Shelley waited expectantly; Nick looked at her and she smiled again, encouragingly. He shook his head and declined Stephen's invitation.

'I'll be here again tomorrow,' he said to Shelley, 'with Miss Unwin. We have a firm of landscape gardeners coming in to do a survey.'

For some reason Stephen said, 'Are you having it all bulldozed, and then beginning again?'

'Certainly not. There are many valuable and rare specimens in this garden.' And with that he bade them good afternoon and strode majestically to his car.

'I told you,' began Shelley when he interrupted her.

'He practically repeated your words. Did you take your strolls around the grounds with him?'

She opened her mouth to say no, then preferred the truth, since after all, that first stroll so long ago was with Nick, when they were both accompanied by Mr. Hawks.

'Yes, as a matter-of-fact, I did.'

'He must have been in a far more mellow mood than he is now,' observed Stephen, eyes sliding to the big car now rolling along the drive—not very smoothly as it was almost impossible to avoid the potholes.

'At the time,' she recollected in a soft, nostalgic tone, 'he was in a mellow mood.'

'Then let us hope he's in a mellow mood when he reads his estimate!' was Stephen's fervent response to that.

Delia stood frowning darkly as Shelley showed her pattern books of wallpapers.

'I'm not really interested, at this moment, Miss Scott. What I am interested in is the other book—the one showing me the bathroom suites.' It was a week since that afternoon when Stephen had said he hoped Nick would be in a mellow mood when he received the estimate. He was, accepting it at once, and so Shelley had really begun to get things moving and already every room in the old manor house was looking even worse than before, as workmen were in—more than a dozen of them. 'I said quite definitely I wanted blue for mine.'

'Mr. Montpelier was firm about having lilac.'

Delia drew a breath and her mouth went tight.

'Order the blue one!' she snapped and Shelley thought how very different she was now from the Delia seen by her fiancé. 'Mr. Montpelier can have what he likes in his own bathroom, but I'm having blue, with the gold-plated fittings as we agreed.'

Shelley gave a small sigh but did not argue. She would see Nick tomorrow; he had phoned the office and told Stephen he wanted to see Shelley. She was at present staying each night at the hotel and she wondered if, by some miracle, Nick would also be staying overnight. She did not think so as there seemed to be no reason for his doing so. Delia, it seemed, had been staying with friends in Glouscester but she was returning to Cheshire later today, she had told Shelley.

'I think you ought to concentrate and choose the wallpaper,' advised Shelley with far more patience than she felt. 'If you're going back to Cheshire then you won't have another chance.'

'I can leave it to you. Besides, the room won't be ready for wallpaper for ages yet.'

'It will be ready in about a week.'

'Then I hope the work isn't going to be shabbily done! A week? It's not possible.'

'Anything's possible when you have enough men on the job.'

Shelley already had a firm of bathroom designers ready to move in; she also had the bedroom furniture and carpet ordered and these could not be brought in until the walls and woodwork were done. Already expert polishers were employed on the woodwork.

'Well. . . .' Delia didn't seem too interested in the wallpaper and Shelley guessed it was because she hadn't been allowed to have the colour she wanted. Nick had seen to that. He had what *he* wanted.

At last Delia made her choice and Shelley instantly objected, saying it was unsuitable but

Delia arrogantly insisted so Shelley wrote down the number.

She saw Delia off the premises and soon after she had driven away Nick's car came bowling along the drive, much to Shelley's surprise. The couple had only just missed one another, she thought, for Delia had been gone less than ten minutes. A very strange setup, she mused, and her doubts about Nick being in love with Delia were strengthened.

It was with a little thumping sensation in the region of her heart that Shelley stood on the steps waiting for Nick to alight from his car; this he did with all the smooth grace and litheness that she remembered.

'Your fiancée's just left—you've missed her,' Shelley told him, hoping her slight stammer had passed unnoticed. Nick seemed untroubled by her information—perhaps *indifferent* would be a better word with which to describe his manner.

'Have you been here all day?' Nick came up the steps to join her at the open front door. He was close . . . closer than was necessary.

'Yes; everything's in full swing now.'

'Let us take a look at the progress.' He flicked a lean brown hand for her to precede him into the hall. 'Ah, so they've managed to get all that varnish off the balustrades,' he noticed with satisfaction. 'This is going to look most attractive when it's polished.'

She just stood watching him as he examined some of the exposed oak and because she made no comment he turned to see if she was still there.

'About the bathroom,' she began. 'Miss Unwin wants blue for hers. I've already ordered lilac but can phone first thing in the morning to change it.'

Nick's eyes were glinting.

'There's no need to change it.'

'What will she say to me, though?'

'Nothing, as I shall already have told her it's to be lilac.'

'The way you and I once wanted it,' she murmured, just to see what effect that would have on him. He smiled sardonically and said, 'That's right; you've a good memory.'

Her blue eyes challenged as they stared directly into his.

'You mean me to have a good memory, don't you?'

'Now what am I to infer from that?' Nick wanted to know.

'Everything you are having done here is what you and I planned. . . . So you too have a good memory.'

He laughed without humour.

'The memory's fading,' he assured her casually. 'Especially now that I've decided to marry.'

'The memory of . . . us?' Soft her tone and gentle. She wanted him so much and although there was time for her to win him back there certainly wasn't much time. As soon as this house was ready they were to be married. Shelley could delay, of course, but not for any appreciable length of time. In any case, it wouldn't be fair to Stephen, since lost time meant lost money; for she could be employed on another job. Besides, Stephen had given a completion date.

'What are you trying to tell me, Shelley?' In contrast to her voice his was hard.

'Nothing—' She shrugged her shoulders, wishing she had more experience, wishing she knew how to flirt with him. But she had no experience at all, for she had never bothered with men since her parting

from Nick . . . and she now knew why. Knew also
why, when she fell to thinking she had not yet met
the right one, inevitably Nick's face would appear
before her mental vision. 'It was just that things
came to mind, which is natural, I suppose. It was a
strange quirk of fate, us being thrown together like
this, at this particular house.' She looked at him
across the small distance and her eyes were wide,
appealing. 'For you, Nick—don't things come to
mind?'

'Such as?' His voice was still hard, and cold.

'Oh, er—things,' she answered lamely.

A faint smile touched the firm outline of his lips
as he came towards her. She felt her heartbeats
increase, and her nerves fluttered.

'You have regrets?' he asked and she saw that his
eyes matched his tone in hardness.

'I suppose one always has certain regrets, Nick.'
She was fighting and yet feeling defeated for after
all another girl was wearing his ring.

'I agree with you, Shelley, but on the other hand,
regrets don't get you anywhere, do they?'

'No, they don't.'

'Because what is done is done.'

Sometimes it could be undone, she thought, but
this was kept to herself because this was not the
right moment to voice a thing like that. She had no
wish that Nick should be provided with the chance
to humiliate her.

'Yes,' she replied flatly, 'what is done is done.'

'I guess you have enjoyed your freedom?'

She looked up swiftly. What was he trying to do
to her?

'I've done well in my job, if that is what you
mean, Nick,' she returned after a slight pause. He
didn't say anything and she heard herself asking,

'What have you been doing with yourself all these years, Nick?'

'I've been in Greece for quite a lot of the time. My aunt died and I had the estate to see to.'

'You like it over there?'

'Very much. Delia and I shall spend part of the year there—probably the spring. Greece is very beautiful in the spring.'

'But spring will be lovely here, in this house. The garden will be full of interest and colour.' A picture of Christmas spread before her eyes . . . logs in the big grate and candles in their holders; a dazzling tree and tinselled decorations, fairy lights and gaily-wrapped parcels. And children laughing. . . .

'Yes, I daresay it will.' Nick glanced around. 'This place certainly has atmosphere.'

'We knew that right away, remember?' Her voice was eager, willing him to soften.

'Did we?' Nick lifted a hand to smother a yawn. 'Does one appreciate atmospheres when one is so young?'

She smiled faintly.

'You were then as old as I am now,' she reminded him.

'So I was—but then a man is so very much younger at twenty-four than a woman is. I'm sure you agree?'

She looked away, feeling defeated again for she did not know how to soften him. He was within weeks of being married so how could she succeed in her efforts to win him back?

It was growing dark and she said flatly, 'I suppose I'd better lock up—' She listened intently. 'I think some of the men are still working upstairs. How can they see?'

'As soon as you get the wiring done we can have

the lights on. Try to hurry that particular firm up, will you?'

'I'm doing my best. It's a big task to re-wire a place like this.' She stopped as two men in overalls came down the stairs.

'Good night,' they said in unison as they passed her. 'Good night, sir.'

'Good afternoon,' corrected Nick easily. And, when they had gone, 'I think there is enough light for me to take a look around. Are you coming with me?'

She hesitated then said yes, she would come with him. He led the way and together they went from room to room. But the light was failing rapidly now and soon they were outside, and Shelley was locking the front door after having carefully checked all the windows and the other doors.

'Are you driving back to London?' enquired Nick as they walked down the steps to the forecourt.

'No, I'm staying at the Angel. Driving to London and back all the time is such a waste. I need to be here, making sure everything's done properly.'

'I'm staying at the Angel too,' said Nick without much expression, 'and so we shall dine together again.'

Chapter Four

It was arranged that Nick should wait for Shelley in the lounge, and she made sure she was not there first. That would show too much eagerness, she decided. She was glad that she had brought an evening skirt with her and a white lace blouse. Not that she had entertained any idea of wearing it, but she had put it into her luggage all the same. And now as she walked into the lounge she knew she was looking attractive, with a little lip-rouge and a touch of the blusher, just to give her face some colour. Her hair shone from vigorous brushing; it made an enchanting halo for a beautiful face. She saw Niek's eyes widen for a fleeting moment as she went towards the table at which he had been sitting, and from which he now rose at her approach. He seemed to absorb everything in that one swift glance before his expression became veiled.

'You look charming,' he complimented and yet his tone was nothing more than that of cool politeness. She sat down and he followed suit, asking what she wanted to drink.

'Martini, please.' She leant back, clasping her hands in her lap. Nick ordered and relaxed against the upholstery. 'It's nice to have company,' she said with a smile. 'I'm usually on my own when dining in an hotel like this.' She could see stars shining as she looked over Nick's shoulder, for the rich velvet curtains had not yet been drawn across the window. Her thoughts flitted to Allswick Manor and she felt it must be a little eerie there just now, with no lights and all the rooms empty and cold. The grounds would present a picture of gloom even though the stars above them were bright. An involuntary shiver caught her companion's notice and he sent her a wide, interrogating glance. 'Someone walked over my grave,' she laughed.

'What were you thinking about?'

'The house, and feeling it must be rather ghostly there at this time.'

'There could be a ghost; many generations have lived and died there.'

'I don't believe in ghosts, you know that.'

'You were a timid child, though, at times,' recollected Nick, moving to one side as the waiter placed his drink before him. Shelley had already picked her glass up and now she was hearing Nick say, 'Cheers . . . here's to happiness.'

Eyes meeting and Shelley's heart beating overrate. Pulses all awry and nerves stretched. She could almost have begged Nick to take her back. They drank, put down their glasses and all at once Shelley felt drained and detached. Why should

she try? What future was there for them, together?

She cheered up somewhat when they were dining
and afterwards they went into the cheery, firelit
lounge for coffee. Then just as Shelley began to say
she was going to bed Nick cut in with a request to
see some drawings of what would eventually be his
study.

'I suppose you have them with you?' he added. 'I
noticed a briefcase in your car.'

'Yes, I have them with me. I'll go and fetch
them.'

'There's no need; we can go to your room. If it's
like mine you have a kind of "lounge" area?'

'With chairs and a settee, yes.'

They went in the lift; Nick took the key from her
fingers and unlocked the door.

'I've put it in the bottom of the wardrobe,' she
said, beginning to move away but Nick's hand shot
out and she was imprisoned. The door was closed
and tingles affected her spine. She had not for one
moment thought about the intimacy when allowing
him to come to her room. He brought her body to
him, tilted her face and took possession of her lips.
His hands caressed and his hard body seemed
locked to hers, so closely was he holding her.

'Put your arms round my neck,' he ordered and
Shelley obeyed, remembering the past excitement
she aroused in him when she feathered his nape
and his ears. She saw his eyes close as his mouth
came down on hers again. It was a timeless interlude of sweetness for Shelley as she clung to him,
heart wildly pounding against her ribs, flooding
warmth a deluge over her whole body. Fire
consumed her when after deftly dealing with the
buttons on her blouse Nick's warm hand found

what it sought and the strong lean fingers closed
tightly, teasing the nipple with the pleasure-pain
which was the prelude to surrender. Wild yearning
fevered through her veins as his other hand curled
far down her back to bring her to him with masterful arrogance and strength. She had no thought of
fighting him; lost was the knowledge that they
weren't married anymore. She felt light-headed
when he lifted her in his arms and carried her
towards the bed. She stood motionless while he
undressed her but lowered her head when
presently she was quite naked before him and his
amorous gaze was feasting itself on her delectable
curves, and resting sensuously on her breasts. He
lifted her, gently, and she felt the coolness of the
cover against her back. She found she could watch
him undress, because it was still as if the years
between had melted into nothingness and they
were again man and wife. Soon he too was naked,
and his hard, muscular body sliding down beside
her own. She slid her fingers right into the mass of
hair on his chest, and nuzzled her face against it,
moaning softly with lips parted on his chest. His
lips caressed, exploring her throat and nape and the
delicate curve of her shoulder. Then he was moistly
possessing her mouth, thrusting his tongue within,
making her aware of its roughness against the
silken skin of her cheek. She quivered from head to
foot, as if in a convulsion, as Nick spread one leg
over her soft warm body. And then the fierce
uncontrollable passion engulfed them and he was
the conqueror, his body imprisoning hers. In shuddering rhythm they soared to the heights of heaven,
lips and bodies locked, volcanic fire in their veins.

Down to earth was as beautiful for Shelley
because sweet memories flooded in and she

wrapped her legs about his slowly settling body. His arms were around her as they went to sleep, and he murmured something she could not catch.

Morning and the sun's cool rays streaming through the drapes they had not bothered to close. Shelley smiled at her ex-husband, and with gentle fingers brushed the dark hair from his brow. So young he looked! Just like before . . . oh, everything was like before! She sighed with gratitude that she had so easily won him back to her. Delia was nothing to him; it had always been her, Shelley, and always would be.

Her smile deepened as Nick opened his eyes. He seemed dazed for a moment and then full awareness came and he sat up.

'What time is it?' He glanced at his watch and slid from the bed. 'Why didn't you wake me? I've to be in London by eleven o'clock.' He seemed angry, she thought and said unsteadily, 'Nick . . . you haven't said good morning—or—or anything.'

'Good morning,' he frowned. 'Mind if I use your bath?'

'No. But—Nick, we—we m-made love last night, and so—'

'I haven't forgotten,' he cut in almost roughly. 'What of it?'

'What of it?' Shelley felt as a sword point had been thrust savagely into her heart. 'Didn't it mean anything to you?'

He had grabbed his shirt but tossed it aside again.

'What should it mean?' He threw the question over his shoulder as he made for the bathroom. 'We wanted a diversion, and enjoyed it. But it's finished so why the haggard expression?' He had turned his head and he was frowning darkly. 'You're a big girl now, Shelley, and I daresay, like me, you've indulged in many such diversions.' He was gone, into the bathroom, and she heard the water running.

It was a week later when the letter arrived at the little mews house. For Shelley it had been a week of self-condemnation, of misery, of anger against the man she loved. He had treated her as nothing more than a pickup, a toy to play with for a few lustful hours. She hated while she loved, and she never wanted to see him again.

She picked up the letter from the mat and stared in some perplexity, for although the postmark was Spain the handwriting was not that of her mother. And her stepfather had never once written to her. With a feeling of unease she slit the thin envelope, vaguely aware that the contents were rather thick. Another envelope dropped to the floor as she took out the single, folded sheet of paper. Stooping, she took up the fallen envelope and recognised her mother's handwriting. Shelley was really perturbed now and she went into the sitting room to read the letters.

Dear Shelley,
her stepfather had written, This is a sad letter, to tell you. . . .

Shelley read on, tears gathering in her eyes. Her mother dead. . . . It didn't seem possible for she was only forty-two. The other envelope was held between trembling fingers. Her mother had told her stepfather where to find this letter, written some time ago when she realised she had a heart complaint. The letter must be sent on to Shelley after her mother's death.

It was some moments before Shelley could open it but at last she had another single sheet of paper before her eyes.

It was a confession and as Shelley read on she kept having to remind herself that her mother was dead, and she, Shelley, must crush this hatred rising within her.

At last she laid the paper aside, and at that moment the bell rang and she opened the front door to see her boss standing there.

'What . . . ?' She opened the door wider, scarcely knowing what she was doing. Her ashen face registered with Stephen and he said with some concern, after entering the sitting room, 'Whatever's wrong, Shelley. You look shattered. Are you ill?'

'Not physically.' She flicked a hand automatically towards a chair and he sat down. 'What is it you want, Stephen?' She felt icy cold, detached from the world.

'Your phone's out of order. Did you know?' Shelley shook her head and he continued, 'I've called to ask you to stay at Allswick tonight, as—'

'Today's Friday,' she cut in to remind him. Unless it was urgent, no one ever worked on Saturdays or Sundays.

'I know, but Mr. Montpelier wants to see you tomorrow at half past ten in the morning. It seems that something doesn't suit him. He sounded furious on the phone so I thought I'd better not tell him we don't work Saturdays. I felt you'd not mind; you can take a day off in the week if you want to.' He paused as she nodded her head, absently. 'Something's wrong, isn't it?'

She glanced at the letter, intending to hand it to him, then realised that Nick's name was mentioned, and so she merely said, 'I've just had word that my mother's dead. A heart attack.' She stood looking down at him with glazed eyes. 'It seems awful, her going as suddenly as that. She never told me she had a heart complaint.'

'I'm so sorry. . . .' Stephen's voice trailed; he was at a loss for comforting words, always was. He felt embarrassed and could only ask the prosaic question, 'Are you going to the funeral?'

She shook her head, wishing she could cry . . . but not for her mother.

'It's all over; she's been dead for over a week.' She noticed that Stephen was looking at the two letters and after a moment of indecision she handed them both to him, saying she would make some coffee and disappeared into the kitchen.

On her return he said curiously, 'Your husband's name was Nickolas—same as our client.'

'Nickolas Montpelier.' Shelley placed the tray on a low table and picked up the coffeepot. 'Is this too strong for you?'

'No—it's fine.' He shook his head, a frown having settled on his brow. 'So your mother was the real cause of the divorce?'

'By her own admission, yes. She—' Shelley broke off and the tears came at last. Stephen shot up and took the coffeepot from her shaking hand; she sat down and covered her face with her hands. 'Nick went to her after some time, begging her to tell him where I was—Mother had sent me away, up to Scotland, to an aunt who has since died—'

Again Shelley broke off, her words having become incoherent as sobs shook her body. Stephen spoke and she listened.

'Your mother told him that you didn't want to see him ever again, that you wanted a divorce in order to marry this man, Paul— He's/the one you told me about?'

'Yes; the one who caused it all. I never really loved him and my mother knew it. But she liked him and she always disliked Nick, and so— so—she. . . .' Great sobs racked her body and Stephen could only sit and stare, helpless in a situation like this. But he managed to speak at last.

'She heartlessly destroyed your marriage!' Stephen rarely portrayed fury but he was certainly furious now. 'How could she, when she must have known how happy you two were!'

'She told me that Nick had called, but it was only to say that he wasn't willing to forgive me and so he wanted his freedom.'

'She deliberately kept you apart!' Stephen's teeth ground together. 'She had to do, if her nefarious scheme was to work. But why, Shelley— why!'

'I've just said; she hated Nick because he was half Greek. She was a strange woman, believing that everyone from the East is uneducated, wild, almost a barbarian. It was so utterly absurd but I didn't care much because she did give her consent to our marriage, after a lot of argument and threats on my part.' Shelley drew forth a handkerchief to dry her eyes.

'Threats?' echoed Stephen, leaning forward to pour her coffee.

'I threatened to leave home and never speak to her again, ever. I also convinced her that I'd marry

Nick the day I was eighteen. And so she gave her consent. I think I've mentioned to you that she was afraid we'd have an affair, or that I'd run off with Nick to Greece.'

'But she knew of his noble English connections?'

'Of course, but they counted for nothing in her bigotry. She had this thing about foreigners. . . .' Her voice failed her and she put the handkerchief to her eyes again. 'I suppose you've guessed that I still love Nick?'

Stephen nodded his head.

'Yes, and also this makes other things clear, too.'

'You can see why I didn't want to renovate that house.' She went on to tell him about Mr. Hawks and that the house was one day going to belong to her and Nick. 'And now—h-he's going to—to live in it with someone else!'

'Shelley, dear—'

'I can't bear it!' she cried. 'Nick hates me now—' She was thinking of that night they'd spent together, and, overcome by physical and emotional fatigue she again burst into tears. Stephen rose and put an arm around her for comfort. He felt unequal to the situation, embarrassed again, but he did draw her head against his breast and speak soothing words to her. And at last she settled, managing to control her sobs, but she felt totally weak and unable to cope with anything—certainly not her job.

'I'll send Monica along to Allswick,' he decided. 'You must stay at home until you feel better.' He sat down again and drank his coffee. Shelley realised she would go mad if she stayed in and said she wanted to go to Allswick after all.

'It will help to take my mind off things,' she added finally.

'You know, Shelley, I'm sure you're wrong in thinking Nick hates you.'

'Well, whether he does or not I've lost him, and through the treachery of my own mother.'

Stephen fell silent for a moment and then, as the thought occurred to him, 'When you saw Nick at the house didn't he seem surprised that you hadn't married this Paul?'

'No; I felt he knew I'd never married him. He merely said that Paul hadn't come up to expectations, or something of the kind. I can't exactly remember.'

'Does he seem to love this Delia? I had the impression that there wasn't an overabundance of affection between them.'

'He says he loves her.'

'You asked him?' Stephen looked at her in some surprise.

'Yes, I did ask him, and he said yes, he loved her. He said she was adorably feminine.'

Stephen made a sound that could only be described as a snort.

'I didn't notice much adorable femininity about her when she came into the office. I thought she was as hard as they come. Mercenary, too. I'd like to bet she's marrying him for his money.'

'Nick would know if she was. He's very astute.'

'No man's astute enough for a clever woman. She's an expert at deception.'

Yes, Delia was that kind of clever woman, an expert at deception, mused Shelley as she recalled how the girl's manner had changed so dramatically when she talked to Nick.

'She's not the one for Nick. . . .' Shelley paused a moment. 'Perhaps she is,' she murmured inconsistently. 'At one time he was softer and kinder than he is now. He's become hard, Stephen,' she quivered, again remembering his heartlessness on the morning after the night they'd spent together.

Stephen looked at her across the table.

'What happened to him would make any man hard, Shelley. He'd repented of his anger with you, was willing to meet you and sort it all out. But he was callously informed that you didn't want to see him ever again, that you wanted a divorce in order to marry another man. He went away bewildered, because he and you had apparently been happy together. He must have been an embittered man—and it's probably that man you are seeing now.'

'But why didn't he make *sure?* He could have tried to find me but he didn't.'

'How do you know? You were away in the wilds of Scotland but your mother had probably told him you were with this other man. Besides, Nick even at that age was obviously a proud man and wouldn't have come begging—'

'I never wanted him to beg!'

Stephen let out an impatient breath.

'We're getting nowhere,' he said unnecessarily. 'If I were you I'd tell him the truth—that your mother lied. I'd show him this letter.'

But Shelley was shaking her head. A week ago, perhaps, before that night, she could have shown him the letter. But not now, when she knew without any doubt at all that he did not care a rap for her, that nothing positive could come from showing him the letter. Too much time had elapsed . . . so many years. . . . Hadn't she herself been convinced that she had recovered completely from her love for Nick? Until she met him again she was sure of it. And it must have been the same with

Nick: he'd fully recovered and was now contemplating marriage to someone else. With him the
meeting with his former wife had had no effect
whatsoever— No, she reflected, that wasn't quite
the case because he had certainly shown *some*
interest in her. However, that interest had proved
to be superficial; the meeting had not had the
impact on him that it had had on her. In short, she
had fallen in love with him all over again, but the
same had not happened to Nick. This she was now
resigned to and she felt she must try, once again, to
forget him.

Stephen moved to pour himself more coffee but
he had glanced at the clock at the same time.

'I'm not showing Nick the letter,' she murmured
in response to his suggestion, 'simply because it
wouldn't do any good. Nick is lost to me. He's
shortly to be married to Delia Unwin. He said they
were only waiting for the house to be put in order.'
Her voice was low and hollow-sounding, her eyes
dark with brooding and pain. 'I'll naturally be glad
when Allswick Manor's finished and I don't have to
see either of them again.'

'It must be agony for you, dear.' Stephen looked
exceedingly troubled. 'Are you sure you want to
see him at all? I've said I can send someone else.'

She shook her head decisively.

'No, I'll carry out the job I've started.' It was her
turn to look at the clock. 'I must be off, Stephen.
I'll stay overnight at the Angel so if you want me
you can phone me there—or leave a message.'

He nodded his head.

'I can't think there'll be any reason for phoning
you but one never knows. How long do you
suppose it will be before the house is finished? You
feel everything's running according to plan?'

'Yes, everything—except this business you've mentioned, about something being wrong—not suiting him. He was angry, you said?'

'Very angry,' replied Stephen with a grim inflection. 'I'm wondering whether to go to Allswick tomorrow morning just to give you moral support.'

'I'll manage,' she said reassuringly. 'It wouldn't be the first time I've seen Nick in a temper.'

Chapter Five

Nick was already on the site when Shelley arrived at twenty minutes past ten the following morning. He was dressed casually in mushroom-coloured slacks and a white, roll neck sweater, and looked so attractive that Shelley caught her breath . . . then felt the tears stinging the backs of her eyes. Why should he belong to someone else! Why should she give up so easily? She had made a resolve to try to win him back, and at the first setback she had accepted defeat.

'I've been waiting for over half an hour,' was his first uncompromising comment as his dark eyes looked her over. 'Where have you been?'

Her chin lifted.

'The appointment was for half-past ten. I'm early, as it happens.'

'The appointment was for ten!'

She blinked at him, recalling that Stephen was a little absentminded. Hadn't he mixed the names of Nick and another client? Yes, on more than one occasion he had shown this absentmindedness.

'Stephen said it was for half past. However, we're here now and so you can tell me what is wrong.'

'Come inside!' He led the way and now Shelley forgot all about her new resolve as her temper rose. Nick had obviously already been into the house because the front door was wide open, and she followed him up to the main bedroom. This door too was wide open, and as soon as they were inside he flung out an angry hand.

'This wallpaper! What sort of trash do you call it? I thought you were an expert at—'

'Your fiancée chose the paper,' interrupted Shelley trying to keep her temper. 'I tried to explain what it would be like—totally unsuitable for this room—but she insisted. I'm here, Nick, to carry out the orders of my clients, and if their tastes are insisted on then mine have to be put aside.' She was a little pale, and a little ashamed, too, because this was one of the very rare occasions when a complaint had been made.

'Delia chose it?' He was frowning heavily, and thoughtfully, and Shelley strongly suspected he had already been in touch by phone with Delia, who had probably denied the choosing of this wallpaper. However, this was merely conjecture and Shelley made no attempt to voice her suspicions. 'Well, you can get it off!' Nick was saying furiously. 'Where's the pattern book?'

'In the room we're having as your study.'

'Then get it!'

She turned on him, eyes blazing.

'When you ask me properly I'll get it! I'm not one of your cringing Greek servants!'

He stared disbelievingly at her; she knew a skin-prickling sensation because she half-feared he would retaliate in some physical way. But she need not have worried; Nick was more surprised than angry.

'I never knew you had a temper like that, Shelley,' he remarked with slight censure. 'So you *have* changed, it would seem.'

'One does change with time. I'm holder of a responsible position where I am used to receiving respect from my clients. Your attitude just now was one of an arrogant master with his servant.' She spoke quietly but with a certain confident firmness that brought a half-smile to his lips, his anger obviously having been dissolved as she was speaking.

'I hadn't meant to treat you as a servant,' he assured her, moving towards the window. Shelley followed his long, sinewy frame with her eyes, noting the erect set of his shoulders, the noble way he held his head. She remained silent and he turned a lean tanned face towards her. 'What made you suppose my Greek servants cringe?' he enquired unexpectedly.

'I've heard of the way you people treat your inferiors—and your women.'

He laughed, surprising her.

'You talk as if I am all Greek.'

'Your mother's Greek.'

He let that pass as he said, 'I can assure you, Shelley, that my Greek servants do not cringe, and as for the way the Greeks treat their women—well, I cannot recall ever treating you badly.'

She looked at him in surprise, profoundly conscious of the change in his manner with her for now he was almost gentle, and his eyes were softer, as was the line of his mouth. Emotion filled her being . . . emotion and love. She was on dangerous ground and yet the resolve came to the fore. She might just win the battle yet. . . .

'You treated me badly only once,' was her softly-spoken reply and at this Nick was swift to remind her that he had cause in plenty. This, she saw, was creating a rift again and she avoided the possibility by saying she would go and fetch the pattern book. But Nick followed her, and he closed the study door behind him. Yet he stood with his back almost touching it, as if he were unsure of himself! The idea staggered Shelley who quickly produced the pattern book and rested it on a bench which the workmen had made from two small ladders and a plank of wood. 'If you will come and look?' she invited, but did go on to add, 'I hope you will inform Miss Unwin of the change. I don't want her coming to me with complaints.' And she added instantly, 'These changes are going to cost you a lot of money.'

Ignoring that he walked towards the bench. But he gave the book only a perfunctory glance—and then Shelley was in his arms and she was being mercilessly crushed to him, the whipcord hardness of his muscles painful against her soft curves. His lips took hers, locking themselves to her mouth then parting it with ruthless mastery. Shelley knew she ought to make some protest, ought to struggle but with all her love paramount she reciprocated to his kisses, thrilling to the entry of his tongue, to the feel of his warm palms on her lower body as he brought her even closer, compelling her to an awareness of his male hardness. And as before the years dissolved and time had stood still.

'Nick,' she whispered. 'Nick, I—' She stopped herself in time, almost horrified that she was going to say she loved him. Mercifully, the memory of his callous treatment of her last week came to her aid, saving her from the humiliation which the folly of an admission of love would have meant.

'Yes?' His lips were feather-light against her temple, his breath the warm caress of a summer breeze. One hand was beneath the fine wool sweater she wore, fingers curled round her tiny waist. 'What were you going to say to me, Shelley?'

For answer she twisted away, taking him completely by surprise after what must have seemed to him a near surrender.

'Nothing. Let us get down to business!' She realised her attitude was absurd after the scene which had just been enacted, and she was not surprised at the sharpness of his voice when he said, 'What the devil's wrong with you, girl? One minute you're ready to let me make love to you and the next you're coldly businesslike!' He paused, regarding her through darkly frowning eyes. 'We made love the other night so why not again?'

Colour flooded her face and she turned away.

'I don't know what came over me—I shouldn't have let you—'

'Rubbish! You enjoyed it as much as I.'

She looked up, eyes moist and mouth quivering.

'But it meant nothing, did it?'

He shrugged his wide shoulders and idly fingered the pages of the thick, heavy book that lay on the bench.

'It was pleasurable for us both, but as for its having some deeper meaning— Well, you'd not expect that, would you? I'm to be married in a few weeks' time.'

'And yet you made love to me!' she flashed, angry because of the pain he was causing her, and because of her own stupidity, and because he was so casual about a night which to her was beautiful. 'You were unfaithful to your fiancée!'

Again he shrugged.

'What the eye doesn't see. . . .' he began to quote.

Shelley gasped and shook her head.

'I'd never have believed you could be like this— uncaring that you'd been unfaithful to the woman you're about to marry.'

Suddenly his manner was one of ruthless enmity. The dark eyes glittered and his mouth compressed.

'*You* talk of infidelity! You!' He raked her contemptuously. 'You appear conveniently to forget your own infidelity.' He half-turned from her. 'A man learns from experience—learns about women and decides they don't deserve much consideration.' He stopped rather abruptly, as if already he regretted this outburst.

'So you don't love her. . . .' Shelley spoke slowly, and to herself. 'Why are you marrying her, Nick?'

'I do love her—'

'No, don't lie. You regret the slip just now but what is done is done. It's very plain that you don't love the woman you're planning to marry.'

He said nothing and she guessed he was furious with himself. He said abruptly, 'Let us get this over and done with. I can't stay here all day!' He flung back the pages and Shelley knew he scarcely looked at the patterns as they appeared before his eyes.

She stood back, not advising or even looking. She was very quiet, her mind steeped in thought as she debated on whether or not to tell him that it was her mother who had caused the divorce, deceiving them both into believing the other was to blame. She could show him the letter as proof of what she was saying. Confusion and indecision; hope superimposing despair, and then visa versa. She said quietly, vaguely hoping for a clue, some form of guidance, 'You and I said we'd have white walls, if you remember? We agreed that velvet-effect embossed paper would be just the thing— There are several designs to choose from in there.'

Silence. He was turning the pages with more interest now.

'This one.'

'This?' Shelley's tone was bleak.

'That's what I said!' decisively and with a harsh inflection. 'And get it done without delay.'

'Yes.' She watched him cross the room and leave it, standing motionless as she heard the car start up and move off the forecourt. Then she moved to finger the page.

Nick had chosen a leaf-green wallpaper.

Steady progress was being made and as the days and weeks passed Shelley realised that soon her task would be completed, and Nick and Delia would be living at Allswick Manor. She had seen little of Nick recently, and when he did happen to be at the house he practically ignored her. Stephen on the other hand was taking a much deeper interest in her than ever before and she guessed he was sorry for her. Nevertheless, she was taken completely by surprise when he asked her to marry him.

'Marry . . . ?' She stared at him across the dinner table, for they were dining at the Ritz. She shook her head. 'Are you serious?' she asked.

'I've never been more serious in my life, Shelley.' His grey eyes studied her face, then moved to the glory of her hair, long and gleaming against the alluring slope of her shoulders.

'I don't love you,' murmured Shelley, a little stunned that she hadn't declined his offer at once

'You've no need to tell me that,' he returned. 'You're in love with someone else.'

She stared at him curiously.

'You don't seem to mind.'

'It's a fact and I accept it. All the same, I do want to marry you, Shelley.'

'But you don't love me.' A statement which he did not attempt to deny.

'I like you very much—we both like each other very much.' She made no comment and after a small silence he continued, 'Look how much we enjoy going out together like this. Look how suited we are businesswise. We've never had a cross word between us, never a disagreement even over the work. You can't remain single all your life, Shelley, pining over a man you can't have. And as for me—well, I've known I'd like to have a wife one day even though I was enjoying my bachelor existence.' His tone was low and serious, his eyes gravely dark. 'Everyone needs someone to be their true friend, dear, someone to share things with, to live with and have as a true partner.'

'Marriage without love. . . .' Shelley felt the tears burning the backs of her eyes; she was suffering agony, thinking of Nick married to Delia and living in that particular house. She had begun to think she would never be able to cast these thoughts from her mind, that they would be torturing her night and day for the rest of her life. But if she accepted Stephen's offer she would have other things to think about. And as he said, they got along so very well together, were the best of pals whether working or taking a break such as this one they were having now.

'Think about it,' Stephen was advising. 'You can't make up your mind in a hurry. But do give my proposal some thought—promise me.'

She nodded her head and smiled across at him.

'I will, Stephen—I promise.'

'Good girl! And now, let us enjoy our meal, and the show I'm taking you to afterwards.'

It was only two days later that Shelley said she would marry Stephen. She had considered his proposal, rejecting it and then accepting it, lying through wakeful hours trying to visualise the future, and a marriage without love. It seemed crazy—and yet on the other hand it seemed a very sensible thing to do. All these chaotic thoughts and disturbance of mind were the prelude to her coming to a firm decision at last.

'You're sure, Shelley?' Stephen looked anxiously at her. 'I rather thought you'd have taken more time than this to come to a decision.'

'I haven't acted hastily,' she assured him with a serious expression in her eyes. 'I've spent hours and hours debating and I feel sure we'll make a success of it.'

He seemed still troubled and she wondered for a space if he were now regretting his proposal. However, his face cleared presently and he was smiling, appearing to be very happy at the idea of marrying her.

'Who knows,' he said, 'love might one day come to us.'

'It's a possibility,' agreed Shelley remembering that, if Nick had not come into her life again she wouldn't now be in love with him. She had recovered . . . or had she? Well, no good could come now of asking superfluous questions. Nick was going to marry his Delia, and she was marrying her boss.

He bought her a diamond solitaire and put it on her finger one day when they were driving through Berkshire to view another house which they were required to renovate. Stephen wanted an opinion from Shelley and so he had taken her off the Allswick job for the day. He drew in at a secluded little lay-by and turned to her.

'I've bought the ring you liked,' he said, not without a degree of awkwardness. 'I hope they've made it the right size; I did give them the ring you let me have as a—pattern, so to speak.' He was still awkward and Shelley's thoughts winged to the day when he had asked her to look at rings and tell him what she liked. She had seen one in the window of Weirs in Cirencester High Street and told him about it.

And now he was putting it on her finger. She closed her eyes against the tears straining for release, and when she opened them again she had managed a smile. Stephen leant over to kiss her cheek and he said a little hoarsely, 'I'm sure we'll never regret it, dear. It's not as if we don't know each other really well, is it?'

'No, Stephen, it isn't.' And she smiled again, noticing his anxiety and wanting only to dispel it. 'I agree with you: We'll never regret it.' And she secretly vowed to do all in her power to make him a good wife.

The following morning she was at Allswick again and looking around with satisfaction at what had been done. The transformation was incredible, even to her experienced eyes. She stood in the doorway of the sitting-room and watched the man on the ladder fixing the Italian brocatelle drapes, helped by his young apprentice. Her eyes moved slowly, taking in the crimson and gold walls— wainscotted below, the tapestries and the exquisite wall lights with two elegant matching standard lamps. Antique furniture and jardinieres, Persian rugs, a cabinet containing Chelsea and Bow, Worcester and Spode. Priceless groups found now-adays only in stately homes or museums.

No money had been spared and the result was going to be perfection.

Shelley went upstairs, drawn to the main bed-room with its two en-suite bathrooms. The lilac one enticed and she went to the door. Dreams. . . . Visions. . . . Of what might have been. Then back to earth and reality as she heard Delia's voice drifting up from the hall. Shelley went to the bedroom window, and saw Nick's car there, on the forecourt. Her eyes wandered a moment. The grounds were fast taking shape and the result was going to be breathtaking.

'Nick, darling, this is just fantastic! Oh, but I'm going to *adore* being mistress of Allswick Manor!'

'Well, it won't be long before you *are* its mis-tress.' Nick spoke rather more loudly than was usual and a slight frown touched Shelley's brow; she was puzzled . . . until she realised that Nick

had seen her car there and knew she was somewhere within the house.

He had wanted her to hear. She suspected that,
from the very first, he had enjoyed torturing her.

She moved swiftly, not wanting to be found in
the bedroom.

'I love your study, Nick. I hope you're not going
to keep me out altogether?'

'I'm used to having a den to myself, Delia, and
so it won't be often that you're allowed in.'

Shelley, on her way downstairs, made a face.
Wasn't it just like Nick to use the word *allowed!* He
had always been masterful, even at twenty-four
years of age. His mother had warned Shelley, 'Nick
will always domineer over you, my dear, so you
might as well resign yourself. It's the Greek in him;
the men of my country can't help themselves. It's
bred in them to be arrogant and dictatorial—that's
why I married an Englishman. I was not cut out to
be a meek, subservient wife.'

'I shall respect your wishes, Nick, darling. You
know that.' The voice, heard from a closer range,
reminded Shelley of the purring of a cat . . . but
then perhaps, thought Shelley, incurably honest,
she herself was merely being catty towards the girl.

'Have no fear,' Nick was saying, 'I shall make
sure you respect my wishes.' He swung around as if
sensing his former wife was at the door. The dark
eyes flickered over her figure, and she knew he was
taking in the slender frame and its curves, the slim
ankles above expensive blue kid sandals. Her dress
was deep blue with a white lace collar and cuffs,
and she wore a plain gold chain round her neck
. . . gift from Nick when she had known him only
a week. His eyes came to rest on it, and became

veiled. Delia broke the silence, saying in a rather cool and patronising tone of voice, 'You've made an excellent job of this place, Miss Scott. I feel that Mr. Montpelier will not hesitate to give you a recommendation.'

Shelley's eyes glinted and her mouth went tight.

'I require no such recommendation, Miss Unwin,' she returned icily. 'My reputation is sufficiently well-known for me to be sure of obtaining the most exacting of clients.' Deliberately she turned away, showing her back to the girl—and to Nick. 'If you'll excuse me—I have to make a few final checks.' These were final only in that they related to certain rooms; others were still requiring the finishing touches but these, Shelley estimated, would be completed within a week—or ten days at most.

And then she would be on another assignment . . . and would probably never see Nick again.

Anger against fate welled up within her. Why had she met him again when she was recovered enough to enjoy life once more? She sighed as she walked away; the garden called and she forgot the checks she had mentioned just now. She wandered along newly-paved pathways and over little bridges, glancing down at the sun-speckled waters flowing merrily along to meet the wider river a few miles distant. Streams had always fascinated her—beginning life as a trickle of water in some high and often remote place, and gathering speed and more water as they sped along, deepening their beds, joining larger streams until, at last, their waters ended up in the sea. This tiny stream meandered through the grounds of the manor, its banks bordered with willows and other ornamental trees, its waters confined within artificial 'levees' of weathered limestone boulders. It was all a part of the landscaping, carried out by experts and with no expense spared. Shelley as she wandered along thought about Nick's ancestral home, where his mother and sister now lived, less than forty miles from here, and although she had been happy there and liked the house and grounds, she could understand why Nick had wanted to settle in something smaller. A massive house could be a liability, whereas this moderate-size manor house was just right, and had about everything to ensure both cosiness for a family and yet possessed the essentials for entertaining.

She paused, listening. Nick was leaving, with his fiancée. Shelley turned back and entered the house, to stand for a long moment looking around, gratified by the incredible transformation even though desolation filled her heart.

She did not know how long she had stayed in the house, moving from room to room, aimlessly and not knowing why she was there at all. It was time to be leaving—had been for perhaps an hour.

'So . . . you're still here.' At the firm crisp voice she wheeled around, having been standing before a glass-fronted display cabinet admiring its antique contents.

'You! I thought I heard your car . . . ?'

'You did. I've taken Delia to the station.'

'She's going back to Cheshire today?' Automatically Shelley glanced towards the brass-faced grandfather clock.

Nick was about to answer when suddenly his eye caught the ring on her finger. He seemed mesmerised, unable to believe what he saw.

'What's this?' He snatched at her hand, his grip painful.

'An engagement ring,' answered Shelley, angrily pulling away. 'What does it look like?'

Nick's mouth went tight and the expression in his eyes, unguarded for a fleeting moment, could only be described as evil.

'Was it there when we were talking an hour or so ago?' he demanded grittingly.

'Of course.' Shelley's nerves tingled; she did not care very much for Nick's manner and she felt the oppressive sensation of knowing she was alone in the house with him.

'You weren't interested enough in me to notice,' she could not help adding in spite of her uneasiness.

'Who's the man?' Nick's jaws seemed clenched and his lips scarcely moved as he asked the question. There was a glowering look in his eyes now as they moved from the ring to Shelley's pale face.

'Stephen—my employer.'

Nick's eyes opened wide.

'He's not in love with you,' he stated in a hostile tone.

Shelley's eyes flashed.

'And what,' she enquired in glacial tones, 'gave you that idea?'

'It's obvious, for otherwise he'd have married you long ago.'

'You know how long I've been working for him?' asked Shelley for the moment diverted.

'I asked him.' Nick subjected her to a measured scrutiny. 'It's to be a marriage of convenience, eh? You're ideally suited businesswise and so this is one way of effecting a lasting partnership. I expect the idea was his,' went on Nick harshly. 'He knew that if you ever married someone else your talents would be lost to his firm.' Nick ran contemptuous eyes over her from head to foot. 'As for your reasons—I suspect—' Unexpectedly he stopped and Shelley endeavoured to guess what had been left unsaid. Did Nick believe she had become engaged to Stephen merely as an act of retaliation towards her ex-husband? Did he surmise she was adopting a 'couldn't-care-less' attitude towards his own forthcoming marriage? She shrugged her shoulders and dismissed the idea. She didn't give a damn what he was thinking, or what conclusions he had come to. It was none of his business anyway.

Shelley broke the silence at last, to ask why he was here.

'Was there something you wanted changed?' she added with an interrogating glance.

'No. I came back to see you.' He was broodingly morose all at once, and a heavy frown knit his brows. 'However, it's of no real importance.' His dark forbidding eyes slid to her finger again and his mouth curved contemptuously. 'I wish you happy,' he sneered and the next moment he was striding from the room, leaving Shelley with tears in her eyes and a leaden weight in the pit of her stomach.

The following day she was at the house very early, having stayed at the hotel but it had been a restless night of tossing and turning as, one moment she was convinced she was making a mistake in marrying Stephen when she loved Nick, yet the next moment she was telling herself that as long as she could never have Nick, she might as well try to make something of her life.

And then she was telling herself that such an absurd reason for marrying could only lead, in the end, to disaster.

She couldn't bear the thought of a second separation; she and Stephen would be sure to get along very well . . . or would they, without love on either side?

It was inevitable that she felt utterly weary and depressed and when, after the last of the workmen had eventually left, she was alone in the lovely house, she seemed automatically to wander up the balustraded staircase to the main bedroom.

The view was wonderful even in the growing dusk. At length she drew the curtains together, remembering that her car was away at the back of the house and that it was rather lonely there after full darkness fell. She must leave at once. But the tiredness seemed to take over and suddenly she decided to take a bath. Yes, it would afford her a certain measure of satisfaction to know that she, and not Delia, had taken the first bath in that luxurious room with its mirrors and plants and gold-plated fittings.

The water was hot, and there were even bath crystals there, in the cabinet, expensive crystals brought by Delia—or it could have been by Nick. Shelley had noticed them when she idly opened the cabinet a few days previously.

The warm bath freshened her up, made her feel almost contentedly relaxed, and she wrapped herself in a huge towel and came into the bedroom where she had left her clothes, on the dressing-stool. She had dried herself and dropped the towel when suddenly her nerves tingled. Someone in the house! Fear brought her heart right up into her mouth. An intruder; someone had broken in, knowing the house was not yet occupied. Footsteps on the stairs and her fear increasing to real terror. What on earth had urged her to take a bath here! She picked up the towel and fled back into the bathroom, but there was no lock on the door—no need for one, since only Delia would be using this, the lilac one.

She heard someone come into the bedroom, heard an exclamation and then . . . Nick's voice. He had seen her clothes on the stool.

'Shelley! What—?' He was striding to the bathroom door. It was wrenched open and Nick stood on the threshold, an unfathomable expression in his narrowed gaze. 'What's the idea—using this bathroom?' he demanded, eyes moving sensuously over a body wrapped in nothing more than a towel.

'I—felt tired—' Shelley drew the towel more tightly around her but she felt naked for all that because Nick's dark gaze seemed to strip the towel from her. She was conscious of damp tendrils of hair on her forehead, and very wet hair down her back, as there had been no cap to wear and she had lain back in the water, uncaring that her hair was floating in it.

'And so you decided to take a bath.' Faint amusement now in Nick's voice, and something else that Shelley did not like at all. 'Well, well, it would seem that I'm in luck.' He stepped back and flicked a hand imperiously. 'Come out of there—' He pointed to a spot in front of him. 'Here.' he ordered briefly. Shelley shook her head, moistening her lips with her tongue.

'I'll g-get dressed if—if you'll go—' Her heart almost stopped at his expression.

'Go?' with a satirical inflection and a lift of one straight black brow. 'My dear girl, I haven't the slightest intention of going. This is my house, remember?'

'Will you pass me my clothes, please?' she said, her glance going past him to the stool where her dress lay beneath her underwear. It was the dress he had recognised, as she had worn it the last time she and he had met here, at the house.

'That,' remarked Nick with exaggerated carelessness, 'is something else I have no intention of doing.' He sent her a mocking glance that yet held triumph as well. 'I said—come here.' Again he pointed and Shelley's temper flared.

'Go to the devil!' she cried. 'I don't take orders from you! Please give me my clothes.'

He turned to look at them; she blushed on seeing his eyes linger on the dainty bra and matching panties—both garments no more than tantalising scraps of lace, she thought with a renewal of her apprehension. Nick hadn't changed; he was still as amorous as ever. She heard him say, in a voice which was slightly hoarse, 'Come and get them yourself—' And he stood aside, sweeping a hand. Shelley stood where she was.

'Only if you promise you'll n-not t-touch me,' she faltered and now he was laughing softly, dark eyes dancing as they again stripped the towel from her.

'Do you really expect that kind of a promise from me?' he quizzed. 'My dear Shelley, you are far too optimistic.'

'You wouldn't dare—'

'Of course I'd dare, and you know it.' He moved and she backed until the bath touched her legs. His hand came forth and long brown fingers gripped the towel. Shelley was compelled to come forward as he tugged, and he made her come slowly, as if he were savouring some kind of exultation at his power to master her. So Greek he was at this moment! Dark and towering; a lean athletic body and an arrogant bearing. His eyes burned into her and on his lips was a twist of sardonic amusement not unmingled with sensuality.

Quiveringly she said, 'You're engaged—and—and so am I. Go away! You can't really mean to—to. . . .' She let her voice trail on noting his expression, for plainly he was laughing at her.

'Seduce you?' with a hint of mockery in his voice. 'It wouldn't be quite that, would it?' The fine lips twitched and the dark eyes were dancing. 'We have been married, remember?'

'But aren't any longer.' Shelley tried to halt his slow progress but she found herself being pulled into the middle of the bedroom floor. 'We're both intending to marry someone else.'

Nick shrugged carelessly.

'What of it? The time is now . . . and you and I are here, together.' His hand came to her shoulder and slid inside the towel. She quivered at the contact of his flesh with hers and she was already half accepting what appeared to be the inevitable. 'The situation might have been made for us. . . .' His grip on the towel tightened as she made to jerk away. 'So intimate— What made you put yourself in such a vulnerable position?'

'I didn't!' she flashed. 'I had no idea you'd be coming back.' Again she jerked, realised she was about to lose the towel and stood stock still, her body close, her face lifted to his. 'Why did you come back, anyway?' she demanded, aware that her pulses were rioting and her heart beating far too quickly for comfort.

'To look over the place,' was Nick's non-committal answer as he bent his head to take her lips. She offered no resistance, aware as she was that she could very easily lose the towel if she began to struggle. The hand within its folds sought and found one firm high breast and closed around it, the nipple caught between Nick's fingers. A shudder passed through Shelley's body and with a sort of compulsive and primitive abandon beyond her control she pressed to him, her mind partly on what he had just said. He had come back to look over the house. . . . And he had expected to be alone. Strange that he wanted to be alone while looking around. Half the enjoyment of such an act ought to be in doing it with the one who would ultimately share his life with him at the manor.

'I don't understand you at all,' she said in a complaining voice when presently he drew away slightly, to look down into her face. Her eyes were wide and limpid and bewildered, her mouth moving convulsively, rosy from kisses which had been none too gentle.

'No?' with feigned enquiry. 'You mean—you don't know what my intentions are?'

Her mouth went tight.

'Stop laughing at me!' she gritted. 'You know very well what I mean! It doesn't make sense for you to want to be on your own here, looking around in the dusk. It isn't as if you haven't been coming regularly, and know everything that's been going on.' He seemed to slacken his hold on the towel and so she began to back away, speedily in order to take him by surprise. He laughed and

jerked her back again, and now his arms were like
hawsers about her, his lips almost cruel in their
mastery. Shelley, soon caught up in the vortex of
his passion, even yet again was conscious of the
dissolving of the years between and she was his
wife. He picked her up and carried her towards the
wide, king-size bed but stopped to take away the
towel before picking her up again and laying her
down on the cover. It was all wrong! Shelley's vivid
imagination brought forth a picture of the future,
when Delia would be here, on this bed, with her
husband. Colour rushed into her cheeks and she
sat up.

'This isn't right!' She made to slide from the bed
but Nick's firm hand with its strong pressure kept
her where she was. 'Don't you care that you're
being unfaithful!' she cried, hoping to make him
drop that cold unsmiling mask that had covered his
face. 'And me—Stephen—!'

'Isn't in love with you so we're not doing him any
harm.' Nick returned calmly. 'As for Delia—' He
lifted one shoulder casually. 'As I said before: what
the eye doesn't see. . . .'

'You've changed! This sort of behaviour's dis-
honourable and you know it!'

'Honour doesn't come into it.' Nick was undoing
his tie, but he was so close to Shelley that even
though she was free there was no chance of escape.
She didn't relish being chased and recaptured as
she ran, naked, to the bedroom door!

'You really mean to—to—carry out your—
intention, then?' she stammered, more colour
flooding into her cheeks.

Nick laughed as he discarded his shirt, tossing it
on to a chair.

'What an unromantic turn of phrase you have,

my dear.' He was calmly dealing with a zipper. 'It
wasn't always like that, was it? I seem to remember
you were a very romantic young lady.' The sarcasm
came through and Shelley turned her back to him.
She wanted some covering and reached down to
get hold of the edge of the lacy bedcover. Nick
gave her a playful slap before she could manage to
throw it over herself, and her cheeks fairly burned
now. She was near to tears and heard herself say
huskily, 'Won't you change your mind, Nick? You
know this isn't right—that two other people are
being harmed.'

'Harmed— Rubbish. Neither of them will
know.' He was undressed now and Shelley felt the
weight of his body on the mattress. There was no
escape . . . but did she really want to get away
from him? Her protests had been genuine . . . as
far as she could make them. For she was
profoundly conscious of being engaged to Stephen,
whom she respected, and who respected her. But
now, as Nick's warm body came against hers after
he had dispensed with the covering, Shelley knew
the fevered excitement of expectation, the unfet-
tered, primordial yearning for the rapture Nick
could give her. His hands roamed over her naked
body, roamed with all the old familiarity and sense
of possession. They lingered with a sort of caressing torment on her breasts before his cool hard
mouth imprisoned one erect rosy tip and his teeth
completed the capture as he practised his finesse,
nibbling gently yet ruthlessly until his desire to
force a little moan from her was satisfied. Shelley
felt weak and subdued, every nerve-cell in her
body aroused in a way that set her flesh throbbing
with desire, and the ache in her loins brought her

shuddering against his manhood . . . and then it was Nick who was shuddering, his passion becoming wildly out of control. For Shelley it was like the outpouring of white hot magma catching her in its deluge, flowing unrestrained over her eager, responding frame. His mouth on her lips was ruthless but when he found her breast she felt that silk was caressing her, so gentle was his way. His tongue traced circles, as if he were enjoying some kind of game, and Shelley arched against him, every motion now an entreaty as wave after wave of desperate longing swept through her aching loins.

'You're as desirable as ever!' Nick's control fled again and he was the masterful, demanding lover she had once known. He cared not for his weight as he thrust himself on top of her, or for the bruises he must be inflicting on her tender lips. But Shelley scarcely felt the pain; she was drugged by desire which was the prelude to rapture indescribable as Nick's primitive energy at last assuaged the frantic craving for fulfilment and she was carried, with her lover, to the very heights of paradise.

How long they lay together, nerves and emotions slowly settling, Shelley did not know. But she was aware of hope in her heart and optimism in her mind, for this was surely too sacred for Nick to pass off as lightly as that other time. Shelley murmured against his chest, ready to tell him about the letter she had received after her mother's death. When he heard what was contained in that letter he would know that the divorce had been engineered by her mother and that she, Shelley, was not so deeply to blame as he had always believed.

'Nick,' she whispered, her moist lips buried in the thick black hair of his chest. 'Nick, there's something I want to tell you. . . .' She paused as he moved his body abruptly. 'You see—'

'It's time we were moving.' Nick's voice was brisk as he reached out to switch on the bedside lamp. 'Lord, it's a quarter past eight!' He lifted his body and slid from the bed. 'Are you staying at the hotel tonight?'

Shelley could not speak for the pain in her heart, the dryness in her throat. So, once again, making love to her had meant nothing. She was just a toy, someone on whom to slake his lust! Shelley felt she hated him in this moment, hated him with a black venom. And she would have liked to hurt him, inflict some kind of crucifying mental pain . . . but how could she inflict pain on a man as insensible as her ex-husband? She said in answer to his question, 'Does it matter to you—whether or not I'm staying at the hotel?'

'It's a long way for you to drive, if you're intending returning to London tonight.' Nick was already getting dressed, and he spoke over his shoulder, having turned his back on her. Tears sprang to her eyes and sheer desolation dragged at her heart. She felt in this moment that she wanted to die, wanted only to find relief in oblivion.

'I might stay at the hotel,' she said flatly. 'I haven't booked in, though, so they mightn't have any vacancies.'

Nick turned and she saw the quirk of amusement on his lips.

'I've booked in, and they've given me a double room. You can share it if you like—'

'Go to hell,' murmured Shelley in a soft voice, and a low laugh escaped Nick as he moved to the door.

'If that's how you feel then perhaps you'd better

return to London tonight.' He turned at the door. 'But mind how you go,' he advised. 'If I remember rightly you didn't care much for driving in the dark.'

And with that he went out, closing the door almost silently behind him.

Chapter Six

Shelley stared at Stephen as if she doubted her hearing.

'Are you serious?' she demanded at last, leaning back in the chair she was occupying on the opposite side of the desk at which her fiancé was sitting. 'Nick actually wants me to go to Greece—to Corfu, and plan the renovation of his house there?'

'That's what he has asked. He feels that you will make a much better job of it than anyone he can employ over there.'

Shelley's eyes narrowed. Just what was Nick's little game?

'He said he was getting married just as soon as Allswick Manor was ready. It'll be finished and handed over to him in less than a week's time, as you know.'

Stephen looked hard at her, the oddest expression on his face.

'I believe he's not getting married until after the house in Corfu's been renovated. It seems it's been occupied by an aged aunt of his who's done nothing at all to it in forty years or more. It requires a lot of work and it could take a long time.' The inflection in Stephen's voice was as unfathomable as the look on his face. 'I've told him that you'll do the job—'

'You've told him!' exclaimed Shelley in disbelief. 'You didn't say so at first.'

'I wanted to see your reaction.'

'My reaction's this: I'm not going to Corfu!'

'It's a job we can't afford to turn down, Shelley.'

Her eyes were wide, disbelieving.

'You know very well how I feel about Nick. Why, if this job at the manor had taken much longer I'd have opted out, and you very well know I would.' Shelley was furious, but greatly puzzled as well, for it seemed incomprehensible that Stephen would expect her to go to Corfu with Nick when he knew how she felt.

'I think you should go.' Stephen rose from the chair and went over to the window, where he stood silently looking out, hands thrust into his pockets. Shelley looked at him in bewilderment for a long moment and then, 'Is there something I'm not being told, Stephen?' she enquired softly.

'That's a strange thing to ask.' Stephen turned as he spoke.

'This is a strange situation,' was her crisp rejoinder. 'You know how I feel about doing work for Nick and yet you're willing for me to prolong the agony by taking on this other job.' She shook her head resolutely. 'It's no go, Stephen,' she told him firmly. 'I don't know what Nick's game is but I'm not joining in it.'

'Something's happened between you two, hasn't

it?' Stephen stared intently, as if he would read her thoughts.

'Nothing that matters,' she answered with well-feigned unconcern. 'I can't think why he wants me to do this other house.' She paused in thought, brow creased in a frown. 'Is his fiancée going over to Greece, too?'

'I didn't ask him. That sort of personal question wouldn't have been relevant anyway.'

Shelley rose from the chair.

'Tell him I've turned the job down, will you, Stephen? If you really feel you must accept the assignment then get someone else to take it on.'

'He wants you . . . or we don't get the job.' Again that peculiar inflection and Shelley drew an impatient breath.

'What the devil's going on?' she wanted to know. 'It almost seems like a conspiracy!'

But Stephen was shaking his head and Shelley was convinced that he was almost as puzzled as she by her former husband's request . . . *almost* as puzzled as she. But not quite. Had he made some kind of a guess as to why Nick should have taken a course like this? She looked intently at him and reached the conclusion that, if Stephen had made some kind of a guess, he wasn't intending to divulge it to her.

'I must go,' she said with a glance at her watch. 'Miss Unwin's made an appointment to see me at the manor at half past three this afternoon.'

'Okay; you'd best be off then.' Stephen paused, watching her open the office door. 'Think about it, Shelley. This job in Corfu could net the firm even more than the Allswick job has done.'

She paused, hand on the door knob, and sent him an oblique glance.

'Doesn't it bother you that your fiancée goes abroad with the man who used to be her husband?' she asked and he was silent for so long that she wondered if he would answer her at all. But at length she heard him say quietly, 'I can trust you, Shelley.'

She drew an impatient breath and left the room. Something, she fumed, was going on! And she intended to discover what it was.

No use questioning Stephen any further, though, so that left Nick.

He wasn't with Delia when Shelley arrived at the house but Shelley was determined to phone him later.

'What did you want to see me about?' Shelley's voice was brisk; she made no attempt to appear friendly. This was business as far as she was concerned—a very different situation from her two previous clients whose weddings she had recently attended.

'It's about my bathroom, Miss Scott! I can't live with that hideous lilac and so it must be redone—a new suite ordered and fitted.' She and Shelley were in the hall and Delia had flicked an angry finger towards the stairs. 'Shall we go up?'

'It won't do much good, will it? Your fiancé made the choice and I merely carried out his orders—'

'I had already given you the order!'

'I'm sorry, Miss Unwin, but you'll have to discuss any changes with Nick—' She broke off but too late. Delia's eyes opened wide then remained unmoving for one disbelieving moment before she said, 'Nick . . . ? You call him by his first name? He allows such familiarity?'

'It was a slip.' Shelley fumbled for something to

say which would sound feasible. 'I suppose it's because, quite often, during long renovations such as these, I do become familiar—or perhaps I should say, friendly—with my clients.'

The other girl's eyes were narrowed.

'I'm not satisfied,' she snapped. 'Nor am I blind! Do you suppose I haven't noticed—things. . . .' She trailed off and Shelley countered at once with the query, 'What things, Miss Unwin?' It was dangerous ground perhaps but Shelley realised with a little sense of shock that she was almost ready to tell this arrogant woman the whole truth.

'He sometimes looks at you in a way I cannot fathom.' Delia turned away, fingering the glossy leaf of an ornamental plant flourishing in an antique brass jardiniere. 'I feel—' She broke off abruptly and Shelley, all female and therefore capable of wanting to 'get back at the other woman,' said in a very quiet and silky tone of voice, 'Surely you can trust your fiancé, Miss Unwin?'

'Certainly!' The girl swung around, eyes flashing, mouth tightened to an ugly line that buried her lips altogether. 'How dare you make insinuations like that!'

'Was I?' Shelley actually knew a dart of spiteful satisfaction as she added, still in that smooth and silky voice, 'I hadn't meant to . . . but it does seem to me that you have certain fears regarding Nick's fidelity.' She had deliberately used his first name again for by now some imp of mischief was taking over and Shelley wanted to rile the girl.

'Nick—again!' Delia almost spat out the words. 'And you needn't give me the same explanation as before!' She turned away again and said over her shoulder, 'I do not have fears about Nick's fidelity!

I feel sure it's you who has deliberately tried to become familiar with him. He's very attractive and most women set their eyes on him.' She stopped rather abruptly as if she regretted the whole of this conversation which, thought Shelley without a trace of pity, must be exceedingly humiliating for the girl.

Should she tell her the truth—that she and Nick had once been married? That imp of mischief urged her to do so but Shelley did manage to remain silent.

Delia changed the subject, beginning to complain again about the colour of her bathroom suite and decor. However, Shelley merely repeated her suggestion that Delia discuss the matter with her fiancé and at last Delia left, her car gears crashing in a way that made Shelley cringe, but she was smiling as she watched the car race along the wide, tree-lined drive. She had rattled the girl and she was glad!

Shelley was alone in the office the following afternoon when the phone rang. Stephen had been called out unexpectedly and he had not been in his office when Shelley arrived there. Stephen's secretary was also absent, having had the half-day off to visit the dentist.

'Hello, is that Steve?' The voice was young and eager, and heard the moment Shelley picked up the receiver, even before she could mention the name of the firm.

'No, he's not in the office—'

'Oh. . . .' No mistaking the disappointment revealed in that one brief word. 'You're his secretary, I suppose? When will he be in? I mean, is he coming in or did he say he'd be out all afternoon?'

Shelley was puzzled, and her nerves became tensed. She wanted to know who this person was, but had no idea how she could go about finding out. She said guardedly, and without disabusing the girl as to the fact that she was not Stephen's secretary, 'I can't say, Miss—er . . . ?'

'Clifton—Wendy. Didn't he say when he'd be back in the office? What he should have told you was that he—we. . . .' The voice broke, as if disappointment choked the words.

'Is it something urgent, Miss Clifton?' Shelley felt this to be a reasonable sort of question a secretary would ask.

'Well, not really urgent, but I'm here waiting for him and he hasn't turned up— What I mean is,' went on the girl, a distinct catch in her voice now, 'We had a date, for afternoon tea at the Ritz and that's where I'm phoning from. I thought perhaps he'd forgotten, being busy, and so I rang to remind him.'

'I take it,' said Shelley aware of a tingling sensation in the region of her spine, 'that you are not a client of his?'

'Oh, no, of course not! We—he—I. . . .' The voice trailed; it was plain that this young woman was now at a loss for words.

Shelley's brow was creased in thought. Stephen had made a date with this girl and had obviously forgotten all about it. Suddenly an idea came to her and she was saying into the receiver, after a swift glance at the clock, 'You're at the Ritz, you say?' The hotel could be reached by taxi in less than ten minutes—traffic permitting.

'That's right.'

'Well, I should wait a little longer if I were you. Mr. Fanchot is obviously on his way—'

'But I've been waiting for over three quarters of an hour.'

'It could be that he stopped on the way to see a client. I should certainly hang on there for at least another twenty minutes or so.'

'All right. And thank you very much.' The receiver clicked but it was some moments before Shelley, a most thoughtful expression of her face, replaced her own receiver.

It was fifteen minutes later when she was asking Michael, the waiter, to take her to Miss Clifton's table.

'Ah, yes; she did give me her name when she came in. She's waiting for Mr. Fanchot.'

'That's right,' smiled Shelley. 'He's been delayed.'

Shelley introduced herself, watching the girl's baffled expression when she sat down.

'But I don't know you,' began the girl, looking at her through the largest brown eyes Shelley had ever seen. Long curling lashes framed them, with delicately curving brows above, and higher still a wide forehead and a glowing mass of honey-brown hair.

'You spoke to me in Stephen's office a quarter of an hour ago.'

'Oh. . . .' The girl blinked uncomprehendingly. 'You're his secretary, but why are you here—? He hasn't had an—an accident?' she faltered and if Shelley had been puzzled before she was truly baffled now. This girl was no more than seventeen —and a very young one at that. And Stephen was thirty-five. . . . Shelley's eyes wandered to the ring on her own finger—Stephen's ring. . . .

Michael was smilingly showing someone else to a

table. Afternoon tea at the Ritz was the 'in' thing and the place was crowded. Nevertheless, being well-known as she was, Shelley was soon being attended to but for the moment she didn't order. She had come here on impulse, to see this girl with whom her fiancé had made a date for afternoon tea. But now she was rather at a loss as to how to proceed. She heard the girl repeat, with almost agonising fear in her voice, 'Steve hasn't had an accident—and—and s-sent you to—to break it to me?'

'He hasn't had an accident,' Shelley was swift to assure her and had to smile at the utter relief that settled on the girl's pretty face. 'Nor did he send me here,' went on Shelley. 'I came merely to see you and to find out what this is all about. You and Stephen are—very good friends?'

'Yes—well, we haven't known one another for very long,' added the girl confidingly and with a smile in her eyes. 'A cousin of mine's having some renovations done to her boutique and I happened to be there when Steve came to look over the place.' She stopped and a reflective silence followed. 'I suppose it isn't the thing for me to talk to his secretary like this, but I was so frightened just now, thinking something awful had happened to him because I just *knew* he'd not stand me up! And so I had to phone—' She stopped suddenly and frowned. 'But you haven't said why you are here? I mean, all you said was that you wanted to find out what it is all about. It has nothing to do with you, Miss— Oh, I've forgotten your name, though Steve did tell me.'

'Miss Scott,' submitted Shelley quietly.

'Scott?' bewilderedly. 'That wasn't the name— no, I'm sure it wasn't.'

'I'm not his secretary—' Shelley paused, undecided. She would have to give the girl some explanation as to why she had taken it upon herself to come here and 'find out what it was all about,' and the simplest thing was to say that she and Stephen were engaged to be married. However, certain aspects of the case stood out, and in the light of this revelation others became equally apparent—or perhaps explained would be a better way of describing it. Shelley regarded the girl through slightly narrowed eyes; she found her quite enchantingly naive, and she could well understand a man being attracted to her . . . but Stephen, the confirmed bachelor, the man who had decided at last to marry more for convenience than anything else? Seemed impossible, but in that short period between putting the ring on Shelley's finger, and this present time, Stephen had met this delightful creature and . . . fallen in love? Undoubtedly *she* was in love with *him*.

'Not his secretary?' The girl spoke at last after waiting for Shelley to continue. 'Then who are you?'

Again Shelley glanced at the ring on her finger. A mistake—for the girl, following the direction of her gaze, lost all colour from her cheeks.

'You're not—not— Oh, I don't believe it! He couldn't! Steve wouldn't do a thing like that to me! Tell me you're not engaged to him!' she cried, and Shelley had to lift a hand surreptitiously to indicate she should keep her voice down.

'Shall we order?' Shelley was playing for time, half inclined to lie to the girl, just to set her mind at rest, but she wanted a moment to consider first. 'We'll talk while we eat—'

'I'm not hungry!' Tears filled the girl's eyes and

her lips trembled. 'You *are* his—his fiancée, aren't you?'

'Do have some tea,' urged Shelley in a gentle tone. 'We shall talk while you have it.'

'All right.' But the voice was flat, and edged with tears.

'I suppose,' decided Shelley with a tiny sigh of resignation, 'that only the truth will serve.' She was going over certain aspects, thinking of the way Stephen had *wanted* her to go to Corfu with Nick. Yes, undoubtedly he had wanted her out of the way for a while . . . so that he could make up his mind about Wendy? It seemed a feasible explanation of Stephen's eagerness to let her go abroad with the man who had once been her husband. Shelley's thoughts switched to the meeting with Delia yesterday and the arrogance of the girl.

It would seem that she needed a lesson! And as Stephen needed to be free of his fiancée's presence for a while the practical thing for Shelley to do was go away with Nick.

But what of Shelley's own feelings? She might be doing what was right for Stephen and this child he was interested in, and she might also be venting her 'spite' on Delia, an act which would undoubtedly afford Shelley a great deal of satisfaction. Nevertheless, to go away with Nick, feeling about him as she did, was just about the most irrational thing she could possibly do.

Wendy had been silent while the tea was being served, and Shelley realised, as she glanced at her, that she was too upset to speak. She believed that Stephen had been philandering with her, playing around while engaged to another girl. She had to smile at the abject figure the girl portrayed. Was this first love? Shelley rather thought it might be.

'I c-can't eat anything, Miss Scott.' The quivering voice broke into Shelley's musings and she sent the girl a reassuring smile and said without much expression, 'Stephen and I are engaged, but it doesn't mean anything at all. We did it for a purpose, Wendy—can I call you Wendy?'

The girl nodded her head dumbly and Shelley went on after pouring herself more tea, 'I don't know how far your affair with Stephen has gone, but it seems plain to me that you're head over heels in love with him.'

Wendy looked up, wide-eyed and bewildered.

'You're so calm about—everything,' she gasped.

'Haven't I just said that our engagement doesn't mean anything? I don't think you were listening,' she added with slight censure.

'I was,' vaguely. 'I'm so confused, you see! Why has Stephen let me down today?'

'I rather think he'll turn up even now—'

'He won't! Not as late as this!'

Shelley was puzzled, for although Stephen might at times be absentminded, it seemed very strange that he would forget such a thing as a date for afternoon tea with a girl as charming as this.

'I'm very sure there is some explanation that will satisfy you,' she offered at last and again Wendy said in some bewilderment, 'You're so calm! I can't believe that your engagement doesn't mean anything. Steve's so—so attractive that—that you're bound to be m-madly in love with him—' She broke off and began seeking for a handkerchief. Shelley frowned and glanced around, half inclined to tell the girl she had to leave. But within seconds Shelley knew she couldn't desert the girl when she was so distressed.

'Don't cry,' she begged, 'not here!'

Wendy looked at her through a mist of unshed tears.

'Please explain, Miss Scott! You must know how puzzled I am!'

Shelley paused, scarcely knowing how to begin. But she soon decided to be totally honest with the girl and tell her that there was no love between Stephen and herself. Wendy listened, and her expression changed so often that Shelley had to laugh.

'You're obviously relieved,' she commented, not without a hint of tartness in her voice.

'Well—er—yes— That is, if you're willing to give him up?'

Amusement brought a light dancing in Shelley's eyes.

'You make me feel quite old,' she said with a tiny sigh.

'I do?' Wendy's eyes opened to their fullest extent. 'Now why should I do a thing like that, Miss Scott?'

'Because you, my child, are so very young!'

'I'm seventeen and a half,' the girl vouchafed.

'And you want me to give up my fiancé because you are fathoms deep in the first emotional situation you have ever experienced?'

Wendy blushed to the roots of her hair.

'You think it's not the real thing?' In spite of her embarrassment Wendy injected an access of indignation into her voice.

'I wouldn't like to form an opinion one way or the other, Wendy.' Shelley paused in thought. 'However, I'll tell you what I'll do: I'll think about this situation we three are in, and I might decide to go away for a while—'

'Go away? You mean, you won't give Steve up?'

'My dear girl,' said Shelley in some exasperation, 'we don't yet know if he wants to marry you. If he doesn't, then why should I give him up?' What a situation this was! Two women—if one could call this delectable female a woman—sitting here, over afternoon tea in London's top hotel, calmly discussing the man who was engaged to one of them but probably in love with the other!

'I feel sure— Oh, but why has he let me down today!'

'I've already said there'll be some perfectly acceptable explanation—' Shelley broke off and glanced up. 'Michael?'

'A message for Miss Clifton,' he said quietly and handed Wendy a small envelope. 'Apparently it was left some time ago but the receptionist who took the message went off duty and forgot to pass the message on to me.' He glanced at Wendy and smiled. 'I hope it's not caused you any inconvenience, Miss Clifton?'

'No—no, thank you. . . .' She was drawing out a folded piece of paper with trembling fingers.

'It's from Steve!' she quivered, her whole expression undergoing a dramatic change. 'He apologises but says he'll be here by about a quarter to five. It's half past four now— Oh, Miss Scott, I knew he wouldn't let me down! He had to see a client, urgently. Miss Scott, you can see now that you'll have to give him up, can't you?'

For the first time Shelley was piqued . . . and not a little possessive. However, she managed to keep her feelings well hidden as she said in her usual quiet voice, 'I can't do that yet, Wendy. I'm not trying to say that he's incontravertibly mine, but on the other hand, I am his fiancée. We agreed to become engaged, and to marry. Now, he might or

might not be in love with you— To be quite honest
I feel you're much too young for him but that's by
the way. As I've said, he might be in love with you
and I might be willing to make myself scarce and
see how things work out. I notice a question in your
eyes: You're wondering how I can disappear from
Stephen's life. Well, a client wants me to go to
Greece to supervise renovations on his home in
Corfu. I have refused, but I could change my
mind—'

'Please do!' Wendy could not help putting in and
Shelley had to laugh despite the fact that she still
felt piqued. This girl was so young, and impulsive,
and she was deep in the throes of what seemed to
be a devastating first love. What the outcome
would be Shelley could not hazard a guess, but she
did know that the idea of fading out of the lives of
Wendy and Stephen was growing stronger with
every moment that passed. She glanced at her
watch and felt the urgency of time being short.
Stephen would be here within a few minutes and
she did not want him to find her with Wendy.

'It's on the cards that I will go away,' she said
quickly. And then, sending the girl a direct look,
'Stephen mustn't know we've met, understand—?
No, don't interrupt! He'll be here directly and I
want him to find you alone—' She beckoned to a
passing waiter and asked him to clear her place. If
he felt any surprise he hid it very well as he said
politely, 'Certainly, madam.'

'You must see,' went on Shelley in haste, 'that if
Stephen were to know what's happened this afternoon he'd feel dreadfully guilty—at letting us both
down. I'll confess that he really is keen on my going
to Greece, which surprised me at the time but it's
explained now: He wanted to be with you. That

doesn't say he wants to marry you,' warned Shelley
as the girl opened her mouth to speak. 'It's my
guess that at this present time he doesn't know his
own mind. If I go away it'll give him the opportunity of discovering his true feelings about you. But
for your part—no mention of having ever met me,
understand?'

Wendy nodded her head and Shelley gave a sigh
of relief. She had half expected the girl to put forth
some kind of argument in favour of their being
totally honest with Stephen.

'Yes, I understand, Miss Scott—'

'Shelley's the name.'

The girl coloured faintly and forced a smile.

'It's a nice name,' she commented shyly.

'It's after the poet—it was bound to be, as my
mother was mad about Shelley.'

This little diversion had taken away any small
amount of tension there had been between the two
girls, and it seemed also to have taken away
Wendy's diffidence. She seemed more cool, and a
little more mature as she said, watching Shelley rise
from the table and sling her bag over her shoulder,
'When will you be going, Shelley? We'll meet again
before then, please?'

'Is it necessary?' Shelley looked down at her and
felt, somehow that, young as she was, she might
after all be the right girl for Stephen.

'Not necessary but I'd like it.'

'But you can't give a reason?'

'I suppose I just want to—well—to thank you.
After all, it isn't every girl who'd be willing to give
up her fiancé for someone else to step into her
shoes.' She stopped abruptly as Shelley threw back
her head and laughed softly.

'You're taking a lot for granted, Wendy,' she said

on a note of warning. 'I hope you're not in for a disappointment.' She glanced around swiftly. 'No,' she added, 'not many girls would go away and leave the coast clear for another. But,' she went on with a quality of tartness to her voice, 'I'm not giving him up, as you appear to think. I shall make that decision when I come back. As for when I shall be going—that depends on the client.'

'I hope you enjoy the time you're away, Shelley.'

Shelley looked at her and drew a breath.

'And I hope you do too,' she retorted with an edge of sarcasm. 'Take good care of *my* fiancé!' And on that parting shot she inclined her head in a gesture of farewell and walked briskly away.

Chapter Seven

It was natural that Shelley should dwell on what had transpired, not only regarding her meeting with Wendy, but on Stephen's attitude and the way she had been puzzled by it. Much had been explained: it was clear that Stephen, having become interested in Wendy, was desirous of 'getting rid' of his fiancée for a while, so that he could be free to see Wendy and allow his feelings for her either to develop or to fade. He wanted to discover just exactly how he felt about the girl, having in mind the whole time that he wasn't in love with his fiancée. Well, that was fair enough, and patently clear.

But what was not so clear was that other baffling aspect of Stephen's manner for it did seem to Shelley that he was hiding something more than his 'duplicity' over herself and Wendy.

Had Nick done or said something that had

supported Stephen's desire for Shelley to go to Greece? Undoubtedly Stephen's whole attitude had been strange, unfathomable when he was talking about Nick.

'Something's happened between you two,' Stephen had said, and she remembered his staring at her in a way that portrayed a strong curiosity. Did Stephen suspect that she and Nick had been intimate? A heavy frown puckered Shelley's brow; she hated the idea of Stephen's knowing about things like that for after all they *were* still engaged to be married. She recalled thinking vaguely that some sort of conspiracy might have been taking place— yet on the other hand, she had had the impression that Stephen was faintly baffled. However, she now felt sure that Stephen had suspected that Nick had some deeper motive for wanting Shelley in Greece than that of renovations to the house. Again Shelley frowned. She hated mysteries and certainly a mystery seemed to exist here. She toyed with the idea of changing her mind again and keeping to her resolve not to go to Greece with Nick.

And it was in this state of indecision that she wandered from room to room the following day as the very final touches were being made to the manor house. Everything looked wonderful, and yet practically none of the ancient atmosphere of mellowness had been lost. A sunblind was at present being fixed over a room at the end of the building, a south-facing room—Nick's study. She was drawn to that room and she opened the door quietly and went in. She could imagine Nick sitting here, at the big Georgian desk, could see his books neatly arrayed on the shelves— Her reverie was cut as the door opened and Delia stood there, tall and lovely, her slender figure immaculately attired in a Réty suit which had plainly cost a fortune. Her bag was of crocodile skin, to match her shoes. Breathtaking was the word which came swiftly to Shelley's mind and she had to admit that the girl would certainly be an asset to Nick in his business career. She stared at Shelley across the room; her mouth went tight, compressed into a thin red line, and the nostrils seemed to quiver and flare. Puzzled, Shelley opened her mouth to ask what was wrong but Delia was before her. She stepped further into the room as she spoke.

'What's all this about your going to Greece with Mr. Montpelier?' she gritted. 'Perhaps you can explain!'

Shelley frowned.

'Nothing's been settled,' she began. 'However—'

'It has been settled, according to Nick! He wants another house renovating, and he insists that no one can do it as well as you! It's the most crazy thing—his wanting to take you over there when we're supposed to be getting married!'

'Supposed to be?' queried Shelley, unconsciously moving a step backwards towards the window, on the outside of which the two men were still working on the sunblind.

'We *are* getting married,' snapped Delia as if impatient with the question. 'But before then Nick's doing this other house up! It doesn't make sense—'

'Nick has told you he's taking me to Greece?'

Delia's eyes blazed at Shelley's way of phrasing the question. Her face was flushed and the slender white hands were clenched, one around the strap of her bag and the other at her side.

'I said before that I've noticed things—the way my fiancé looks at you, in a way I can't fathom—'

'Then why,' broke in Shelley with an acid-sweet smile, 'didn't you ask Nick about it? Surely he'd be willing to explain.'

'Explain what?' the other girl countered, eyes glittering now and her chest heaving as if she was having some difficulty with her breathing.

Shelley gave a small, impatient sigh. Why was she standing here arguing with the girl? After all, hadn't she almost made up her mind not to go with Nick to Greece? She could set this girl's mind at rest by telling her so . . . but for some reason she could not explain Shelley remained silent, and in any case, Delia was speaking again, and this time her voice was somewhat muffled, as if her throat was full, choked.

'You call him Nick, in that familiar fashion! And from the first you've tried to make him notice you—I've already told you I'm not blind! You've deliberately engineered this trip to Greece—I know it! But—' She advanced slowly across the room and for one stunned moment Shelley steeled herself against physical attack. But the girl stopped, body visibly quivering and it was plain that she was under the influence of an emotion that was creating chaos within her. Jealousy was breeding frenzy and despite her intense dislike of the girl Shelley could not help feeling sorry for her. 'But,' she went on with a glowering stare, 'it is not going to happen! You'll tell him you're not able to go—do you hear!' The last three words were screamed, almost, and Shelley turned her head to see if the men outside had heard. Yes, they were both staring into the room. Shelley said quietly,

'My advice to you, Miss Unwin, is to have this out with your fiancé—'

'He won't talk about it, or listen—!' She broke off abruptly but knew it was too late, and humiliation gave even more colour to her face.

'If he were my fiancé,' Shelley could not help saying, 'I'd make him listen.'

Delia looked at her, teeth gritting and the sound pressing on Shelley's nerve-ends.

'Even this is familiar—the way you're talking, I mean. Is this the way you discuss all your clients?'

'Don't be absurd. My clients' fiancés are not in the habit of approaching me in the way you have.' Shelley paused, frowning with impatience. She was more puzzled than ever now, but one thing she did know . . . she was being urged, by some unfathomable force within her, to go to Greece with Nick.

'You're impertinent!' Delia swung away and made for the door. 'I shall take your advice and make Nick explain! But you,' she added on reaching the door and turning her immaculately-coiffeured head, 'will do as I say and tell him you are not able to go!' And with that she went out, slamming the door behind her.

Shelley stood motionless for a long time, until she suddenly became aware that the two men had gone and it was beginning to rain, the drops loud and heavy against the window.

Soon it was a downpour, bringing a dimness to the room and, outside, creating a depressing metal-greyness over the whole landscape. A lake in the distance was soon being lashed, and twigs broken from trees were floating on its surface. Silence but for wind and rain. . . . Shelley felt the awful oppression of loneliness, of isolation, and the house seemed all at once to be forlorn and unfriendly.

She sighed, and almost without knowing it opened the top centre drawer of Nick's desk. Unseeingly she stared at the few papers lying there, vaguely thinking they couldn't be important, seeing that Nick had not bothered to lock the drawer. The small gilt key was in the lock. The weight of oppression was still pressing on her; she did not know what was the matter with her—this unwanted restlessness sweeping over her, and a sort of fatalistic sense of helplessness because of a reappearing indecision regarding this trip to Greece. Nick surely had some ulterior motive, since the action did not make sense in the light of his imminent marriage—or at least, it was supposed to be imminent, as they were only waiting for the manor to be finished.

And now that it was finished, Nick was deliberately postponing the wedding, and not only that, but he was taking his former wife over to Greece!

Another sigh, and a frowning glance through the window. Did it have to rain today, adding to her depression? It came down with undiminished vigour and the grounds seemed to take on an almost eerie aspect. Shelley felt a shiver run along her spine and she wished she had left before the downpour began. The two men who had been working had gone off in their van and she was alone in the house . . . alone with ghosts of its ancient past?

Ghosts? Why a thought like that? She loved this house . . . or did she? Delia's presence was here, even in this room which was essentially to be

Nick's. Delia seemed to be everywhere, thought Shelley, now that she began to dwell on it. Delia in the bedroom, the bathroom, the lovely drawing room. . . .

No ghost, but reality, and Shelley wanted to get away from the house, eager to leave for the very first time. She made to close the desk drawer, then a box caught her eye, not a jewel box exactly, but a very attractive, suede-covered box which had been made for—what? Curiosity became strong but a sense of honour fought it and she stood there, undecided, longing to know what the box contained and feeling convinced that curiosity would win in the end. But just as she was putting her hand into the drawer she swung around and there was Nick. His eyes flickered to the drawer; without a word he moved with his customary lithe grace and closed the drawer. Shelley felt the blood hot in her cheeks, opened her mouth to make some wild excuse then closed it again, aware that Nick, no fool, had guessed at her intention.

But he made no comment on that guess as he said, 'Everything all right? I see the men doing the sunblind have been rained off.' He glanced towards the window, hair glistening, jacket and slacks darkened in places by rain. He brushed a hand through his hair and brought out a handkerchief to dry his face. 'You look . . . strange.' Eyes flickered again to the drawer and she rather thought he was now wondering if she had already looked into the box and had been putting it back when he entered the study. 'You're not unwell, I hope?' He sounded anxious, she thought and shook her head to reassure him.

'I'm fine.' She paused a second or two and then

added, looking straightly at him, 'Miss Unwin's been here; she can't understand why you want me to go to Greece with you—and, in fact, neither can I.' The two had again just missed one another . . . so very strange.

'Didn't your—er—fiancé explain—' Nick's eyes wandered to her left hand, and the ring sparkling there. 'I want to renovate the house my aunt left me and you're the one for the job; it's as simple as that.'

'Simple, is it?' She shot him a challenging glance. 'And what of your marriage? Miss Unwin's very upset—'

'What did she say to you about it?' broke in Nick curiously.

'How cool you are!'

He only laughed at that and responded lightly, 'When can you be ready to come with me to Greece?'

'When—!' Shelley gaped at him. 'I haven't even said I'll come,' she managed to retort at last. 'I want a reason first.'

'Do you?' he murmured with a strange inflection, and with those piercing, metallic eyes fixing hers. 'Do you, really, Shelley?' It was almost as if in his mind he was adding, 'You know very well you want to come, and it's not only to spite Delia.' But aloud he went on, 'I've given you a reason, Shelley. I want that house done up to perfection and no one will be able to do that except you.'

'You haven't experienced the work of others in Stephen's employ,' she pointed out but Nick was shaking his head.

'I want you,' he stated emphatically. 'And that ends the matter.'

'It does not! I haven't made up my mind.'

Ignoring that Nick looked at his watch.

'Have dinner with me tonight,' he said and the inflection was imperious. 'We'll stay at the hotel—'

'I'm going home!'

'In this storm?' with a lift of his straight dark brows. 'If I remember rightly you were as reluctant to drive in bad weather as you were in the dark.'

'The storm will abate soon,' she asserted but, glancing through the window to the oppressive ash-grey sky she very much doubted it. Everywhere was so bleak, and suddenly she felt tears behind her eyes and saw Nick's own eyes open wide.

'What's wrong?' he asked almost roughly. 'You're upset about something?'

'I'm a little depressed, that's all— Don't ask me why!' she cried as he was about to interrupt. 'I can feel *down*, can't I, without having to supply an explanation!' It was a childish outburst but she wasn't prepared for the result. For Nick's voice was almost tender as he said, holding out a handkerchief as a tear rolled down her cheek, 'Stop being all tight inside, Shelley. Just let yourself go, and enjoy the trip to Greece.'

'I haven't said—'

'No more argument,' he interrupted in that old familiar way of speaking, and with the same masterful expression in his dark eyes. 'Your fiancé— employer's agreeable; I want you, and so you have no choice.'

'Oh, yes, I do have a choice.' Shelley dried her cheek, blew her nose vigorously and handed him back his handkerchief, which he accepted gingerly but with a gleam of amusement in his eyes. Shelley had no idea just how young she looked at this moment, how forlorn and tired. 'Another thing,' she went on after a while, 'is the puzzling fact that Stephen actually wants me to go with you. What did you tell him to make him so eager for me to go away with another man—and the one I'd been married to. It doesn't make much sense to me.' She was being a little specious, she knew, because she had already decided that the main reason for Stephen's wish was that he could be with Wendy.

Nick was pausing, as if carefully choosing his words.

'It was perhaps as much what he said to me as what I said to him, but I'm not intending to expand on that, Shelley, so you needn't insist as it'll get you nowhere.' Imperious the tone and firm. She said with a hint of anger, 'You've not changed a bit, have you? Still the domineering male as you were before.'

'Before . . . ?' He smiled enigmatically. 'I was the domineering *husband,* remember?'

She was puzzled by this comment and it showed in her expression.

'You remind me that we were once married . . . why?' Nerves were tingling and pulses erratic. Had she a chance with Nick after all? Could they possibly get together? It was said that no one should ever go back, but conversely with this was the undeniably truism that mistakes should be rectified if at all possible.

And she knew the divorce had been a mistake . . . but did Nick? It was hard to tell. Would she gain anything by telling him of her mother's treachery? No, now was not the time . . . but. . . .

'Do I need to remind you that we were once married?' Nick's tone was dry, his expression one of amused satire. 'I think not, Shelley.' A pause but she made no comment. 'Well, are you dining with me or not?'

'I thought you'd decided definitely that I was.'

He laughed.

'So you like to be bossed about—'

'No such thing!'

He gave a small sigh but was still amused.

'Let us cease this bantering and settle a couple of things. One, you *are* coming to dinner with me, and two, you *are* coming to Greece with me. And now, get your coat and we'll make a dash through this storm to my car and drive into town.' He looked over her shoulder and frowned. 'What a climate! Why do we live here when there's so much sunshine elsewhere?' He seemed almost to be talking to himself and she stared a moment before saying slowly, '*You* can live elsewhere, Nick, but most people can't.'

'Very true.'

'Besides, you've had this house done up so obviously you intend settling in England.'

He turned to the door, ignoring what she had said.

'Come on—is your coat in the hall?'

'Yes; I'll get it. I want my briefcase as well. It's in the lounge.'

'I'll. . . .' His voice trailed as his eyes wandered to the desk. 'Go and fetch it, then,' he said abruptly and held the door open for her.

She glanced back; he was going towards the desk and she knew of course that he had been going to say he would fetch the briefcase for her but had changed his mind. He wanted to lock the desk drawer—or perhaps he was removing that little box altogether. Either way, he was making sure that she would have no opportunity of assuaging her curiosity.

Chapter Eight

They had flown to Athens and from there to Corfu, and now the plane was descending towards verdent forests and golden cornfields as it glided over the lagoon. The sun was shining and the view downwards seemed full of promise and Shelley gave an unconscious little sigh, bringing her companion's eyes around, an interrogating expression on his face.

'What was that for?' he wanted to know and without stopping to think she had revealed the picture in her mind.

'It's as if a warm smile hovered over everything.' And she stopped somewhat abruptly, delicate colour mounting her cheeks. Nick's eyes, unmoving, remained on her with a mask-like expression she would have given anything to interpret.

'You have a rather charming turn of phrase,' he commented at last and with a tinge of amusement.

'So you're favourably impressed with the island it would seem?'

'It certainly looks attractive.'

'You'll like the house,' he said, turning to glance down as they came in to land.

Shelley said nothing; this whole expedition savoured of something unreal, as if she were dreaming it. Nick, her ex-husband with whom she had again fallen in love, here with her in Greece, his mother's country.

And Nick was engaged to another girl; she, Shelley, engaged to another man. How had this situation come about? She would have been simpleminded had she been content to accept what was on the surface which was that Nick, desiring to renovate the house left him by an aged aunt who had occupied it for over forty years, had enlisted the services of a girl whom he could trust to carry out the work efficiently, since she had already proved her worth. Oh, yes, that part of the situation was simple enough. But Shelley had a very strong suspicion that something much deeper—and more important—lay beneath the surface. She sent him a slantways glance as they touched down on the runway and wondered again if she had any chance with him. His profile showed a set, firmly chiselled outline so strongly portrayed in the statues of Greek gods and heroes which were to be seen in most of the museums of the world.

His was an enigmatic personality; he hid his thoughts and intentions well; this much Shelley had learned during that brief period of their marriage.

The small village of Catones, high above Paliokastritsa, was their destination and they arrived there in the hired car which Nick had previously ordered and which was ready for them at the airport.

Nick drove, while Shelley was engrossed in the scenery. As they neared Paliokastritsa she became aware of thousands of olive trees, their gnarled and twisted trunks indicative of their great age. Cypresses, too, often dominated the view on the landward side. On the other side the sea shone like a million diamonds, using the captured sunlight to enhance its surface. At times, though, colours could be seen—pale aquamarine and amber, pearl and blue and sometimes a hint of gold. It looked warm and velvety. Crags came into view, and with them the impression of invisible danger. In a cove hereabouts legend had it that Nausicaa, 'Tall, pale and beautiful as a goddess' found the naked Ulysses and took him to her father's palace.

Shelley's thoughts were cut into as her companion spoke, asking what she was thinking about.

'As a matter-of-fact, I was away in the distant past, in the realms of mythology,' she answered with a laugh. 'Nausicaa and all that.'

Nick caught her humour and laughed.

'If mythology interests you then you will really enjoy yourself here in Greece.'

'But I haven't come for enjoyment,' she reminded him softly. 'I'm here to do a job of work.'

'Of course,' briefly as he negotiated a dangerous bend in the road. He changed the subject to say, after awhile, 'It becomes hot here but we do have a breeze coming in from the sea. You'll find the food different, too— But you like fish so you'll enjoy the seafood meals they serve in the restaurants.'

'I thought you said we were staying in the house? You said you had servants—'

'We're living in the house, yes, but we'll certainly not be eating much there. I've no one who can cook properly so we'll eat out for the most part. Definitely we shall eat out at night.' He continued by telling her of the way of life in the village, with the men going out in the evenings to spear octopuses and squid, helped by the light from flaring carbide lamps fixed to the front of the boats. And, when they passed a woman carrying a heavy load he seemed unable to suppress the comment, spoken with an unmistakable hint of mocking amusement, 'Another thing you will find in Greece: Peasant women are subject to the rigid rule of male authority.'

'Oh—and don't you wish you were all Greek?' she inquired tartly.

'What exactly does that mean?' Nick slowed down to take another nasty bend.

'That you could assert your rigid rule of male authority over your poor, downtrodden wife.'

Nick threw back his head and laughed.

'Getting at me, eh? You've gained confidence, my girl. At one time you'd never have spoken to me like that.'

'At seventeen one doesn't have much courage at all.'

'But now you do have courage.' He was in a narrow lane now and it was bordered by masses of oleander bushes, the delicate flowers of white and pink and red moving gently in the breeze. A gate at the end of this lane led them off to a sort of track, and on the left the low, sprawling villa came into view. Shelley grimaced and said, 'It's large, but not very prepossessing.'

'I told you it had been sadly neglected.'

'It'll be a bigger challenge than the manor

house.' The car had slid to a standstill and she alighted before Nick could come round to open the door for her.

'And a vastly different one,' commented Nick as he came to her side and stood for a long moment staring at the house. It was difficult to form any sort of picture as to what it would eventually look like because practically the whole of the front wall was covered with a smothering creeper which had reached right up to the roof, and sprawled over it to hang down in numerous places, many of the shoots bare of leaves and so resembling the down-hanging roots of the banyan tree. Shelley turned her head to look up at the owner and again grimaced.

'Where do we start?' she wanted to know.

'You'll have all the help you need,' he assured her, adding that the outside was not her problem anyway. He would hire a firm of landscape gardeners.

It was the following day that Nick said, a curious inflection in his voice, 'You've never asked me why I haven't brought Delia with me.'

'Because it isn't any concern of mine.' Shelley hoped she sounded casually indifferent.

'But surely it seems rather odd?'

'I'm here to carry out work, Nick, not to question your private actions.'

'And you're not curious?'

They were in a little *taverna* on the beach, eating kebabs and delicious fresh salads and washing it all down with a fruity local wine. They had been looking over the villa for the whole of the morning and nothing had come into the conversation that did not concern the task in hand. Now, however,

Nick was bringing a personal element into it and it was as if he were attempting to force Shelley to admit to being curious about Delia's not being here.

Shelley hesitated before answering his question and when eventually she did it was immediately followed by a question of her own.

'It is natural that I should consider it a little strange that your fiancée is to have no say whatsoever in the renovation of a house in which she will be spending some of her time—' She broke off to look up into his lean, saturnine face with its very dark eyes and taut, masterful jawline, its sensuous mouth and thrusting chin. 'You appear to be eager to explain, Nick, so I'm willing to listen. Tell me why you have left Miss Unwin behind.'

Nick's lips twisted in a smile.

'I knew you were curious. Why did you have to be prompted before you could bring yourself to question me?'

'I don't think I understand your attitude,' she almost snapped. And she concentrated on her food, then lifted her glass to sip her wine. Two men came out on to an improvised stage and began to dance the *syrtaki* to the strains of *bouzouki* music coming from a tape recorder whose speaker was somewhere in the trees. Shelley was in reality waiting for Nick to explain but to her disappointment he was now fully interested in the dancers and she knew she was not going to get an answer, at least not today.

Two more men came out, linked together by a handkerchief clasped in their fingers, their olive faces intensely solemn as they dipped and rocked with movements far more slow and serious than those of the first two men. For this was the *tsamiko*, and the strains of the music had become mournful and much less vibrant.

As they were walking back to the villa the topic reverted to the alterations which were proposed there and it suddenly struck Shelley that everything she had suggested up till now had been accepted unconditionally by Nick. So after awhile she said without much expression, 'Do you think that Miss Unwin would want the saloon to be in blue—the carpet and drapes, I mean?'

'Oh, I should think she'll like it well enough.'

'And white walls?'

'White walls give one the opportunity of hanging pictures to great advantage.'

'I was asking if Miss Unwin would like them to be white.'

Nick changed the subject, talking now about the garden and what he proposed doing with it.

Shelley merely listened, and when they were back at the villa she went off on her own with a notebook and pencil. The two people who had been caretaking were Costos and Eleni Levendis, married and aged about forty-five or so. Their children were all married and the reason why Costos and Eleni were here, residents in this villa, was that they had been forced to give up their house and land as a dowry for the youngest daughter, or otherwise the girl would not have been able to find a husband. Costos and his wife and one son had worked for many years, scheming and scraping to save every *drachma* to provide dowries for the other three daughters. Now, the couple were without a home of their own but Nick, who had decided to keep them on after inheriting the property, had hinted to Shelley that he would have a small building done up for them. It was a sort of workshop and Nick felt it could be made habitable and very bright if Shelley would plan its transformation. The couple would still be in Nick's employ and spend most of their time at his villa, but they would also have a home of their own.

Costos came up to Shelley as she was busily sketching on her pad. She glanced up with a smile and he returned it, gold fillings revealed as he parted his dry lips.

'You're wanted on the telephone, miss,' he said. 'It's a call from England I think.'

'Thank you, Costos.' From England? Stephen, she supposed, and it was.

'How are things going?' he wanted to know.

'It's early days and we haven't managed to get any further than sketches and suggestions.'

'How about supplies?'

'They don't present any real difficulty here. This is a very civilised island, more Italianate than Greek—or so it seems to me.' Shelley did believe that with certain commodities she might have difficulty in obtaining supplies but she felt there was nothing to be gained by mentioning this to Stephen.

'And—er—our client?'

The hesitation was not lost on her and she said curiously, 'Is there any particular reason for asking, Stephen?'

'Why—no, of course not,' swiftly and followed by the prosaic, 'What makes you ask?'

She had to smile as she returned, 'Forget it, Stephen.' And then, without much expression, 'Are you having a good time, without me?'

'Er . . . I'm very busy, of course.'

Shelley had to laugh, but she covered the mouthpiece with her hand. Stephen was speaking again,

saying that Miss Unwin had been into the office to
see him and complain about several things at the
manor.

'I told her to see Mr. Montpelier,' he ended and
a moment later Shelley was replacing the receiver.
She was in the room designated at Nick's study—a
charming airy room with windows facing the sea
and a display case containing seashells and other
marine curiosities. On a shelf were two ikons and in
front of them two candles in pewter candlesticks.
Nick came in just as she was about to leave and he
asked to see her sketches.

'Hmm . . . And now let us take a look at the
dining room.'

'I think I ought to tell you that Miss Unwin's
been into Stephen's office to make complaints.'

'How do you know?'

'He's just phoned me.'

'What are the complaints about?' Nick strolled
casually over to the shelf and took down one of the
ikons to examine the work.

'Stephen didn't say. He told her to get in touch
with you.'

Nick glanced up, the ikon still in his hand.
Shelley drew a breath. How tall and straight, with
that distinguished air which alone seemed to set
him above any other man she had ever met. Why
had she ever let him go!

'I'll have a word with her later. Meanwhile. . . .'
He paused and glanced through the window. 'I feel
like a swim. You can come with me.'

Her heart leapt. But she mustn't appear to
eager.

'I'm here to work, Nick—'

'There's not much you can do until supplies
arrive.'

'But I haven't ordered any. If I make the list out then I'll know exactly what I want for each room, how many workmen, and—'

'It'll keep,' imperiously as he replaced the ikon. 'Get rid of these,' he said as if the idea had just occurred to him. 'But don't throw them away; they're valuable. Give them to Costos for his new home.'

The water was like silk on Shelley's skin, the air crystal clear, and warm in the golden light of mid-afternoon. Nick was swimming strongly towards some rocks and Shelley came out of the water and picked up the towel, her eyes, narrowed against the brightness of the sun, following his progress, a brooding expression in their depths. If only Nick would give her a hint of his feelings, just one small clue which would provide the optimism for her to reveal her mother's treachery. Nick never even mentioned the past or the divorce— well, scarcely ever. It was as if he still harboured a grudge and yet had no real wish to let her see it . . . at least, not nowadays. At first he was almost spiteful in his desire to hurt her by making her do up the house which he and she had so wanted for their own. He seemed to have been driven to punishing her, but gradually she had seen that he no longer wanted to punish her—but as she had told herself already, this changed attitude did not mean he wanted her back. Shelley had to face the fact that he was after all engaged to another girl and that he had given no indication that he had any intention of jilting her. That he was not in love with her seemed plain, but deep love was rare these days anyway, and from what Shelley had seen, many couples adopted this casual way with one another.

So different it had been with her and Nick! Their love had been so deep that they had had to show it. And yet, if it *was* deep then how was it that they'd not only parted but gone the whole way—as far as divorce?

Nick was calling and lifting a hand. He wanted her to go back into the water but she stayed where she was, allowing the sun to finish off the drying process. She wanted to get a tan while she was here if that were possible and she now lay back, resting on her arms, and still watching Nick. He came out at last and she handed him the other towel, her eyes meeting his and becoming locked for a long moment before he looked down, to strip the scanty covering from her and laugh softly at her heightened colour.

'We *have* been married,' he couldn't help reminding her with a hint of mockery in his voice. 'Also, we've made love more recently so I fail to see why you should be shy with me.' He was using the towel; she became profoundly conscious of his powerful muscles as he dried thighs and legs, vitally aware of his sex appeal as her eyes wandered. . . .

He watched her intently, the sensuous mouth curved in a smile of amused satire, the dark metallic eyes narrowed and gleaming with a kind of fire which was by no means difficult to interpret. There was no one else on the beach and he reached down, a swift masterful movement which brought her to her feet and to the cool dampness of his body. Shelley tried to pull away but his arms were hawsers, one palm flattened on her back and the other preventing her from moving her head as his mouth came down to possess hers. She had no wish to struggle; on the contrary, she eagerly parted her lips for his tongue to enter her mouth, and as eagerly lifted her arms to slide them round his naked shoulders. His voice was throaty and low as he said, 'Let us go in, Shelley. . . .' and she nodded her head and gave him a lovely smile.

But as they walked back to the villa both knew that the moment was lost, and so the rest of the afternoon was given over to business. Then they went out to dine at the Castello Hotel which overlooked the sea. They had a variety of roasted meats and salads, and Shelley was adventurous, trying the cucumber in yogurt, with dill and garlic. Wine was a rosé, medium-dry and very much enjoyed by them both. It was almost as if the years between had never been, except that Shelley did not feel like seventeen again any more than she looked it, and Nick was older, too . . . and they both were wiser. Should she speak, voice the question which would change her whole life if answered the way she hoped? But no. Nick was charming with her but she could not help recalling his callousness after they had made love, letting her know that it had meant nothing more than an interlude of pleasure and satisfaction . . . there was nothing deeper than the erotic joy of sex.

'Shall we go?' His voice broke into her musings and she gave him a smile. Her heart was beating far too quickly; her pulse was erratic. She swallowed convulsively for her throat felt tight and very dry.

'It's been a wonderful evening.' Shelley rose as she spoke.

'Yes; I've enjoyed it, too.' He took her arm, just like before—oh, so long ago it seemed now and the years between increased to eternity. Shelley was so affected by emotion she wanted to cry . . . on Nick's shoulder, with his strong arms about her, his tender words to comfort her, his gentle touch flicking away her tears.

They were at the car; he stood looking down into her eyes and a sigh seemed to accompany the frown between his eyes. What were his thoughts?

'You look tired,' he observed and suddenly he was touching her cheek. 'And you're pale.'

'I think the weather—I mean, I'm unused to the heat.'

'You find it hot here?' He seemed faintly anxious, she thought and wondered why. 'You don't like heat?'

'I do—yes, of course. But I'm not used to it yet. In another day or two. . . .'

He helped her into the car and soon they were driving along the road leading to the villa. The track was reached and Nick turned into it, and the villa in the moonlight looked friendly and inviting, warm and welcoming. Shelley's thoughts winged to the manor, and the way it had seemed weird, no, eerie, in the dimness.

'But we both loved it—' Shelley spoke her thoughts aloud and then stopped abruptly, a little stunned at what she had done.

'Loved what?' Nick slowed down as he slanted her a glance.

'I was thinking of the manor—and comparing it— Take no notice,' she added hastily and with a hint of impatience. 'I spoke without thinking.'

'The manor, and comparing it with this?'

'There is no real comparison.' Shelley depressed the door handle as the car slid to a stop on the rough gravel outside the front door.

'No, there isn't.' Nick came round to her side

and looked at the dark facade where the creeper flourished. 'This is a typical Greek villa and Allswick Manor is a typical English medieval house.'

'Both have a charm of their own.'

'The charms of this villa haven't been brought out yet.'

'They will be.' Shelley could not imagine Delia here; she belonged to everything that was British, somehow.

'And soon.'

'We haven't made a start yet.'

'Tomorrow we shall have all the basic details mapped out.'

She looked up at him.

'You mean, you're going to take a hand in the planning of the renovations?'

Nick gave a nod of his dark head.

'You and I shall plan everything together . . . down to the last detail.'

Nerves tingling and heart racing; hope and fear alternating in rapid succession. She just had to say, 'Supposing—supposing your fiancée doesn't—like what we've planned?'

'My fiancée. . . .' His voice seemed taut, but there was nothing to be read from his expression. 'She'll like it, all right.' Something cryptic in the tone? Shelley felt impatient with herself for her inability to understand him.

'Shall we go in?' she suggested and moved away. The light was on in the hall and in the sitting-room but there was no sign of life when they entered the villa after Nick had used his own key to unlock the door.

'Oh, Mr. Nickolas!' It was Eleni, looking apologetic. 'You should have rung the bell.' She spoke good English, almost as good as her husband. 'Sorry for not being here to open the door for you.'

'It's all right, Eleni. You can go. We don't want anything tonight.'

She smiled at them in turn.

'I go, then, *Kalinikta!*'

'*Kalinikta,* Eleni.'

He was smiling down into Shelley's face as the woman walked away.

'No, I don't speak Greek, but one should always be able to pass the time of day, wherever one is.'

'I expect you did learn a little Greek when you were over here?'

'A little,' he admitted, 'but not as much as I shall learn.'

'Shall?' with a swift glance of inquiry. 'You aren't intending to live permanently in Greece, are you, Nick?'

'I might, who knows? You must admit we have a deplorable climate in our country.'

'You'd live in Greece. . . . So this villa's really being done up as your permanent home? Your fiancée—'

'Shall we go into the saloon?' suggested Nick deliberately lifting a hand to hide a yawn which, Shelley suspected, was not there at all. 'I know it isn't very comfortable but we can sit down and have a drink.'

'It can be a beautiful room,' Shelley was remarking as she cast a professional eye around her. She had been given her drink and she was sitting back in her chair, shapely legs crossed, glass in hand. 'Very beautiful, Nick.'

'Comfort is more important than beauty, but if we can achieve both so much the better.' He had been standing by a cupboard which was an improvised cocktail cabinet but he moved slowly towards where she was sitting, tall and lithe, his slim frame erect. An arresting figure, an aristocrat . . . Shelley caught her breath, willing him to come closer.

As though he read her desire Nick placed his glass on a low table and came slowly towards her, an enigmatic half smile lifting one corner of his mouth, his eyes locked to hers with an expression of mockery in their depths.

Stooping, he took the glass from her fingers and put it on the small, occasional table at her elbow.

'You're no longer tired.' The observation was voiced with a touch of satire as he pulled Shelley to her feet. Quivering at the nearness of him, deeply affected by the male aroma of him, she made no attempt to resist when with an imperious gesture he tipped back her face and bent his dark head to take her lips with that sort of masterful possession which she knew so well from those days of her marriage— and more recently. His sensuous mouth explored moistly before his tongue began to probe and she parted her lips, a spasm of pleasure rippling through her as his tongue caressed hers. Instinctively she arched herself towards him, vitally aware of the flexed muscles of his thighs, whipcord hard against her soft and pliant curves. She felt him shudder slightly, and his heart was beating as unevenly as hers.

His hands moved in sensuous exploration, sliding slowly along her curves in their progress downwards, while Shelley's own hands were not idle, and she was aware of his heightened emotions as she caressed his nape, and the sensitive places beneath his ears. She began to feel the desperate longing for fulfilment as Nick's practised hands explored more and more intimately, stimulating her erotic senses by his previous knowledge of what aroused her. His mouth widened, devouring hers, and the tip of his tongue was caressing the inside of her lips and cheeks. She uttered a little moan of pleasure as his tantalising hands curved around her body, to bring it even closer to compel her to an awareness of his hard masculinity.

'Shelley . . . you're even more desirable now—' Suddenly his voice roughened and so did his actions, and Shelley felt the blood pounding in her head as she was drawn helplessly into the vortex of a passion that was all Greek in its demanding ruthlessness. She was swung off her feet and right up into his arms. She relaxed against him, lost in the sublime realm of physical love and expectation. His rhythmic movements in themselves were exciting and she clung to him as he carried her along the wide corridor to the bedroom she had occupied, and in which there was a large divan bed.

He undressed her gently, as in the old days, savouring the removal of every garment until she was clad only in two scanty bits of lace. He held her at arms' length, his eyes glittering fiercely as they roved over her. She coloured delicately but smiled, too. And after a long silent moment she shyly took his hand and placed it on her breast, and her eyes were tenderly pleading as they gazed into his.

She saw a darkening of his eyes as passion flared again within him; she noticed a pulse-beat uncontrolled at the side of his throat. His mouth came down, slowly, tantalisingly, and the hand on her breast curled and the erect little nipple was trapped between his lean brown fingers. A quiver that was both pain and pleasure shook her slender body and within seconds she was once again drowned within the deluge of his passion.

It was a long while later that she said huskily, 'Do you love, Nick?'

No answer. The man beside her was sleeping. . . .

Chapter Nine

There was a wistful expression on Shelley's face as
Nick, having wakened with the dawn, immediately
slid from the bed after no more than a cursory
glance at his wife. She had been awake for some
time, had lain there with growing expectancy,
waiting for Nick to open his eyes. She had eased
herself up on one arm to savour the masculine
appeal of him, for she knew what he looked like in
sleep. All the familiar hauteur was there but the
noble face, relaxed in slumber, had a softened
look, and the sensuous lips seemed faintly to smile
in an enigmatic sort of way that in itself was oddly
appealing to the girl who adored him.

How strange that she should have believed she
had recovered. She had in recent months dwelt on
the possibility of finding someone else with whom
she would fall madly in love and with whom she
would make a new and more lasting marriage.

And then fate had stepped in and she was now as wildly in love with Nick as she had ever been. Wildly in love, yes, but not quite in the same way as before, for now she was older, more mature, and she knew her love was stronger and deeper . . . and it would last forever. If Nick was not to be hers then she would remain single for the rest of her life. It was a gloomy prospect and now it seemed gloomier still because of Nick's action in going off to the bathroom without one word of greeting, and because she had recently cherished hopes of a reunion, and a remarriage.

She flung back the covers, slipped from the bed and put on her dressing gown. There was the sound of splashing water and she sighed; Nick was taking a bath . . . and he was singing quietly. Shelley went over to the window and pulled back the drapes. The garden was wild but many of the original bushes and trees had survived the invasion of weeds, and in the morning sun an hibiscus hedge glowed red, like fire newly fanned, and oleanders reared above a mass of ground creepers. A spectrum of anemones with their dazzling mauves and lavenders, crimsons and yellows and whites and purples and blues . . . a few brilliant red poppies too, and then the trees: jasmine and jacaranda and pencil slim cypresses rising to the sky, like sentinels guarding the border. So peaceful, with the sea not any distance away in the other direction, its 'wine-dark' waters stealing light from the sun to create a million stars flickering on its surface. Shelley's eyes became pensive; she was conscious of a little shock of surprise.

She could live here . . . she actually preferred this house to the manor in which she had believed she could have settled till she died.

Turning, she encountered the tall figure of the man who had once been her husband, the man with whom she had slept last night. His expression was impassive in response to her own of eager expectation, and her face fell. Her throat felt full and she could not have uttered a word even if she had been able to find something to say. Was Nick playing with her? Was he doing this only to punish her in retaliation for her leaving him and—as he believed —deciding to divorce him?

Nick had a towel around him and his hair was wet.

'I've finished with the bathroom, if you want it.' His voice was as unreadable as his expression as he moved towards the chair on which his clothes lay. 'We'll have an early breakfast so that we can get started. I want to get on with this job and see it finished within a month—'

'A month? That's not giving me very long.'

'There'll be plenty of labour. I reckon it can be completed in a month.'

She went into the bathroom, moving swiftly because of the tears in her eyes which she did not want him to see.

It was no use, she told herself; there was no hope for her at all, and she determined never to allow Nick anywhere near her again. She was no toy! If it was only a woman to assuage his lust that he required, then he could find plenty of women in the town! Anger gradually grew within her and when she eventually met him at the breakfast table there was a sparkle in her eyes which immediately brought a question from her companion's lips, 'Is something the matter?' and it served only to add fuel to the fire.

'Only that I want you to understand that there'll

be no repetition of last night! And if you don't like it I can return to England and you can find someone else to do this place up for you—and the woman you're going to marry!' She hadn't intended saying anything like that but fury and jealousy had loosened her tongue in a way she immediately regretted.

'I don't think I understand, Shelley.' Nick helped himself to toast and began buttering it. Shelley set her teeth; she could have thrown something at him!

'Then you're obtuse!' she retorted, her chest heaving with the anger consuming her.

'I must be, since I can see no reason for this anger.'

She drew a deep breath and suddenly decided that an altogether different approach was required if she were to save her face.

'Forget I ever spoke, Nick. I guess I was a little piqued by your manner earlier on but there was no need to be. After all, what occurred was no more to me than it was to you—just a pleasant interlude as you once intimated. And now, we really must concentrate on these plans if this job is to be completed in the time you've stipulated.' She smiled sweetly as she reached for the coffeepot. 'Can I help you to some more?' she asked, holding the pot aloft. Nick merely nodded his head, watching her with an intent gaze. And on his lips was the ghost of a smile that was a mingling of amusement and perception.

By the time another week had passed there was already a transformation taking place at the villa as a veritable army of workmen toiled at their various jobs. Shelley was in the saloon discussing drapes

with the representative of a firm in Athens, from
where all the carpets and curtains had been
ordered. The saloon was ready for these things,
and as soon as they were completed the furniture
would be put back—most of it, that was, but a
lounge suite and some additional armchairs were
on their way from a large store in the capital. The
rest of the furniture was old and beautiful and both
Eleni and Costos had been hard at work cleaning it
and restoring the patina of age.

'I think that is all,' the man was saying. 'I'll now
do the dining room if you don't mind. It's just to
make quite sure we have all the measurements
correct.' He glanced at his notepad as he spoke,
then moved away towards the door.

Shelley let him go alone; she was in a mood of
deep depression because of the speed with which
things were progressing. Undoubtedly Nick was in
a hurry and she could think of only one reason: He
was anxious to get married.

He came in while she was standing at the window, staring out to where the gleaming white
campanile of a church raised its head among the
palms. Beyond was the sea, with something magic
about it today for the colours were more positive—
cobalt blue and aquamarine, silver and cerulean
and emerald-green, all in motion and all created by
the wispy cirrus clouds hovering and snaking and
curling in the brittle Grecian sky above. A yacht's
white sails added to the magic, and down by the
harbour several little fishing-boats were bobbing
about, their owners sitting on the waterfront bang-
ing octopuses or mending their nets. Shelley turned
at the sound and a frown creased her brow before
she could stop it. She didn't want any conversation

with Nick at this time; she had been savouring the scenery and the peace, her mind off her troubles for a brief space.

And now Nick was here, wearing that impassive mask of unsmiling severity.

'I thought I'd just mention that Delia's coming over the day after tomorrow,' he said casually. 'Perhaps you will see that a room is made ready for her.'

'She's—coming over here?' Strange that such a possibility had not occurred to her, thought Shelley, but she supposed Nick's initial attitude towards herself had been the reason. She now looked at him across the lovely room, her face pale and disturbed. She heard herself say in a tight little voice. 'I'll have the room ready, Nick, yes—but I feel that it is best for me to leave here before she comes.'

'Oh, and why?' His eyes were formidably narrowed, his mouth compressed.

'Well—' Shelley bit her lip, searching for words. 'I might as well be honest,' she decided at length. 'Your fiancée and I do not get along and, therefore, I'm leaving before she arrives.' Her shoulders were squared, her head tilted proudly and her gaze challenging.

'Do you have to get on?' he enquired with what to Shelley was maddening calm.

'I'm leaving,' she repeated, 'and that is all there is to it. I'm not entering into any argument—'

'I wasn't aware of an argument,' interposed Nick with a lift of his brows.

Shelley drew an impatient breath and repeated, 'I'm leaving, Nick, and nothing you can say will make me change my mind.' He was now subjecting her to an intense scrutiny and it did seem that there was a hint of satisfaction in his eyes not unmingled with mockery.

'So you're jealous of Delia, it would seem.'

Shelley turned away; she was sadly recalling how she and Nick had once belonged to each other, and now he was telling her she was jealous of the other woman who had come into his life, to take her place. She recalled, too, how they had clasped hands one day, soon after they were married, and made sacred vows to love one another forever and never ever to give each other the slightest cause for jealousy. How young they were then! How idealistic and trusting!

'I mean what I say, Nick.' She turned again and confronted him bravely in face of his formidable manner and the almost threatening light in his eyes. His chiselled jawline was taut for a moment before he spoke, in tones authoritative and firm.

'You'll stay because I say so, Shelley. I've employed you, through your firm, and if you should default on the agreement which I drew up with your employer then I am legally entitled to refuse payment for what has already been done.'

'You—!' Shelley stared at him in disbelief. 'But thousands of pounds have been spent! You can't do this—' Her eyes narrowed with suspicion. 'I don't believe you are legally entitled to refuse payment. You're just threatening me—and wanting me to stay here for some reason of your own—and I know what it is!' she added without thinking and was not surprised when Nick said with a curious inflection, 'You do, Shelley?' His voice was very quiet, his eyes searching as if he would read into her very soul. He seemed strangely expectant, too, a circumstance which puzzled Shelley immensely.

It was almost as if he were waiting for her to say

she loved him! So he could laugh in her face? Yes, undoubtedly that was his reason—if of course her guess was correct and he really was waiting to hear that kind of confession from her. Her chin lifted and her face, pale but composed, wore an element of proud hauteur Nick had never encountered before.

'I am not going into any discussions or arguments, Nick,' she stated firmly. 'Nor does your threat make any difference to my intention of leaving. I shall phone the airport and see if I can leave sometime tomorrow.'

'I should ring your employer first, if I were you,' was Nick's advice as he turned to leave the room.

'My *fiancé!*' she snapped. 'I notice you always refer to Stephen as my employer.'

Nick turned his head and she noticed the dark frown knitting his brows. He opened the door and went out without another word.

Shelley phoned the airport and found she could book a flight for ten-thirty the following morning, and this she did. But as the next few hours passed she found she could not get Nick's warning out of her mind and at last she decided to phone Stephen.

'Oh, hello!' was his greeting before Shelley could say more than her name. 'How's everything at the villa?'

'Going according to plan—or even better. I want to ask you something, Stephen.'

'Yes?'

'If I come home—leave the rest of this renovation to someone else, can Nick evade payment for what's already been done?'

'Come home? What the devil are you talking about?' The voice carried a strange, unfathomable

inflection . . . and also, Shelley had the odd conviction that, prosaic as they were, he had
previously rehearsed them!

'I believe I made myself clear,' she said crisply.
I'm coming home tomorrow; I've booked my seat
on the plane.'

'You can't leave the job,' he snapped. 'Nick can
refuse to pay. I signed an agreement with him and
it has to stay.'

'An agreement whereby it was *I*, and I alone who
must carry out his work at the villa?'

'That's right.'

'You've never done a thing like that before.
Supposing I were ill?'

'You're not ill,' with some asperity, 'so the
question doesn't arise.'

'You're deep,' she complained. 'I'm being kept
in ignorance about something.'

'Don't be melodramatic—'

'And don't you go on taking me for an idiot!' she
flashed. 'I'd been totally lacking in intelligence if I
didn't sense something was going on between you
and Nick!'

'Shelley,' he said with a deep sigh of impatience,
'just you get on with the job assigned to you and
see it through to its conclusion, as is customary.
We've never changed operators midstream and I
am not starting now. Think of the losses—'

'I don't believe for one moment that Nick would
default in payment. I know him, remember!'

'Do you, Shelley . . . ? Are you quite sure?' Soft
the tone and it was almost as if Stephen were trying
tacitly to convey something to her.

'That question only deepens the mystery as far as
I am concerned,' she said. 'You must know that.'

'I only know that when Nick phoned earlier—'

He cut abruptly but of course not soon enough and Shelley naturally seized on what he had said.

'So he rang you earlier today, did he? What time?' She knew the approximate time without being told; it was soon after Nick had thrown his ultimatum at her, and advised her to phone Stephen. Nick had in fact gone in first!

'It doesn't matter,' snapped Stephen, obviously furious with himself for the slip. 'Just do as I say and remain there until the job's done.'

She set her mouth.

'I wish I hadn't phoned you!' she gritted, and Stephen instantly came in with, 'It wouldn't have made any difference because I was intending to phone you.' He paused but only momentarily. 'I wanted to tell you that I can't go through with our engagement. I've fallen in love at last.'

'I see. . . .'

'You don't sound surprised.'

'Should I be surprised? We both knew that the engagement didn't have any depth and that if you did happen to meet someone else before the marriage took place then it would be all off between you and me. I wish you every happiness . . . with Wendy; she's a delightful girl, and crazy about you. I'll let you have the ring back when I come home.' And without giving him time to reply Shelley replaced the receiver on its hook.

Nick insisted on taking Shelley out to dinner even though she told him she would prefer to dine at the villa.

'Alone!' she added just because it afforded her a measure of satisfaction to add the word.

'Well, you're not dining here alone. Don't be so damned perverse. I could tan that hide of yours without much provocation, the way I feel. In fact, I ought to have done it years ago!'

Colour rushed up to suffuse her cheeks.

'Don't you dare to threaten me!' she seethed. 'I've said I'll stay but I could just change my mind!'

'You won't.' The conviction in the mocking voice only added fuel to the fire of Shelley's wrath and before she quite knew it she was hitting out at him and then actually winced at the sharp sound of the slap. Nick seemed momentarily stunned and in those few seconds of his inaction Shelley bit her lip at the angry red mark she had made on his cheek. Whatever had made her do a thing like that? She was asking herself when suddenly her eyes dilated and she stepped back strategically towards the door.

'Nick, I'm very s—'

'You little vixen!' With the agile leap of a jungle beast he was across the room and Shelley put both hands behind her back because she knew he intended grasping her wrist. The action seemed to increase his already inflamed temper and he swung her around, so roughly that she gave a little cry of protest and pain. Her clasped hands were held in a vice-like grip as Nick dragged her, struggling, to a chair, and sat down. A couple of minutes later she was released and set on her feet, crying as much with anger as with pain.

'You fiend!' she cried across the distance now separating them. They were in the saloon to where Nick had come to tell her they were dining out that evening. 'You—beast! You're nothing better than your domineering, brutal, heathen Greek ancestors!'

Nick's manner underwent a dramatic change and he gave a hearty laugh.

'That,' he said in some considerable amusement, 'was a very entertaining string of adjectives.' His dancing eyes moved to where Shelley was unconsciously rubbing herself. 'You asked for it, Shelley,' he said and now his voice was serious and his eyes frowning a little. 'I'm not going to apologise, nor even to express the slightest degree of regret. I rather think you'll hesitate the next time you feel like slapping my face.'

She averted her eyes, affected in some strange way by his gravity, and she felt convinced that despite his little stricture he was in fact regretting the chastisement he had inflicted on her. He came to her, and tilted her head with a proprietorial hand beneath her chin. She swallowed convulsively and the tears came again, much to her chagrin. He took out a handkerchief and dried them, somewhat clumsily, she thought.

'You are staying,' he told her with a kind of gentle firmness. 'And now, run along and get yourself ready. I've booked a table for eight o'clock and we'll have aperitifs first. . . .' His eyes, travelling over her, suddenly came to rest on the hand hanging loosely at her side. 'Your . . . ring,' he said and lifted his eyes to stare penetratingly into hers.

'Stephen and I aren't engaged anymore,' was all she offered and to her surprise Nick merely nodded —just as if he had expected this to happen—and refrained from saying anything more about it.

Delia arrived the following day and Nick went to the airport to meet her. She was all poise and confidence as she looked around the villa before being shown to her room by Eleni. And a short while later she came to Shelley in the garden and said arrogantly, 'I can't say I care for some of the—er—improvements, you've been making, Miss Scott. There's too much evidence of the previous owner about the rooms—especially the saloon.'

'Nick didn't want to take everything of his aunt's away. Most of her furniture is antique, and it's beautiful now that it's been thoroughly cleaned and polished by the servants here.'

'I don't care all that much for antiques,' interrupted the girl rudely, blowing out the smoke from her cigarette with little regard for Shelley's comfort, for it was going directly into her face. 'I shall have to talk to my fiancé and see if we can't scrap some of it.'

Shelley said nothing; she knew that Nick would never part with the lovely furniture which his aunt had left him. He was sentimental about it, apart from anything else, and so Shelley strongly suspected he would have put up with at least some of it even had he not liked it. But he did like it and so did Shelley; they both agreed that it suited the style of the villa, which itself was far from modern, having once been part of a vast estate owned by a Venetian in the days when a sort of feudal system existed on the island. Now much of the land was divided up, and other villas had been built over the years, but Nick still had large grounds surrounding the house, and a *perivoli* where grew a great deal of citrus fruits and olives. Shelley loved this orchard and she had suggested the planting of thousands of flower bulbs so that there would be a carpet of colour in the spring next year. Nick had readily agreed—just as he had agreed with practically every suggestion she had made here—and gardeners had already begun the planting.

Delia was speaking again and Shelley turned to look at her, noting the perfectly-coiffeured hair, the flattering use of colour on lips and cheeks, the long slender hands with their brilliant red nails. The girl wore an expensive cotton dress with tight-fitting bodice and flared skirt, its colour a flattering shade of lime-green with large crimson and yellow flowers—poppies, they looked like to Shelley. She could not help but admire the girl's appearance and half wished her own job required more attractive attire. As it was, she usually wore denims or corduroy slacks and a white shirt, open at the throat. Today, however, she had chosen to wear a summery outfit of blouse and skirt in a shiny-surfaced cotton—deep turquoise trimmed with a lacy white collar and cuffs to the short sleeves. It was becoming, she knew; nevertheless, she felt inferior beside the other girl's total sophistication. Delia spoke, a hint of anger in her tone.

'Didn't you think it odd that my fiancé should not have asked me to accompany him—and you—over here?'

'I didn't give the matter a thought, one way or the other,' was Shelley's guarded reply.

'It was because I couldn't come at that time, but I'm free now and so I rang him to say I was coming.' Shelley said nothing but it had of course registered that the invitation to come over had not come from Nick. 'I expect you've been trying all sorts of tricks to make him notice you,' added Delia spitefully at length.

'But I thought you'd already decided that your fiancé *had* noticed me,' Shelley couldn't resist saying in an acid-sweet way, and she smiled with satisfaction when Delia's colour heightened. The girl drew heavily on her cigarette and blew out the smoke.

'You're impertinent!' she snapped. 'You seemed to have forgotten your place right from the start. You're a servant, nothing more, and don't allow yourself to forget it!'

'And you, Miss Unwin, are about the most ill-mannered woman client I have ever had. I don't know what Nick sees in you.' And with that she swung around on her heel and strode away, leaving Delia watching her through narrowed eyes, a look of sheer hatred on her face.

'I'll think of something. . . .' She inhaled deeply of the smoke from her cigarette, the half-closed eyes still following Shelley's slender figure as she walked briskly in the direction of the side entrance to the villa. 'Yes, Miss Scott . . . I'll think of some way to prevent you from taking Nick from me. . . .'

Chapter Ten

That evening the three of them dined at the country club and Nick seemed bent on paying attention to Delia and practically ignoring Shelley except at those times when the conversation touched the subject of the renovations. Only then was she brought in. Delia seemed elated at this treatment of the girl she now regarded as her enemy, but at the same time she was puzzled, and watched with concentrated intentness any small glance that passed from Nick to Shelley. She set her mouth once or twice; she was convinced that Shelley had 'set her cap' at Nick and was trying to get him for herself.

The atmosphere in the club restaurant was romantic and quiet. Only the low murmur of voices and the soft strains of *bouzouki* music being played by four men on the slightly-elevated platform at the far end of the room. Candles were the only illumination, and on the table were flowers—delicate bunches of cerise bougainvillaea, a delightful flower of warm countries. Glass and silver shone in the candlelight . . . and Shelley wished she were alone with Nick. This intimate atmosphere was nostalgic and she felt almost too full to enjoy her food.

Several times Nick shot her a glance, which was seen by Delia and Shelley did wonder what she was thinking. But Shelley was angry with Nick, who seemed to be playing the kind of game she would never have believed he could play. He was deliberately causing both girls to wonder just what he was up to.

The following morning she saw Delia talking to one of the outside workmen some distance away from the house, and Shelley, deciding that the girl was giving the man some sort of instructions thought no more of the matter. Nick had gone off for the day to an office he had established in the capital very recently, a circumstance that set Shelley wondering if it was in fact his intention to settle on Corfu permanently and she could not help speculating on how Delia would settle here. The girl liked London and all the hustle and bustle and the plush shops and hotels. This village where the villa was situated was quiet, a little backwater which to Shelley could be sheer heaven. . . .

Delia came in at last and Shelley wondered if she were imagining it or whether there really was something furtive about the girl. Shelley did not like the way Delia kept glancing at her while they were discussing the decor of the larger drawing-room, one which would be used only when there were a number of guests in the house.

'I must have wallpaper,' decided Delia. 'I can't stand this panelling.'

'It's beautiful; you can't have it all taken away.'

'I am the one who says what shall be done, Miss Scott!'

Shelley shrugged her shoulders and wished with all her heart that it was all finished and she could go home.

She felt she must have a day off anyway; she hadn't had once since coming to the island and so had not seen anything outside of the village and the beach at Paleokastritsa. She told Nick when he arrived back and he made no demure. He did ask where she intended going and she said she would like to see the palace of the Empress Elizabeth. He nodded as if he had already expected her to say she wanted to see the home of the beautiful and neurotic empress who had renovated a decaying Venetian palace and named it the Achilleon after her son, Achilles who committed suicide at Mayerling. The palace was his memorial, and dolphins' heads were a prominent feature of the decorations as the dolphin was sacred to Achilles's mother, Thetis. Nick took time to tell Shelley all this and ended with an amused, 'It was all mythology, of course—the original Achilles and Thetis and the dolphins.'

Shelley went off early after hearing Nick say he was going to his office again and would not be back till late afternoon. He was leaving Delia on her own. . . .

Shelley hired a taxi in the village and drove through a landscape of olives and myrtle and tall cypress trees, with the driver chatting and turning his head right round as he drove, scaring the wits

out of Shelley who was such a careful driver
herself. So she was breathing a sigh of relief when
at last she was paying the driver—and politely
refusing his offer to wait so that he could drive her
back to the villa again.

It was less than half an hour later that Shelley
saw Nick and her heart seemed to turn a somer-
sault. Why had he come here? He was smiling
faintly as he walked towards her with that familiar
lithe grace which made every step so smooth that
he seemed to be walking on air.

'You look surprised,' he remarked.

'Well—of course I'm surprised. Why have you
come?'

'I, too, felt I'd like a day off.' He stood at her
side, looking down at her, an amused expression on
his face.

'So you thought you'd come to the palace?' The
question in her eyes increased his amusement.

'You're wondering why,' he said.

'Naturally.' Shelley's heart was beating overrate
but she contrived to remain calm. 'It's so
unexpected—seeing you here.' She paused but he
did not speak; he was looking her over from head
to foot as if he would take in every single thing
about her—what she was wearing, her face, her
hair. . . . 'You knew I was coming here,' she added
at last and Nick nodded his head, still not saying
anything and she went on, 'I should have thought
you'd have invited your fiancée to come with you.
She's all alone.'

Nick merely shrugged and said, 'She'll keep
herself occupied.' He looked around. 'Have you
seen all you want to see?'

'I've been all over the palace, yes.'

'Then let's go outside.' He took her arm and urged her towards the door opening on to the formal gardens where statues abounded—the row of the nine muses were spectacular even though to Shelley the sculpture was not of the best. There were also busts of ancient Greeks like Euripides and Plato, Sophocles and Homer. Woodlands sloped towards the sea and a quaint little *taverna* sat invitingly among masses of hibiscus and oleanders, its chairs and tables shaded from the fierce sun by a canopy of vines. 'We'll have something to drink.' Nick glanced down to see if this suggestion found favour and she nodded and smiled. She was happy and it was revealed in the brightness of her eyes, and that ready smile. It seemed so natural that they should both be here, that his fiancée should seem as if she were non-existent. Nevertheless, Shelley could not help a fleeting moment of speculation as to how the girl would react were she to know that Nick had come here especially to be with his ex-wife.

They were greeted by a brown-faced waiter whose smile revealed a couple of gold fillings. His round, good-natured face was lined, his wiry black hair sprinkled with grey. He wore a white jacket and black trousers, and lightweight shoes that gave evidence that he was a dancer. Shelley hoped he would entertain them with a few of the traditional Greek dances and she was not disappointed. Greek men seemed mad about dancing and performed at many of the cafés and restaurants.

Nick drank *ouzo* but Shelley had fresh lemonade. Nick seemed faintly ill-at-ease—a circumstance that amazed Shelley who had always noticed how self-possessed he was. However, when he spoke it was with all the old familiar self-confidence, and certainly with the hint of arrogance which was an essential facet of his makeup—inherited from both his noble English father and his Greek mother.

'You seem to be rushing this job, Shelley. I particularly want perfection, understand?'

She coloured at the censure but nevertheless managed to assume a cool, composed front as she replied, 'I'm doing my best, Nick. Don't forget that here on an island one doesn't altogether have the scope for choice that one has in a place like London.'

'You can order from London if you want.' His eyes were coolly brilliant as they looked straightly into hers. 'I thought I'd made it clear that no expense was to be spared.'

'You did, but there are still limitations to what can be done. If I begin ordering fittings and the like from England the job will take ages. You said earlier that you wanted it done as quickly as possible, remember?'

'I did—' He frowned at the reminder as if he now regretted asking for speed. 'But I want a perfect job for all that.'

Shelley said nothing for she did not understand this strange mood of his. And Nick himself seemed to shake it off and was soon smiling as he asked her if she wanted another glass of lemonade. She shook her head, and after a few moments of silence as they watched the lone dancer they wandered into the palace grounds proper and walked around, enjoying the flowers and the sunshine . . . and for Shelley, Nick's company. Several times she sent him a sidelong glance but always his jaw was rigid and so there was nothing to be read from the mask-like profile.

Once back at the place where Nick had parked his car Shelley paused and said hesitantly, 'Hadn't I better take a taxi?'

'Whatever for?' Nick's face registered surprise.

'It might upset Delia if she knows we've been together.' She just had to say this because she wanted to see what Nick's reaction would be. He seemed indifferent and stepped forward to open the car door; a gesture invited her to get in.

'Delia won't mind.' Nick's voice was devoid of expression. 'Why should our being together upset her?'

'Perhaps it's best I didn't tell you.'

Nick closed the door after having given his ex-wife a little shove which forced her into the passenger seat of the car.

'Now you have me intrigued.' He turned on the ignition and slanted her a glance at the same time. She leant back against the upholstery and crossed her legs. 'I'm curious,' he prompted when she did not immediately speak.

'Delia's suspicious of us.' Shelley couldn't have said what urged her to utter those words. Was she becoming desperate in her hopes? Was she willing to make a deliberate attempt to win Nick back by any possible means—fair or foul?

'She is?' with a frown as Nick made no attempt to start the car. 'In what way, might I ask?'

Again Shelley was driven by some force beyond her control.

'She thinks I'm setting my cap at you, to put it bluntly.'

'And vulgarly.'

'Does it matter?' Shelley turned her head to let him see her frown.

'So she's actually been accusing you of—er—trying to come between her and me?'

'She doesn't trust you, obviously.' Shelley bit her lip. Why was she being so rotten?

'She said so?' sharply and with a grim inflection.

'Not categorically, but she as good as told me to lay off.'

'She did!' Nick seemed highly amused suddenly as he said with a hint of mockery, 'Sounds as if you two have been at one another with claws extended. Tell me some more; it's entertaining.'

'Just what is your game, Nick?' Shelley asked bluntly. 'I felt at first you hated me, wanted to punish me for—for the divorce. But now. . . .' If Nick caught the plea in her voice he chose to ignore it. In fact, he seemed bored with the subject—this after only seconds ago having declared it was entertaining. He drove the car off the park and Shelley pressed her lips together. What an exasperating man he was! Why hadn't he answered her question? But perhaps he didn't know himself what his game was!

Delia was in the garden when Nick's car came bowling along the drive, and Shelley gasped at the girl's malevolent expression as she took in the situation. But a swift and dramatic change took place as she transferred her eyes to Nick, and she was smiling with her customary charm—put on, thought Shelley with spite, especially for Nick's benefit—as she tucked her arm into him immediately he stepped from the car.

'Where have you been, darling,' she purred. 'You've obviously given Miss Scott a lift home.'

'I've been busy. And, yes, I have given Miss
Scott a lift back. It saved her the expense of a taxi.'
His eyes met Shelley's then became veiled by his
long lashes. Delia sent Shelley a narrowed, malicious glance and her mouth had tightened to an
ugly line. Shelley excused herself and moved away,
dwelling on Nick and his unfathomable behaviour.
Drat the man for being so mysterious! Could it
possibly be that he couldn't make up his mind
which girl he really wanted! It would serve him
right if he lost them both!

Shelley surveyed her handiwork and felt happy
indeed at the result. She had been a little dubious
about the fireplace in the dining room, as it seemed
at first glance far too large for the room. But once
the mass of excess furniture was out the effect was
vastly different, with the fireplace—having been
cleaned up and polished by Eleni and Costos—
being now the most charming and arresting focal
point of the room. The cerise wall-to-wall carpeting
matched the drapes in colour, while the walls were
white for the most part but with the merest shading
of cerise coming up from the carpet for about
eighteen inches and gradually fading delicately and
almost imperceptibly into the white above it. The
effect which Shelley wanted to achieve was the
illusion of a reflection from the carpet to the lower
walls, and she had succeeded. Nick praised it,
though Delia said with some heavy disparagement,
and when Nick wasn't there,
   'It's gimmicky! I dislike it, Miss Scott. It's lacking in taste and I shall soon be having it altered.'
   The saloon was now also finished, as was most of
the rest of the house. Just the east wing was left,
and this was the most neglected part of all as Nick's

aunt had closed it up and shut it off from the rest of the villa more than five years previously. Shelley sighed as she entered the main room of this wing. Nick had suggested it be renovated with the idea of a nursery in mind. To Shelley it was at the present time dim and bleak but it was also a challenge and she began to get down to the work and to consult Delia as to what she wanted.

'I know exactly what I want,' said the girl with an insolent raking of Shelley's body. She felt a tramp but was not unduly worried. Her denims and open-necked white shirt were practical for the job she was doing, as both would wash easily and both required the minimum amount of ironing. It was all right for Delia to be immaculate in a cream linen trouser suit and with her hair stunningly gleaming as if less than an hour ago it had been in the hands of an expert hairdresser. 'And I hope you will carry out my orders to the letter! I've had enough of my ideas being shelved in favour of something quite hideous!'

'You must remember that Nick has done much of the choosing.' Shelley's voice was terse.

'With your persuasion, Miss Scott! But now we shall see what *my* ideas turn out like.' She proceeded to outline her plan for the nursery, now and then searching Shelley's face as if she would read her thoughts. Shelley adopted a nonchalant mien, smoothing her hair, glancing at her finger-nails, even suppressing an imaginary yawn rather in the way Nick would have done, had he been bored. Delia set her mouth and her eyes were coldly brilliant. She was furious—and Shelley was enjoying herself!

'I'm a bitch,' she told herself but without the faintest trace of shame or remorse.

'And now the verandah. . . .' Delia's voice underwent a change and Shelley glanced swiftly at her, a puzzled look in her eyes. Delia was avoiding her gaze as she pointed, indicating the open French door to this upstairs room situated right on the end of the east side of the villa. 'I want it made into a sort of play space, with colourful little animals—rabbits and squirrels and little deer—sitting on a pretty stone wall. The animals can be made of stone, too, or perhaps of wood. . . .' She paused in thought and Shelley stared at her. Was the girl advocating a low wall which could never be safe for a young child who must at some stage be tempted to climb on to it. Obviously the wall was to be low—Shelley frowned and shook her head.

'How high is this wall to be?' she wanted to know, staring out at the wooden rails which were occupying the space where the stone wall was going to be.

'Oh, quite low. Otherwise the children won't be able to see the animals—not while they're small, that is.' Delia spoke as if her thoughts were on something else and again Shelley was puzzled.

However, all she said was, 'That's what I thought, Miss Unwin. And has it not occurred to you that small children are in the habit of climbing low walls?'

Delia's mouth twisted and she raked Shelley's slender frame contemptuously.

'I knew you'd find fault, Miss Scott. Trouble with you is that you have no real imagination. How you managed to get where you are is a complete puzzle to me. You're a fraud! I guess it's a case of 'if you can make people believe you're clever, then you *are* clever.''

'Your opinion of my talents is of no interest to

me,' returned Shelley in tones of ice. 'What does concern me is that I'm not carrying out any plans here that would endanger a child's life.'

Delia gave a deep sigh. She changed her manner, though, and even yet again Shelley was puzzled . . . and suspicious without knowing why.

'Well, perhaps you have some suggestions? I do want to make good use of this verandah.' She flipped a hand. 'Let's go out and take a look.' She deliberately stepped aside. 'You go first,' she urged.

'What do we need to go out there for?' Shelley stared at her. 'We can see all we want to see from here.'

'What I meant was—you can take some measurements and then suggest what can be done.'

Shelley's suspicions increased as she sent her a searching look. Only moments ago the girl was laying down the law most firmly, stating emphatically that she was having things done *her* way. . . . And now she was almost cordial in her request that Shelley should make suggestions. It was all too baffling, and for some reason Shelley felt she ought to be on her guard . . . but against what?

Delia was speaking again, repeating what she had said about taking measurements as a preliminary, and as this was reasonable enough Shelley agreed and went off to get her measuring tape. Delia wasn't there when she arrived back so she went out on to the verandah alone. The boards creaked and she grimaced. The whole structure would have to be dismantled and rebuilt and this meant that alterations in measurements could be effected. In other words, the verandah could be made wider, which would be an asset if as Delia

wanted, it was to be a sort of small playground—
Shelley's musings were cut abruptly and she flung
out a hand as the floor began to give way beneath
her. She flailed the air, gave a strangled scream as
the boards under her feet collapsed and she
dropped in a crumpled heap to the marble floor of
the patio below.

Shelley's eyes fluttered open and she gave a small
moan and lifted a trembling hand.

'Oh, my head! What—what happened . . . ?'
She was alert now, remembering everything in a
flash. 'The verandah—' She glanced up as someone
came swiftly to the side of the bed. 'Nick, the
verandah wasn't safe.' She closed her eyes and
again a stifled little moan issued from her pale lips.
'My head—I must have banged my head.'

It was throbbing and she felt sick; she tried to
struggle to a sitting position but a strong hand
forced her back on to the pillow.

'Be still, darling, the doctor is on his way.' Nick's
voice was hoarse and unsteady. Shelley forgot her
pain for a second as she stared up into his drawn
face and wondered if she had heard aright. She
started to say, 'You called me—me—' and then
stopped and began to cry.

'Don't, love—oh, my Shelley, don't cry like
that!'

Love now. . . . She couldn't be dreaming . . .
or could she? Her mind was fogged so it might be
that. The pain was excruciating so that might be the
reason she was imagining things—imagining those
beautiful words, and this strain on Nick's face that
was causing it to have a distinctly greyish tinge.
Was she really imagining all this?

'Nick. . . .' His hand was cool on her temple and she put her own small one on top of it to keep it there.

He smiled then, a thin and twisted curve of his lips that held no humour.

'Where the hell can that doctor be!'

'How long have I been here, Nick?' Shelley had no idea just how weak her voice was or how it affected the man standing over her, looking down into her face so anxiously.

'About twenty minutes,' he replied then shot a glance at the window. 'The doctor's here,' he said as the car crunched to a halt down below on the gravel. 'Thank God!'

Dr. Demetrious was a stocky man neatly dressed in a suit of dark grey serge material and when he opened his mouth to speak the usual gold fillings appeared. He took Shelley's pulse, examined the gash where the hairline met her forehead and gave a small grunt.

'It ees bad! But it could be worse—yes. I haf dressing with me but maybe you prefer that she go to the hospital?'

'Not unless it's absolutely necessary.' Nick's voice was a mixture of firmness and query. The doctor said that although the wound was nasty it was not dangerous, and after asking for hot water, and a razor to shave a little of the hair away, he applied the dressing. Bruises were examined, grunted over but not commented on. He was a silent man, this Greek doctor from the village. He made out a prescription but did have some tablets with him and these he handed in a box to Nick. 'This verandah you talk about,' he said to Nick as he prepared to leave, 'it should haf been tested before anyone go on to it. Madam Amelia who lif here many years never do anything to that part of the house—'

'Yes, we know that, Doctor,' broke in Nick impatiently. 'Thank you for coming so promptly. You'll call again tomorrow?'

'Of course. Gif the *kore* the tablets and she sleep long time. That verandah is not safe,' he mumbled as Nick showed him out. 'But it very strange to gif way because that *kore* is not very heavy. . . .'

Delia came up to the bedroom when Shelley was almost asleep. Nick having given her two of the tablets immediately on the doctor's departure.

'What's happened!' she exclaimed. 'Ireni said there'd been an accident and Miss Scott was injured?' Her wide eyes travelled to the bed where Shelley was endeavouring to keep awake, just to see if Nick would say nice things to her again once this unwanted girl was out of the room. 'Oh, you poor thing!' Delia came silently towards the bed. 'How did it happen? Ireni said you fell from that verandah.'

'That's right, Delia, she did.' Nick's voice was strained, but the sigh that escaped him seemed to have nothing to do with his anxiety about Shelley. 'The supports were obviously rotten and gave way under her weight. . . .' His voice trailed; he was thinking of the doctor's words . . . about that girl not being very heavy.

'How awful,' Delia was saying as she moved closer to the bed. 'Is she injured badly?' The voice was faintly harsh, thought Shelley, then wondered if she could be mistaken. After all . . . she was almost . . . almost asleep. . . .

'Miraculously, no,' from Nick with a deeply-drawn breath. 'It's a bad gash on the head she has, plus some nasty bruises, but that's all.'

'She's been lucky.' Delia's voice sounded tight, decided Shelley still attempting to keep awake.

'Very lucky.'

'Is there anything I can do?'

'No, Delia, thank you—nothing. Shelley's had some pain-killing tablets and she'll be asleep in a few minutes.' It was plainly a request for Delia to leave the room and this she did, without another glance at the girl on the bed.

Several hours later Shelley awoke and a sigh of relief escaped her. The pain was gone. And she did not feel too bad at all.

Nick was there, instantly beside her as she moved.

'You've had a good sleep—' He put a hand on her forehead and looked down into her eyes. 'How are you feeling, dear?'

'Not too bad at all.' A smile came slowly to her lips. 'You called me dear,' she added then coloured up, feeling foolish.

'Thank God you're all right. Shelley, what a fright you gave me!' No veneer now, or arrogance or mockery. Nick was just as Shelley had once known him—gentle and tender, and anxious about her.

She said, feeling very young again, and shy, 'How did it happen, Nick? I'd been on that verandah before, you know—when I first looked over the villa—' She paused, brow puckered in recollection. 'You were with me!' she exclaimed. 'And there was no sign of any weakness then.'

'No.' He too became thoughtful. 'No, there

wasn't. I do remember thinking a great deal would have to be done to that east wing, but I had no indication at all that any part of it could be unsafe.'

'I must investigate when I get up.' She paused, feeling her head and pulling a wry face. 'I've lost some of my hair. I wonder how long it will take it to grow?'

Nick had to laugh.

'If that isn't just like a woman! She's escaped what could have been a very serious injury and all she can think about is her looks! Vanity, my child, is a sin. Didn't you know that?'

She was smiling with tears in her eyes.

'You love me, don't you, Nick?' she murmured simply, her mouth moving with little convulsive jerks. 'Oh, my husband—my darling husband—I love you too!' She struggled to a sitting position, received a stern command to lie down again and instead of obeying she flung her arms around his neck, forcing him to bend lower. She offered her lips, which he took so tenderly, just as if by kissing her with too much force or passion he would hurt her.

She laughed joyously and said, 'It's only my head that's injured, Nick, not my mouth!'

'Brazen hussy!' and this time he very efficiently satisfied her craving, kissing her till she was breathless and fighting for release.

'You haven't said you love me, Nick?'

'Apparently there isn't any need— Don't look like that, my dearest darling. Of course I love you. . . .' His voice dropped to a hoarse whisper as he repeated, close to her cheek, 'I love you, my own darling Shelley, love you to distraction! Why did we ever part like that?'

She told him about the letter, promising to show it to him later. The fury created by the information almost frightened her and she shook her head, reminding him that it was all in the past, and the future was theirs.

'But why didn't you tell me before this?' he demanded and she was sure that, had she been perfectly well, Nick would have shaken her. 'Why, I say?'

'The time didn't seem right,' she quivered on the point of tears. 'You were engaged—' She stopped abruptly as Eleni knocked and opened the door.

'Phivos wants to see you, Mr. Nickolas.'

'Phivos?' Nick's expression was blank. 'Who's he?'

'One of the outside workmen.' Shelley vouchsafed the information before Eleni could answer.

'I see.' Nick frowned and hesitated. Shelley said it might be something important. The man might be waiting for some specific instructions.

Nick went out in Eleni's wake and Shelley leant back, nestling her head in the soft pillow. Life was good!—so very good! She closed her eyes, half inclined to get up and put on her clothes. But Nick would be sure to order her back to bed, she thought ruefully, and decided to stay where she was.

When he returned she gasped at the glowering expression on his face. That he was in a raging temper was more than obvious. She asked anxiously, 'What's wrong, Nick? What did Phivos want?'

It seemed for a moment that he could not speak; Shelley saw a muscle jerk in his throat; she saw too that his hands were clenched tightly at his sides. He looked at her and for a moment she panicked, fearing that she had done something to anger him. But he spoke at last, saying harshly, 'That verandah— The supports were taken away—at least, three out of the four were.'

Shelley blinked at him, unable to assimilate this information.

'I don't understand?' was all she could find to say.

'Delia—' He stopped as if finding the greatest difficulty in carrying on. But he continued presently, 'Delia had told this man, Phivos, to dismantle the verandah—'

'She—!' Shelley stared disbelievingly at him, while at the same time aware of an intruding recollection—that of Delia in conversation with Phivos outside, in the garden. 'But she wouldn't have let me go out there.' Shelley shook her head vigorously. 'It was Delia who asked me to measure up the verandah.'

'She told Phivos to dismantle the verandah, but when he had taken away three of the supports she then told him to leave it. He could finish it another day. He was worried, saying that it was not now safe but she assured him that no one would go on to it. Obviously she convinced him because he went away to carry on with the job he'd been doing before she took him off it.'

Shelley still could not believe that Delia had tried to injure her . . . or had she hoped the accident would be . . . fatal? Sheer horror filled Shelley and she could not speak. Nick went on after a space, 'You intimated that Delia was jealous of you—'

'No! Oh, I'm sure she'd never— It's too awful to think about! I can't believe that anyone would go as far as that, Nick. You must know there's some explanation—'

'Explanation?' he broke in harshly. 'What explanation?'

'I don't know—' Shelley shook her head. She didn't want to believe that Delia could be capable of wanting to injure her—and yet, wasn't the evidence damning against her? 'Where is Delia now?'

'I've told Eleni to find her and send her to the saloon.' Nick's eyes were brittle, his mouth harshly compressed. Shelley felt a quiver pass along her spine. She had seen Nick in this kind of a fury once only before. . . .

'Phivos obviously didn't know of the accident until now?'

'He's been working on the hedge running along the road outside. Costos told him what had happened when he took his sandwiches and coffee out to him. Phivos came straight away; he's most concerned and wishes he'd come to warn me of the danger.'

'If—if Delia did do this thing, then surely she must have known that Phivos would give her away.'

'It's my guess that she assumed he'd be so frightened he'd keep silent.'

'Because of his omission in giving us a warning?'

'That's right.' Nick paused, his expression dark and glowering. 'But instead, he was so upset when he heard of the accident that he came straight to me.' Nick turned his head as Eleni knocked on the door.

'Miss Unwin's in the saloon, Mr. Nickolas.'

'Thank you, Eleni.' Nick's voice was taut. He seemed consumed with fury and a shiver rippled along Shelley's spine. She felt she would rather give ten years of her life than be in Delia's shoes at this moment.

It was four days later—Shelley's birthday—and she was looking down at the exquisite snuff box given her by Nick; it was the one she had not been able to afford. And it was in the box she had seen in the drawer of Nick's desk. He'd bought it weeks ago—for her birthday.

'It's beautiful,' she breathed. 'Dear Nick—thank-you!'

He took her in his arms, smiling down at her with infinite tenderness.

'Don't cry, darling!' he exclaimed on seeing the unnatural brightness of her eyes. 'It's a happy day.'

She managed a weak smile and nodded her head.

'I know. And there are many more happy days for us. Oh, Nick, never let us be so foolish again, will you?'

He held her close to his heart, a hand gently stroking her hair above the dressing, his lips caressing hers.

'I promise— But why should we even visualise a repetition? We're both older, and much wiser.' He kissed her passionately and for a long while there was silence in the saloon where they were standing together by the high wide window, outside of which several men were busy laying lawn turves, while some distance away two others were putting the finishing touches to the fountain which had been erected. 'You're sure, sweet, that you want to live here permanently?'

'For ever and ever . . . with you,' she answered fervently.

'It's strange that you had the same feeling as I about the manor,' he said reflectively.

'I suppose I put some of my unhappiness into it,' was all the explanation she would give, but she now knew that there was too much of Delia in it, and in addition there was the fact of Nick's original unkindness in making Shelley renovate a house which, years earlier, they had both loved, and badly wanted for their own. Shelley felt that too much heartache had been experienced there—not only by her but by Nick who very soon realised that it was his ex-wife he loved and not the girl with whom he was intending to share the manor house.

'Yes—that and other things,' murmured Nick and as she looked up into his grim countenance Shelley knew that his thoughts had been running along the same lines as her own. He drew her close, bending his dark head to possess her softly-parted lips.

'When are you going to marry me, my darling?' Nick asked the question after an interlude of love-making that left Shelley breathless . . . and craving for more. She said tremulously, 'As soon as you like, Nick.'

'That doctor seems to think I can wait forever!' A frown darkened Nick's brow. 'I'll have a talk with him when he comes today.'

Shelley had to laugh.

'Forever? It's only four days since the accident!'

His smile transformed his face and the dark eyes softened with tenderness as they looked down into hers.

'I know, love, and I'm a brute to be impatient; but we've lost so much, fools that we were, and all I want now is to get right back to where we were.'

Shelley thought about this for a few moments and then, curling her arms around his neck, she looked into his eyes and said seriously, 'There's no going back—in fact, one should never ever contemplate such a thing. We're making a new start, darling, and we'll go forward from now on . . . together.'

'You're so right, my love,' agreed Nick almost immediately. 'What is past is past and only the present and future are ours.' He took her face in his hands and kissed her with infinite tenderness and love, a love which she knew, came from deep within his heart. 'Yes, you and I are beginning all over again, in a new home in a new country where the sun always shines— Oh, my beloved, I don't deserve this second chance!'

Shelley put tender fingers to his lips.

'A new beginning, darling,' she reminded him, her eyes limpid and trusting and reflecting the depth of her love for him.

'A new beginning,' he echoed fervently. 'Together.' His lips claimed hers in a kiss that was as savage as it was gentle, and his arms were strong about her. She arched towards his body and gave herself up to the fierce intensity of a passion he could not control. And it was a long while before they drew apart.

'Oh. . . .' she breathed, dreamy-eyed and still floating back to earth after the flight into the realms of ecstasy. 'I'm so happy!'

'That,' he said with a tender smile, 'makes two of us.'

They clung to each other again, sitting close on the sofa, Shelley's head against his shoulder. Silence reigned for a while and Shelley found her thoughts turning to Delia who had wanted to do

her the sort of harm that would preclude forever
any chance of her taking Nick from her. This she
had confessed to Nick during the scene that took
place between them—a scene which Shelley had
built up in her imagination from small things
mentioned by Nick, and of course by recollections
of the scene which had been enacted by Nick and
herself all those years ago. Delia, knowing she had
lost Nick forever, admitted her jealousy and was
told that Nick and Shelley had been married before. And now Delia was gone, not only from the
island but from their lives. Stephen had phoned,
been told what had transpired, and offered his
congratulations but at the same time bemoaning his
loss of the best assistant he had ever had. But he
ended on a happy note. He and Wendy planned to
marry quite soon and would like Nick and Shelley
to be at the wedding.

'Darling, you're a long way from me. . . .' Nick's
voice broke Shelley's reverie and she twisted her
head to meet his inquiring gaze. 'Where are you,
sweet?'

'I was thinking of Stephen,' she began when he
interrupted her.

'The man you became engaged to just to make
me jealous.'

She shook her head, laughing softly.

'No, that wasn't the idea,' she denied. 'I felt it
would take my mind off you . . . and the thought
of your marrying someone else.' She touched his
lips with hers before saying with a hint of mischief
in her voice, 'But it worked another way, didn't it?
It did make you jealous and so you made me come
here—away from Stephen.'

He nodded his head and murmured reflectively,
'I spoke to Stephen, though, and told him I wanted

to have you to myself, so I could decide if what I felt for you was really genuine. He agreed—and in fact I learned from him that he actually coerced you into coming here with me.'

'Yes, he did, and I thought there was something funny going on.'

'But you didn't guess what it was?'

'In a way. . . .' She nodded but frowned at the same time. 'I had begun to wonder if you were regretting your engagement to Delia.'

'The trouble was, love, that even then I was stubbornly determined to remember what I believed to be injuries to me. I'd approached your mother—almost humbly, which was difficult for me—'

'I'll bet it was!' Shelley could not help interposing and received a little shake for her trouble.

'Your mother said you were finished with me and would be happier with this fellow, Paul. You wanted a divorce and I have—all these years—considered myself as the injured party.' He sighed and caught his underlip between his teeth. 'I know now I should have ignored everything your mother said and determinedly set out to find you, when I could have discovered for myself whether or not you wanted a divorce. Pride!' he added with a scowl and another sigh. 'Stupid pride!'

'On both our parts,' she put in generously for it hurt to let Nick shoulder all the blame. He said nothing to that and soon she was saying, 'All the time you were punishing me you were at the same time beginning to have doubts about your engagement, weren't you?'

'That's right, but yet I still drove myself to continuing the punishment until at last I knew I had to examine my feelings and not make another major mistake in my life. That's why I wanted you here.'

She thought about this for a while before saying, 'And all the renovations here . . . they were for us, you and me.' It was a statement rather than a question and Nick nodded his head ruefully.

'I admit it,' he said with a reflective smile. 'As soon as I saw this house I knew that, one day, I'd like to live here. But I couldn't see Delia leaving the glamour of London so the house in the Cotswolds seemed to be a wise choice. This villa would have to be kept as a holiday home and, therefore, I hadn't any intention of doing much to it at all.' He paused and Shelley made no attempt to break into his thoughts. At length he looked down into her lovely face and went on, 'Then you and I met again and I soon began to realise that you could still affect me even as you had before. But all I wanted to do was punish you and it seemed that fate had played right into my hands: a long-desired wish had come true. I had the opportunity of hurting you—' He broke off and a heavy frown creased his brow. 'You see, darling, I very soon realised that you cared for me—you'd never have made love so wonderfully if you hadn't—'

'It was wonderful . . . to you as well?'

'So wonderful it hurt!' He crushed her to him and his kiss was far from gentle. 'Yet, such was my obsession to make you pay that I forced myself to act as if you meant nothing to me—' He broke off, the frown reappearing. 'Dearest, why did I do it—to you, whom I loved so deeply?'

'People in love do sometimes hurt each other, Nick.'

'Well, it's the last time either you or I will hurt one another,' was his fervent rejoinder.

'I can understand how you felt, thinking I was with Paul. Stephen once suggested Mother had told you that—Stephen's known all about us for some time,' she went on after a slight pause. Nick said nothing and Shelley ventured to ask if he had ever loved Delia.

A pause followed before Nick spoke.

'I was drawn to her,' he admitted reflectively. 'I believe it was purely a physical attraction.' He paused and Shelley nodded understandingly. Delia certainly had sex appeal—in plenty! 'But the moment I saw you again, Shelley,' Nick was saying, 'I knew that what I felt for Delia was a shallow emotion in comparison to what I felt for you years ago.' Again there was a pause: Nick smiled down into Shelley's face and then bent his head, to take her lips in a long and tender kiss. 'You remember the day I came back to the manor?'

'You said it was to see me,' she recalled, looking enquiringly at him.

'I felt we must talk—thrash things out and discover how we now felt about the divorce. But then I saw Stephen's ring on your finger. You were engaged, so there was nothing to discuss after all.'

'Oh, if only I'd known,' cried Shelley regretfully. 'It was you I loved and Stephen knew it.'

'Yes, but *I* didn't know all this at that time. Later, when I said I wanted you to come to Greece to renovate this house he guessed there was some underlying reason. I suppose he didn't think it natural for me to want to delay my wedding while I took my ex-wife abroad with me.' Nick laughed then and Shelley caught his humour.

'What puzzled me at that time was how you could get away from Delia—I mean, didn't she make any objections?' Shelley was thinking of that scene with the girl when Delia had been so furious at the idea of Nick and Shelley going off to Corfu.

'I explained that I had to do something to the villa before its condition worsened. She wasn't pleased but she had known me long enough to accept that my word was law, my wishes paramount.' He laughed at Shelley's sudden grimace and after kissing her thoroughly he assured her that she would have nothing like that to fear. At which she chuckled and said with a shake of her head. 'You'll always domineer over me, Nick, and you know it. You do have some of your mother in you, remember.'

'I shall put the manor up for sale,' murmured Nick presently. He touched her cheek with his lips, and his hand was gently cupping her breast. Shelley closed her eyes as rapture spread over her. She wanted Nick to make love to her, and was even contemplating asking him to do so but he spoke again, reflectively. 'I found myself resenting even the smallest suggestion made by Delia and so I knew then that it was you I wanted.'

Shelley spoke after a long silence, asking Nick how he would have managed to break his engagement if Delia, by her malicious act, had not made it easy for him.

'I'd have been frank,' he returned almost indifferently. 'She knew there was nothing really deep between us and so I don't think for one moment she'd have suffered any hurt.'

Shelley felt that any other explantions could be dealt with some other time. For now, she breathed a deep sigh of thankfulness that she and Nick had met again and were now together . . . for always.

She snuggled closer to him and curled her arms about his neck. She was full up, emotion making speech impossible even though she knew what she wanted to say.

So she remained silent, the invitation being in the softly-parted lips, and the expression in her eyes. . . .

IT'S YOUR OWN SPECIAL TIME

Contemporary romances for today's women.
Each month, six very special love stories will be yours
from SILHOUETTE. Look for them wherever books are sold
or order now from the coupon below

$1.50 each

☐ 5 Goforth	☐ 28 Hampson	☐ 54 Beckman	☐ 83 Halston
☐ 6 Stanford	☐ 29 Wildman	☐ 55 LaDame	☐ 84 Vitek
☐ 7 Lewis	☐ 30 Dixon	☐ 56 Trent	☐ 85 John
☐ 8 Beckman	☐ 32 Michaels	☐ 57 John	☐ 86 Adams
☐ 9 Wilson	☐ 33 Vitek	☐ 58 Stanford	☐ 87 Michaels
☐ 10 Caine	☐ 34 John	☐ 59 Vernon	☐ 88 Stanford
☐ 11 Vernon	☐ 35 Stanford	☐ 60 Hill	☐ 89 James
☐ 17 John	☐ 38 Browning	☐ 61 Michaels	☐ 90 Major
☐ 19 Thornton	☐ 39 Sinclair	☐ 62 Halston	☐ 92 McKay
☐ 20 Fulford	☐ 46 Stanford	☐ 63 Brent	☐ 93 Browning
☐ 22 Stephens	☐ 47 Vitek	☐ 71 Ripy	☐ 94 Hampson
☐ 23 Edwards	☐ 48 Wildman	☐ 73 Browning	☐ 95 Wisdom
☐ 24 Healy	☐ 49 Wisdom	☐ 76 Hardy	☐ 96 Beckman
☐ 25 Stanford	☐ 50 Scott	☐ 78 Oliver	☐ 97 Clay
☐ 26 Hastings	☐ 52 Hampson	☐ 81 Roberts	☐ 98 St. George
☐ 27 Hampson	☐ 53 Browning	☐ 82 Dailey	☐ 99 Camp

$1.75 each

☐ 100 Stanford	☐ 114 Michaels	☐ 128 Hampson	☐ 143 Roberts
☐ 101 Hardy	☐ 115 John	☐ 129 Converse	☐ 144 Goforth
☐ 102 Hastings	☐ 116 Lindley	☐ 130 Hardy	☐ 145 Hope
☐ 103 Cork	☐ 117 Scott	☐ 131 Stanford	☐ 146 Michaels
☐ 104 Vitek	☐ 118 Dailey	☐ 132 Wisdom	☐ 147 Hampson
☐ 105 Eden	☐ 119 Hampson	☐ 133 Rowe	☐ 148 Cork
☐ 106 Dailey	☐ 120 Carroll	☐ 134 Charles	☐ 149 Saunders
☐ 107 Bright	☐ 121 Langan	☐ 135 Logan	☐ 150 Major
☐ 108 Hampson	☐ 122 Scofield	☐ 136 Hampson	☐ 151 Hampson
☐ 109 Vernon	☐ 123 Sinclair	☐ 137 Hunter	☐ 152 Halston
☐ 110 Trent	☐ 124 Beckman	☐ 138 Wilson	☐ 153 Dailey
☐ 111 South	☐ 125 Bright	☐ 139 Vitek	☐ 154 Beckman
☐ 112 Stanford	☐ 126 St. George	☐ 140 Erskine	☐ 155 Hampson
☐ 113 Browning	☐ 127 Roberts	☐ 142 Browning	☐ 156 Sawyer

$1.75 each

☐ 157 Vitek	☐ 170 Ripy	☐ 183 Stanley	☐ 196 Hampson
☐ 158 Reynolds	☐ 171 Hill	☐ 184 Hardy	☐ 197 Summers
☐ 159 Tracy	☐ 172 Browning	☐ 185 Hampson	☐ 198 Hunter
☐ 160 Hampson	☐ 173 Camp	☐ 186 Howard	☐ 199 Roberts
☐ 161 Trent	☐ 174 Sinclair	☐ 187 Scott	☐ 200 Lloyd
☐ 162 Ashby	☐ 175 Jarrett	☐ 188 Cork	☐ 201 Starr
☐ 163 Roberts	☐ 176 Vitek	☐ 189 Stephens	☐ 202 Hampson
☐ 164 Browning	☐ 177 Dailey	☐ 190 Hampson	☐ 203 Browning
☐ 165 Young	☐ 178 Hampson	☐ 191 Browning	☐ 204 Carroll
☐ 166 Wisdom	☐ 179 Beckman	☐ 192 John	☐ 205 Maxam
☐ 167 Hunter	☐ 180 Roberts	☐ 193 Trent	☐ 206 Manning
☐ 168 Carr	☐ 181 Terrill	☐ 194 Barry	☐ 207 Windham
☐ 169 Scott	☐ 182 Clay	☐ 195 Dailey	

$1.95 each

☐ 208 Halston	☐ 218 Hunter	☐ 229 Thornton	☐ 240 Hunter
☐ 209 LaDame	☐ 219 Cork	☐ 230 Stevens	☐ 241 Wisdom
☐ 210 Eden	☐ 220 Hampson	☐ 231 Dailey	☐ 242 Brooke
☐ 211 Walters	☐ 221 Browning	☐ 232 Hampson	☐ 243 Saunders
☐ 212 Young	☐ 222 Carroll	☐ 233 Vernon	☐ 244 Sinclair
☐ 213 Dailey	☐ 223 Summers	☐ 234 Smith	☐ 245 Trent
☐ 214 Hampson	☐ 224 Langan	☐ 235 James	☐ 246 Carroll
☐ 215 Roberts	☐ 225 St. George	☐ 236 Maxam	☐ 247 Halldorson
☐ 216 Saunders	☐ 226 Hampson	☐ 237 Wilson	☐ 248 St. George
☐ 217 Vitek	☐ 227 Beckman	☐ 238 Cork	☐ 249 Scofield
	☐ 228 King	☐ 239 McKay	

_#250 THERE MUST BE SHOWERS, Hampson

_#251 AFTER AUTUMN, Wilson

_#252 UNTAMED, Roberts

_#253 TWO OF A KIND, James

_#254 DARLING ENEMY, Palmer

_#255 CAPRICE, Smith

SILHOUETTE BOOKS, Department SB/1

1230 Avenue of the Americas
New York, NY 10020

Please send me the books I have checked above. I am enclosing $_____
(please add 75¢ to cover postage and handling. NYS and NYC residents please
add appropriate sales tax). Send check or money order—no cash or C.O.D.'s
please. Allow six weeks for delivery.

NAME _____

ADDRESS _____

CITY _____ STATE/ZIP _____

6 brand new Silhouette Special Editions yours for 15 days–Free!

For the reader who wants more...more story...more detail and description...more realism...and more romance...in paperback originals, 1/3 longer than our regular Silhouette Romances. Love lingers longer in new Silhouette Special Editions. Love weaves an intricate, provocative path in a third more pages than you have just enjoyed. It is love as you have always wanted it to be—and more —intriguingly depicted by your favorite Silhouette authors in the inimitable Silhouette style.

15-Day Free Trial Offer

We will send you 6 new Silhouette Special Editions to keep for 15 days absolutely free! If you decide not to keep them, send them back to us, you pay nothing. But if you enjoy them as much as we think you will, keep them and pay the invoice enclosed with your trial shipment. You will then automatically become a member of the Special Edition Book Club and receive 6 more romances every month. There is no minimum number of books to buy and you can cancel at any time.

PRAISE FOR

THE COLTER SHAW SERIES

"Jeffery Deaver creates insanely devious plots calculated to make your head explode. . . . [*The Never Game*] dazzles with its crafty twists and turns."

—*The New York Times Book Review*

"Deaver introduces a fascinating new character in the methodical Colter Shaw. Nothing is predictable in the case, and like a curvy mountain road, the twists are intense. Hopefully more stories with Shaw are in the future."

—Associated Press

"[A] superb series launch from Thriller Award winner Deaver. . . . Fans of twisty suspense that pushes the envelope of plausibility without inviting disbelief will be enthralled." —*Publishers Weekly* (starred review)

"The story is—this will come as no surprise to Deaver's many fans—full of twists and right-angle turns, and a second Colter Shaw novel feels not just inevitable but mandatory. Deaver is a hit maker who always delivers the goods." —*Booklist*

"Award-winning author Deaver introduces an engaging new protagonist with staying power. Colter's backstory is fascinating and his persona as much a part of the tale as the crime itself. This is a sure bet for fans of suspense and will find a home with those who like their protagonists to be a central part of the mystery." —*Library Journal*

"As always, Deaver gets you in his stealthy grip on page one, and then takes you on a wild and inventive ride . . . this time with new star character Colter Shaw. No one in the world does this kind of thing better than Deaver."

—Lee Child

"With a twisty plot, riveting characters, and relentless suspense, *The Never Game* fires on every single cylinder. Readers will delight in this compelling new character from one of the finest suspense writers in the field. I always look forward to the new Deaver, but this one tops them all." —Karin Slaughter

"Lightning-fast and loaded with twists, *The Never Game* is a thrill a minute from one of the best. Don't miss it."

—Harlan Coben

"Jeffery Deaver is a one of our most exciting storytellers, and *The Never Game* pulls off the remarkable feat of intertwining a devilish plot with unforgettable characters, fascinating disquisitions with propulsive action, every element conspiring to make it almost impossible to not turn the page. I absolutely loved it." —Chris Pavone

"Jeffery Deaver knows how to deliver exactly what a reader wants. He has a gift for place and character and, here, the tension ratchets up, page by page, as we follow the exploits of a new hero. Crisply plotted and fraught with danger."   —Steve Berry

"Terrific writing, vivid and raw, Deaver grips from the very first line and never lets up. He is, hands-down, one of the finest thriller writers of our time."   —Peter James

"*The Never Game* is the very definition of a page-turner."
—Ian Rankin

"Grabbing you from the first page, Jeffery Deaver crafts a devilish plot that unfolds with breakneck speed. An excellent start to a new series, Colter Shaw has comfortably nestled onto the bench with Lincoln Rhyme and Kathryn Dance—one of our best literary puppet-masters at the end of all their strings."   —J. D. Barker

"Jeffery Deaver scores yet again with a fascinating new detective, Colter Shaw, and a plot as full of thrills and twists and turns as you would expect from him. With *The Never Game* you know you are in the hands of a master. But be warned—don't start this too late in the evening because sleep would be an annoying interruption once you've started reading!"   —Peter Robinson

Stand-Alones

The October List	The Blue Nowhere
No Rest for the Dead *(Contributor)*	Speaking in Tongues
Carte Blanche *(A James Bond Novel)*	The Devil's Teardrop
Watchlist *(Contributor)*	A Maiden's Grave
Edge	Praying for Sleep
The Bodies Left Behind	The Lesson of Her Death
Garden of Beasts	Mistress of Justice

SHORT FICTION

Collections
A Hot and Sultry Night for Crime *(Editor)*
Trouble in Mind
Triple Threat
Books to Die For *(Contributor)*
The Best American Mystery Stories 2009 *(Editor)*
More Twisted
Twisted

Stories
"Buried"
"The Second Hostage"
"Verona"
"The Debriefing"
"Ninth and Nowhere"
"Captivated"
"The Victims' Club"
"Surprise Ending"
"Double Cross"
"The Deliveryman"
"A Textbook Case"

THE
GOODBYE
MAN

JEFFERY
DEAVER

G. P. PUTNAM'S SONS

NEW YORK

PUTNAM
— EST. 1838 —

G. P. PUTNAM'S SONS
Publishers Since 1838
An imprint of Penguin Random House LLC
penguinrandomhouse.com

Copyright © 2020 by Gunner Publications, LLC
Excerpt from *The Final Twist* copyright © 2021
by Gunner Publications, LLC

The Library of Congress has catalogued the
G. P. Putnam's Sons hardcover edition as follows::

Names: Deaver, Jeffery, author.
Title: The goodbye man / Jeffery Deaver.
Description: New York: G. P. Putnam's Sons, [2020] | Series: Colter Shaw |
Identifiers: LCCN 2020011584 | ISBN 9780525535973 (hardcover) |
ISBN 9780525535997 (ebook) | ISBN 9780593189177 (international)
Subjects: GSAFD: Suspense fiction. | Mystery fiction.
Classification: LCC PS3554.E1755 G66 2020 | DDC 813/.54—dc23
LC record available at https://lccn.loc.gov/2020011584

First G. P. Putnam's Sons hardcover edition / May 2020
First G. P. Putnam's Sons international edition / May 2020
First G. P. Putnam's Sons premium edition / March 2021
First G. P. Putnam's Sons international mass-market edition / March 2021
G. P. Putnam's Sons international mass-market edition ISBN: 9780593332634

Printed in the United States of America
1   3   5   7   9   10   8   6   4   2

For Jane Davis, with boundless gratitude

What a journey I have made, the things I have seen . . .
Give me a jug of water and human flesh. Give me air to
breathe and a strong sailing wind when I rise from the
underworld.

BOOK OF THE DEAD, EGYPTIAN FUNERARY TEXT

THE
GOODBYE
MAN

ONE:

THE MAN ON THE CLIFF

1.

Seconds to decide.

Swerve left? Swerve right?

A steep drop into brush? Or a narrow shoulder that ends in a cliff wall?

Left.

Instinct.

Colter Shaw spun the wheel of the rental Kia sedan hard, braking intermittently—he couldn't afford a skid. The vehicle, which had been doing forty along this stretch in high mountains, plunged into foliage, narrowly missing a collision with the boulder that had tumbled down a steep hillside and rolled into the middle of the road before him. Shaw thought the sound of a two-hundred-pound piece of rock rolling through brush and over gravel would be more dramatic; the transit was virtually silent.

Left was the correct choice.

Had he gone right, the car would have slammed into a granite outcropping hidden by tall, beige grass.

Shaw, who spent much time assessing the percentage likelihood of harm when making professional decisions, nonetheless knew that sometimes you simply had to roll the dice and see what happened.

No air bags, no injury. He was, however, trapped inside the Kia. To his left was a sea of mahonia, otherwise known as Oregon grape, benign names both, belying the plant's needle-sharp spikes that can penetrate cloth on their effortless way into skin. Not an option for an exit. The passenger side was better, blocked only by insubstantial cinquefoil, in cheerful June bloom, yellow, and a tangle of forsythia.

Shaw shoved the right-side door open again and again, pushing back the viney plants. As he did this, he noted that the attacker's timing had been good. Had the weapon fallen sooner, Shaw could easily have braked. Any later, he'd have been past it and still on his way.

And a weapon it must have been.

Washington State certainly was home to earthquakes and seismic activity of all sorts but there'd been no recent shivering in the vicinity. And rocks that are this big usually stay put unless they're leveraged off intentionally—in front of, or onto, cars driven by men in pursuit of an armed fleeing felon.

After doffing his brown plaid sport coat, Shaw began to leverage himself through the gap between door and frame. He was in trim fit, as one who climbs mountainsides for recreation will be. Still, the opening was only fourteen or so inches, and he was caught. He would shove the door open, retreat, then shove once more. The gap slowly grew wider.

He heard a rustling in the brush across the road. The man who'd tipped the rock into Shaw's path was now scrabbling down the hillside and pressing through the dense growth toward Shaw, who struggled further to free himself. He saw a glint in the man's hand. A pistol.

The son of a survivalist and in a manner of speaking a survivalist himself, Shaw knew myriad ways of cheating death. On the other hand, he was a rock climber, a dirt bike fanatic, a man with a profession that set him against killers and escaped prisoners who'd stop at nothing to stay free. The smoke of death wafted everywhere around him, constantly. But it wasn't that finality that troubled him. In death, you had no reckoning. Far worse would be a catastrophic injury to the spine, to the eyes, the ears. Crippling his body, darkening the world or muting it forever.

In his youth, Shaw was called "the restless one" among his siblings. Now, having grown into a self-professed Restless Man, he knew that such incapacity would be pure hell.

He continued to squeeze.

Almost out.

Come on, come on . . .

Yes!

No.

Just as he was about to break free, his wallet, in the left rear pocket of his black jeans, caught.

The attacker stopped, leaning through the brush, and lifted the pistol. Shaw heard it cock. A revolver.

And a big one. When it fired, the muzzle blast blew green leaves from branches.

The bullet went wide, kicking up dust near Shaw.
Another click.
The man fired again.
This bullet hit its mark.

2.

S haw was piloting his thirty-foot Winnebago camper through the winding streets of Gig Harbor, Washington State.

With about seven thousand inhabitants, the place was both charming and scuffed around the edges. It was, to be sure, a harbor, well protected, connected to Puget Sound via a narrow channel through which pleasure and fishing craft now glided. The Winnebago motored past working and long-abandoned factories devoted to manufacturing vessels and the countless parts and accessories with which ships were outfitted. To Colter Shaw, never a sailor, it seemed like you could spend every minute of every day maintaining, repairing, polishing and organizing a boat without ever going out to sea.

A sign announced the Blessing of the Fleet in the middle of the harbor, the dates indicating that it had taken place earlier in the month.

PLEASURE CRAFT NOW WELCOME!

Perhaps the industry was now less robust than in the past, and the organizers of the event wanted to beef up its image by letting lawyers and doctors and salesmen edge their cabin cruisers up to the circle of the commercial craft—if that geometry was in fact the configuration for fleet blessing.

Shaw, a professional reward seeker, was here on a job— the word he used to describe what he did. *Cases* were what law enforcement investigated and what prosecutors prosecuted. Although after years of pursuing any number of criminals Shaw might have made a fine detective, he wanted none of the regimen and regulation that went with full-time employment. He was free to take on, or reject, any job he wished to. He could choose to abandon the quest at any time.

Freedom meant a lot to Colter Shaw.

He was presently considering the hate crime that had brought him here. In the first page of the notebook he was devoting to the investigation, he'd written down the details that had been provided by one of his business managers:

> *Location: Gig Harbor, Pierce County, Washington State.*
>
> *Reward offered for: Information leading to the arrest and conviction of two individuals:*
>
> *—Adam Harper, 27, resident of Tacoma.*
>
> *—Erick Young, 20, resident of Gig Harbor.*

Incident: There have been a series of hate crimes in the county, including graffiti of swastikas, the number 88 (Nazi symbol) and the number 666 (sign for the devil) painted on synagogues and a half-dozen churches, primarily those with largely black congregations. On June 7, Brethren Baptist Church of Gig Harbor was defaced and a cross burned in the front yard. Original news story was that the church itself was set on fire but that was found to be inaccurate. A janitor and a lay preacher (William DuBois and Robinson Estes) ran outside to confront the two suspects. Harper opened fire with a handgun, wounding both men. The preacher has been released from the hospital. The janitor remains in the intensive care unit. The perpetrators fled in a red Toyota pickup, registered to Adam Harper.

Law enforcement agencies running case: Pierce County Public Safety Office, liaising with U.S. Justice Department, which will investigate to determine if the incident is a federal hate crime.

Offerors and amount of reward:

—Reward one: $50,000, offered by Pierce County, underwritten by the Western Washington Ecumenical Council (with much of that sum donated by MicroEnterprises NA founder Ed Jasper).

—Reward two: $900 offered by Erick Young's parents and family.

To be aware of: Dalton Crowe is actively pursuing the reward.

This last bit of intelligence wasn't good.

Crowe was an unpleasant man in his forties. Former military, he'd opened a security business on the East Coast, though it wasn't successful and he shut it down. His career now was freelance security consultant, mercenary and, from time to time, reward seeker. Shaw's and Crowe's paths had crossed several times, on occasion violently. They approached the profession differently. Crowe rarely went after missing persons; he sought only wanted criminals and escapees. If you shot a fugitive while you were using a legal weapon in self-defense, you still got the reward and could usually avoid jail. This was Crowe's approach, the antithesis of Shaw's.

Shaw had not been sure he wanted to take this job. The other day, as he'd sat in a lawn chair in Silicon Valley, he had been planning on pursuing another matter. That second mission was personal, and it involved his father and a secret from the past—a secret that had nearly gotten Shaw shot in the elbows and kneecaps by a hitman with the unlikely name of Ebbitt Droon.

Risk of bodily harm—*reasonable* risk—didn't deter Shaw, though, and he truly wanted to pursue his search for his father's hidden treasure.

He'd decided, however, that the capture of two apparent neo-Nazis, armed and willing to kill, took priority.

GPS now directed him through the hilly, winding streets of Gig Harbor until he came to the address he sought, a pleasant single-story home, painted cheerful yellow, a stark contrast to the gray overcast. He glanced in the mirror and brushed smooth his short blond hair, which lay close to his head. It was mussed from a twenty-minute nap, his only rest on the ten-hour drive here from the San Francisco area.

Slinging his computer bag over his shoulder, he climbed from the van and walked to the front door, rang the bell.

Larry and Emma Young admitted him, and he followed the couple into the living room. He assessed their ages to be mid-forties. Erick's father sported sparse gray-brown hair and wore beige slacks and a short-sleeved T-shirt, immaculately white. He was clean-shaven. Emma wore a concealing, A-line dress in pink. She had put on fresh makeup for the visitor, Shaw sensed. Missing children disrupt much, and showers and personal details are often neglected. Not so here.

Two pole lamps cast disks of homey light around the room, whose walls were papered with yellow and russet flowers, and whose floors were covered in dark green carpet, over which sat some Lowe's or Home Depot oriental rugs. A nice home. Modest.

A brown uniform jacket sat on a coat rack near the door. It was thick and stained and had LARRY stitched on the breast. Shaw guessed the man was a mechanic.

They were doing their assessment of Shaw as well: the sport coat, the black jeans, the gray button-down shirt. Black slip-ons. This, or a variation, was his own uniform.

"Sit down, sir," Larry said.

Shaw took a comfortable overstuffed armchair of bold red leather and the couple sat across from him. "Have you heard anything about Erick since we talked?"

"No, sir," Emma Young told him.

"What's the latest from the police?"

Larry said, "He and that other man, Adam. They're still around the area. The detective, he thinks they're scraping together money, borrowing it, maybe stealing it—"

"He wouldn't," said Emma.

"What the police said," Larry explained. "I'm just telling him what they said."

The mother swallowed. "He's . . . never. I mean, I . . ." She began to cry—again. Her eyes had been dry but red and swollen when Shaw arrived.

He removed a notebook from his computer bag, as well as a Delta Titanio Galassia fountain pen, black with three orange rings toward the nib. Writing with the instrument was neither pretense nor luxury. Colter Shaw took voluminous notes during the course of his reward jobs; the pen meant less wear and tear on his writing hand. It also was simply a small pleasure to use.

He now wrote the date and the names of the couple. He looked up and asked for details about their son's life: In college and working part-time. On summer break now. Lived at home.

"Does Erick have a history of being involved in neo-Nazi or any extremist groups?"

"My God, no," Larry muttered as if exhausted by the familiar question.

"This is all just crazy," said Emma. "He's a good boy. Oh, he's had a little trouble like everybody. Some drugs—I mean, after, well, after what happened, it's understandable. Just tried 'em is all. The school called. No police. They were good about that."

Larry grimaced. "Pierce County? The meth and drug capital of the state. You should read the stories in the paper. Forty percent of all the meth in Washington is produced here."

Shaw nodded. "Was that what Erick did?"

"No, some of that Oxy stuff. Just for a while. He took anti-depressants too. Still does."

"You said, 'after what happened.' After what?"

They looked at each other. "We lost our younger boy sixteen months ago."

"Drugs?"

Emma's hand, resting on her thigh, closed into a fist, bundling the cloth below her fingers. "No. Was on his bike, run into by somebody who was drunk. My, it was hard. So hard. But it hit Erick in particular. It changed him. They were real close."

Brothers, Shaw thought, understanding quite well the complex feelings the relationship generated.

Larry said, "But he wouldn't do anything hurtful. Never anything bad. He never has. 'Cepting for the church."

His wife snapped, "Which he didn't do. You *know* he didn't."

Shaw said, "The witnesses said it was Adam did the shooting. I haven't heard where the gun came from. Does Erick own one? Have access to one?"

"No."

"So it would be his friend's."

Larry: "Friend? Adam wasn't a friend. We never heard of him."

Emma's ruddy fingers twined the dress hem. A habit. "He's the one did the cross thing too, burning it. And the graffiti. Everything! Adam kidnapped Erick. I'm sure that's what happened. *He* had a gun and made Erick come with him. Hijack his car, rob him."

"They took Adam's truck, though, not Erick's."

"I was thinking about that," the mother blurted. "Erick did the brave thing and threw his keys away."

"He had his own bank account?"

The boy's father said, "Yes."

So they wouldn't know about withdrawals. The police could get that information, what branches he'd been to. Probably already had.

"You know how much money he has? Enough to get very far?"

"Couple thousand, maybe."

Shaw had been examining the room, observing mostly the pictures of the Youngs' two boys. Erick was handsome with bushy brown hair and an easy smile. Shaw had also seen pictures of Adam Harper, posted as part of the reward announcement. There were no mug shots, though in both of the photos in the press he was looking into the camera with caution. The young man, whose crew cut was blond with blue highlights, was gaunt.

"I'm going to pursue this, try to find your son."

Larry said, "Oh, sure. Please. You're nothing like that big guy."

"Didn't like him one bit," Emma muttered.

"Dalton Crowe?"

"That was his name. I told him to leave. I wasn't going to pay him any reward. He laughed and said I could stuff it. He was going after the bigger one anyway, you know—the fifty thousand the county offered."

"When was he here?"

"Couple days ago."

In his notebook Shaw wrote, *D.C. present at offerors' house. June 9.*

"Now, let me tell you how I approach this. It won't cost you anything unless I find Erick. No expenses. If I locate him, you'll owe me that $900."

Larry said proudly, "It's $1,060 now. One of my cousins came through. Wish it was more but . . ."

"I know you'll want me to bring him home to you. But that's not my job. He's a fugitive and I'd be breaking the law if I did that."

"Aiding and abetting," Emma said. "I watch all the crime shows."

Colter Shaw tended not to smile but when meeting offerors, he occasionally did, to put them at ease. "I don't apprehend. I deal in information, not citizen's arrests. But if I can find him, I won't let the police know where he is until there's no chance he or anybody else'll be hurt. You'll need a lawyer. Do you know one?"

They regarded each other once more. "Fellow did our closing," Larry said.

"No. A criminal lawyer. I'll get you some names."

"We don't have . . . I mean, we could work out a home equity thing, I guess."

"You'll have to. He needs good representation."

Shaw reviewed his notes so far. His handwriting was

small and had once been described as balletic, it was so beautifully drawn. The notebook wasn't ruled. Shaw didn't need guidance. Each line was perfectly horizontal.

For another twenty minutes Shaw asked questions and the couple responded. Over the course of the interview, he noted that their adamant view that their son was innocent seemed objective; they simply could not accept that the son they knew had committed this crime. The idea bewildered them. The sole perp had to be Adam Harper.

When he felt he had enough information for the moment, he put away the pen and notebook, rose and walked to the door. The parents agreed to send any new information they heard from the police or friends or relatives Erick had contacted for money or other help.

"Thank you," Emma said at the doorway, debating hugging him, it seemed. She did not.

It was the husband who was choking up. He fumbled whatever he was going to say and just gripped Shaw's hand. Larry turned back to the house before the first tear appeared.

As he walked to the Winnebago, Shaw was reflecting on the one subject he had not mentioned to Emma and Larry: his policy not to accept a reward from family members if the search revealed that their missing loved one was dead. No reason to even bring up the possibility, even though it seemed more or less likely to Shaw that their second child had been murdered as soon as Adam found he had no more use for the boy.

3.

Why should I talk to you?" the man scoffed.

Dressed in a faded jacket of cracked brown leather, jeans and boots, Adam Harper's father, Stan, continued to stack cartons of motor oil on a dock. He was a ship's chandler, an outfitter, and apparently getting an order ready to load onto a delivery boat when it arrived back in the berth.

The air was richly scented, pine and sea waste and petroleum.

"I'm helping Erick Young's family find their son. The last the police knew, he and Adam were together."

"You're after that reward, I'll bet."

"I am, yes. Now, is there anything you can tell me about Adam that could help? Where he might go? Friends, relatives he'd be staying with?"

"Put that away." Nodding at the notebook and pen in Shaw's hand.

Shaw slipped them into a pocket.

"Don't have any idea." Harper was solid as a tree,

with sandy-gray hair and a rosy complexion, nose slightly ruddier than cheek.

Erick's family had offered money for someone to find their fugitive son; Stan Harper had not. As far as Shaw knew, he might hope his son successfully escaped from the law. There was no reason for him to say a word. Still, he wasn't stonewalling. Not exactly. Three stacked cartons later, Harper turned. "He was always a problem. Moods this, moods that. Said it was like bees buzzing around him all the time. Made it hard on us too, you can believe. He didn't get that. It was all about him. Trouble at school, counsellors calling all the time. Had some fights, him and me." A glance toward Shaw. "But that's fathers and sons. Happens to everybody. Easier for us when he quit school and started working trades. Day labor, mostly. If he was on staff, he'd get fired in a split."

Shaw would tread lightly with his next question. Bigotry, he'd found, was often handed down from parents to children like hair color and heart trouble. He had no problem calling out a racist, but at the moment his mission was to gather information. "The incident at the church? The cross, the graffiti. Did he ever talk about doing anything like that?"

"Never heard him. But I gotta say, me and him, we didn't talk about much of anything. After Kelly passed— after my wife passed—he went even further away. Hit him hard. I was like, *it's coming*, her passing, and I tried to get ready. Adam, he just didn't think she'd ever . . . Denied it, you know?"

"Any friends in supremacist groups? Was he a member of any community like that?"

"What're you, like a bounty hunter?"

"I make my living finding people."

Whether this answer satisfied or raised questions, Shaw couldn't tell. Harper hefted two big cartons at once with little effort. They must've totaled fifty pounds.

Shaw repeated the question about neo-Nazis.

"Not that I ever heard but he was . . . you know, was impressionable. He met some musicians once, and for a year that was all he was going to do. Be a heavy metal star. That was the whole world to him. Then he gave it up. Was going to build skateboards and sell them. That went no place. Fell in with a bad crew in high school, shoplifting and drugs. He did whatever they wanted.

"You know, when I heard from the cops about the church, I wasn't surprised. Not like *oh shit* surprised. I figured he'd snapped. I could feel it coming. Since his mother died."

Stan walked to the edge of the dock and spit, wiped his mouth with the back of his hand.

"That Erick kid, you oughta check him out."

Shaw replied, "He doesn't seem to have any connection with supremacists. No history of hate crimes."

Harper's eyes narrowed. "You know, Adam took off for a while. He was away for three weeks, a month, I don't know. After we lost Kelly. He just disappeared and when he came back he was different. He was better, his moods. I asked him where he'd gone. He said he couldn't talk about it. Maybe he hooked up with some of those assholes then."

"Where?"

"No idea."

"Can you give me the names of friends I can talk to?"

A shrug. "Couldn't tell you. He wasn't a boy, you know. He had his own life. We didn't chat on the phone, like he did with his mama." Harper received a text and then replied. Looked over the still water of the harbor. Then back to the cartons.

"Was he straight?" Shaw asked.

"You mean . . . like, not being gay?"

Shaw nodded.

"Why you wanta ask something like that?"

"I need all the facts I can get."

"Only ever saw him with women. None of 'em for very long." A sigh. "We tried everything with him. Therapy. Yeah, that was a joke. Medication. Always the most expensive ones, naturally. And that was on top of Kelly's bills too. Doctors and hospitals." He nodded toward the shack that was the corporate headquarters for Harper Ship Services, Inc. "I look like I can afford Cadillac health insurance?"

"Nothing worked for Adam?"

"Not much. Just being away wherever he went, that three or four weeks." The crowning carton was placed on the stack. "Maybe he got a kick out of learning to burn crosses and spray paint churches. Who the fuck knows? I got paperwork to do."

Shaw gave him a card with his number on it. "If you hear from him."

The man slipped it into his back pocket and gave a cynical smile, which meant: Helping you get your blood money.

"Mr. Harper, I want to get both of them back safe."

Harper turned but paused halfway to the shed.

"It was so damn frustrating. Sometimes you just wanted to shake him and say, 'Get over yourself. Everybody's got the blues. Just live with it.'"

Back in the Winnebago, Shaw brewed a cup of strong Honduran coffee, poured in some milk and sat down at the table.

He spent the next half hour or so calling some of the Youngs' relatives. They were sympathetic but had no helpful information. Then on to Erick's friends. Those willing to talk could offer no insights into where he might have gone and generally expressed dismay that he'd been implicated in a hate crime. One classmate, however, said that since his brother died "he's just like . . . he's not really himself, you know what I mean?"

Shaw spoke to Tom Pepper, a former FBI special agent and a friend with whom he rock-climbed occasionally. Pepper may have been retired but he was just as connected in law enforcement now as he had always been and was current on a robust security clearance. He also enjoyed staying in the investigation game and Shaw sometimes called Pepper for an assist. He now asked for the name of somebody involved in the investigation, either in the Pierce County Public Safety Office or the local FBI field office.

A reward seeker's relationship with the police is complicated. Law enforcers have no problems with tip lines, like Crimewatch, whose purpose is to gather information from those who have personal knowledge of an incident.

Cops are, however, reluctant to give much assistance to an active investigator like Shaw. Reward seekers, as opposed to tipsters, have been known to muddy up cases, occasionally even resulting in a suspect's escape when police were close to an arrest. Seekers also sometimes end up injured or dead, which complicates a cop's life to no end.

Still, Pepper's name carried some weight and so did his assurance that Shaw wouldn't get underfoot and could even possibly prove helpful. The Pierce County detective running the case, Chad Johnson, spent ten minutes filling Shaw in on the details, which Shaw recorded in his notebook. Johnson provided particulars on Adam Harper, supplementing what the young man's father had said.

When they disconnected, Shaw made another cup of coffee and flipped through the notebook.

> *June 7. Around 6:30 p.m. Erick Young went to the Forest Hills Cemetery on Martinsville Road in Gig Harbor. This is where his brother, Mark, who died sixteen months ago, is buried. He went to the gravesite frequently.*
>
> *At some point shortly thereafter, Erick was seen in the company of Adam Harper in the cemetery, according to witnesses. Erick had no apparent prior connection with Adam.*
>
> *At around 7:30 police responded to reports of a shooting at Brethren Baptist Church. Victims— a lay preacher and a janitor—reported that two suspects, later identified as Adam and Erick, had placed a cross in front of the church and set it on*

fire. The church was also defaced with Nazi swastikas and obscenities.

When the preacher and janitor ran outside to try to tackle the suspects and hold them for police, Adam drew a gun and shot at them, hitting both.

The suspects fled in Adam's ten-year-old red Toyota pickup truck, registered in Washington State. Erick's car was found parked near the cemetery.

None of Erick's social media posts suggest racist leanings. Adam has no FB, Twitter or Instagram account.

Neither is gay; unlikely there was a sexual encounter.

None of Erick's other family members or friends have heard from him. There is no particular location he might have run off to that his parents and friends know of.

The authorities were forensically able to link the defamatory graffiti on the Brethren Baptist Church to similar incidents in Pierce County over the past year and a half.

The suspects are believed to still be in the Tacoma area, since both Adam and Erick emptied savings accounts over the past several days, and there have been two sightings of the pickup via video surveillance. Probably gathering money for a long-distance escape from the area.

Erick Young has been working part-time in a rehabilitation center for troubled youths and getting a B.A. at a local community college. He excelled in math, history and biology. But after his brother's death, he became moody and his grades dropped and attendance at work became a problem. His girlfriend broke up with him because of his moods. Parents described him as "confused and vulnerable."

Adam Harper has a history of depression and other emotional problems. A drifter. He's taken classes at community college but never graduated. He's worked trades most of his life.

He has been arrested on shoplifting and minor drug possession charges. He has no obvious history of white supremacist or racist organizations, though father pointed to his disappearance for 3 to 4 weeks out of town. Hooked up with a group then?

Adam has few friends and the ones the police contacted, as well as a couple of family members, were unaware of anyone or anyplace he would be inclined to flee to.

His residence, a small apartment on the east side of Tacoma, was searched. There was no evidence of any extremist affiliation.

Firearm used in the shooting was a Smith & Wesson .38 Police Special, registered to Adam's father.

Neither of the suspects' phones are active.

Both men have passports. Erick's is still in his parents' home.

A video of a currency exchange showed two
men, in sunglasses and wearing hoodies, chang-
ing $500 U.S. into Canadian. They matched the
general builds of the suspects.

Shaw scanned these notes, sat back, closed his eyes, digesting what he'd read, drawing conclusions about the incident and the people involved.

His phone hummed. It was Chad Johnson.

"Detective?"

"We've got them, Mr. Shaw."

Fastest reward job on record. No money. But the good news was that he could now return to his other mission: tracking down his father's secret.

Echo Ridge . . .

"Anybody hurt? Did they resist?"

A pause. "Oh, we haven't apprehended them yet. I mean, we've *located* them. They're in Adam's pickup. There was a sighting of it headed north on I-5. Then they turned off on surface roads and were still heading north. Making for Canada, of course. We've got a taskforce on the apprehension detail. Ten person."

The last word stumbled out. Johnson had recently been trained not to use the male gender if possible, Shaw guessed.

"Should get them in the next hour."

"Good."

"Sorry about the reward, sir."

He didn't sound too sorry, Shaw thought. Maybe the Ecumenical Council and the high-tech wunderkind

Ed Jasper were contributing the bulk but the rest of the cash would have to come out of his budget.

Shaw thanked him. He sipped a bit more coffee, then sent a text to Mack McKenzie, his D.C.-based private eye, requesting three items of information. Shortly after, she responded, answering all of them with the level of detail that she was known for.

Shaw read the reply closely and, after scanning a map, fired up the Winnebago's engine. He pulled out of Harper's parking lot, surveyed the vehicles nearby—those parked, as well as those in motion—then drove onto the uneven road. He steered east out of Gig Harbor, his GPS directing him to a trailer camp, where he'd park the Winnebago and Uber to a car rental agency to pick up a sedan or SUV. He edged the camper as far over the speed limit as he dared without getting pulled over.

He couldn't afford any delays. Time was vital.

An hour later Shaw was steering his rental Kia along a mountainous route fifty miles east of Tacoma in the beautiful country approaching Mount Rainier National Park. Winding roads, panoramic views, verdant forest, formations of rock shiny and pitted as wet bone.

He eased out of a climbing switchback and onto a straightaway, a hillside face on his right, and began to accelerate.

Then a moving shadow caught his attention.

The boulder was cartwheeling toward the road directly in front of him.

Seconds to decide.

Swerve left? Swerve right?

4.

T *his bullet hit its mark . . .*
      A golden eagle, troubled by the sharp crack of the
pistol rolling through the valley, lifted off and descended away from the human disturbance in stately urgency.

Colter Shaw glanced down, noting the sizable gunshot hole in the Kia's right front tire. The car knelt.

Now free from the vehicle, Shaw pushed through the
forsythia and watched the shooter walk across the road,
dusting away pollen and burrs from his sleeves and jeans.

Fully bearded, Dalton Crowe was two inches taller
than Shaw's six feet even. Broad shoulders, ample chest,
both encased in a black and red plaid lumberjack shirt.
Camo overalls. His belt was well tooled and well worn,
shiny and unevenly dark. The holster for the long-barreled
revolver was cowboy style, brown and glossy and chrome
studded.

Each of the men had bestowed scars upon the other,
about the same number, the same length, the same depth.

The bruises had long fleshed away. The confrontations were not intended to be lethal but simply to derail the other's success in finding the suspects in reward jobs. In one instance, Crowe wanted to stop Shaw so he could get one hundred percent of the money for an escaped prisoner; Shaw wanted to stop Crowe from gunning down the trapped, unarmed man.

Crowe ambled across the road and looked at the tire. "Hmm."

"You fired in my direction," Shaw said. His tone was scolding only; he hadn't felt himself in much danger. He'd known to a certainty that the rock-tipper and shooter was Crowe and not the suspects, Adam Harper or Erick Young.

For a big man who would look right at home in Hells Angels attire, Crowe had an eerily high voice. "Nup, Shaw. None of that. I was saving you from a snake." He was from Birmingham, Alabama, and came equipped with the accent. "Timber rattler and a damn big one."

Shaw glanced down. "Don't see him."

"Aw, I just fired to scare him off. Which I did, as you can see. I like all of God's creatures, rattlers included. Sorry about your tire."

Shaw looked at the boulder, completely blocking the highway.

Crowe didn't bother to spin a tale about that.

"These boys're mine, Shaw. Adam and Erick. I'm going to find 'em and I'm going to bring 'em in. I got to Gig Harbor 'fore you did. So dig yourself out and head on home."

"How'd you find me?" Shaw asked.

"I'm the best, that's how." Crowe slipped his gun away. Shaw wondered if he ever twirled it on his finger like gunslingers do in the movies. Shaw had once seen somebody shoot himself in the armpit doing that. Human stupidity has no bounds.

"You heard my piece. That's all there is to it. I've got a yellow Volkswagen to catch up with."

Shaw's brows compressed. "How'd you know they were . . ." His voice faded, as if he'd slipped up, confirming a fact that Crowe hadn't known for certain.

"Haw. Now get that tire of yours fixed, call Triple A or man the jack yourself." Crowe looked around, at the boulder, then back to Shaw. "On these roads, in that breadbox of a car . . . you could come to real grief. Not from me, of course, saving your ass from rattlers. But somebody aiming at *you*. I'd hate to see that happen."

The threat delivered, Crowe turned and plodded up the road, then disappeared into the bushes. A moment later his silver SUV drove onto the road, on the other side of the boulder, and turned away from Shaw and the rock. A hand appeared from the driver's window of the Bronco. The gesture seemed to be a wave but it might have been ruder.

He called 911, reporting the fallen boulder to the state police. The obstacle was in the middle of a straightaway and could be seen fifty yards away from either direction. Still, Colter Shaw was hardwired to save people from disaster, even if it was their own failings that put them in peril. Someone cruising along while texting might deserve the air bag slap; his or her children did not, however.

Shaw spent a few minutes checking the tires and backing out of the razorish weeds. It took some rocking and some tire spinning but eventually the car rolled onto the road again.

Once on the asphalt, he changed the tire and searched the wheel wells. He found the GPS tracker Crowe had hidden. He clicked the off button and stowed the device in his backpack.

Then he turned around and sped back the way he'd come, the exact opposite of the direction that Dalton Crowe was headed. Shaw checked his map and estimated that he should intercept Erick Young and Adam Harper in less than a half hour.

5.

t had taken some effort, and time, but the problem of Dalton Crowe had to be eliminated.

The man's assessment of his own skill—"I'm the best"—was just plain wrong. Crowe was a functional, not talented, tracker, and he was just plain lousy at surveillance. Shaw knew Crowe had been dogging him from the moment he'd arrived in Gig Harbor. He'd noted the silver SUV as soon as he'd arrived at the Youngs', parked at the curb several doors away, in front of a house with a FORECLOSURE SALE sign in the lawn. Not necessarily suspicious. He merely tucked the observation away.

When he'd left, he'd pulled past the SUV and seen the driver bending toward the glove compartment, as if avoiding being seen. Then the Bronco had pulled away from the curb and followed the Winnebago all the way to Adam's father's chandler business on the waterfront.

It was obviously Dalton Crowe, who would have been staking out the Young residence since he'd arrived in the harbor town on the chance that the boy, known to be still in the area, would return.

At that point, Shaw's mission had doubled: get rid of Crowe, *then* find Adam and Erick.

Shaw had come up with a plan to do both.

The Public Safety Office believed the young men were headed north from Tacoma, presumably en route to Canada, given the currency exchange intelligence.

Shaw was eighty percent certain, however, that Adam and Erick were not in the red pickup.

Anticipating the suspects' most logical plan, Shaw had sent the email to Mack. The questions he'd posed were:

1. What neighborhood in Tacoma has the highest gang activity?

2. Where's the main bus station in or near that neighborhood?

3. Where are cars likely to be taken for chopping in the Seattle-Tacoma area?

The reply had been: the neighborhood of Manitou, a Western Express bus terminal on Evans Street, and any number of places, though there was a concentration of junkyard/chop shops on the south side of Seattle.

Shaw believed that they'd donned costumes and exchanged U.S. dollars for Canadian to trick investigators into thinking their destination was north. That alone wasn't enough, though. They had to keep the law's focus on Adam's truck. Since Erick worked with troubled youths, he was likely familiar with the underworld of

Pierce County. He would have known where to leave the pickup—with the keys "hidden" under the front seat or in a wheel well—where it would quickly be perped by some bangers and driven to south Seattle for butchering into parts.

Meanwhile, Adam and Erick had walked a few blocks to the bus station on Evans Street, bought tickets and left town.

After leaving Harper's seaside company, Shaw had driven the Winnebago to a campground east of Tacoma, and parked it there. He'd Ubered to a nearby car rental agency and gotten the Kia, which he'd then driven into the Manitou neighborhood, with Crowe clumsily tailing all the way.

Shaw had parked in front of the Hermanos Alverez bodega. He had gone inside the store, and for a twenty-dollar bribe and several bags of groceries he didn't need, bought the right to slip out the back door.

From there, to the bus station, at which the ante increased significantly, and it cost him five hundred dollars to learn the destination of the tickets the two boys had bought—a little town called Hope's Corner, eighty miles southeast of Tacoma, near Mount Rainier National Park.

This fact was good news. They were both alive.

He'd returned to the car, out the bodega's front door, dumped the groceries in the trunk. When he pulled into traffic, Crowe's SUV was not far behind. It had been while the car was parked in front of the store that Crowe had clamped on the tracker.

Then the fun began.

Shaw had driven a circuitous route in the general direction of Hope's Corner, though he had stopped every fifteen miles or so, buying water or coffee or snacks or yet another unnecessary road map. And always asking the clerks and customers the same question.

"Say, you notice a yellow Volkswagen bug coming through here? It's my two buddies. We were going fishing at Wuikinuxv Falls but there's been a change of plans and I can't reach 'em. Those boys're just not picking up their phones."

The point of this exercise was to misdirect Crowe as to the suspects' means of transport and their destination. Now, having used the boulder to clear the field for himself, the man was speeding in pursuit of a gaudy, nonexistent car, to a town whose name was hard to pronounce and harder yet to spell . . . and that lay in the exact opposite direction of Hope's Corner, where the suspects really were.

Colter Shaw now rolled past the Hope's Corner WEL-COME TO sign and surveyed the burg. The downtown embraced a diner, a mechanic's garage, a general store and two gas stations, one of which was also a bus way station; it would be there that the suspects disembarked.

The tiny place also featured an overlook from which you got a grand view of Mount Rainier, the tallest peak in the state. It was designated a Decade Volcano, one of the most hazardous in the world. Shaw knew this because he and Tom Pepper had once considered climbing it. But while the threat of eruption wasn't a deterrent, the surfaces were. They were largely ice and snow, and that made for a specialized technique that didn't interest them much.

Shaw steered the Kia into the pump area of the larger

gas station, refueled and examined the damage to the car from his boulder-avoiding plunge. Cosmetic only. Expensive, of course. But Shaw wasn't concerned; he always bought the loss/damage insurance. When finished at the pump, he drove the car into a shaded spot at the side of the general store. Climbing out, he went to the trunk, opened it and, after looking round and seeing no humans or security cameras, removed his concealed carry weapon—a single-stack Glock 42, the .380 caliber, in a Blackhawk holster. He chambered a round and fitted the holster inside his right waistband, making sure the securing hook snugly held his belt; the fastest draw in the world is pretty useless if the holster comes along for the ride.

Now, to determine where exactly were the suspects.

Shaw considered the timing. The bus was scheduled to arrive thirty minutes ago. Had they hiked out from Hope's Corner? Had they met some friends near here?

Neither Adam nor Erick *appeared* to be neo-Nazi but what if they were operating undercover? After all, the defamatory and racist graffiti had persisted in Pierce County for more than a year, and no one had been caught. Now that they'd been identified and were in the open maybe they'd come here. Washington State had an unfortunate history of hate groups and white supremacist organizations, Shaw knew from several reward-seeking jobs on the West Coast. There were nearly two dozen active extremist groups in the state, including two KKK chapters.

From the overlook, Shaw gazed at the massive expanse that could easily hide a militia compound.

Or had the boys simply panicked after the shooting

and fled as far as their money would take them, or to the home of a friend who'd shelter them—a friend that no one back home knew about?

So, Shaw told himself, assess.

The odds that they had arrived, disembarked and hiked out into the wilderness? Fifteen percent. This territory would require some serious gear and a level of fitness and knowledge of the outdoors that the young men didn't seem to have.

The likelihood that they were planning to meet somebody to drive them elsewhere? Forty percent.

Hitching down one of the crossroads that went east and west out of Hope's Corner? Possible, though a challenge; there was little traffic on either road. He gave it twenty percent.

Sheltering with a friend? Fifteen percent.

There was another option as well. Were they still here, in Hope's Corner?

Shaw had donned his brown sport jacket. To make sure his concealed stayed concealed, though, he took the added step of untucking his shirt. His pistol permit was valid in the state but he didn't need the attention that would ensue if someone spotted the grip of his weapon.

He began a stroll through the town, eyes scanning for the two.

They weren't in either gas station.

The general store was next. He stepped onto the low, saggy wooden porch and pushed inside, hand low, near the gun. No Erick, no Adam.

He entered the restroom, which he had to use anyway; they weren't there.

The establishment was a combination store and restaurant, where a half-dozen diners sat at a chipped linoleum counter. He snagged a can of Fix-a-Flat, being spare-less now, and perched on a stool to order a turkey sandwich and a large coffee to go. When the order was up he took the bag and the can to the register. He handed the check to the middle-aged man in a beige polyester shirt embroidered with a pattern of chains.

Shaw set down a hundred-dollar bill.

The man grimaced. "Sorry, mister, I can't change that."

"I don't want change."

Eyes cautious now.

"The son of a friend of mine's run off. I'm helping find him. He was with another guy. Think he might've come in on that bus from Tacoma."

One of the reasons Shaw shaved before a job, polished his shoes and dressed in a sport coat and pressed shirt was to give the impression of legitimacy. The sort who really would help a friend find a boy. He shot the man another stage smile.

"Here's his picture." He displayed a photo of Erick. The boy was in his football uniform.

Shaw wondered if the clerk watched the news from Tacoma and had heard of the shooting at the church. Apparently not. He asked only, "What's he play?"

"He's a receiver," Shaw vamped. "Can catch a pass one handed."

"No."

"He can."

"Why'd he run off?"

Shaw shrugged. "Being a kid."

The bill vanished into the man's pocket. "Yeah, they were here, thirty minutes ago. Bought some food and water. Bought a disposable phone too. And a prepaid card for the minutes."

"You overhear where they were going?"

"No."

"Where could they get from here on foot?"

A *who knows?* shrug. "There're a dozen cabins in the foothills." Another shrug meant: Good luck finding them.

"Any towns in walking distance?"

"Depends on who's walking. It's a trek but there's one they could make in a day. Snoqualmie Gap. Used to be called Clark's Gap. After Lewis and Clark. But got itself changed to Snoqualmie. That's a word, Indian word. Means 'fierce tribe.' Some folks were pissed off they changed it. You can go too far, this PC crap." He'd looked Shaw over, perhaps registering "Caucasian" and guessing it was okay to offer the comment—not knowing Shaw did in fact have some Native American in him. "Funny thing is, don't make no difference either way."

Shaw didn't understand. He shook his head.

"Lewis and Clark never got here, and the Snoqualmie River's nowhere near either. So might as well call it New York, Los Angeles or Podunk. Maybe those boys were headed there." He frowned briefly. "You know, there's this place in the mountains outside of it—Snoqualmie Gap. Some people ask for directions."

"Place?"

"This retreat."

"Separatist thing? Neo-Nazis?"

"Don't think so. More, some New Age bullshit. Hippies. You're too young."

Shaw had been born in the Bay Area long after flower children and the Summer of Love, 1967. But he knew about hippies.

He looked at a map on the wall. He saw Snoqualmie Gap, a small town, about ten miles from Hope's Corner. Quite a hike in the mountainous terrain.

"Where's the retreat?"

The clerk squinted. "About there, I guess." Tapping a valley in the mountains beside a large lake. Shaw estimated it was six or seven miles from Snoqualmie Gap, accessed via a state route and then the narrow and eerily named Harbinger Road.

Walking, it would take them three to four hours to get to Snoqualmie, and another three to get to the retreat, if that's where they were headed.

"I didn't see much traffic on the way here. Going that way, to Snoqualmie, could they hitch a ride?"

"Somebody could. *They* couldn't."

"Why's that?"

"That guy with your friend's son? I wouldn't pick him up on a dare. Something about his eyes."

Shaw thanked the man and started for the door.

"Hey, mister?"

He turned.

The clerk was frowning. "You forgot to pay your bill." He looked at the check and said, "That's eleven twenty-eight you owe me."

6.

n ten minutes Colter Shaw's job was over.

He found Adam Harper and Erick Young on Old Mill Road, about two miles from Hope's Corner and still a ways to go to Snoqualmie Gap.

Shaw stopped on a narrow shoulder and looked down, to his left. Here the road was made up of switchbacks because of the dizzyingly steep grade. It descended to a valley in which a river glistened, blue and silver. On the other side, the road rose into the hills once more.

The young men were fifty feet below Shaw. They were trudging along like college kids on a weekend hike. Each had a backpack. Adam was holding a large refillable water bottle. Erick pointed to the steep uphill climb they'd have once they crossed the bridge. Adam said something and Erick nodded.

Strolling, not a care in the world.

Shaw carefully examined them; he couldn't see the profile of a pistol, or a protruding grip, in the pockets of either.

Erick dug into his backpack pocket and pulled out a plastic bag. Jerky, Shaw believed. He ate a piece and offered some to Adam, who declined with a shake of his head. The suspects came to the end of the straight portion of the switchback and followed the road, curving to the left. Shaw watched them emerge. They got halfway along this stretch of road and stopped where it swelled with a broad shoulder on a cliff. It was a substantial drop; boulders had been placed here to serve as guardrails. The two sat down on one of these, the size of a park bench. Erick ate more jerky. Adam made a phone call.

Shaw examined his Rand McNally map and discovered that they were in Hammond County. He placed a call to the sheriff's office. He was connected to the sheriff himself, a man named Welles, and explained about the crime in Pierce County and told him that he'd just found the two suspects. The sheriff hesitated a moment, taking in the information, then asked for Shaw's location.

"I'll be at the intersection of State Route Sixty-four and Old Mill Road."

"Okay, sir. Let me check this out and we'll be there soon."

Shaw turned the Kia around and drove back up Old Mill to the intersection, about a half mile away. He preferred to meet the law enforcers in a place separate from Erick and Adam's actual location. He didn't know the procedures—or style—of the deputies here and didn't want them blustering up, sirens wailing, acting all tough cop. That might spook the pair into shooting . . . or taking to the brush. If that happened it would be a true chore to track them, especially if they split up. And, equally worrying, this was dangerous territory: steep cliffs, hazardous slopes, torrential rapids. The river below was beautiful. Shaw knew it would be cold as January metal and guessed the speed of the current was twenty miles per hour.

Shaw parked where Old Mill and the state route met and soon three official vehicles and one private—a mud-stained SUV—arrived. Shaw and the men climbed out. Five of them. They varied from youthful twenties to middle age. Welles, the sheriff, was around fifty, rotund. Blond hair and—curiously, given the shade of the strands on his head—his eyes were brown as aged leather.

All wore gray uniforms, except the tallest, a lean and bony bearded man in green-and-black camo, his dark tan baseball cap sitting backward on his head. He radiated military and, at early forties, he might've recently retired. You serve twenty and you're out. A faded name tag sewn onto his jacket was crooked, cut from one uniform and stitched onto his hunting garb. DODD, J. The SUV was his. He appeared to be civilian, though Shaw noted a blue light affixed to the Pathfinder's dashboard. While the others gazed at Shaw and his sport coat and city shoes with curiosity, Dodd's gaze was expressionless.

Welles approached. A paw of a hand embraced Shaw's. "You BEA?"

"No." Shaw had never considered being a bond enforcement agent, whose days were usually spent tracking down bail-jumping druggies—men, usually, who were stupid enough to hide out at their parents' or girlfriend's bungalow.

He explained about the reward.

This raised an eyebrow or two.

He expected the next question to be "How much?" But that query wasn't forthcoming. Instead, one of the deputies asked, "You don't bring 'em in yourself? Why call us?" A solid, jowly man, Welles had a fitting voice, like distant thunder.

"I don't apprehend. I only find the whereabouts. The rest is up to the person or agency offering the reward, or local law enforcement."

The sheriff said, "My, that sounds formal."

"Say, Sheriff, we get any?" one of the younger deputies asked.

"Any what?"

"Of that reward?"

"Tell me, Bo: you didn't go and find anybody, did you?"

"Just asking."

"Now, now." To Shaw, Welles asked, "You armed, sir?"

"I am. I'll show you my ticket." He slowly extracted his wallet and displayed a Utah concealed carry permit, which was recognized in Washington State.

"Do me a favor and keep your piece tucked away, will you?"

"Sure. My job's pretty much done here."

Another deputy: "You tracked 'em all the way here from Gig Harbor?"

"I did."

Welles said, "I checked with the Pierce County public safety chief. He confirmed they're fugitives and there's a reward. He didn't know about you."

"I was in touch with a detective there, not the sheriff. Chad Johnson."

"He told me these boys shot up a man of God, burned a church."

"Partly true. There was a burning cross, and they defaced the place. Some graffiti. No fire damage to the building itself. A janitor and a lay preacher were wounded."

"They skinheads or Nazis or what?"

"They don't seem to be. The main suspect's Adam Harper, late twenties. I can't piece together Erick's role. He's only twenty."

"Whatever," Sheriff Welles muttered, waving aside one or two of the persistent mosquitos, "the warrants're for both of them."

"That's correct."

"Any trouble from 'em on the way here?"

"None that I saw or heard about."

"Why are they headed this way?"

"No idea. Maybe meeting some friends. And I heard there's a retreat near Snoqualmie Gap. Maybe they were headed there."

Welles considered this. "Yeah, there is that place. I don't know much about it. Different county, not our watch. Anybody?"

None of his officers was familiar.

Welles said, "If it's a church thing, they might be planning to shoot it up too."

A deputy said, "Or Thompsonville. A couple of churches there. Long walk, but they could hitch."

Welles looked pensive. "Thompsonville. Yeah. That'd be a target for sure." He clicked his tongue. "Men who disrespect Christ? That's baked into the bone. They have mischief in mind, I guarantee it. All right, we'll take over from here, Mr. Shaw. You said they're armed."

"Have to assume so. It's a .38 Police Special."

"Mule kicker," somebody said.

"Where can we find them?" Welles asked.

"Last I saw they were taking a break. They were headed down into a valley about two klicks from here."

"A valley?"

Shaw noted that the sheriff's eyes met Dodd's, whose head dipped a fraction of an inch.

Shaw said, "You have a map, I can point it out."

Welles muttered to a deputy nearby, the youngest, "Glove compartment, kid."

With a brisk nod the officer scurried to the sheriff's squad car and disappeared inside. He returned with a map, handing it to Welles, who unfurled the sheet on the nearest car hood, underneath which the engine ticked as it cooled.

A lover and collector of maps, Shaw studied this one carefully. The crisp, unstained paper explained that the sheriff and probably the rest of the deputies didn't get out here much. This rugged terrain was within the county they oversaw but much of the land was state park. Shaw supposed that the rangers were the main law enforcers. There was also a national forest around here, with boundaries that ran in and out of the county's turf.

Looking down at the map, he tapped a site. "They were there, having some water and food. I don't know how long they were going to rest, though even if they started hiking again right away after I left, they couldn't be more than a half mile north." Another tap. "That'd put them about here, at the farthest."

Welles turned toward his men. "Here's what we're gonna do. They're moving north. I want somebody to circle around to Abbott Ford, fast, get ahead of them and come back south. TJ and B., you do that."

"Sure, Sheriff."

"Me and Jimmy'll go north."

One deputy said enthusiastically, "So we catch 'em in a pincer movement."

Which wasn't exactly what the sheriff was describing.

"Exactly."

The sheriff turned to gaunt, unexpressive Dodd. "And you get yourself up Scatterback. On the ridge. Get a good position. To cover us."

"K." The lean, laconic Dodd asked Shaw, "They have long guns?"

"No."

Dodd gave a nod.

Welles folded the map. "'Preciate your help, Mr. Shaw. You've earned every penny of that reward." A faint laugh. "Though easy for me to say; I'm not the one writing the check." The smile faded. He looked over the deputies. "Gentlemen, I am serious now. We've gotta stop 'em. The chief in Tacoma told me victims at the church there were black, true, but they were still children of God. Now, let's get to it."

Shaw returned to the Kia. He heard a whisper of "Reward." And some chuckles. As he sat in the driver's seat he watched the sheriff and the uniformed deputies walk to their cars, which soon sped off, leaving a haze of mustard-colored dust behind them.

Dodd remained. The man loped to his personal SUV, lifted the tailgate and uncased a big-bore Winchester rifle, fitted with a Maven telescopic sight—an expensive one, probably equal to one of the deputy's paychecks. He opened a metal ammunition box and lifted out a package of bullets. Big ones, .308. Sniper rounds.

The wiry, unsmiling man began loading the magazine. His eyes, which had been dead until now, brightened considerably as he clicked each lengthy, lethal slug home.

7.

As Shaw sped back down Old Mill Road to the place he'd left Erick and Adam he thought:

Never underestimate the power, for good and bad, of religion.

This was not one of his father's rules; Shaw had come up with it himself over a decade of reward-seeking. (He had significantly supplemented the Never rulebook since Ashton Shaw's death, some years ago.)

He understood what God's protector, Sheriff J. Welles, had in mind. The sheriff's and one other car would block the road south, while the third would do the same from the north, boxing Adam and Erick in. Dodd, on high ground, would understand that his instruction to "cover us" really meant "shoot to kill."

Maybe Adam would lift his hand in surprise at the officers' presence.

And Dodd would drop him with one of the big rounds.

"I observed a threat to the officers on the ground and I acted accordingly."

And Erick?

He'd instinctively turn to the wounded Adam.

Another shot.

"I observed the second suspect reaching for the weapon of the deceased individual and I was concerned that he would use lethal force against the officers who were present."

And there would be no body cams or witnesses to give a different story.

Having seen the look that passed between Dodd and Welles and guessing what they had in mind, Shaw had tapped a spot on the map miles from the shoulder on Old Mill Road, where the two young men actually were.

What exactly he would do when he found Erick and Adam, he couldn't yet say. But he knew he had to keep them out of the reach of Welles and his Christian soldiers.

He now piloted the Kia back to the hill where he'd parked when he spotted the two for the first time. Shaw backed off the road into thick, stalky growths of pine and sedge and tangled brush. The vehicle was hardly an SUV but it did have four-wheel drive and if he kept it on packed earth he was confident it wouldn't get stuck.

Leaving his jacket in the car, he climbed out and rearranged brush to obscure the vehicle yet more, then he walked to the road's edge, looking down the steep, grassy slope to the shoulder where the boys sat, about sixty feet below. Now, he tucked his shirt in, exposing the Glock on his hip, facilitating a fast draw.

He studied Erick and Adam. They still were sitting on the roadside boulder, facing the road and the hill beside it, not the spectacular view behind them: the rocky valley and gushing river at the bottom of the ten-story cliff. When Adam turned, Shaw could see that, yes, he did have the pistol; sitting had pushed the grip slightly out of the pocket of the close-fitting jeans. This was good for Shaw. Adam's Smith & Wesson featured a hammer, which was notorious for catching when one drew it quickly.

The suspects were speaking to each other. Then conversation paused at the sound of a default ringtone. Adam pulled out the mobile to take the call. He looked around, orienting himself and noting a road that branched off Old Mill. Shaw's impression was that the boys were expecting someone driving from that direction. The Rand McNally was in the car but he called up the GPS map on his phone. The road was Highland Bypass: narrow but a good shortcut to Snoqualmie Gap.

This added a complication. Who was coming to meet the suspects? How many were there? If Shaw's undercover theory was right, might they be armed extremists?

How long until they arrived?

And when would Welles and his deputies assume the young men had slipped out of their trap—or figure that Shaw had lied for one reason or another? A half hour tops, he guessed.

No time to waste. He'd have to get to the young men, disarm Adam, and zip-tie their hands. Then, into the Kia and get the hell out of Hammond County.

I deal in information, not citizen's arrests . . .

Not this time.

Picking his footsteps carefully, Shaw worked his way down the hill to the road on whose wide shoulder the two sat. From behind a tree, he assessed the scene. To approach them straight on, either from across the road or from the asphalt itself, he'd have to cover an unprotected field of fire. He'd be some distance away when he'd call for them to surrender, which might encourage Adam to draw and shoot. He was probably a better shot than Adam but that wasn't certain, and in any event the last thing Shaw wanted was a firefight.

Odds of success with that option: thirty percent. Not good enough.

Stay under cover and just call for them to surrender?

No, they'd shoot or run, probably both. The cops would hear the gunfire and move in, guns ready. Dodd would move to high ground and target them with his heavy weapon.

That tactic had only a ten percent success rate.

Take them by surprise, from behind?

Yes, the best option.

Of course, that approach carried a complication of its own: "behind" was essentially a cliff face a hundred feet above the rocky valley floor.

When the boys were looking away, Shaw, crouching, hurried across the road and peered over the edge. The face was not a smooth sheet of vertical rock. It cantilevered downward at a forty-five- or fifty-degree angle to the rocky floor below. There were ledges and shelves and outcroppings along the way.

Shaw recalled a book he'd read as a boy about warring Native American tribes. Flinging enemies from cliffs was a popular way for tribal people in mountainous regions to dispatch their victims. Let gravity do the work. Saves arrows and effort. The human body can withstand an impact of about thirty-five to forty miles an hour if the surface you land on has some give. You achieve that speed in about ten to twelve yards of free fall. Farther than that, combined with a rock landing, you've pretty much had it.

Never tense up in a fall.

Ashton would remind the children of this rule before he had them jump from eight-foot-high ledges onto the ground. You would have far less damage from impact if you went rag-doll limp. Shaw had been on a reward assignment one time when a kidnapper tried to escape from him by leaping from one roof to another. He missed and fell thirty feet to the grass. The man was uninjured, except for a broken pinkie. The EMS tech confirmed that a likely reason for this was his completely relaxed state— thanks to half a bottle of vodka.

If Shaw lost footing, he would tumble the hundred-foot length of the cliff face. Possibly fatal but more likely, he foresaw, broken bones. The fact was he would prefer death to a cracked back or neck—and being forced to live out his life the opposite of itinerate: chairbound.

He would go over the side, execute a free solo descent for about ten feet, then climb sideways and ascend behind them. He'd move in fast, disarm Adam and have them zip-tie each other's wrists.

If he wasn't heard, wasn't spotted.

And if he didn't fall.

He had no chalk or climbing shoes. He knew how to climb barefoot but he needed to keep the Eccos on. If it came to a pursuit on the gravel-strewn road, he wanted the protection.

He estimated this approach to offer a seventy-five percent success rate. Importantly, of course, the twenty-five percent failure possibility incorporated more than simply not collaring the boys; it embraced a debilitating if not lethal tumble to the valley floor.

But no other choices.

So get to it.

Now.

8.

Shaw looked down, studying the face he would have to negotiate to come up behind Adam and Erick.

It was what climbers loved: craggy and cracked. He now did what all good climbers do first: planned his route. He lay on his belly and backed toward the edge, his feet finding outcroppings he'd noted before and memorized. Descending from the top of a cliff was always more difficult than ascending; you can't brush or blow off the dirt covering hand- and footholds. Without chalk on your hands, even a faint dusting of soil can be deadly. Shaw usually rappelled to the ground, rather than climbing.

He started down. Farther, farther, his feet searching for places to support his weight. His hands gripping rocks and branches to hold him in case his shoes slipped. Finally he was far enough over he could look down, which was a huge relief. Now, thanks to rocky protuberances, two- to three-inch cracks and a conveniently placed—and sturdy—branch, he descended the eight feet to the ledge.

Then he moved sideways slowly to the spot just below where he estimated the suspects to be. The ledge angled downward and the boulder on which they sat was at this point about twenty feet above him. He looked up and plotted his climb. He reached up and brushed soil from a handhold, then gripped and pulled himself up. He kept his hip against the rock, which brings the shoulder close too, which in turn meant that his body stayed vertical— the best way to climb. He was edging with his feet, and using cracks into which he'd insert his hands and spread his fingers and palms. Then he'd bend a knee, find a foothold and straighten his leg to move up a foot or so at a time.

Not too fast. Fast is noise. Fast is mistakes. Fast is the black muzzle of a gun awaiting you at the crest.

He came to a smooth portion of the face that was about five feet square. On a normal climb, he would "smear"—use the soles of his shoes for traction by keeping the heel down and pushing the rubber hard against the face. You need good handholds for this, and while there were adequate ones here, he didn't trust the street shoes for the maneuver. He executed a side pull to go around the smooth portion, then up a rough slab with plenty of handholds, then he did another side pull, in the other direction, to put him back on vertical course.

Now he was three feet below the crest. He rested for a moment and controlled his breathing, preparing himself for the contortion that was coming next: a mantle—the maneuver climbers use to top out at the summit. He gripped a crack with his left hand, brought his left foot then right up to a nub nearly even with his elbow. His right hand aiming for an outcropping near the top, he extended both legs from the crouching pose and rose to the edge, grabbing the rock he'd sought.

Shaw slowly lifted his head. He half-expected to find Adam aiming at him.

No, the suspects were ten feet away, still facing in the other direction.

Adam: "I don't know. Probably twenty minutes. They weren't sure."

"My parents're going to be worried."

"I keep telling you: this'll be worth it."

"I just wish I could get them a message."

"Not after that shit at the church."

Shaw's left hand found a secure oak sapling and he pulled himself to the surface, breathing hard . . . while trying to do so silently. This was not easy.

He crouched, tapped the Glock with his hand to remind himself exactly where it was holstered. He then moved toward them, glancing back and forth from Adam's hands to the ground in front of himself, aiming for the most quiet places to step.

Nine feet, eight, seven. Shaw paused as the boys looked up the road.

Were the neo-Nazis approaching?

Or Welles and his band?

Don't worry about it now.

Just like he'd planned the ascent, he planned the takedown.

And executed it.

Keeping his Glock in the holster, he came up behind Adam and in a fast, firm gesture gripped the stubby re-

volver, pushing downward first so that the hammer
wouldn't catch and pulling it free.

"The fuck!" Adam rose and turned. Before he could
even draw back to slug the intruder, Shaw's fist slammed
into his gut. The young man grunted and dropped to his
knees, cradling his belly.

Shaw pocketed the Smittie and drew his Glock, aiming toward, though not at, Erick.

"No, man, please . . . No!" His eyes were wide.
"Who—"

"The fuck," Adam repeated. "I'm going to puke."

"Then do it and get it over with. We don't have any
time. You're both in danger."

"You hit me."

Erick whispering, "Who are you? What's—"

From his back pocket, Shaw handed Erick two of the
zip ties he always carried with him. "On his wrists, hands
in front. Then do your own. Now."

Wide eyed, Erick took the off-white nylon strips. He
glanced at them, figuring how they worked.

Adam grunted, "You're a cop, you gotta identify
yourself. Otherwise an arrest isn't legal."

"That's not true, and I'm not a cop." He said to Erick,
"I'm here because of your parents."

"Mom, Dad?"

He pointed at the zip ties. "Now. I'm not going to tell
you again. There're men nearby who want you dead. I
can save you. Do it."

Erick eyed Adam, who rose slowly. He said nothing
but looked both sick and disgusted.

"You have to—"

"The wrists. Now!"

Erick zip-tied Adam and then held his own hands out to Shaw.

"No, do it yourself."

He did, and Shaw gave a tightening tug. Their hands secured in front of their bodies wasn't as secure but it was a safer way for them to climb to the Kia, which was fifty feet above them on the steep hill.

Adam said in a harsh, desperate voice, "Please, man. Let us go. You have to! This is all fucked up. You don't understand."

"We'll talk later. Now, move!" Shaw gestured them along the road. "We have to get up that hill."

The three of them broke into a jog, Shaw ready to grab or trip either of them if they tried an escape.

Erick whispered, "My parents?"

"They offered a reward to find you."

This seemed to bewilder him.

"I couldn't call them. The police would be tapping their phones." A nod toward Adam, who was apparently the source of this warning.

"I'm parked on top of that hill." Shaw gestured. "We have to get up there now."

"Who wants to hurt us?" Erick asked.

"Local deputies. I thought they'd arrest you and hold you until detectives got here from Tacoma. But I'm pretty sure they want to kill you instead."

"Why?"

"Later. On the drive." They were almost to the spot where they could start the climb to Shaw's car.

He said, "I saw you on your phone. You were calling somebody to meet you here. Who?"

"Nobody."

The young man was lying—a conclusion that was obvious both from his tone and from his glance at Highland Bypass, the road from which presumably the "nobody" would soon emerge to meet the boys.

Shaw glanced at Erick, who said only, "I . . . Nobody."

Didn't matter, Shaw supposed, as long as they were out of the area in the next few minutes.

At the shallowest portion of the hill, where Shaw had walked down from his car, he had them stop. He pointed. "Up there. Climb slowly. The grass can be slick."

Erick looked up and began to climb, his palms ahead of him gripping large clumps of grass and plant stalks to pull himself forward. He slipped and Shaw climbed up a few yards to help him to his feet.

Shaw glanced at Adam. "You. Now."

The young man was looking around him. Shaw wondered if he was going to sprint down the road, and he tensed and readied himself to pursue.

"Hey, dude!" Adam called out. Erick looked down at him. "Remember what I told you. Your brother and everything? It'll be all right. I promise." A gentle smile crossed his face. He was muttering some words. One was "Goodbye"—and then something else that Shaw couldn't hear.

He started sprinting away—but not up the road. He sped directly toward the cliff's edge.

"Adam! No!"

Erick cried, "Hey, man, what're you doing?"

Shaw ran after him.

Adam didn't hesitate. He reached the cliff at full speed and launched himself into the air.

Breathing hard from the run and the shock, Shaw stopped just shy of the edge and watched the young man spiral to his death.

9.

Sheriff Welles's car eased to a stop on the shoulder of Old Mill, near the boulder the suspects had been sitting on.

A hundred feet below, Adam's body was lying face-down, utterly broken, one leg twisted at a horrible angle. Blood pooled and glistened brightly in the sun, mocking the nearby river.

The sheriff climbed out of his sedan. The passenger door opened as well, as another man got out. It was Dodd, the sniper. His face was just as emotionless as before. Or was it? Did he register just a hint of disappointment that he hadn't had a chance to shoot any heretics?

Both men hitched their belts simultaneously, as if it were procedure to do so upon exiting an official vehicle in Hammond County. They walked toward Shaw, the sheriff's shoes scraping on the asphalt. Dodd wore rubber-soled hunting boots; his transit was silent.

When they stopped they too turned their gazes to the valley floor far below. The other deputies were there, near the bridge over the speedy river. Shaw would have thought they might cover Adam's corpse. But no. Then he realized: Why bother? No passersby to shock. A blanket would also interfere with the selfies. He felt a wave of disgust, watching them click photos.

What the hell had happened? Killing himself? Adam must've understood that he'd get a fair trial back in Pierce County. Also, he might have hoped for a chance to escape from Shaw, given that he was only in wrist restraints and Shaw's transport wasn't a paddy wagon but a Kia sedan.

Why just give up and leap so casually to the flinty ground below?

Shaw was furious with himself. He knew that Adam was unstable. He should have kept the man closer to him, though he'd hardly expected his lightning-fast sprint to the cliff's edge.

Welles said, "So. Guess they weren't where you sent us."

When would the man ask why Shaw had zip-tied the prisoners and had taken custody when he'd told them specifically he wasn't here to apprehend? He wondered if he himself would see the inside of the Hammond County lockup.

Dodd asked, "Where's the other one?"

"After Adam jumped I went back for Erick but he was gone." Shaw pointed to a trail that led into the woods. "Went down there."

"You zip-tie him too?" Welles asked.

"Yes."

The sheriff was looking over the shoulder and the cliff. "He jumped, did he?"

"That's right."

"Not an accident, you sure?"

"No. We weren't near the edge. He had to run for it. I have no idea why."

"Where's the weapon?"

"It wasn't on him when I found them," Shaw lied.

All three men gazed downward for a moment more, then Welles looked in the direction Shaw had pointed, the trail down which he'd said Erick had escaped. The sheriff asked, "You're *certain* he went that way."

Meaning: You lying to us again?

"Positive."

The sheriff seemed to believe him. "Okay." He pulled a walkie-talkie off his belt. "Jimmy?"

Clatter. *"Sheriff."*

"You and somebody, head over to Morgan Road. The second boy's probably gonna show up there, a half hour or so. He's on the logging trail. He's in zips."

"His feet?"

"Of course not his feet. What's he doing, hopping like the Easter Bunny?"

"Sure, Sheriff. Roger that."

Welles slipped the unit back onto his service belt. "We'll track him down. No hurry. Even if he gets scared and hides, don't suppose a punk like that, from Gig Harbor, knows the lay of the land here. He'll get hungry and break for the road, sooner or later. We'll get him."

Welles added in a low voice, "You sure pulled one over on us, Mr. Shaw."

Here it comes.

Welles gave a wry smile. "But don't you worry, sir. We'll back you up."

Dodd nodded and offered a semblance of smile. Shaw could tell it was an alien expression for him.

Welles stuck his hand out.

Mystified, Shaw gripped the lawman's palm.

"I'm proud of you, sir," Dodd said.

"I'm sorry?"

"Oh, I know, you have to play it that way." Welles gave a knowing grin. "I was thinking, at first, gotta say, I thought you were trying to send us in the wrong direction so you could snag those boys and get 'em to a do-gooding liberal lawyer."

"Fuck them," Dodd muttered.

Welles's voice was now dropping in decibels even further, as if spies, or reporters, lurked. "I mean, you're a sharp one. Calling us in the first place and reporting them boys here, and then sending us off." He snapped his finger. "You made it all seem on the up-and-up."

Dodd: "Was smart."

Welles frowned. "Course, I woulda liked to do the honors myself. But we all got the result we wanted, didn't we?" A nod toward the cliff's edge.

Shaw now realized his meaning. The sheriff and his deputies believed that Shaw had planned this out—killing the boy intentionally and making it look like a suicide: wreaking private vengeance upon the preacher shooter.

As disgusted as it made him feel, Shaw gave a smug smile. "Oh, I could hardly say that, now, could I?"

"Lips sealed."

Dodd the sniper said, "Sir, I must say, I do regret not being able to end that sinner's life. But, if I was the one to handle the task, he never would've felt an instant of pain."

A bullet travels at close to three thousand feet per second.

"But, thanks to you, that sad excuse for a human being had a most unpleasant time between you shoving and him hitting."

Shaw gave an amused frown. "Oh, you're thinking I shoved him. I'd never do that. He jumped."

Welles said, "And that's what our report'll show. You'll still get that reward of yours?"

"I will."

"God bless and well earned. A shame they *both* couldn'ta jumped. Like a pact, you know? You see that some."

Shaw said, "Keep in mind, it was Adam did the shooting. Not Erick."

"I'll do that." Welles shook his head, smiling. "Sharp one you, I was saying. You let that boy run off first 'fore you took care of Adam. Right? No witnesses. Naw, that boy's hide is safe. But I assure you he will have a most uncomfortable time in our hospitality suite. I promise you that. I mistook you, sir. At first. Dressed up like you were. We get people from not around here who don't see eye to eye with us. Look down on us some."

"A shame, that," Shaw said, fully in his role.

"Thinking you were one of those city sorts, even with that piece of yours." He nodded toward Shaw's waistband, where his Glock resided. "But you're one of us."

How we hear what we want to hear and see what we want to see.

"Where do you pray?" the sheriff asked.

"First Baptist," Shaw said. "The wife and I've been going there for years."

He picked that denomination because even if Welles was inclined to check, there'd be thousands of them throughout the country.

And all good churchgoing men need *the* wife.

Welles nodded to Dodd, then lifted a hand when the deputy didn't seem to understand. "Oh, right." He dug into his pocket and handed Shaw a napkin. Inside was the bloody zip tie that had been cut off Adam's wrists.

Welles said, "Thought it might go better that wasn't found. A zip-tied man *could* jump off a cliff but . . ." His sun-brown face creased more than it already was. "Just better not to raise any questions. The inquest'll be handled here. Which is good. The coroner's one of us. Poker buddy too. It'll go good. Don't you worry about nothing."

"Appreciate that."

Ironic that the sheriff's and medical examiner's "cover-up" report would present what actually happened.

He jumped, did he . . . ?

"Okay, we'll get on finding that other boy. He'll probably surrender. There are mighty bugs this time of year. And, course, snakes. Now, that is a most unpleasant way to go. Just ask J. P. Gibbons, my predecessor. Spent a bad last month. 'Cept, I guess you can't ask him anything now."

"Was he a man of God?" Shaw asked.

"Not enough, it seems. You take care now, Mr. Shaw."

10.

Shaw watched the sheriff's squad car amble down the road, rocking on the tortured asphalt.

He walked to the edge of the cliff once more and looked down. The sight remained difficult; Adam's body still lay, uncovered, where it had landed. The deputies lounged about, waiting for the coroner. Two played cards on the hood of a squad car.

Shaw climbed the steep hill and returned to the Kia. He'd just arrived when he heard the sound of an approaching vehicle from the Highland Bypass—the road on which Adam seemed to have been expecting visitors. He'd forgotten about them.

Armed neo-Nazis?

He'd have to call Welles. However unpleasant the man and his crew might be, Shaw wasn't going to let them be ambushed. From the shoulder here, gunmen would have a turkey shoot.

He checked the Smith & Wesson. In the five-round cylinder were four spent shells. One live slug remained.

He slipped the gun back into his pocket. In the Glock, there was one in the chamber and six in the single-stack magazine. Returning to the brush for cover, he pulled out his phone and prepared to call Welles.

A black van pulled into view and braked to a stop on the shoulder, near where Adam and Erick had been sitting. On the side was the mathematical infinity symbol, a logo of some sort. The door opened and two men and two women got out.

Not Nazis.

More like . . . Amish.

They were wearing identical uniforms—dark slacks or skirts and powder blue shirts and black slip-on shoes. Only one variation in costume: two of the men wore unmarked baseball caps, and one of this pair had orange sunglasses. Most of them seemed to wear necklaces. He expected crucifixes but, no, it was something else, which he couldn't see from this distance. Shaw supposed they were from the retreat near Snoqualmie Gap, the one that Adam and Erick were apparently headed for.

The driver stepped from the van too. He wasn't tall but was quite broad and built like a wrestler—though not the lean, zero-body-fat athletes Shaw had competed against in college. He was clearly in charge and looked around impatiently, then barked orders. The others fanned out.

A soft cry. One of the women was staring down the cliff. She'd seen Adam's body on the road below. She was compactly built, a brunette with dark curly hair. Her hips were broad, though she was otherwise slim. An alluring face. Not a model's; more like that of a thoughtful, art-house actress. Her eyes were light, though he couldn't tell the exact shade. Her complexion ruddy.

The driver, a man and the other woman joined her and gazed down at the corpse. Unlike the brunette, they glanced down without any reaction. Utterly nonchalant. The driver actually grimaced, irritated, as if the trip here had been a waste of time. He shooed the others back to the van. The brunette remained were she was, though, wiping tears. The driver strode up to her, taking her roughly by the arm. He was angry and he whispered something, his face dark. She bowed her head submissively, nodded. A reprimand. Why? For displaying emotion at the death of someone? Possibly a friend? She and Adam might have had a connection in the past.

The driver continued to whisper. More nodding. He glanced to the van and when he noted that the others weren't looking his way, he moved his hand from her arm to her neck, the backs of his fingers. Then around to her throat, where, it seemed, he touched the chain or necklace. The hand then started down her chest. She turned abruptly and walked to the van. He frowned and called after her. Shaw caught the words ". . . or demerits."

She paused, looking crestfallen, then continued into the vehicle.

Looking around once more the blunt man called out softly, so as not to draw the cops' attention. Shaw caught what might have been two names: maybe "Jeremy." Definitely "Frederick."

Not far away there came a rustle and a snap of footfalls, as the man in the orange sunglasses trooped down the hill. Apparently he'd stepped away to look for Adam and Erick before learning of Adam's death. Had he seen Shaw? Maybe. At the van he stopped and looked back. Shaw crouched. The man climbed inside. The engine started and the driver made a careful three-point turn and the curious assembly vanished back the way they had come.

Shaw climbed into the Kia and fired it up. He drove slowly back up Old Mill in the direction he'd come. He passed through Hope's Corner and then five miles farther until he was out of Hammond County.

There he pulled over onto the shoulder and climbed out. He walked to the rear of the car and used the remote to pop the trunk. He looked down at Erick Young, who was blinking against the bright blue sky.

Shaw said, "Let's get you out of there."

11.

He was driving fast, though only a few miles over the limit. He didn't need to be stopped by any associates of Sheriff Welles, even if he had the apparent blessing, one might say, of the man. He was glancing in the rearview mirror; nobody was pursuing so far.

His mind returned to the brunette who, unlike her companions, had reacted with such shock and dismay to Adam's death.

Who was she and what about the group she was with? Was it the retreat he'd heard about?

Hippies . . .

Erick, in the passenger seat of the Kia, whispered, "Why would he kill himself?" The young man was staring out the window. His hands were now zip-tied behind him. Shaw was still armed and didn't want to risk a wave of desperation within the boy driving him to lunge for the weapon. Or to leap from a car in motion.

Saving Erick Young from the deputies had been a

gamble, though he could hardly leave him to be found and arrested by Welles.

"Come with me," Shaw had called to Erick, after Adam had jumped. "Fast." He'd helped the shocked young man up the hill to his car and opened the trunk. "Get in and stay quiet. You stay with me and I'll get you back to Gig Harbor. Your parents. Find you a lawyer."

"Okay," the young man had replied, his voice a whisper.

With yet another county between them, Shaw began to relax. He checked the navigation system on the car. It would be an hour and a half back to Pierce County. Shaw had plenty of gas in the car and water for them, and they didn't need food. As for a restroom, it would be brush by the roadside. There was no unsuspicious explanation to a gas station clerk as to why your traveling companion was zip-tied when you carried no badge.

"They were going to hurt us, you said? The police?"

"That's right. They weren't interested in just arresting you."

"Who are you?"

Shaw reminded him about the reward offered by his family, and the one offered by the county.

"Mom and Dad wanted you to catch me?"

"They wanted you brought in safe. Running with an armed fugitive was a stupid idea."

"It's just . . . I had to go with him."

"Why?"

"I just did." Looking at the pines zipping past. "He jumped," Erick repeated. "Why would he do that?"

"Maybe he couldn't take going to prison."

"But we didn't do it."

The most popular defense in the world. Shaw asked, "Which part?"

"All of it. I mean, yeah, Adam shot those guys. But it was self-defense."

This caught Shaw's attention. "Tell me about it."

"Okay, there's this cemetery where I go to. To visit . . . Well, my brother died last year."

"Mark. I heard. I'm sorry."

"I kind of go talk to him, you know." The boy seemed embarrassed. "Sounds stupid but I do."

An image of Shaw's own brother, Russell, floated into his thoughts. "No, not stupid at all."

"I was standing by his grave and I was crying, I guess." He glanced at Shaw and saw a sympathetic face. "Adam was there too. He walked over to me. He was . . . I knew he was kind of weird. But he seemed like he was worried about me. He asked if I was all right. I told him about Mark. And he didn't say anything at first, then he pointed to a grave. It was his mother. He said when she died he got all fucked up.

"He said there was this group. They had a place in the mountains. It had helped him a lot. He said maybe him and me, we could go there together. You spend, I don't know, three weeks or a month or something. Like therapy, I guess."

Shaw remembered Adam Harper's father telling about the young man's improvement after spending some time away from Tacoma. This would have been what he was referring to.

"I thought, can't hurt to try. Nothing else was working. He said it was expensive but I said I could get some money. School was out and I could take time off work, so I said, 'Sure.' Then, all that shit went down at the church." He was breathing hard. "Oh, man . . ."

"Go on, Erick."

"We were walking back to our cars and talking about when we could leave and go to this place when we saw the fire. We went to see what it was."

"The cross in front of the church?"

"Uh-huh. Like the KKK, you know? These two men came out and one of them—the janitor, William, I heard—he had a gun, and he starts shooting at us."

Shaw frowned. "He fired first?"

"Yeah. I'm on the ground and Adam's screaming, like, 'Stop, *we* didn't do it!' But he just keeps at it. Adam pulls out his gun, the one you got, and he shoots back and we run. I saw the news later and it didn't say anything about them shooting first."

If it had happened as Erick said, then the janitor had committed a felony; you can't shoot a nonthreatening trespasser. If you weren't preventing use of deadly force, it's a crime to even display the gun, let alone pull the trigger. After the janitor was hit, he probably gave his gun to the lay preacher and told him to hide it. An unregistered weapon, Shaw supposed.

Shaw asked, "What was this group he was talking about?"

"It's something Foundation. Up in the mountains somewhere, where we were headed. Some of them were coming to pick us up. I kind of lied when you asked. But Adam said there was nobody, so I didn't know what to say."

"You were saying it's like therapy?"

"I guess. It's expensive and you have to pay up front. That's why we didn't book outta town right away. I needed to get some cash together. At first I was thinking scam, you know. But Adam was all: No, it'll really work. It helped him get over his mother's death and there were some problems with his father too. Adam really wanted me to feel better. It was important to him." His voice grew muffled. He was crying. Shaw pulled over, put his gun and holster in the lockbox in the trunk and helped Erick out. He rezipped his wrists in front of him and offered the boy a wad of napkins from the food he'd bought earlier.

They resumed the drive.

Miles rolled past before Erick said, "I don't know whether it was crazy or not. I wanted to try it. I just miss him a lot, my brother. Every day. You ever feel that way, Mr. Shaw?"

He didn't answer. He slowed for a speed trap, easing through Evansville right on the nose at thirty miles per hour.

Soon the Kia was back up to sixty-five.

Picturing the brunette, her reaction. And the others' glazed, sheeplike gazes as they looked at the corpse far below. Shaw asked, "The people Adam called to get you? Did he mention who they were?"

"I don't remember if he did. I didn't pay much attention when he was on the phone." Erick's lips tightened. "I'm going to go to jail, aren't I?" He wiped his eyes again.

Colter Shaw had once thought of practicing law. When the family, for their own safety, abandoned the San Francisco Bay Area for eastern California, his father had carted along hundreds of books, many of them legal volumes. As a boy, Colter devoured them. He liked casebooks in particular, the compilations of trial decisions, many of which read like short stories.

From his knowledge of criminal law, Shaw knew Erick was in trouble, certainly, even if his story was true. At a minimum: flight, obstruction of justice, aiding and abetting, but he'd have a good chance of acquittal or a suspended sentence. His prints would not be on the Smith & Wesson. The police might find the janitor's gun and could locate the bullets in the ground near where Adam and Erick had been. Under interrogation, the janitor—if he lived—or the lay preacher might recant their account and tell the truth. There might be witnesses supporting Erick's story.

Shaw said, "You'll have your day in court."

"Lawyers're expensive, aren't they?"

"Good ones are."

This discouraged him. He asked, "How far to home?"

"An hour, little under."

"I'm going to sleep, I think."

"Are the restraints too tight?"

"No."

"I have to leave them on."

"Sure." The young man closed his eyes.

12.

Shaw pulled his phone out of his pocket and, hesitating only a moment, placed a call.

"Hello."

"Is this Stan Harper?"

"Yeah. Help you?"

"It's Colter Shaw. I talked to you earlier about your son."

"I remember."

Shaw had had these conversations several times in his career. There was no way to buffer them. "Mr. Harper . . . I'm sorry to have to tell you that Adam died an hour ago."

No response.

"He took his own life."

"What?" A gasp.

"I was going to bring him and Erick in to surrender to the police."

"But you said . . ." The voice faded.

"I know I did. I'm sorry."

I want to get Adam back safe . . .

"Did he shoot himself?" Perhaps the thought of a son using his father's own weapon to end his life was unbearable.

"No, he jumped off a cliff."

"Jumped?" The voice said he didn't understand.

"The police will be in touch so you can make arrangements." When the man said nothing more, Shaw continued, "Mr. Harper, I've been speaking to Erick Young. It's possible they were both innocent."

"They didn't burn the cross, didn't shoot anybody?"

"Adam fired, yes, but it might have been self-defense."

"So he would have gotten off?"

"Seems likely, or been convicted on minor charges."

"Then why did my son kill himself?"

"I don't know the answer to that."

Silence rolled up. Through the phone Shaw could hear a ship's horn, the caw of an angry seagull.

"Mr. Harper?"

Five more seconds of silence, then the man disconnected.

You ever feel that way, Mr. Shaw . . .

As he drove, Shaw silently responded to Erick Young: *More often than that, actually.*

Colter Shaw and Erick Young shared this in common: mourning for their brothers. Dead, in Erick's case. As for Shaw's, Russell was long gone, though dead or alive, Shaw had no clue.

Ashton and Mary Dove's three children assumed very different personalities. Their daughter, Dorion, the youngest, was the clever one. Colter was the restless one. Russell, the oldest, was the reclusive one.

Ashton Shaw died years ago—ironically, just like Adam Harper, tumbling from a cliff in a foreboding place known as Echo Ridge. That death, however, had decidedly not been a suicide. Not long after their father's funeral, Russell had disappeared. Colter Shaw made a living by finding people, and he was good at this profession. Yet Russell had managed to elude him since that day. Neither Mary Dove nor Dorion had had any contact with son or brother in all those years either.

A father's loss is tragic, especially under suspicious circumstances. At the end of his life, though, Ashton was growing increasingly demented and paranoid. Shaw—a teenager during those times—recalled moments when the man grew dark and dangerous. His death may have been premature but it seemed a natural conclusion to the complicated life he'd embraced in his later years.

Russell's disappearance had been much harder on Shaw. The absence was bad enough but aggravating that sorrow were certain questions. First, was he alive or dead? Mourning is a different process in each instance.

And then there was the so-very-difficult question of what drove Russell away from the family.

Shaw had resigned himself to the fact that his brother was gone forever and did what he could to cope with that pain. He'd noted how hopeful Erick had sounded when he talked about this group, the Foundation, and how their brand of therapy might dull the loss. Treatment like that, however, was not a remedy that had any appeal whatsoever to Colter Shaw.

Odd how a rewards job in the wilderness of Washington State triggered memories and emotions with roots from a very different life, in a very different era.

Ah, Russell . . . Where are you? What are you doing at this moment?

If you're doing anything at all.

Now, as Erick dozed beside him in the sedan, Shaw piloted the smooth-driving vehicle west.

Forty-five minutes to Tacoma.

His brother and father occupied his thoughts for a good portion of the drive.

Other images intruded occasionally. The group of curious men and women in their blue and black garb.

The brunette in particular, her run-in with the thickset bully.

And, of course, Adam Harper.

Whose death rested squarely at Colter Shaw's feet.

13.

He thought it best to take Erick Young directly to the Pierce County Public Safety Office to surrender.

He'd considered reuniting him with his family and then calling the authorities but the case was already fraught with changing narratives and actors. He did, however, call the boy's parents ahead of time and tell them that Erick was all right, and that they should meet him at the PSO.

Shaw's private eye, Mack, had tracked down a seasoned criminal attorney and sent Shaw the man's number. The two had a brief conversation about the nature of the crime and what Erick had told Shaw on the drive— his version of the incident at the church, which Shaw believed.

"Well, this's one for the books," the lawyer, Bob Tanner, had said in a courtroom-ready baritone.

Shaw had left it to the attorney to coordinate with the parents and the detective about the surrender to the authorities. Now, in the rental, parked a few blocks away from the Safety Office, Shaw felt his phone hum.

"Mr. Shaw?" said Tanner.

"Yes."

"I'm here in the back of the station, with Erick's parents. The detective you talked to, Johnson, he'll be handling the processing. I know him. He's a good man. No games, no showboating, no perp walks. The press is still in the dark."

"We'll be there in five," Shaw told him and disconnected. "Erick, you ready?"

The boy was looking at an old-fashioned diner. Acme Chili and Sandwich Company. "Mark and I went there, I guess, a couple of times. We had brown cows. You know what that is?"

"No."

"A root beer with ice cream. Like we were kids again. And fries. Yeah, I'm ready."

Shortly, they were pulling up behind the old redbrick building—an early twentieth-century police house if ever there was one. Erick's parents stood beside two older men, both large and unsmiling and in dark suits. The lawyer's garb was more distinguished, though the other's was accessorized by a shiny gold badge on his belt.

Shaw climbed out and helped Erick from the car, the detective lifting his eyebrow at the restraints. Shaw cut the zips off and soon the boy was in proper cuffs, hands behind his back. Then the detective looked toward Erick's mother and nodded, a prearranged signal for a permissible hug. She threw her arms around him. His father stepped forward and embraced the two of them.

"Sorry, Mom. I'm . . . sorry." The boy's eyes swelled with tears.

Crying as well, Emma Young stroked his cheek.

Detective Chad Johnson was a calm man in his forties. He said to the parents, "We'll get to processing. He'll be arraigned and there'll be a bail hearing. He'll be able to call you at some point soon."

Shaw went to the rear of his car and opened the trunk, where he'd put the paper bag holding the Smith & Wesson he'd taken from Adam. "Detective?"

"Yessir?"

"It's the weapon."

Johnson took the bag.

"You'll want my prints for comparison."

"We have them, Mr. Shaw."

When you get a concealed carry permit, your prints are scanned and sent to a national registry. Interesting that the detective had gone to the trouble already.

Shaw added, "It hasn't been discharged since I've been in possession."

"That's helpful to know. We'll want a statement from you about Adam Harper too."

"Anytime."

Johnson and Erick started away, along with the attorney. Erick stopped, turned back. "Mr. Shaw. Thank you. You, like, saved my life." Then, without waiting for a response, he was led by the detective through the station's back door.

Shaw returned to the parents. He said, "I don't know how it's going to fall out. His story's different from what we thought at first."

"Mr. Tanner told us. I checked him out. He's a good lawyer. Really good."

Mack's connections were always really good.

"Somebody else burned that cross." Emma's face was staunch. "I knew it. And that poor boy, Adam. He was innocent too. Self-defense. But he still killed himself. What on earth was that about?"

What indeed?

Picturing him diving from the ledge, the leap, the arc, the fall.

Picturing too the smile on his face just before.

A voice from the street in front of the PSO. "Where is he? Ah, I'll bet that's him there!"

The man turned out to be short, round and dressed in a dark, pinstripe suit. His age was around fifty. With him was a woman in a pink and yellow floral dress and a black cotton coat that covered only three-fourths of the frock. She was around the same age as her companion.

"Mr. Shaw. You're Mr. Shaw?" He walked past Erick's parents.

"I am."

The man and the woman were both smiling. Their eyes were intense.

"I'm Lucas Slarr, executive director of the Western Washington Ecumenical Council." He thrust a hand out and they gripped palms. "This is Kitty McGregor, WWEC president." She too shook, just as firmly as Slarr, though more enthusiastically. They nodded to the Youngs, clearly not caring who they were. Shaw was the hero in this feature film.

"Kitty, do the honors."

She withdrew an envelope from her sizable beige purse. "Mr. Shaw, we've received confirmation from Hammond County that you successfully apprehended Adam Harper."

"I found him, yes."

Slarr added, "And the Public Safety press office here said that Erick Young's been brought in."

McGregor said, "The terms of the reward offer had nothing to do with the fact that one of the suspects in that terrible crime died. That wasn't your fault."

No, he thought, it was entirely my fault.

"On behalf of all the churches in the western Washington area, I'm pleased to present you with this."

Shaw took and opened the envelope. Inside was a certificate on parchment paper, 5 by 7 inches, depicting a radiating cross and an image of Jesus in the center, looking earnest and kind and more than a little Aryan.

> To Mr. Colter Shaw, for courage in championing the cause of Jesus Christ Our Savior.

In addition to the parchment sheet of paper, there was a check in the amount of $50,000.

In the law of contract, a binding agreement can be made by an offer and an acceptance—with words only. Fred promises to loan Sam money, and Sam promises to repay. Bang, that's a contract, enforceable by both sides.

But a reward is a special kind of contract; it's unilateral, meaning that it does not become binding until the reward seeker completes the job. Shaw had had no obligation to pursue the young men but once he'd succeeded, a contract magically came into existence, and he was owed the money.

That the facts at trial would probably show that the Ecumenical Council had posted a reward for tracking down the wrong individuals did not negate Shaw's right to the money. They'd wanted Adam and Erick, and that's whom they got. Shaw had collected perhaps three hundred or so rewards over the years. He didn't think he'd ever earned one for a crime the suspect had *not* committed. Under other circumstances he might have returned it, or a portion, but not today.

Slarr: "Do you think in the last minutes of his life, Adam repented his sins?"

Shaw suspected not, largely because it appeared he hadn't sinned at all. "One can only hope."

"Amen," Kitty McGregor said. They shook Shaw's hand again and walked up the alley.

As he turned back to the Youngs, he heard a booming voice. "You son of a bitch!"

Colter Shaw had only a few seconds' warning before the palm slammed into his back, knocking him forward. Not quite to the ground but almost.

He turned to face a furious Dalton Crowe.

14.

"Oh my," Larry Young said.

He seemed to be considering confronting the man but Dalton Crowe outweighed Erick's father by fifty pounds. He was intimidation personified. The big, swarthy man shot him a warrior's glare and Larry stayed put.

Shaw regarded Crowe calmly. He knew that the man wasn't going to do more than try to rough him up a bit—especially given that they were within shouting distance of the Public Safety Office.

The Youngs now relaxed somewhat, noting that Shaw didn't seem troubled by the slap or bluster or glowering face.

"Dalton," Shaw said pleasantly.

"You led me on a wild goose chase."

A phrase coined in *Romeo and Juliet*, by the witty and doomed Mercutio. *Wild goose chase* . . . While there was no TV in the Shaw household on the Compound, the children read and read and read. And often acted out plays, Shaw's specialty being *Henry V.*

Crowe continued, "There was no yellow ▓▓▓▓▓ Volkswagen Beetle. That wasn't sporting. You owe me that money." A nod toward the check in Shaw's hand. "That's mine."

He reached for it. Shaw leaned forward and looked with utmost—and unnerving—calm right into Crowe's eyes. The man eased back.

Shaw could very well have waited until later: the privacy of a hotel or in his Winnebago or in the Youngs' own living room. But because Adam Harper had died under his watch, and because Erick Young was sitting scared as a mouse in a holding cell and because Shaw's shoulder still hurt from Dalton Crowe's love tap, he decided that now was the perfect moment. He pulled his fountain pen from his jacket pocket. He looked to the Youngs. He asked, "Your bank account, it's joint?"

"Our . . . ?"

"Your checking account, both your names on it?"

"Oh." Emma looked perplexed. "Well, yes. But—"

Crowe grumbled, "What's this?"

Shaw endorsed the check over to the Youngs and handed it to Larry. This is why he had no intention of returning the reward.

"The fuck?" Crowe snapped.

Shaw said to the couple, "Tanner won't come cheap."

Emma said, "I know. But we'll get a bank loan. We can't accept this."

Crowe: "They can't accept it."

"It's done," Shaw said.

Crowe bristled, then seemed to sense this was a battle he could not win. He pointed a finger at Shaw. "I will get you for this, my friend." He stalked off down the alley.

Larry waved the check. "If there's any left over—"

"Get Erick some help. Better therapy than he's had."

"We will," Emma whispered.

Shaw wanted to be gone. He said goodbye to the Youngs and walked back to the rental car. In his mind he heard the exchange between Stan Harper and himself.

Then why did my son kill himself?

I don't know the answer to that.

He now supplemented his response: *Not yet.*

15.

Through the windshield Shaw stared ahead at the red-brick walls of the Public Safety Office. He powered up his router and computer and went online, then composed an email to Mack.

He started the car and pulled out of the alley.

A half hour later he was back at the Tacoma RV park, after dropping the poor Kia at the rental company, offering a mea culpa that was heartfelt but not of much significance, given the damage waiver. The new paint job would be on Hertz. The clerk was unfazed.

Stepping inside the homey Winnebago, he was thinking of what lay ahead. As he'd sat in that comfortable lawn chair in Silicon Valley not long ago, he'd been considering which of the two missions to strike out on: going after the reward for Erick and Adam, or driving back to the Compound in the Sierra Nevadas and pursuing the mystery involving his late father.

A professor and amateur scientist—both the political and the natural variety—Ashton Shaw had made a discovery, one so significant and controversial that his life and those of his colleagues were put in danger. He warned his associates about the risks, and promptly moved his wife and three children to a large spread in the Sierra Nevada Mountains. There he learned survival skills and trained the children in the same edgy arts.

Ashton appeared to the world to have given up exploring his discovery, while all the time secretly continuing to pursue it. He would travel to places unknown, presumably looking into more details surrounding his finding—whatever it might be.

Shaw might have put his father's concerns and secretive efforts down to the man's growing breaks with reality had not several incidents occurred. First, there was Ashton's untimely death and the deaths of several colleagues. Second, just last week, Shaw's own close call with the people he believed were responsible for the deaths. They were a ruthless woman named Braxton and her hired killer, Droon, whom Shaw had been thinking of earlier. Shaw had evaded the pair and learned that his father's discovery was hidden somewhere on the family land, near where Ashton had died, Echo Ridge.

Shaw needed to find the secret. What on earth could it be? Something that exposed corruption in the government? Evidence of other crimes? An invention, maybe a drug that could topple a big pharma company? A military mystery?

He didn't try to guess.

Never speculate without substantial facts.

A good rule, one of his father's. Shaw followed it closely much of the time.

Yes, the secret was a burning question and, now that the reward job here was done, his plans to return to the quest would have put him on the road at first light.

Would have . . .

The quest would have to wait. Plans had changed.

Because of an image seared into Colter Shaw's mind: Adam Harper's eerily calm leap into eternity.

His phone dinged with an incoming email. He read the thread, which began with his query to Mack.

To: MMack333@dcserversystem.net
From: ColterShawReward@gmail.com
Re: Request for information

Please find any available information about a self-help-style organization called "Foundation" or "the Foundation." Logo is an infinity sign. There's a facility located near Snoqualmie Gap, Washington State.

To: ColterShawReward@gmail.com
From: MMack333@dcserversystem.net
Re: Request for information

Probably the Osiris Foundation, a California C corporation (for profit; unusual, since most of these organizations prefer 501(c)(3) status, nonprofit). Link to the home page for their website is below. Self-help operation of some kind. Very little information on Clearnet, nothing on the dark web. No Wikipedia listing. No social media accounts—Facebook, Twitter, YouTube.

That is unusual too. I found several online ads for the organization on websites offering help for bereavement, terminal or serious illness, depression and anxiety. Likely the Foundation wants to control its public image and employs scrubbers to eliminate references online.

Shaw scrolled down to the link and clicked on it. He was directed to the site's home page.

THE OSIRIS FOUNDATION

Where the Yesterday Is the Key to a Better Today and a Perfect Tomorrow™

Are you depressed, grieving because of losing a loved one, anxious, troubled, lonely, overwhelmed? Are you plagued by regret and the bad decisions you've made?

The Osiris Foundation may be just what you're looking for. We'll teach you to make fundamental changes in your approach to life so that you'll find the happiness, contentment and comfort you deserve. You'll never be troubled again.

Our program, called the Process™, is an intensive three-week course at our beautiful mountainside camp in Washington State. The Process™ brings together traditional spiritual teaching and modern medical and psychological methods. It's helped hundreds of people achieve a happy and contented life.

Read the testimonials of those who have successfully completed the Process™ by clicking here: Testimonials.

Contact us for an application by clicking here: Applications.

About our founder and director: Master Eli created the Osiris Foundation four years ago. Orphaned at a young age, he graduated from prestigious schools and pursued a successful career in business. But he was troubled by all the suffering and discontent he saw around him: both professional and personal. He sold his businesses and traveled the world, studying philosophy, theology, medicine and science. From those experiences, he developed the Process™. Master Eli oversees the training at the Osiris Foundation camp from May through September. In the fall and winter months, he travels to the Far East, meditating and studying with renowned spiritual leaders.

Mack's email continued:

Eli is probably David Ellis, 41. His internet presence is largely scrubbed too. No web or social media imprint I could find. But corporate and government filings link him to the limited liability corporations that own the Foundation. History of real estate development and running brokerage houses in Florida and California but no records of filings since the inception of the Osiris Foundation. No criminal record.

He read the promo piece again and recalled the uniformed crew in the van parked on the ridge where Adam had died. Smelled like a cult.

An impression borne out by another link Mack had included: to an article from *The San Francisco Daily Times.* The story was about cults preying on the vulnerable for money or sex, or simply because the leader was hungry for the power that comes from adulation and obedience.

The piece was long, and the author dissected a number of cults. There was a mention of the Osiris Foundation, though a very brief one.

> *Some organizations appear to be cults, as they have charismatic leaders, demand absolute loyalty, teach spiritual or emotional advancement and require significant financial commitment. However, they are so shrouded in secrecy that it is impossible to say exactly what they are: predatory cults taking advantage of the vulnerable and gullible, or legitimate self-actualization groups. Among these are WayForward and the Thompson Program, both of which are in California, and the Osiris Foundation, in Washington State.*

Shaw decided to call the article's author, Gary Yang, and see if he could tell him more about the Foundation.

But when he scrolled to the next page of Mack's email he read:

> Note that Yang was killed in a robbery outside his town house in the Mission District of San Francisco.

The death had occurred one week after the article had appeared.

Never accept coincidence at face value.

Shaw put a connection between the reporter's death and the article at forty percent, high enough that he felt it was worth looking into.

He went online and called up news stories about the crime. Yang's killer was Harvey Edwards. He'd shot Yang after demanding his wallet. Then he fled. He was subsequently shot to death by police. A day laborer at the time of the robbery, Edwards had a troubled past, including criminal convictions for assault, burglary and drug possession.

On the surface, the murder seemed to be a typical mugging gone bad. Shaw wasn't convinced. Why shoot someone who'd cooperated and handed over his cash? He did some more searching. He found next to nothing about Edwards, only several social media photos from years ago. The killer wasn't what Shaw had expected. Not a sullen or shifty visage, not a glare of suspicion and anger. He was good-looking, athletic, cheerful of expression. The images were of him on a beach somewhere, squinting into the sun, smiling. An attractive blonde sat beside him.

Shaw was about to log off when he froze.

In the photo Harvey Edwards was wearing a necklace. It was a thin black cord, and from it dangled a piece of jewelry: a purple infinity symbol.

The logo of the Osiris Foundation.

16.

om."

Shaw was sitting at the banquette of the Winnebago, speaking to his friend, the former FBI agent Tom Pepper.

The man asked, "We still climbing Two Wolves Face? Weather permitting."

"Weather? Don't you worry," Shaw replied. "I'll hold the umbrella for you"

"Haw."

The three-hundred-foot cliff, in the Sierra Nevada chain, had been on their free-climb to-do list for some time, and they'd planned it for August.

Shaw said, "Need the name of another detective."

"Tacoma?"

"No. This one's in San Francisco."

"Hmm. Lot of homicides out there. Lot of detectives. You know, Colt, you'd think, being so pretty, the Bay, the bridges, Ghirardelli Square, all those old hippies singing Jerry Garcia, nobody'd want to tap anybody."

Shaw explained about the journalist.

Pepper grunted. "Now, that pisses me off. Free press has to stay free. And alive."

"I need the lead detective."

"Give me five."

Shaw brewed a cup of coffee. He made the beverage as he always did: the old-fashioned way, boiled water poured through a filter. Capsules were not his favored technique; convenience always comes at a price. He added some milk. One sip, two. Pepper called back with a name and number. Shaw wrote it down, thanked his friend. A third sip, then he punched the number into his phone.

"Detective Etoile." A rich, vibrating baritone. Shaw imagined that that voice could shake confessions out of suspects within a dozen words.

"This is Colter Shaw."

"Oh, Mr. Shaw. Yes, your associate, Tom Pepper, just called."

Associate. Somewhat true. Shaw let it stand.

"This's about the Gary Yang murder?"

"That's right."

"Mr. Pepper said you're a private investigator."

This too was close enough. Shaw said nothing about his reward-seeking work.

"Detective, can I ask how the murder happened?"

"It was pretty straightforward. Plenty of witnesses. The victim was approached outside his townhome, robbed and shot. The suspect fled. Responding officers cornered him in a convenience store. He didn't surrender. There was a firefight. He was killed. No one else was injured."

"Edwards had no history of violent crime?"

"No history of *arrests* or *convictions* for violent crime," Etoile corrected.

"I've found out that Yang had written an article about cults. One of the groups he mentioned was the Osiris Foundation in Washington State. I think Harvey Edwards was involved with it."

Etoile was silent for a moment. "The implications being that (a) the robbery was a cover-up for a hit and (b) others might have been involved."

"Did you find anything in the investigation about the Foundation? Literature? Anything with an infinity sign on it?"

"Like the number eight on its side?"

"That's right. It's their logo."

"Nothing I recall. But we didn't toss . . . we didn't search Edwards's place much. No need. You heard the facts. Homicides don't get any more open-and-shut than that. You're probably interested to know if we looked at the new stories that Yang was working on, for possible motives."

Shaw said, "And the fact you raised the point tells me no, you didn't."

"Correct. Like I said, open-and-shut. What is this group, Osiris Foundation? Like the Manson Family?"

"Doesn't seem to be. Talks about self-help. That kind of thing."

"And what exactly is your interest, Mr. Shaw?"

"One of the followers of this outfit killed himself. Adam Harper. Tacoma Public Safety has the details. And

I saw another follower, a woman. I didn't like the way she was being treated."

"What's her name?"

"I don't know."

Silence in response to this too.

"I just want to make sure nobody else connected with this outfit gets hurt."

"You clearly have some law enforcement experience, sounds like, so you know once a case's closed, brass treat it like used chewing gum."

"I'm sure."

"I'll ask some questions. Give me your contact information."

Shaw did so and thanked him.

They disconnected the call.

More coffee. He looked up a third website that Mack had sent. There was a "Contact Me" email address at the bottom of the page. Shaw composed a brief note and sent it off. He wondered if he'd hear back.

Three minutes later, he did.

17.

"O siris Foundation? Not one I'm familiar with." The person looking back at Shaw, via Skype, was a handsome businesswoman sort, with trim hair, a dress blouse and a gold chain around her neck. Middle age. "And, frankly, I'm familiar with most of them."

Anne DeStefano was among the top cult experts in the country. A doctor in psychology, she advised law enforcement about such organizations, testified as an expert in trials, and deprogrammed— "de-brainwashed," as she put it—followers who'd escaped from cults and other oppressive organizations and individuals.

"What does this Foundation do?" DeStefano was in her Los Angeles office. Shaw could see a half-dozen certificates from various institutions and schools on the wall behind her.

"You have another computer?" Shaw asked.

"Yes, a desktop." She glanced to her left. "You sending me an email?"

"No. There's a website."

"I'll just Google it."

"They scrub their name from search engines and so-cial networking sites."

DeStefano lifted an eyebrow. "That's a technique you see with some of the more troublesome cults. What's the URL?"

Shaw recited it and DeStefano turned away, typing on the other keyboard.

Eyes to the left, she read the Foundation's homepage. "Hmm. Hard to say from this. Most true cults want you and your loyalty for life. A three-week session? More like a dude ranch or yoga camp. Have some fun in the country, listen to lectures, sit around a campfire and sing 'Kum-baya.' At worst, you've wasted some time and money. But then there's 'Osiris'—the Egyptian theme. That's a bit occult. And *Master* Eli. A lot of the more culty leaders give themselves titles like that. You know anything about him?"

"Not much. His data's scrubbed too. Was a business-man a few years ago, then gave it up to run the Founda-tion. I saw some of his followers. They were all wearing matching clothes."

"Then it's *not* your typical self-help outfit. But that doesn't mean it's a cult."

"What exactly *is* a cult?" Shaw asked.

DeStefano chuckled. "Somebody once said a cult is a religious or a social movement that you don't happen to like."

Shaw smiled.

"Well, what's a cult and what isn't?" she mused. "For me, it's like that Supreme Court justice who said he wasn't going to try to define porn but he knew it when he saw it. People with common interests and goals get together every day. You could say a sports team with a mesmerizing coach is a cult. You could say the Catholic Church is a cult. The Shriners, the Lions Club, the Masons. Me? I define a cult as a group that presents a potential physical or mental danger to the members or those outside.

"I borrow my test from a book by Margaret Singer and Janja Lalich, *Cults in Our Midst.* For them, a cult, one, controls the environment of the followers; two, has a system of rewards and punishments; three, creates a sense of powerlessness among the followers; four, uses fear for control; five, promotes dependency on the leader or cult; and, six, has a mission to reform followers' behaviors.

"There's another element too: nearly every cult is headed by a single controlling leader. He—it's usually a man—has a consuming ego, attacks his enemies, lashes out in anger, has an absolute belief that he's correct, won't listen to advice or criticism, is paranoid and craves worship and adulation."

DeStefano's eyes cut left to the second computer. "This Osiris Foundation?" She shrugged. "Can't really say without more information. It seems to fall into the category of a personal improvement and transformational cult—the least harmful. Usually the followers are people who're sick of their jobs or can't find satisfactory romance. The leaders'll use hypnosis, meditation, dream study and encounter sessions to change your outlook on life. The lack of a social media presence is troubling, though. Are they hiding anything?"

"You mentioned categories of cults. What would those be?"

DeStefano stretched back. "The majority are religious, drawing on traditional sects, hybrids or made up out of whole cloth. Then the political ones—we can thank 8chan and the internet for most of those. There are business-oriented cults that suck in members for get-rich-quick schemes. Then the really bad ones: racist, like the KKK or Aryan Nations. Militant separatists. White suprema-cists. Psychopathological cults—Charles Manson, for instance. Black magic. Satan worship, animal and human sacrifice. There are more of these than you'd think."

The deprogrammer leaned forward and eyed Shaw. "Can I ask why you're interested?"

He told DeStefano about the murder of the journalist Gary Yang and the likelihood that the killer had been a member of the Foundation.

This drew a frown. "Yang wrote an exposé on it?"

"Not really. It was just one reference to the Founda-tion. But the piece suggested that the group might be a cult. Yang was killed a week after the article ran—by someone who probably had been a member."

"So the killer either wanted to get revenge for what Yang wrote, or he was afraid that Yang might be plan-ning to write more, maybe revealing some secrets."

"I was thinking that."

DeStefano thought for a moment. "There's a phe-nomenon in all organizations called the isolated negative. Let's take a benevolent group whose purpose is to help people, Transcendental Meditation, for instance. Something like that. The leader or teacher's not on any power trips, truly wants to better people's lives. There's no abuse, the fees are reasonable, its programs are uplifting and positive and effective. No control. You meet every Tuesday night and go out for cocoa after.

"But the group exists to help people who, to a greater or lesser degree, are troubled—otherwise, they wouldn't be there in the first place. Right? That means the membership contains a higher percentage of individuals more likely to act out, sometimes violently. That goes against the entire purpose of the cult but they don't care. Those individuals are 'isolated negatives.' I've seen them in completely harmless organizations. They're fine . . . until they snap and assault and sometimes kill fellow followers or outsiders."

"There was another death involving a member. He killed himself."

Her brow furrowed at this news. "Do you know why?"

"History of depression. Lost his mother recently. He was about to be arrested, though I think the charges would have been dropped. He should've known that. Still, he took his own life."

"Some cults—especially the transformational ones like this Osiris outfit seems to be—can be tough on the unstable. Encounter sessions can amount to institutionalized bullying."

That word resonated. He explained about the treatment of the brunette by the driver of the van.

The woman was silent for a moment. "Mr. Shaw, I get

your concern. But, my two cents: there's something that happens when people fall under someone's spell. Jim Jones convinced over nine hundred followers in his Peoples Temple to murder hundreds of children and then kill themselves with poisoned fruit punch—not Kool-Aid, by the way, another brand. Up until 9/11, it was the largest civilian loss of American life in a single non-natural event.

"Charles Manson told four of his followers to slaughter complete strangers in the most gruesome way they could and they didn't blink twice before doing just what he asked. David Koresh, founder of the Branch Davidians, convinced his followers to battle it out with the FBI. Seventy-five people died. Warren Jeffs was the head of a fundamentalist Mormon cult. They believed in polygamy and marrying children as young as twelve. He had eighty-seven wives. He's now in jail for life.

"Cults brainwash. There's another name for brainwashing: menticide. Murder of the mind and the personality." A wave at the offstage computer to her left. "This Process that the Osiris Foundation talks about might've turned its members violent or even homicidal. Even if it's beneficial on its face, it could still be home to dangerous isolated negatives.

"I haven't even touched on the hundreds of anti-cult organizations out there. They attack cults, the cults attack back. And cults fight one another, competing cults. It's a running battle, often physically dangerous.

"So, Mr. Shaw, the situation is filled with risk." De-Stefano lifted her hands. "My advice is this: if you don't have a personal stake, just stay away. I mean it. Far away."

TWO:

THE BEST
IS YET
TO COME

18.

June 15

Colter Shaw was driving the pickup truck along a gravel drive, past a modest sign, purple type on a white background:

∞

THE OSIRIS FOUNDATION

Shaw continued toward the main entrance, through a narrow gap in a rock formation that was fifty feet high. It reminded him of a scene in a series he'd read and reread as a boy: *The Lord of the Rings*. The image that had come to mind was the forbidding entrance to some ancient kingdom. Shaw noted that a rockslide here—at the hand of nature or man—would effectively block the only way into and out of the Foundation by vehicle. He had pored over maps of the area; no other roads, not even old logging trails, serviced the Foundation's camp.

Once through the rock wall he saw ahead of him a

six-foot-high chain-link fence. He drove to the guard-house beside the motorized gate. The shack was about ten feet by ten feet. A chimney protruded, which told Shaw the gate was manned constantly, whatever the hour; eve-nings would be chilly in this mountain valley, even in the summer. He recalled that the Foundation camp was closed in the fall and winter. Harbinger Road would be impass-able for much of the colder months.

A solidly built man in black slacks and an odd gray shirt—a tunic that reached to mid-thigh—stepped up to Shaw's window. He wore the curly earbud of security people and TV talking heads, and a walkie-talkie rode on his hip. Out of instinct, Shaw scanned the uniform, if that's what it was, but could see no outline of a weapon because of the loose cut of the cloth. On the man's chest was a tag that read ASSISTANCE UNIT.

"Afternoon." The man offered an easy smile.

"Hi," Shaw said. "I have an appointment."

"Name?"

"Carter Skye."

A pad was consulted and its touchscreen touched, and Shaw's undercover identity was recognized.

"Good to see you, Mr. Skye. Now, you have any weap-ons, liquor or drugs with you, or in the vehicle?"

"No. Just clothes, shaving kit, the usual."

Another touch to the pad.

He'd been honest about his possessions, if not his name, and it was just as well. Across the parking lot were two men in similar uniforms, carefully searching an SUV. One held a mirror on a long handle, examining the undercarriage. This was how security forces searched for bombs, and drug agents for controlled substances.

The guard walked to the back of the Silverado and jotted something on an envelope, license plate number and make probably. If anyone checked—not that there'd be a reason to—the truck had been leased in a corporate name. Suitably anonymous and hardly suspicious. He handed the envelope to Shaw. "Park anywhere, put the keys inside and go through the main gate. There'll be somebody there to direct you. Be sure to keep your application form with you."

"Got it."

Another tap on the touchpad screen and the gate opened with a faint grind.

After parking, he climbed out and foraged in his backpack for the application, slipped it into the inside pocket of his tattered windbreaker. He also wore a wrinkled white T-shirt, faded blue jeans and scuffed Nocona boots, dark brown. Picking up the luggage, he turned toward the camp entrance. The chain link wasn't the only barricade protecting the Osiris Foundation. Shaw was looking at a tall, pressure-treated stockade fence. The gate in this barrier was made of dark metal bars and over it were words in wrought iron:

YESTERDAY, TODAY, TOMORROW

The gate's panels, each six feet wide, were open. He walked through them and a man who could have been the first guard's brother gave him a smile, took the key envelope and his luggage and directed him through a metal detector.

On the other side, Shaw turned back to him. The guard pointed to a path and said, "Follow that into the camp. Administration is the third building on the left."

He reached for his backpack and gym bag.

"We'll take care of that for you, sir."

"I'll hang on to 'em." A bit diffident. Carter Skye had some rough edges.

"We'll take care of them, sir." Another smile. Of sorts. No way in hell was Shaw getting the bags. He hesitated. Then exchanged them for a claim check.

The guard tapped his touchpad.

Shaw followed the footpath for about a hundred feet through woods fragrant with pine and eucalyptus and jasmine. When the foliage ended, Shaw stopped and examined what lay before him.

The Osiris Foundation's camp nestled in a valley of grass and woods, about thirty or so acres in total. High, rocky cliffs covered three sides and, to Shaw's left—which was east—stood a forest crisscrossed with paths. Beyond that there was a steep drop-off. Though you couldn't see it from here, on the other side of the cliff was the large lake he'd seen on his maps. Through the trees he could see in the distance a spectacular panorama of mountains.

Shaw counted scores of buildings, most of them single-story. One, though, dominating the southern end of the camp, was larger than the others. It had three floors and was crowned by an octagonal glass gazebo.

This structure was on the back boundary of the compound, south. Shaw could guess who lived there.

All of the buildings, which had peaked roofs to stave off snow-weight damage, were fashioned in log-cabin style but had not been constructed on-site from hand-hewn timber; the pieces were too even and well seated. These were the result of prefab kits. Shaw knew the process. The whole camp could have been set up in a month, and the bill would have been substantial.

He thought of the place as a *camp* because that was how it was described in the material he'd been sent with the application. Having just finished a job in Silicon Valley earlier in the month, he found the word curious; there, most corporate grounds were called *campuses*, as in college. *Camp* had a different connotation. There was summer camp, of course, but also boot camp. Detention camp too.

And then, chilled at the thought, Colter Shaw realized that the arching words in wrought iron over the entrance gate were reminiscent of yet another facility, infamous, from the past century.

The place was, at the same time, beautiful and unsettling. Anne DeStefano, the deprogrammer, had warned him to stay away. But he couldn't. He hadn't shared with her that he did indeed have a personal stake.

Adam Harper—who had risked everything to eradicate Erick Young's sorrow—had died because of him.

And he now knew the death couldn't be because of the crime at the church, which was a justifiable act of self-defense.

Everybody's got the blues. Just live with it.

Adam's father's ironic phrasing. But sometimes you just *couldn't* live with it, and Shaw should have known that.

His death was a question that had to be answered.

Another image lingered too: the brunette, alone among those at the site of Adam's death, who was so deeply saddened by his demise. And the hulking van driver's whipcrack words to her . . . a correction of some sort. Then her shrinking, in revulsion, from his unwanted touch. Was she too at risk, like Adam, because of something at the Foundation?

Were other followers endangered as well?

Shaw's career as a reward seeker, no, his *essence* was about survival. Saving lives. Finding the kidnap victim, the imperiled runaway, the serial killer stalking the sales clerk or college coed. And here he'd failed. Adam was dead. He needed to know why. And he needed to know if anyone else here was at risk.

Shaw looked at what he was doing as a reward job like any other, just without the reward. He'd come here to investigate. And, if anyone needed rescuing, he'd rescue them. If abuse needed to be exposed, then that's what he'd do.

"You're looking for Administration, Mr. Skye?" A voice from behind. It was another gray-tunicked man. Also smiling. Also with still, careful eyes. He scanned Shaw's rough-and-tumble outfit carefully, even though the metal detector would have reassured him that Shaw had nothing threatening on his person.

And how does he know my name?

From the tablet, of course, which he now slipped into a small shoulder bag.

He muttered, "I see it. Just looking over the place. Nice view."

"Yessir." The man remained impassive.

Shaw took the hint—the equivalent of a cop saying, "Move along"—and continued down the path. He passed a building marked LUGGAGE STORAGE, then a larger one, ASSISTANCE UNIT.

The next was Administration. It was larger than the others he'd just passed. He walked into the spotless, stark lobby and was greeted by a brunette at a reception desk. She was in her early thirties. Her outfit was the same as those worn by the women in the van who had driven down Highland Bypass to pick up Adam and Erick: pale blue top and black skirt.

And she wore a necklace—a purple infinity sign, just like Harvey Edwards, the killer of the San Francisco journalist, had. Almost certainly answering the question of whether he'd been affiliated with the Foundation. This would be the necklace that the followers in the van had worn—the ones he couldn't identify clearly in the distance.

Down a long corridor behind her, Shaw noted doors marked INTAKE, BUSINESS AFFAIRS, PLANNING, MEDIA. There were other offices too, though the corridor was dim and he couldn't read those signs from here.

Yet another tablet was consulted. "Mr. Skye, go right on in." Nodding to the INTAKE door.

This was an equally pristine room, about 40-by-40 feet. On the white-painted walls were unimaginative photos of sunsets or sunrises. On the back wall was stenciled in black ink:

THE OSIRIS FOUNDATION
WHERE THE YESTERDAY IS THE KEY TO A BETTER TODAY AND A PERFECT TOMORROW™

On the side wall was another:

THE BEST IS YET TO COME

At the receptionist's desk, near the door, sat another woman, presently on the phone. She was a blonde in her late twenties. She smiled and held up a *just wait a sec* finger. Three other desks lined the back wall, and two were also occupied by young women, looking over their own pads. The tablets were mounted in stands so they could be viewed like monitors. These women also wore the blue and black outfits, along with the infinity jewelry. The only difference among them was in nail polish and accessories. All three women in the room were attractive and had radiant smiles and calm eyes. They, like everyone else Shaw had seen so far, were white.

There were several other applicants present as well. At the far desk was a balding man in a business suit, answering the employee's questions. Speaking with the woman in the middle desk was a couple, apparently married, both middle aged and looking mildly embarrassed. They too were providing information, which was being recorded on this worker's tablet. There was a third desk, on the far right, unoccupied. A tablet sat on this desk too, facedown.

When the receptionist hung up, she said, "Welcome, Mr. Skye." She glanced at the pad and hesitated briefly. His sense was that she'd noted it had taken him a bit longer than normal to walk from the parking lot to Administration, as he'd stopped to assess the place.

"Your Intake specialist has been called away. It'll just be a moment or two. There's a bench outside. The weather's not too bad today. Why don't you wait there? I'll come get you when she's returned."

He didn't have much choice. There were no chairs in Intake or the Administration lobby.

"I guess. How old's this place? Buildings look new."

"Oh, I don't really know. It'll be ten minutes, tops." Another of those smiles.

Shaw stepped out of Intake. As he passed the initial receptionist and nodded, she too smiled back. He noted that she turned her tablet slightly away.

On the porch he was greeted by the damp scent of pine sap once more, which never failed to take him back to his youth. In this instance, the memory was of stripping off his belt, slapping it around a tree and using it as a climbing sling to escape from what was pursuing him. Bears climb too but unless they're really hungry they can be as lazy as anyone else. This one debated for a minute, seemingly confused about a prey that could both run and climb—and do both quickly. A new breed of predator maybe. Might be trouble. The creature had wandered off.

Musical tones rang out through the camp, the well-known opening fifteen-note theme of the "Ode to Joy" choral movement of Beethoven's Ninth Symphony. They were played on a synthesizer, in a low register. The last note stretched out until it faded to silence. Then a woman's soothing alto called out through speakers, "The time is four-thirty p.m."

Just as he was about to sit on the rustic bench on the porch, he stopped, hearing an urgent call from behind the Administration building. It was a man's and it was raw and troubled. He couldn't make out the words at first. Then louder:

"No! No! Stop!" Followed by a faint cry: someone was in pain.

19.

S haw glanced about and saw no one was nearby—
and no security cams, at least none visible, pointed
his way.

He walked along the side of the building, ducking
when he passed windows. He crouched behind a thick
stand of myrtle and camellia, which was in brilliant red
bloom.

In a grassy strip that separated the buildings on the
east side of the camp from the woods, a slim blond man
in tan slacks and a blazer and T-shirt stood between two
others, big men, both in the gray tunics and both wearing ASSISTANCE UNIT badges. They gripped the civilian by
his upper arms as a third man approached.

It was the driver of the van that had come to collect
Adam and Erick, the one who'd dressed down the brunette and tried to grope her.

Also tunicked, he was about five-six, with thinning
brown hair. Broad chested, swarthy of complexion. A
placid, unflappable look on his face. He wore two badges.

In addition to ASSISTANCE UNIT, there was SUPERVISOR. Unlike the other Assistance Unit men Shaw had seen, he wore an infinity amulet; his was silver.

Another person was present as well: a young woman similar in build, age and appearance to those Shaw had just seen inside the Intake room, wearing the same outfit as they. Maybe the third desk was hers, and this was to be his specialist.

There was one difference, though, between her and the women inside. She was not smiling and her eyes were cold, contracted dots.

The supervisor walked forward. He regarded his tablet and then nodded to the two guards. They released their grips. The man in street clothes slumped and rubbed his arms. "What's this all about? They just *assaulted* me!"

The supervisor looked over the captive. "Mr. Klein, I'm Journeyman Hugh. I'm in charge of the Assistance Unit." The voice was calm, a monotone. "Now, you've tried to gain access to the Foundation illegally. On the application, which you signed, it states clearly that entry under a false identity is prohibited and any attempts to do so will make you guilty of trespass."

False identity? Shaw tucked that away.

"There's some mistake. My name is Briggs. You saw my ID. You've got me mixed up with somebody. This is embarrassing. And frankly, I'm pissed off. You can't touch me like that. I know my rights."

Hugh nodded toward the woman. "Journeyman Adelle here was interviewing you when a facial recognition scan came back with your real identity."

Oh, hell. Hadn't figured on FR.

Adelle said, "It was doubly confirmed."

Hugh said, "You're Jonathan Klein, an investigative reporter for NewsCircle. We run sixty-point facial recognition. The algorithms are rarely wrong. To confirm, though, we called the publisher of your newspaper and were told you were away on assignment for a week, and when I called your house—"

Klein gasped. "My house? How did you—"

"—I got your wife to tell me you were away for a week in the mountains of Washington State on a story. She wasn't sure where."

"You fucker." Klein leaned forward, his palms balling up.

The two large men in tunics looked at their boss for direction. Hugh shook his head. "What we do here at the Foundation is provide intense self-help treatment for individuals who are coping with a number of problems. Their issues are extremely sensitive. I've read your rag. Like most media, you take things out of context and inflate and distort. You'd jeopardize the treatment of people in our care just to sell a few internet ads. We care too much to let that happen."

Klein snorted at this claim. "You're not getting away with this."

"Here's what comes next, Mr. Klein. You never arrived here. You'll drive back through Hope's Corner and keep going twenty miles, then turn around, head in this direction and drive off the road."

Klein blinked in surprise. "Hold on a minute."

"Make it look real. The crash, I mean. When you get

out of the hospital, and back to work, you'll move on to other stories and you'll make sure that no one from your news site tries to cover the Foundation again. I don't know how you'll do that but that's in *your* lap."

"Hospital?"

Hugh handed his tablet to Adelle—then lunged forward and, before the reporter could lift a protective arm an inch, Hugh delivered a palm-open blow to Klein's nose. The reporter barked a scream. Hugh then pointed to the man's mouth as he glanced at one of the Assistance Unit men, who stepped behind him and wrapped his hand over Klein's lips. Hugh moved closer, gripped the reporter's left wrist and twisted—Shaw, a champion wrestler in college, knew what was coming. He didn't hear the sound as the shoulder popped from the socket; dislocations are loud internally but not to the world. Klein's second scream was higher pitched, though muffled from the slab of a palm pressed against his face. He sagged.

Hugh gestured and his man lowered his hand, withdrew a tissue and wiped Klein's blood from his fingers. Hugh adjusted his stance, centered himself briefly and, lightning fast, drove a fist into the reporter's cheek. This time Shaw could hear the bone break.

Klein went out for a moment. The Assistance Unit men kept him upright.

Hugh leaned forward. "Can you hear me, Mr. Klein?"

"Wh . . . why?" He spit blood. He was crying. "No more. Please, please . . ."

"Can you hear me?"

The reporter started to lift his arm and wipe the blood

that streamed from his nose and mouth but screamed again; he'd used the arm with the dislocated shoulder.

Hugh grimaced, apparently irritated at the sound. "You understand what I said?"

"No stories."

"And no police. Other than to tell them about your accident. Because if you say anything more"—he gestured at Klein's shattered face—"there'll be consequences."

"No, no, please." Sniffing. "I'll do anything."

Hugh nodded to the others.

The men guided the staggering reporter into the forest behind the Administration building. Shaw could see that they turned left toward the parking lot. Apparently there was a path there that ran north and south, hidden by foliage. Via this route they could get to the lot and not be seen by anyone in the camp. Shaw backed away through the bushes and returned to the front of the Administration building.

This changed everything.

Hugh and the other three might be the isolated negatives the deprogrammer had told him about. After all, Hugh seemed to take the reporter's incursion like a personal violation, and his sadistic response was absurdly out of proportion. Everyone else in the camp could be helpful professionals. Still, the fact that anyone here would resort to violence like that, when they could easily have called the police to report a trespasser, told Shaw that this was no place for anyone vulnerable and suicidal.

He'd stumbled when it came to protecting Adam Harper. He needed to find out how much danger the other members here were in.

Of course, there was a problem.

Facial recognition . . .

The initial application to the Osiris Foundation required a picture; it made sense to match that against the applicant who arrived in person. But they were using recognition software that prowled through public—and likely private—databases to weed out undesirables and catch intruders, like reporters and spies from competitors.

If the FR system failed to identify him, he'd stick with the original plan: participate in the Process himself and see what this place was all about—find out if Adam had been bullied enough that he found suicide a better alternative to dealing with the police.

Of course, if the recognition came back labeling him as Colter Shaw, he supposed he could just sprint for the gate, make a camp in the surrounding woods and reassess from there.

Forget the luggage. He'd lose his computer but he'd lost computers before.

Never put inanimate objects before your hide.

So, leave the truck, sprint to the parking lot and vault the chain link, take to the forest. Follow Harbinger Road back to Snoqualmie Gap. Call Mack, have money wired. Then buy what he needed and trek back here, setting up a base nearby, and start his surveillance.

That is, if he wasn't beaten so badly that would not be an option.

The front door opened. It was the Intake receptionist. She seemed to take note that he was standing, not sitting on the bench. "Please come in, Mr. Skye."

He was glancing toward the path that would take him back to the parking lot. He saw three tunicked Assistance Unit guards standing in a circle in front of their building. How many were there in total? And how many subscribed to their boss's bare-knuckle approach to security?

"You all right, Mr. Skye?"

"Yeah. Fine."

"Please follow me."

She led him to the third desk. He sat in the chair previously occupied, he assumed, by the now-severely-injured investigative reporter. It took a few seconds to spot the pinhole cameras. The one recording him was in the letter *M* of TOMORROW on the wall behind the third desk.

The back door opened and in walked the blond woman he'd seen outside.

She sat down, placed her tablet in the stand and touched it to life. Her lips smiled. Her eyes remained concentrated dark circles, like gun muzzles.

"Mr. Skye, I'm Journeyman Adelle. Let's get started, shall we?"

20.

Handing over the application form he'd downloaded and filled out, Shaw noted a trilogy of blood spots on the side of Adelle's blue blouse, just below her right armpit. Hugh's blow to Klein's nose had been powerful, the spatter significant.

The Intake receptionist got a call. She said to the other women, "The gate'll be closed for a half hour."

Adelle said, "I know."

Shaw asked bluntly, "The gate? Everything all right?"

Her glance contained a hint of cautious curiosity. Why would he ask? "Everything is fine." She corralled a smile and continued to keyboard on her tablet.

Well, he figured, play your part for now. So far, his joints and cheekbones were intact and Adelle was smiling, even if that smile had no more substance than her makeup.

The woman spread his application in front of her and began transcribing information from it into the tablet.

There'd been an initial online process, in which Carter

Skye had sent the picture of himself and a brief memo about why he sought admission to the three-week-long Initial Training Period at the Osiris Foundation.

He based Skye's life on both the San Francisco journalist's killer, Harvey Edwards, and Adam Harper. Skye's history was one of depression and anger. He'd had run-ins with the authorities, drug offenses, occasional fights. He was "on the spectrum" somewhere: OCD, attention deficit, Asperger's, anger issues. His romantic relationships had all ended quickly and presently he doubted that he and the woman he was seeing would be together for much longer. (This portion of the play was inspired by someone else, Margot, and was largely nonfiction.) Skye's job—like Shaw's after college—was working in the forestry business, surveying. Both Shaw and his alter ego liked the solitary nature of the work. He was a drifter, working temporary assignments. He didn't do well with bosses.

The next day he'd received an email from the admissions director reporting that if he wanted to attend the session beginning the following Monday, he should complete the attached and bring it to the camp, along with a nonrefundable application fee of $1,000 and, if he chose to sign up for the course, the full fee would be $7,500.

Adelle posed a few questions, which he answered quickly—he'd memorized Skye's bio, backward and forward.

The camera in the letter *M* was minuscule but to Shaw it was like a sniper scope aimed his way. He kept his head down at first but then gave up on the suspicious posture.

It didn't matter. He was sure the lens was of the highest resolution and already had recorded a dozen perfect, rich-pixel images of him. They were being carried by clever software through databases. Perhaps a digital eyebrow was presently being raised regarding a curious lookalike, one Mr. Colter Shaw.

If he got busted, how would it play out? They'd presumably take him to the clearing and do the same thing as they'd done to the reporter, beat him and then get rid of him. Shaw would come up with a story. Yes, he'd used a fake name but he was embarrassed about seeking help. He'd be passive. They'd let their defenses down. He'd incapacitate Hugh first. The supervisor was talented in Eastern martial arts but Shaw's father had taught the children grappling, and Shaw's wrestling skills from college had never left him. He'd use surprise to get the man on his back fast and relieve him of any weapons—a gun, if he was lucky. Then, covering them, he'd sprint for the woods.

Shaw found himself tense.

Then he thought of one of his father's Never rules.

Never give away what you're about to do.

He relaxed and sat back.

He'd fight if it came to fighting, escape if it came to escaping, continue the performance if the facial recognition autobot gave him a pass. Now, stick to the role: troubled guy in his thirties unhappy with life and hoping for a quick fix.

Shaw noted Adelle's nails were the same shade as that of the three dots of dark blood. What would her reaction be if she noticed the stains tonight? Would she be troubled at the memory of the beating, or would she think it was all in a day's work?

She finished transcribing the information and slipped the paper application away in a drawer. "Now, if you decide to go forward with the ITP you'll discuss the financial arrangements with your interviewer but I'll take the application fee now. How will you pay?"

Cash—in that amount—is automatically suspicious. In the post-9/11 world, anonymous credit cards are hard to come by; banks and Homeland Security remain vigilant. But checks? Not so difficult. Shaw dug in his wallet and handed over one for $1,000 already made out to the Foundation. It was drawn on one of his LLC accounts but his PI, Mack, had ordered starter checks and had printed on them Skye's name and a post office box number.

Adelle put the check in the drawer too, ticked another box on the tablet. She started to turn toward him but at that moment her eyes flicked back to the screen and she froze.

Had an inquisitive bot returned the message: *He's really Shaw, Colter, 7832 Vista Trail Road, Okachee, FL, professional reward seeker?*

The woman came to life and tapped some more on the tablet then, tellingly, turned it over, as she'd done before stepping outside to watch the reporter's pounding. Apparently his interview was over; the applicants at the other two desks were still in the chairs where they'd been for forty minutes.

"If you'll excuse me for a moment."

Shaw shrugged.

Adelle vanished through the door to the back. She

started to speak to someone on the other side before the panel closed.

Shaw glanced at the front desk. That receptionist was no longer there. He noted that one of the Intake clerks—at the desk next to Adelle's—glanced at him quickly, then returned her attention to the couple who was still being tableted. They seemed less awkward than before. At the far end, the bald man still was morose.

And his strategy of claiming an innocent motive for the pseudonym? He decided to rethink it. If the facial recognition had in fact returned a positive, Hugh would probably have guessed a reward seeker was akin to a soldier of fortune or a mercenary. Maybe working for a competitor. The expert, Anne DeStefano, had told him about the rivalries among cults. Shaw might be considered more of a threat than the reporter.

Then the back door was opening and the person walking through it was not blood-spattered Adelle but Hugh himself. Closer now, Shaw could see that the man was not handsome, his face pocked, his nose broken and badly set long ago. But he wore a bulletproof confidence. His shoulders were broader than the earlier view had indicated and his thighs thicker, hands meatier.

"Hello." A pleasant voice, calm as could be.

Shaw nodded, standing.

Never fight from a position lower than your opponent's.

"I'm Journeyman Hugh."

"Carter Skye."

The palm that Shaw shook was thick with calluses. Many martial artists spend hour upon hour punching and kicking bowls of dry rice and gravel to sheathe-up the striking portions of appendages. "If you wouldn't mind following me, please, Mr. Skye." Nodding toward the back door, the one through which reporter Klein had presumably walked to meet his fate.

Shaw glanced toward the front door. Twenty feet away. No. Play it out.

He'd be oblivious till the end, then use surprise to try to take Hugh and the others. Get into the woods. They'd chase. That was fine. The wilderness was *his* world.

At the door Shaw paused, his eyes doing an "After you."

Never let your opponent get behind you.

Hugh wasn't going to make an issue of position. He had plenty of backup, not to mention lethal hands. The man walked through the door first, and Shaw followed.

They'd bypassed the main reception area of the Administration building and Shaw found himself walking down the dim corridor he'd seen earlier, extending to the back of the building.

At the end of the hallway, Hugh stopped beside an unmarked door and typed a number into the code pad, waited for one green light. Then he typed another. Shaw had never seen this type of lock before. Hugh pushed the door open, meaning Shaw should precede him, and this time he did. As he walked forward, he brushed Hugh's right hip, trying to feel for a firearm. None. And the man was right-handed; that was the side on which a trained shooter would holster his gun.

Never cross-draw a pistol.

Inside, Shaw looked around. This was a very different room from Intake. The walls were painted violet and hung with bas-reliefs, paintings and plaques. Egyptian was the motif. A deity—Osiris, probably—was depicted in many. Shaw tried to summon what he'd learned in high school about Egyptian civilization. He was unsuccessful.

At one end of the room was a large wooden desk, behind which sat a tall-backed chair made of shiny dark-brown leather, affixed to the frame with brass buttons. Across from the desk were two matching chairs, though smaller, and a round table between them. Against the right side wall was a couch, also matching, in front of which was a coffee table. The furniture legs ended in talons gripping metal balls.

Shaw grunted. "Weird place."

"Have a seat, please."

Shaw half-expected Hugh to use his real name.

He sat in the chair across from the desk.

Was this where the initial "interview" of the reporter had occurred? It was hardly the spot for interrogations; the place resembled the office of an Egypt-obsessed CEO running a small but successful medical or office supply company.

The door opened and Shaw found himself looking at a pudgy man wearing the male version of the regulation uniform: blue shirt and black slacks. The infinity amulet he wore was, like Hugh's, silver. His face was moon round and his thinning hair was combed back, accenting the shape of his head. He wore disks of glasses, also contributing to the spherical image. In his thick hand was yet another tablet, in which he was absorbed as he walked to the desk and then behind it.

The man eyed Shaw up and down. "We have a few things to talk about, sir."

21.

Shaw rose and separated his feet and rocked forward—a fighting stance.

"No, no, no. Sit, my friend."

After a moment Shaw did, though he kept his weight forward, poised to leap. The pudgy man looked around. "Some room, isn't this? Elegant. Small, though. Do you know where the word 'claustrophobia' comes from?"

Shaw eyed him, said nothing.

"'Claustro' is Latin for 'bolt,' as in bolting the door. And who doesn't know what 'phobia' is? All those *Jeopardy!* questions. Do you watch *Jeopardy!*?"

"No."

"Of course you don't. No time. Busy, busy man. So, I apologize for the"—he lifted his arms—"windowless chamber. Master Eli is security minded. Insists that we all be. You, me, all God's children. Our Assistance Unit boys sweep for listening devices. Did you know that you can buy high-tech bugs on *Amazon*, of all places? And get next-day delivery if you order within four minutes and seventeen seconds."

Shaw eyed him warily because that's what somebody of Skye's background, suspicious of authority and being in a closed space like this, would do.

The man seemed genuinely cheerful. However, Shaw thought: he's softening me up. Shaw kept part of his attention attuned to the door behind him. He wondered if Hugh might come up with a Taser or choke hold, which when properly applied can render one unconscious in six seconds. Death rarely takes longer than ninety.

He glanced around, as if viewing the room. The head of the Assistance Unit had left silently.

Curious.

The man's fat fingers typed on the tablet. Then he looked back to Shaw. "I'm Journeyman Samuel."

Shaw looked for improvised weapons. The chair, the tablet, a pen. All would work. None well.

And "Journeyman" again. What was that about? It was a title, obviously, not a name—but what did it indicate?

More reading on the tablet. "There are certain applicants that Master Eli likes to flag, Mr. Skye."

So they believed his fake identity.

Shaw offered silent thanks to Mack McKenzie.

Colter Shaw had had occasion to use false identities in the past; it's not illegal if you're presenting yourself as someone else to private citizens, and if you're paying your way. Mack was an expert at ginning up documentation to turn you into someone else: driver's license, nonactive credit cards, employer ID and insurance, and shopper loyalty and AAA cards.

The real problem isn't the documentation, though. It's the damn internet, the place where everybody first turns to see if you're really who you say you are.

Shaw hadn't anticipated facial recognition but he had guessed that his cover would be checked, and Mack had worked hard to shore it up. When he'd decided to go undercover, she'd placed a call to one of her specialists: a "massager," he billed himself. His bots would roam the Clearnet and dark web and eradicate or deeply bury references to his clients. Shaw's own reward-seeking website was temporarily suspended and many of the news stories about him were either scrubbed or weighted down with so much autobot baggage that his real name sank to the bottom of Google and Bing and Yahoo.

At the same time, the savvy software would flood the web and social media sites with a phony identity: in this case, real and Photoshopped pictures of Shaw—as Carter Skye—on vacations, in news stories (fake news was de rigueur nowadays, of course, and so very easy to produce and place), employment and education records, blogs, Twitter and Facebook posts, Instagram, Snapchat. Like pregnant spiders, these bots would populate that ethereal world with gigabytes of data about Carter Skye.

Like Adam Harper, Skye had a troubled background— petty crimes. And like Harvey Edwards, there'd been some violent offenses in his past, assaults, including one with a deadly weapon.

Samuel now looked him over, a grandfatherly gaze.

"People like you are perfect for the Foundation. You've got a bit of a past, if you know what I mean."

"You mean, the law?" Shaw frowned. "Half of it was trumped up. Cops give you shit. I don't put up with it."

"Understood, understood. See, some people come here on a lark. Not really committed. You're the kind of person that'll keep your head down, do the work. You want to get better. I can feel it. You'd be a credit to us. And"—he lowered his voice slightly—"Master Eli likes those in his flock who are, let's say . . . presentable. And you, Mr. Skye, are not hard to look at."

A bit of flirt laced Samuel's words. Shaw gave a cautious nod, simultaneously acknowledging the man's meaning and gently rejecting the overture.

The matter was settled, and no harm done.

"This means, I'm pleased to tell you, that if you want to sign on for the training, you'll be placed in our expedited program. We feel you'd be an asset to the Foundation."

"Well, I . . . Sure. Why not?" Still wary.

"Excellent. Now, let's get to the nitty-gritty, shall we?" In the manner of all good salesmen, Journeyman Samuel devoted himself entirely to the task. He set the tablet down and looked Shaw in the eye. "The Process is expensive but you get—"

"—what you pay for."

"Indeed, indeed, indeed! Master Eli is committed to making the Process available to everyone so he's created an ingenious fee structure. Yes, there's a large payment for the ITP, the Initial Training Period. The seventy-five hundred you saw on the application. Master Eli knows it's substantial but that guarantees commitment. You put that kind of money into *anything*, you'll follow through. Think about those health club memberships—you force yourself out of bed at five a.m. not because you want to work on your pecs but because you don't want to waste those two thousand buckolas. Am I right?"

He charged ahead without waiting for Shaw's response. "Now, if you're satisfied with the Process, the Foundation offers one-week refresher training sessions. Most people return at least two or three times a year."

"What's that cost?"

"Two thousand a week. But we offer a lifetime enrollment plan. You pay a nominal fee for expenses—a few hundred—every time you attend and you agree to leave the Foundation five percent of your estate when you die. For that, you can come back as often as you like. I'd recommend that. A number of people sign up."

Shaw gave a scoffing laugh. "Maybe it's something to think about. I don't have any money. It was all I could do to scrape together the seventy-five hundred. But a will? I don't even have one."

"We'll take care of that for you."

"Well, you really want five percent of a 2006 pickup and my CD collection, be my guest. But . . . well, is there a guarantee of some kind about this Process?"

This brought a smile to Samuel's round face. "As you'll see, a guarantee wouldn't really be practical. But once you go through the Process, you'll know that it works. Depression, loneliness, anxiety . . . They'll be things of the past."

"I don't want drugs. I got into trouble before."

"None of that. What you need to cure your ills is already within you. Master Eli simply gives you the skills to fix yourself. And it works. Oh my, it works. So, Mr. Skye, I'm pleased to say that you've met all the criteria for the training. I do hope you'll sign up. However, first . . ."

Samuel extracted from the top desk drawer a single sheet of paper. "You'll have to be comfortable with the rules. Master Eli has found that the Process works best when we're on a smooth ship. Or a tight ship. Whichever one, you get the idea." Samuel chuckled.

Then the smile vanished, as he grew serious. "And I must tell you: infractions *do* have consequences." He slid the piece of paper toward Shaw.

22.

Welcome, Companions!

The cornerstone of your training, the Process™, is a completely immersive experience. Master Eli has developed a series of simple rules to guarantee that you will get the most you possibly can from your time here. We ask that you follow them at all times.

The Rules

1. You cannot leave the camp for any reason during your three-week ITP (Initial Training Period). There is a medical team on-site, which can provide treatment for nearly all illnesses and accidents. If necessary, we have access to excellent local medical care.

2. You cannot make or receive any phone calls or emails during the ITP. You will leave your cell phone, computer and other electronic devices with the Assistance Unit.

We have arrangements to get messages to you, in the event of a true emergency at home.

3. You will wear your provided clothing and your amulet at all times.

Provided clothing? Required jewelry? Shaw was once more wondering what he'd gotten himself into.

4. You will not consume alcohol or use drugs, other than prescription medications.

5. In the Osiris Foundation, we are not "members" or "followers." Staff, trainers and trainees are to be referred to as "Companion." We use given names only and precede them with the status of the Companion you're addressing: Novice, Apprentice or Journeyman. Those in the Inner Circle should be referred to as "Journeymen." Using these titles is in keeping with the Foundation's philosophy of equality among genders, sexual orientation, races and nationalities.

6. You will not engage in relations with other Companions or staff.

7. You should spend your hours of Introspection meditating and reflecting in solitude, not groups.

8. You cannot leave your dormitory between the hours of 10 p.m. and 6 a.m. This is because of the risk presented by wild animals.

Shaw had an amusing image of a hungry wolf noting angrily that the time was 9:45 in the evening; he'd have to wait fifteen minutes for dinner.

He skipped to the end of the rules.

13. Once you have completed the training, you may tell others about the benefits of the Foundation but nothing about the Process™ itself or the specifics of your training. You will not post anything online regarding the Foundation, the staff or your experiences here.

14. You will do nothing to disparage the integrity of Master Eli, the staff, the Foundation or the Process™.

Weren't two of the Ten Commandments about not worshiping other gods and taking the name of the Lord in vain?

Tapping the sheet, Shaw asked, "'Companions'? What's that about?"

"Master Eli believes the term best captures the spirit of the Foundation. It connotes camaraderie and equality."

Didn't people refer to their dogs as companions? Shaw's sister, Dorion, had. He recalled another use of the word: he'd once rescued the teenage daughter of a prostitute, when the local police had little interest in finding the missing girl. In describing possible suspects, the hooker had referred to her clients as "companions."

Shaw scanned the sheet once more.

"We can't leave?" Frowning.

"Master Eli has found the Process works best when you're wholly focused."

"No phone?"

"We allow one phone call to let your loved ones know that you'll be incommunicado for three weeks. Beyond that, Master Eli likes to say that the Foundation will be your family for the time you're here. Besides, you're single, have no children." Samuel knew this without looking at his magic tablet. "Well, what do you think, sir? We'd be happy to have you on board."

A practiced salesman, Samuel said nothing more. He knew not to oversell. He removed his glasses and cleaned the lenses with a tissue. Replacing the specs, he cocked his head and gazed at Shaw.

As if debating, Shaw studied the desktop, noting in the troubled wood an image of a lopsided Mount Fuji. His brow was furrowed. It was a smart arrangement. Applicants had already paid a nonrefundable fee. Of course they'd sign up; who'd want to flush a thousand dollars down the drain for this ten-minute spiel?

"Okay. I guess. And I'll think about that, you know, will thing. For the future sessions."

Samuel beamed. "Plenty of time for that. And the fee? Credit card or check?"

Shaw withdrew a second check from his wallet, made it out and handed it to the man.

The tablet revolved toward Shaw, and Samuel indicated where he should sign with his finger.

He did so, hoping the device wasn't set up to capture fingerprints.

"Now, make that phone call. And let's get started!" Samuel slid a card toward Shaw. "This is an answering service. Twenty-four hours. Give this number to whoever you want. If there's an emergency, he or she can call and leave a message. Somebody from the Assistance Unit will contact you."

Shaw placed a call to one of Mack's burner phones, one she never picked up. The answering message was the default; it gave no name, just the number—which was helpful now, in case Hugh or someone was listening in. Shaw left a message for his "mother." He would be away for three weeks, getting some help he needed. He'd be out of touch for that time. He gave the Foundation's answering service number. He said he loved her.

Samuel held out a hand, took the iPhone and, after powering it off, placed it in an envelope, which he then sealed.

"Do you have any other devices? Wristwatch—smart or conventional? A tablet, computer? . . . They'll be coming up with iToothpicks one of these days," Samuel said with a wry laugh.

"Just my laptop. It's in my backpack. It's off."

"Good." Samuel then added, "Your luggage will remain in storage for the time you're here. You'll be provided everything you need."

That they were going to dress him rankled almost as much as the absence of communications gear.

Another envelope appeared, similar to the one his mobile had disappeared into. "You'll need to leave your wallet, credit cards and cash too." He tapped a red stripe seal on the envelope. "Everything will be safe in here."

Because no one's ever stolen a sealed envelope before.

"I can see you're troubled, suspicious. Some of our Companions, like yourself, the independent ones, have trouble with the conformity and giving up control. Master Eli has spent hours and hours determining what's best for all the Companions. He's decided that anything that reminds us of our lives outside the camp is a distraction. We can't have that. So, we'll put all this in your backpack or gym bag."

Shaw noted the reference to his specific pieces. And Samuel hadn't asked for a key; he'd known they were unlocked.

"In our four years here, we haven't had a single incident of theft. Now! Bet you're dying to know! Let me give you an overview of what's going on here. The ITP. You'll be working with a trainer. For the first week, that will be me."

Training. Speaking of dogs.

What was that part of the deprogrammer's definition? *A cult has a mission to reform followers' behaviors* . . .

"There are three levels in the Process. You start out a Novice." He handed Shaw an amulet, a thin blue metal infinity symbol, on the end of a black leather string. "Put this on and wear it at all times."

Shaw had never worn a necklace. No jewelry, in fact. He'd come close, once. That involved Margot. But in the end, his finger remained free of metal.

"Rule Three." Shaw recited this without looking at the sheet.

"Ha! You're a sharp one. Well, you start the Process as a Novice. The trainer decides when you'll move on to the next level. That's Apprentice. You'll get a red amulet. Usually takes five, six days. Sometimes shorter, sometimes longer. After that, you'll move up to the final level and become a Journeyman.

"Most of the expedited Companions like yourself consider advanced training after the ITP is over. You can move up to the next level, and become an IC—Inner Circle." He tapped his own silver infinity symbol.

For, of course, another $7,500. Maybe more.

Samuel rose, as did Shaw. "One last matter. We don't shake hands here. We don't embrace."

He moved his right hand, open, to his left shoulder. "It's our greeting and our farewell. So much easier and more respectful, isn't it? Do I kiss this woman, do I hug this man? Do I try a bone crusher handshake?" He now gave the gesture once more. Shaw reciprocated.

"Ah! Like you've been doing it all your life. Well, welcome to the Osiris Foundation, Novice Carter."

Shaw sighed, like a reformed criminal suspicious that *he* was being robbed. "This better work."

The back door opened and Adelle appeared, from where she'd apparently been waiting.

"Journeyman Adelle will show you to your dormitory."

Why weren't they Journey*women*?

"You can change, freshen up, relax. Dinner is served promptly from seven until eight. Attendance is mandatory."

As he followed her out, Shaw paused, turned. "One question?"

"Yes?" Samuel asked.

"Your website doesn't really say anything. What *exactly* does this Process do?"

With a dash of reverence in his voice, he said, "Nothing less than completely change your life . . . forever."

23.

Shaw and Adelle walked through the camp, over a gravel path. The place was now making him think of an army base, though one from the nineteenth century.

He noted a dozen people on the rustic grounds, carrying notebooks: a middle-aged couple, several men by themselves, all in their forties or fifties. They appeared to be businesspeople. He spotted a cluster of three women, all in their twenties, Shaw guessed, looking like cheerleaders returning from practice, especially in their matching blue and black uniforms; their skirts were short, above the knee. There were several men too, in the gray tunics of the Assistance Unit, all solidly built.

Shaw wondered about the light blue blouses and high-neck sweaters of a matching shade. Maybe because the color would be easily spotted in the forests and fields surrounding the camp. Not as obvious as orange but helpful for pursuers, in case that became necessary. This would have been an outrageous thought . . . if not for the vicious beating he'd just witnessed.

He noted several more men and women wearing the silver amulets, then more of the tunics, who wore no necklaces. How many of the Assistance Unit, he wondered, were like Hugh and his two thugs? Maybe most people here were like Samuel, intelligent, humorous and devoted to helping those who'd signed up to battle their daily woes. Maybe they were no different from, say, some workers at the internet companies he'd met on a recent job in Silicon Valley.

Shaw corrected himself; he'd thought: Hugh and his two thugs—and another person too.

He was walking beside her at the moment.

A golf cart passed. This was the only means of mechanized travel within the grounds. He spotted several of them, driven by those with the Assistance Unit, in their tunics, or by followers in the blue and black uniforms.

"How long have you been in the Foundation?" he asked Adelle.

"A few years."

Silence.

"So you're like full-time."

"I'm on staff."

"You like it, huh?"

"Master Eli is a genius in providing the best solutions to the problems we all face. I'm proud to be a part of it."

He was curious about her personal life. An employee, she'd be here all summer. Despite Rule Six, the full-timers must have romantic relationships or at least the occasional liaison. Some might even be married. And what of the brunette on the roadside where Adam killed himself? Was she close to anyone?

Never miss an opportunity to gather relevant facts. They're usually better tools and weapons than hammers and guns.

"So nobody leaves? Not even to get to town for a few hours?"

Her answer: "The rules."

Shaw studied the camp carefully, looking for entrances and exits, the number of Assistance Unit people.

And looking too for the man in the orange sunglasses, who had, possibly, seen Shaw beside the Kia near where Adam had died. Shaw now realized that he'd thought the man had two names: Jeremy Frederick. Now, he knew he'd misheard. It would've been *Journeyman* Frederick.

"Novice Carter?"

"Yeah?"

"You're admiring the camp?"

"It's something."

Had he been busted doing surveillance?

Possibly not. Her face exuded pride as she said, "Master Eli designed it himself. He studied architecture, you know."

"I didn't." He glanced again at the peaked roofs. "So you're not open in the winter."

"No. But even if we were in a warmer area, the Foundation would be closed from fall to spring. Master Eli needs that time to go to the Far East. He's always exploring and learning and refining the Process. He says it will never be complete. He's helped me so much. He's the smartest and most generous man in the world. I lost my baby two years ago."

This was an electric jolt, all the more shocking because she delivered the stunning words with a faint smile.

"█████ I'm like, I'm sorry."

"Oh, no, it's all right. Master Eli *made* it all right. Here's your dorm."

Shaw, unable to think of a word to say, proceeded with her to Building C. Like all the other living quarters, it was a long, nondescript structure with a covered porch in the front, accessed by two steps up. Like the others, the style was the faux log cabin he'd noted earlier. Four teak rockers, aged to gray, sat facing outward. Shaw followed Adelle through the unlocked front door and into a corridor, with four doors on each side. No decorations on the walls, as in the Administration hallway. Shaw's room was the last on the left. She opened the lock—a simple one, easily picked, but this was noted merely in passing. If any staffers wanted to get in, they'd get in. As for anyone else? What did Shaw have left to steal?

Adelle handed him the key. "You'll find your clothing inside. They assessed you for size, and they're always right. But if something doesn't fit, just let someone in Admin know and they'll get it sorted out."

They . . .

"There's a bag for those clothes inside." She gestured vaguely toward his torso. "You can leave all that outside the door."

"I can't hold on to them?" he asked, though he knew the answer.

"I'm afraid not. It's part of the Process. Master Eli says we should leave everything in the past behind. They'll be laundered and waiting for you when you leave."

"Sure."

The Beethoven notes sounded again and Shaw glanced toward the window. The woman's voice echoed from loudspeakers again. "The time is five-thirty p.m."

Adelle said, "They sound every quarter hour from six a.m. to ten. Master Eli feels that that's as much time-telling as we need. He says there's too much control by the corporations and the government. They dictate everything, even the time to the second."

Another, though different, *they* . . .

He said, "Those clocks sure can screw around with you."

Adelle didn't reply but, after a pause, she explained how to get to the dining hall and added, "Tomorrow's schedule will be inside on your desk." Then her eyes turned suddenly shrewd. "It's different here, different from what you're used to, Novice Carter. As much as you want help, because of Minuses in your life, you resist. It's natural. However, the sooner you let go, the sooner you'll embrace the Process and everything will be wonderful."

Her words had been a gentle but unmistakable leash jerk. Shaw realized that maybe he deserved it. Perhaps he'd allowed some tone of condescension to slip into his time reference. He simply could never step out of character again.

He gave a faint exhalation—about the only apology that street-hardened Skye was capable of. "Just, this whole thing is . . . Never done anything like it."

Her face softened. "You'll do fine. Master Eli has all of our interests at heart. That includes you now." She nodded to his amulet. She turned, paused and glanced back. "And read the rules. They do take them seriously."

Shaw closed the door after her and looked around his

room. He had never been in prison—well, not to serve a sentence, though he'd been detained a number of times—but this room was probably what a minimum-security cell would be like, the abode of check kiters and low-seven-figure inside traders.

There was an austere bed—a futon on a raised platform—a rickety desk and a chair. Several matching lamps, cheap ones. The bathroom was small and on the narrow shelf were the basics: soap, a sealed toothbrush, a packet of disposable razors, tubes of relevant lotions, soaps and creams. Thin towels. On a shelf sat a coffee maker, and a tray of generic brands of coffee and tea and packets of sugar and Coffee Mate. A microwave too. A basket of trail bars, cookies and nuts. A small fridge contained bottled water.

He washed his face and hands, dried off on the limp towels and looked over the room more carefully. Shaw used surveillance equipment in the reward business occasionally and knew where to plant cameras and what to look for. There'd be none here, he was sure. A webcam video of someone traipsing back naked from the shower? That could put somebody behind bars for a long time. As for microphones, those were possible, though his search revealed none. But of course they could be embedded in the walls, invisible and, if hardwired, undetectable by scanners, even if he'd had one.

He'd just assume everything he said here was being listened to.

Looking over his uniform, laid out on the desk. Even underwear. The articles were in the manufacturer's plastic wrap with size tags attached: new, not laundered. He had a ridiculous thought that he'd be allowed to keep them when he left—souvenirs of My Month in the Cult.

Shaw dressed. The outfit was comfortable and fit perfectly. *They* had even gotten the shoe size right. One aspect of the clothing was curious: there were no pockets. What was the point of that?

Shaw could see no practical reason. He assumed it was just one aspect of control the Foundation asserted over the members.

He slipped the clothing that he'd worn here into the linen bag and set it in the corridor.

On the desk sat four 8-by-10 spiral notebooks: on the cover of each was printed, *The Process™*. A half-dozen pens rested next to it. He opened the book, expecting a rambling treatise or a lesson plan for the next three weeks.

Nope. All blank pages. He'd be attending lectures, he guessed, or encouraged "to journal"—a word he simply did not accept as a verb.

Also on the desk were three sheets of paper. One was a copy of the rules. Another read:

Day One Schedule for Novice Carter

8 a.m.	Breakfast
9 a.m.	First Discourse by Master Eli
10 a.m.	Introspection
11 a.m.	Training Period Building 7
12 noon	Lunch
1 p.m.	Introspection
2 p.m.	Second Discourse by Master Eli
3 p.m.	Introspection

7 p.m.	Dinner
8 p.m.	Introspection
10 p.m.	Lights out and curfew

The last was a small sheet meant to orient newbies:

Remember, at the Osiris Foundation we are "Companions."
Novice (blue amulet)
Apprentice (red)
Journeyman (purple)
Inner Circle—"IC" (silver)
Those in the gray uniforms are members of the Assistance Unit—"AUs." They are here for your help and safety.
Always refer to Companions by their ranks and first (given) names only, never "Mr." "Mrs." "Ms." "Dr." etc.

Shaw memorized this and set it down, looking over his schedule for tomorrow once more. He recalled that the hours devoted to Introspection were to be spent alone, according to the rules. He wondered if this was to keep members separate during the times they were not herded together and under the watchful eye of Eli and the minders.

Control, of course.

In any event, this was good for him. He wanted the freedom to roam the camp for his investigation.

Which was exactly what came next on his agenda.

24.

In unfamiliar and potentially hostile territory:
   Never be without an escape route.
   Never be without access to a weapon.

These were among his father's most fundamental rules.

The unfamiliar part was a given. Hostile? Let's just make that assumption, thank you, Journeyman Hugh.

Shaw's first task was attending to the escape plan. He strolled through the grounds of the camp, as innocent as a freshman on campus, examining the place. The valley wasn't landscaped. Dotting the grassy grounds were clusters of trees and spheres of wild foliage. The bulk of the property was field, whose grass had been chopped short by a wide stand-on mower, sitting under an open tent near the Administration building. No flower beds or decorative plantings.

The late afternoon sky was cerulean and within it floated thick cotton clouds. The sun was well behind the cliffs to the west and the air was chill, redolent of pine, lake decay and swamp gas.

Expecting the Assistance Unit minders to be eyeing him closely, Shaw noted that they weren't—or at least didn't seem to be.

He scanned the grounds for security cameras again but saw none. This struck him as odd in this day and age. But then he considered: Why bother with expensive, hard-to-maintain equipment when your flock was fenced in, miles from other human beings? A flock, by the way, that believed—or would come to believe—that it was the gravest of sins to transgress against the deity known as Master Eli.

Rule 14 . . .

He reflected too that there was another reason that some organizations didn't use security cameras. They recorded evidence that the outfits didn't want committed to digital record. Hugh would prefer his summary punishment of intruders remain a secret.

Shaw considered how easy it would be to get his backpack and gym bag, wallet and phone. The luggage building was closed and dark now. The front and back doors didn't seem alarmed but he'd have to be careful if he chose to break in that way; he could be seen by anyone in front of or beside the Assistance Unit. There were windows in the luggage facility, side and back; those would be the logical points of entry.

Now, the truck keys?

He strolled back in the direction of the gate that read, YESTERDAY, TODAY, TOMORROW. He paused beside the

Assistance Unit. Inside the well-lit building, which resembled a functional police department, he could see a lockbox. Inside were pigeonholes containing the key envelopes. The box featured thick security doors and an impressive lock. He could probably bludgeon the thing open, given a crowbar or hammer. But three Assistance Unit thugs sat at desks. He guessed that the building would be occupied all day, all night.

Forget the pickup truck.

He strolled the perimeter, eyeing the buildings, taking note of every detail. There were a number of dormitories like his and other structures that seemed to be classrooms. Most were presently occupied, members—no, *Companions*, he reminded himself—were sitting in circles inside, jotting in notebooks like his.

One building sat to the south of the dining hall. It was larger than the dorms and its windows were painted over and barred. A sign on the front:

BUILDING 14
PRIVATE

Two gray tunicked men sat on the porch in front, unspeaking, eyeing everyone who passed. They glanced at Shaw without reaction. He kept his eyes forward and passed by without pausing. Was it a detention facility? A storeroom, containing sensitive data? Or something dangerous?

Weapons? Nearly every wilderness outpost had a rifle, in case of animal intrusion, but was there more? Shaw continued along the sidewalk until he was out of sight of the guards, then circled back. Like the others, Building 14 had a back door and the grass leading to it was tamped down from golf carts and foot traffic—presumably staff, making deliveries. He tested the knob. Locked and there was no give. It had a simple lock that could be picked but doing so would take time.

The windows were gridded by sturdy iron bars, fixed to the frames with screws whose heads had been filed down so screwdrivers were useless to remove them. The paint on the glass was thick; he could see nothing inside.

Building 14 would have to remain a mystery for the time being.

He headed for the south side of the camp, where the large residence building was situated. He noted that the majority of people he passed wore red amulets—Apprentices, the second level in the Process training. Some were Novice blue.

Of the two dozen people he'd observed, every one of them was white. Seemed to be out of keeping with Rule 5, but it wasn't surprising.

Occasionally one of the Companions would send a dewy-eyed smile his way and give that odd gesture—touching their left shoulder with right palm. Shaw made sure to return the salute in kind.

Continuing to the back of the residence, he surveyed a tall rock face soaring eighty feet into the air. The face was amply cracked and fronted with outcroppings; Shaw could easily free-climb it—the technique of using ropes to prevent falls, not to assist in the ascent. It was also conducive to free soloing—climbing without any ropes at all—if one were so inclined. Shaw was not. Free soloing was incompatible with his central philosophy of life: survival.

So, south was not an acceptable escape route.

Neither was west, which was another cliff: the soaring Lord of the Rings formation whose gap he'd driven through on the driveway from Harbinger Road to the Foundation's gatehouse.

North was the stockade fence and the parking lot, protected by the chain link. Climbing a wooden fence, even an eight-footer, isn't impossible. However, this one was easily ten. That would be too difficult to surmount without a ladder, of which he'd seen none. And he knew the gates would be manned, maybe all of the time. North was out.

The eastern edge of the camp was the forest leading to the high bluff, with the lake beyond. In the clearing atop the cliff to the east, benches sat every fifty feet or so, overlooking the splendid view of mountains. Two miles or so that way—east—lay a state route, Shaw knew from studying Google and his Rand McNally. Along the highway were gas stations every ten miles or so, which meant a fair amount of traffic. Hitchhiking was a possibility, or trekking to one of the service stations and calling Mack to arrange for a ride.

But how to walk out of camp in that direction? He walked along the cliff's edge; the face was too smooth to climb down. He stared at the sheer bone-yellow stone, and couldn't help but think of the two people who had died by falling from such a place: Adam Harper at Hope's Corner and, at Echo Ridge, Shaw's father, whose death had been engineered by those he thought of as the Enemy—

the woman named Braxton and Ebbitt Droon . . . and the others who worked with them. It represented too Shaw's missions. It rankled some that he'd had to put the search for his father's killers on hold. But there was no choice. Whatever had driven Adam to his death might imperil others. The quest to uncover the secret behind his father's death would have to wait.

Turning away and continuing north, toward the front of the camp, he came eventually to the eerie gate and the tall wooden fence and followed it east. Where it ended deep in the woods a six-foot-high chain-link barrier ran from the fence to a steep drop-off onto rocks far below.

Eli sure didn't want anybody leaving.

Or, Shaw reflected, entering without permission.

There was a padlocked gate in the chain link. Shaw debated. The lock was rusted, and the gate entwined with vines, the ground around it undisturbed. No one had been here for months. He found a rock and with a half-dozen blows broke off the hasp. The gate opened freely.

He could jog to the highway in twenty minutes.

So he had his escape route.

A weapon?

Beethoven echoed through the camp. Then: "The time is six forty-five p.m. Dinner will be served in fifteen minutes."

Shaw returned to his dormitory, sat on the porch and sketched out a map of the compound.

In case the notebook was examined, he added some notes about what Samuel had told him in the initial interview—to make it seem that he was taking the whole thing seriously. When he was done, Shaw scanned the map, noting the locations of his dorm, the central square and stage, the Assistance Unit, Building 14, the three-story residence. And of course, the escape path to the east.

Shaw was going to put his book back in his room but then remembered one of the rules.

Osiris Compound

1 - Driveway to Harbinger Road   9 - Building 14
2 - Parking lot   10 - Central square
3 - Wooden barricade   11 - Stage
4 - Luggage Building   12 - Eli's residence
5 - Assistance Unit   13 - Path
6 - Administration   14 - Bluff/benches
7 - Dorms/classrooms   15 - Lake
8 - Dining hall

Keep your notebook and a pen with you at all times...
He headed for the dining hall and queued, nodding to and chatting with other Companions. And keeping an eye out for Frederick, the man with orange sunglasses,

who had possibly seen him at the site of Adam's death. Trouble was, Shaw wasn't sure he'd recognize the Companion without the eyewear and hat.

He searched too for the brunette.

No sign of either.

Had she left the Foundation?

On the one hand, that would be a setback: her reaction at Adam's suicide suggested they had a connection. She might help him fill in the dots about his death. On the other, it would mean she was out of harm's way.

Another possibility. After her rejection of Hugh, had there been repercussions? Shaw recalled the man's face contorted with anger and then his snide smile and threat of demerits as she walked away from him, and his sadistic glow as he broke the reporter's bones. He was a man who obviously took pleasure in inflicting pain. Was she hurt? Or worse? Was Building 14 a morgue, and the brunette's body was stashed there, after Hugh's retribution got out of hand?

Anywhere else, anytime else, that idea would be absurd. Not here. Reality was suspended within the web of the Osiris Foundation.

The windowless, mysterious structure might very well be a house of the dead. Colter Shaw, though, suddenly learned that the woman was not a resident. Head down, she walked directly past Shaw and joined the end of the dining hall line. Without a word of greeting to anyone, she opened her densely filled notebook and began to write.

25.

The iconic fifteen notes composed by the nearly deaf German genius sounded, echoing through the cool, dank evening.

"The time is seven p.m. Dinner is being served. All Companions please report to the dining hall."

The doors opened and the crowd of about seventy shuffled into the brightly lit room that resembled any one of a thousand school cafeterias around the world. The smell was of grilled meat or fowl. The perfume of Lysol could be detected.

Just inside the doors was a large board: a seating chart. Since everyone—all three levels of Companions: Novice, Apprentice and Journeyman—stopped to look, Shaw guessed that Eli shuffled diners around. Was there a strategy to this? Maybe helping out newcomers who could benefit from the company of mentors.

Or keeping potential troublemakers separated.

Or was it merely another muscle flex on Master Eli's part?

The majority of Companions were men in their thirties,

forties and fifties, many with wives of about the same age. The next most common were young women, twenties and thirties. Shaw had expected more hippies—or hippies 2.0. At last, he noted a few Latinxs, Asian Americans and African Americans. A total of five.

Shaw spotted his place, Table 4, near the door, the opposite end of the room from the buffet line, which was on the far wall, near the kitchen. Shaw ignored his assignment and held back, watching where the brunette was going to sit.

She made her way to Table 7, several away from his. She sat, never looking up from her notebook. The pages were thick from the moisture of hands, humid air, ink. It seemed that she'd filled almost every page.

The tables were segregated by rank. Most of the diners wore the red amulets of the second level. There were three tables of Journeymen, and two of Novices. The Inner Circle Companions, sporting silver amulets, were not seated but stood against one wall, chatting among themselves.

When most people were seated, Shaw strolled up to Table 7 and sat, leaving one empty chair between him and the brunette. He nodded to the others: an older man, another who was tall and slim, and two women in their late twenties or early thirties. They regarded him with cautious politeness, as if he'd accidentally stepped into the wrong private dining room at a nice restaurant.

He turned to the brunette. "I'm Novice Carter."

She looked up, blinking in surprise. Her pale gray eyes dipped to his blue amulet and grew wide with concern. She seemed speechless.

"How's it going?" Shaw asked, giving the shoulder salute. He looked around. "What's on the menu? Doesn't smell too bad. Haven't had a hot meal for a couple days, unless you consider a Big Mac hot." He whispered, "Wouldn't mind a beer, but I guess the bartender's off duty. Permanently." He laughed at his own feeble joke.

"I'm . . . I'm sorry but this is an Apprentice table." She pointed to her red infinity sign. Her eyes held his momentarily, then fled to the oilcloth.

"Huh?"

She stammered a repetition. "An Apprentice table."

"Oh." He lowered his arm, feigning confusion.

"What do we have here, Apprentice Victoria?"

A familiar voice: Adelle's. She'd changed her blouse. No blood. "Novice Carter."

"Journeyman Adelle." He frowned. "Something wrong?"

Victoria said, "I'm sorry, he just—"

Adelle: "There are assigned seats, Novice Carter."

"There are?"

"The chart." She pointed.

"Oh. Hey. Wasn't paying much attention."

She chided, "It's one of the rules."

Read them carefully. They do take them seriously . . .

"And Apprentice Victoria, you *must* remember that if someone breaks a rule, you call an AU or an IC immediately."

Shaw recalled his cheat sheet: IC was Inner Circle. AU, Assistance Unit.

Adelle was continuing to speak to Victoria, her voice

dull-edged but firm. "If you don't call one of us right away . . ."

"That's a violation of the rules too. I know that!" Victoria's eyes were cast down. "I was caught off guard. I was journaling . . ."

"It's a minor infraction. I don't think I need to call Journeyman Hugh in for a decision."

"Oh, thank you, ma'am."

Hell. Shaw realized how his little tactic here had nearly gotten her disciplined by the very person he was trying to protect her from. He resolved to be more careful.

Victoria winced. "And I won't say 'ma'am.' Or 'sir.'"

Shaw recalled the rule.

"That *has* been a mistake of yours in the past. Not grievous but something to watch." Adelle's head cocked a small degree. "And *he* doesn't need to know about this either."

The reverential emphasis told Shaw that Adelle was probably referring to Eli.

"Oh, thank you, Journeyman Adelle."

Her breathless submissiveness galled Shaw, especially as Victoria seemed several years older than Adelle.

Victoria returned to her notebook. Her hands were tremoring.

Adelle accompanied Shaw to the seating chart. "There you are, Novice Carter. Table Four."

"I'll take a look at those rules again."

With a nod, she peeled off and headed to a Journeymen's table.

He found a place and sat. Pitchers of water and iced

tea were on the table, which was set with cheap metal utensils and paper napkins. Like all the others, this table was covered with a dark purple cloth. Shaw suddenly realized that the colors of the lower-level amulets, blue and red, combined to make purple, the shade of the Journeymen's infinity signs. Maybe purple represented something significant in ancient Egypt—he still didn't know how Osiris figured in the scheme. Or maybe the shade was part of Eli's personal mythology.

Shaw greeted the other Novices at his table. There was a couple in their sixties, Walter and Sally. The balding man from the Intake office earlier that day was Henry. He was fit, his grip firm—they shook hands before mutually recalling that it wasn't allowed.

Shaw whispered, "You ever done anything like this before?"

"Never. Little bizarre. You from here, Washington?"

"No. California. Travel around a lot. I'm a surveyor. Forestry."

"I live on the East Coast." Henry looked around the room and his morose expression from earlier that day returned. "Hope this works." He fell silent.

The others at Table 4 were Todd, a sullen man in his early thirties, crew cut, trim. He was inked, probably a sleeve, but Shaw couldn't see more than an inch's work at his wrist, disappearing under the uniform. Abby was a pretty brunette with a somber face and fidgety manner. She couldn't've been older than nineteen or twenty. A tanned, curly-haired man in his late twenties sat hunched forward over the place setting. His name was John.

At 7:10 the Inner Circle Companions, equal numbers men and women, stepped away from the wall and fanned out, each sitting at a different table. Apparently they were chaperones.

Or guards.

Spies was another option, Shaw supposed.

The Inner Circle Companion assigned to Table 4 approached, striding stiffly. The mid-thirties man sported hair that was perfectly trimmed and gelled into a businessman coif. He stood erect and looked them over. He said in an oily, practiced voice, "Greetings, Novices. I am Journeyman Quinn. And I'm proud to be your table host for this evening." His glasses were of the sort you don't see much: wire frames with half lenses.

He touched his left shoulder with his right palm. Ignoring the absurdity he felt, Shaw did the same. He summoned a shy smile—as if proud to be part of the family, even if a newcomer.

Quinn made a show of lifting the iced tea pitcher and the water, one in each hand, and leaning close to the diners. "Preference for a beverage?"

Shaw opted for tea. Quinn poured for everyone—the other ICs were doing the same—and then he sat.

A voice from the overhead speakers announced: "Let us give thanks." Most knew what was coming and spoke along: "For what we are about to receive, our thanks to you, Master Eli, and all that you *have* taught us, you *are* teaching us, and you *will* teach us. From the Yesterday, a better Today. From the Today, a perfect Tomorrow."

Shaw and Henry mouthed along as best they could.

He noted that Quinn was watching them make the effort. Then the voice from above called out, "The best is yet to come!"

Applause filled the room, though not what you'd hear at the end of a concert. Several of the Inner Circle had started a coordinated slow clapping of their cupped palms, carefully timed, one strike per second. This lasted for a very long half minute.

"Now, Journeymen may approach the buffet."

The senior Companions did so. Only when they had filled their plates and sat down was permission granted to the Apprentices. Finally the Novices.

Control . . .

The food was what Shaw had expected: steam table chicken, hamburgers, vegetarian lasagna, salads and side dishes. Parker House rolls, butter. He was hungry from the effort of the trip here and his quick-march surveillance of the camp, so he piled the plate high.

As he ate, Shaw would glance at Victoria. Her brunette hair was in double braids, disappearing down her back. The ends were bound in thin red ribbons, the bows carelessly tied. Her face oval in shape. Over her blue uniform blouse she wore a blue vest. No wedding ring or other jewelry. Shaw scanned the room; no one wore any, it seemed, none that he could see. Surely some of these people were married. Maybe they'd had to check their rings, like the cell phones. Getting rid of reminders of the outside world. He couldn't tell if Victoria was wearing makeup. Her face had the slightly ruddy shade he recalled from the other day. Maybe a tan.

Shaw looked away just as she lifted her head and

started to glance his way, as if she'd felt she was being observed. He struck up a conversation with his table-mates. He and Henry were the only Novices at this table to start today. Abby had been here for ten days. John, Sally, Walter and Todd had been studying the Process for a week. Shaw noted that Walter did the talking for the couple; Sally was retiring and uncertain. Abby was constantly in fidgety motion, Todd was suspicious, John was rueful.

When they had finished the main courses and were toying with substance-less devil's food cake for dessert, Quinn wiped his mouth and set down the napkin.

He looked over everyone with his cool lizard eyes. Finally, he said, "Now it's time to share."

26.

'm Walter and this is Sally."

Quinn tilted his head, a corrective tap.

"Ah, I meant to say, *Novice* Walter and *Novice* Sally. My apologies."

With thin white hair and slim build and only a faint swelling of belly, Walter had the mannerisms and serenity of a successful businessman transitioned to retirement. He now explained as much: "We're from Chicago. I owned a manufacturing company that made parts that went to Detroit and disappeared into cars. I wouldn't've made 'em if the government didn't say they had to be in your horseless carriages, so I did, and that put the kids through college, thank you very much."

The sharing, the Inner Circle Quinn had told them, was about letting the others know why you'd come to the Foundation, what you hoped to get out of the experience. This helped "facilitate the Process."

Walter continued, "Now, I do some consulting, which means, gettin' paid to shoot my mouth off. And Sally's such a good gardener that she's got green fingers in addition to thumbs."

Sally smiled at the mention of her name. Gray haired, a heart-shaped face, the woman was trim too, with wattles at the chin. Maybe a recent weight loss. Shaw wondered about cancer, but her skin had a healthy pallor.

Walter continued his narrative, to make sure she didn't have to chime in. "I'd say she's got green toes, but that's an unfortunate image, so we'll let it go. We've been married forty-two years and have three children and four grandchildren."

A frown crossed Sally's face as she looked down at her left hand, resting on her husband's. She was gazing at her naked ring finger, and her eyes darted about, panic filling her face. She'd be thinking the piece had gone missing. Walter didn't notice.

Shaw understood why they were here.

Walter confirmed this with: "We've had a few health issues that're making life a little tricky and we read about the Foundation when we were doing some research about getting ourselves a little better. We heard how people said the Process makes them happier. Who doesn't need more happy in their life? So here we are."

Sally whispered to her husband, lifting her left hand. He smiled and told her something in return. She grew calm again, comforted that her missing engagement and wedding rings were accounted for.

Alzheimer's . . .

Quinn said, "Thank you, Novice Walter. And, Novice Todd?"

"Yeah, that's me." The man ran his hand over his

short hair. His eyes brown, his complexion dark—Latinx, maybe, and definitely military, Shaw decided.

"I'm from San Diego. Encinitas. Did a couple of tours. Was all right, no big shit. But I lost a couple of buddies overseas. Kind of, everything kind of went to hell when I got back." He unbuttoned his cuff and exposed his skin. It wasn't a sleeve tat, it was a knife and the words EVER FORWARD. A gothic typeface. "Did some VA shit. Some private docs. Nothing helped." He shrugged. "Heard about this thing in a bereavement group. Thought I'd give it a shot."

"Very good, Novice Todd. But remember . . ."

"Yeah, yeah. Sorry. Not 'thing.' The Foundation."

"You'll learn."

"Medicine didn't work, doctors didn't work. I hope the Process will."

"Is it, Novice Todd?" Quinn asked, head back, eyes down, looking at him closely over his half-rimmed glasses. "Do you think it's working?"

"I think so, yes."

There was a hesitation in his voice. If Shaw noticed it, so did Quinn.

"Thank you for that. Now." Quinn turned to the slim, bald man beside Shaw. "Share."

"I'm Henry. *Novice* Henry." He was embarrassed. "This is my first day."

"Welcome, Novice Henry."

"I'm a researcher for a drug company in RTP—Research Triangle Park, outside of Raleigh, North Carolina." A deep breath. "I . . . uhm, I lost my wife eight months ago." His voice trembled. He brought it under control. Flustered for a moment, he gave a hollow laugh. "I work on oncological drugs. You know, chemotherapy drugs. Karen had cancer. A different kind from what I specialize in. But it's kind of ironic, I guess, so I thought I'd mention it." A look toward Quinn.

The IC encouraged, offering that smile that everyone on the staff here was so good at—partly embracing, partly distant.

Henry swallowed and said, "It's kind of hard to cope. Every day is hard. So. That's what I'm hoping to fix. I've tried bereavement groups, therapy, drugs. They're not working all that great. Maybe this'll be better. Tomorrow will be better. That's what they said."

"Very good, Novice Henry. Now you, Novice Abby."

"That's me. Uhm . . . This is my second week. You know, same old. You've heard it." She seemed edgy, upset. She played with her food. Hadn't eaten much.

"Our new Novices haven't," Quinn said evenly. "Please enlighten them with your tale, Novice Abby."

Eyes down, she was digging one fingernail into a cuticle. "Just, stuff, you know."

"Go ahead. Remember: don't shy from the Minuses. You can do it. Master Eli says you've made good progress."

Her eyes widened slightly, and she seemed moved that the leader of the Foundation had commented about her.

"Go on," Quinn nudged.

"Okay, like, I'm in college, studying communications." She didn't make eye contact with anyone. "So. The thing is, at home, it's kind of sucky. I stay away as much as I can. I got in with this crowd. I mean, they're okay. *Sort of* okay. But there was some Oxy action, you know. Other shit." She stopped abruptly.

Quinn pulled a smile, fast as a gunslinger. "It's all right. Say what you feel."

"They got me into all kinds of stuff. Like, finally I got clean. It's not so easy. And I'm pretty freaked that I'll lapse. You know, go back. I've got this friend and her mother came here and it was, like, it helped her. So I kind of sent my application in and I got accepted." She shrugged, then slouched back in her chair. "And it's pretty cool. Master Eli is, like, the best."

"Thank you, Novice Abby. And, Novice Carter?"

Shaw spun his fictional account of hard times, not being able to hold down work, his emotional problems. He channeled Adam Harper and Harvey Edwards, along with some of the tougher fugitives he'd pursued in his reward-seeking business. He skirted the criminal past—largely because he hadn't written a very detailed script about that portion of Skye's life.

Shaw stuck with the tale that Carter had a family history of depression. The drugs, the anger issues. He always started out hopeful with a girl, but then—he gave a thumbs-down—he'd hit the road and never see her again. "Trying to outrun the blues, I guess. Sometimes I do, sometimes I don't."

"Good," Quinn said. "Thank you for that."

John, the thirty-something, had no professional issues. He was a successful coder and software designer in Los Angeles. He liked his work. He was good at it. Then his voice dropped in volume. "So, a year ago I was on PCH—Pacific Coast Highway—with my buddy. My best friend. I was hotdogging in my Porsche." His voice caught. "We went off the road, hit a tree. He was killed. I didn't get a scratch . . . Not a ▆▆damn scratch. I'm trying to get over Dale. It's not so easy. My trainer says I can. Master Eli too. He says I'll be okay. Eventually. I believe them."

"You should," Quinn said. "He'll take care of you. You'll be all right."

As Quinn looked them over, Shaw wondered: Could a human being sit up any more upright?

"Very good, everyone," Quinn said. "You can be confident that the Process will bring you comfort. Would you like some more beverage, Novice Carter?"

He'd noted that Shaw's iced tea was half-empty.

"No. I'm good. Thank you, Journeyman Quinn."

Conversation at the table resumed—but only momentarily. A silence descended in the room, punctuated by Companions' whispering. Eyes had turned toward the front of the dining hall. Through the windows, Shaw detected movement along the path leading to the building. It was hard to make out anything specific in the dusk. Lamps on wooden poles lined the paths but the illumination was subdued and yellow. The lanterns added to the nineteenth-century feel.

A whisper: "Is that him? Is he coming in?"

"Sometimes he does at dinner."

"Let's hope."

"Here he comes!"

Two AUs opened the door, and in walked an entourage, led by a man in a white tunic. He strode slowly into the hall. Spontaneously, the slow, rhythmic clapping of earlier broke out.

Master Eli paused, smiled and offered the shoulder salute to his flock.

27.

Shaw knew from Mack's research the man was forty-one. He seemed younger. Though not tall, he was in solid, sportsman's shape, perfectly proportioned. When he walked he was perfectly upright.

His broad, handsome face was well tanned. The eyes were piercingly blue, similar to Shaw's though lighter, ethereal, and the upper lids dipped slightly, imparting what was sometimes described as bedroom eyes. The thick black hair was carefully trimmed and parted on the side. It was a politician's cut. He wore an infinity amulet; his was gold.

Shaw glanced at those who'd accompanied him. The two AUs who'd opened the door for him had watchful eyes and were, Shaw supposed, bodyguards. Also, there was a woman in her mid-forties with auburn hair. She too wore a white tunic, and her amulet was purple.

Entering last was a young, diminutive balding man, about Eli's height, in the standard blue Foundation uniform. He too wore a purple amulet and carried a thick notebook—leather bound, not like the ones the Companions had been issued. Eli paused and turned to him, whispering. The man drew a pen and jotted in the opened book. He had eager rabbit eyes.

As Shaw scanned the crowd, the differences in the reactions among those present as they looked the leader's way were intriguing. Most of the Novices were curious about the man to whom they were paying $7,500. Those with purple and red amulets gazed his way with adoring eyes and some seemed to puff up, in hopes of being seen by the man. Those with the silver necklaces, the Inner Circle, didn't look at him at all but studied the crowd, as if gauging their reactions.

Shaw took in the bodyguards. One was broad and dark, not particularly tall. The other was angular and well over six feet and had the stern, lined face and gray crew cut of a former drill instructor. It was impossible to imagine either of them smiling. Shaw named them Squat and Gray. Like the AUs, they wore gray tunics and no amulets.

Why protection? There'd been the metal detector, the safety of the checked luggage and car searches, facial recognition. How much danger could a self-help guru be in?

Eli circulated, smiling and pausing at tables, leaning down to speak with various Companions. Once, he gave a hearty laugh. Later he picked up a woman Apprentice's notebook and read a page, while she blushed.

He moved on. Shaw heard him say in response to a question, "I came up with that myself! No, really. It was my own idea." Then: "Nobody else could figure out how to do it. It wasn't easy, but I did."

As Eli looked their way, many of the Companions offered the shoulder salute. Sometimes Eli returned it,
though usually he just nodded—the way a military officer
chooses to respond to an enlisted man's salute or not.
Shaw's impression was that the dining hall was an off-duty
area and there was less formality here than during the
daytime.

The auburn-haired woman who accompanied Eli was
attractive, with high cheekbones and carefully tended
brows. She wore purple lipstick and foundation makeup.
Her posture was good and her walk studied. A former
model maybe.

Eli would whisper to her occasionally. She'd give a
smile or offer a reply.

A voice in Shaw's ear: Walter's. "That's Anja."

"His wife?"

"Don't know about that. Nobody gives away very
much here. But whoever she is, she supposedly helped
him found the place."

"And the bald kid?"

"Journeyman Steve. Personal secretary, keeper of the
details. I've never seen him without that notebook. Carries it around like a mother with her baby."

Shaw would have to be careful. He felt a tendency to
fall into his real identity around Walter; he liked the man.
He couldn't afford to trip up.

When Eli came to Victoria's table, she grew nervous
and animated. Her face radiated a very different self, one
of adoration. She could look his way only for a few seconds without breaking eye contact, and she seemed
breathless. Her face was flushed. While Shaw sensed she

was taciturn by nature, now she engaged Eli in a nonstop monologue, as if—should she fall silent—he'd escape.

Steve whispered to Eli, who silenced him with a wave of the hand and continued his conversation with Victoria. She wanted to show him something she'd written; she held her notebook out. He read the passage silently, then bent close and spoke to her. She beamed and saluted; he did the same. Victoria seemed deeply moved by this. Her adoring eyes followed him as he left.

I prefer another name for brainwashing: menticide . . .

Then Eli moved toward Shaw's table.

"Greetings, Novices Walter and Sally, Abby, John and Todd. And, Novices Henry and Carter—welcome on your first day here."

Impressive. He knew them all.

They all mumbled various forms of hello. Shaw gave the shoulder salute, which brought a smile to Eli's face.

"Novice Carter, in our expedited program."

"That's right, Master Eli. I was surprised. I didn't exactly excel in school. I'll do better here. I promise."

"When I created the Process, I decided we needed to make special arrangements for some of our Companions. I have every confidence in you."

This comment drew murmurs from the nearby tables. Eyes turned on Shaw. Some seemed impressed and pleased for him. But there was jealousy too.

Shaw himself was troubled that he'd drawn attention, the last thing he wanted. He noted Victoria looking his way.

Eli glanced at the picked-over dinner plates. "I hope you're finding the meals acceptable. Remember, the fulfillment that the Foundation promises is emotional and psychological, not gastronomical." Drawing gentle laughs. "Good luck with your training. I'll see you tomorrow. You're going to love what I've got in store for you."

The entourage moved on.

A young redheaded woman nearby called, "Thank you, Master Eli. For everything. I'm so . . ." Concluding words eluded her.

"It's Apprentice Andi. Am I right?"

"Yes . . ." The redhead was breathless. She mouthed, "Thank you."

"Thank *you* for being a part of the Foundation family."

Shaw whispered to Walter, "He's memorized everybody's name."

"Not exactly," the older man said. "Gets prompts from his shadow." A nod toward Steve.

Eli and his entourage left via a side door, and conversation within the dining hall resumed immediately. Many of the Companions seemed to be dissecting what Eli had said and to whom.

Shaw looked toward Victoria. Her head was down, as she jotted notes.

The lights dimmed, simultaneously with the loudspeaker tones outside, then the keeper of the clock's melodious voice: "The time is eight p.m. Dinner is concluded."

The Companions rose, bused their own dishes into gray bins and ambled out the doors. Shaw did the same.

The sun was down and a faint iridescent blue glow

filled the sky. Bright stars radiated, visible because of the muted lamplights. The air, steeped in pine and wood smoke, was bracing.

Shaw paused just outside the door, looking about, as if to orient himself, though he knew exactly where he was and in what direction his dormitory lay. He was looking for Victoria. His excuse to speak to her would be to apologize for getting her into trouble because of his breaking the rules.

After a few minutes, though, the hall was empty of Companions; only the cleaning crew remained. She hadn't passed him.

Then Shaw spotted her, walking up the steps to her dorm, across the central grounds from his. How had she gotten there? It had to be via the side door, the one that Eli and those with him had used, even though doing so meant a longer walk. It was almost as though she'd been intentionally avoiding Shaw.

28.

After breakfast the next day, Shaw strolled across the grounds as the brilliant rising sun poured over the landscape.

He'd planned on eating quickly and then approaching Victoria afterward. But he'd arrived late. He'd had to return to his dorm for his notebook; an AU had noticed him barehanded and reminded him of the rule that you kept your notebook with you at all times. "You might," the man said, "have an insight." As if speaking of finding a pot of gold.

By the time he was back in the hall, Victoria had left. Only ten minutes? Maybe she'd forgone the steam-table food—understandable—and had picked only juice, coffee or tea.

The tones of "Ode to Joy" filled the camp.

The angelic voice: "The time is nine a.m. All Novices please report to the Square for Master Eli's First Discourse."

A command, Shaw noted. The word *please* didn't mitigate.

A moment later: "All other Companions who wish to hear Master Eli may attend as well."

The Square was a 50-by-100-foot clearing in the portion of the camp near Eli's residence. At the south side was a broad stage, whose backdrop was a purple banner with the words in dark gold: YESTERDAY, TODAY, TOMORROW, the same as the wrought-iron gate topper. Above the middle word was a large infinity symbol, also gold.

The stage was about thirty feet across and bare except for three armchairs at the far right. Anja sat in one, Steve in another. The chair closer to center stage was higher. A throne.

Shaw looked for Victoria. He couldn't spot her in the crowd, which numbered maybe eighty or ninety people. Some of the Companions were chatting, some were silent and serious, some had smiles on their faces. In the center were the Novices, Apprentices and Journeymen. On the outskirts were the Inner Circle Companions, about two dozen of them. They were arrayed in fact in a circle.

The entire camp appeared to be here, even though attendance was mandatory only for Novices.

Synthesizer music suddenly filled the air: this time the entire "Ode to Joy" theme from Beethoven's Ninth, a more rousing and, yes, *joyous* composition could be found nowhere in the classical repertoire. The ICs began clapping in time to the music, and Shaw realized that the meter was that of the clapping from last night. Everyone, including Shaw, joined in.

For a minute or so the musical notes echoed through the valley, then they ended abruptly—though the clapping did not. The ICs kept it up, encouraging—requiring—the whole assembly to do the same. Finally Master Eli strode onto the stage, arms raised, radiating a smile. Anja and Steve were on their feet too and slapping their palms together like everyone else.

Not all of the ICs were participating, though. Some held tablets and from time to time made notes or took videos of Eli and the crowd.

Voices in the audience would yell, "Master Eli!" There were cheers and impassioned cries whose words Shaw couldn't make out because of the cacophony.

Eli would occasionally point to someone in the audience and smile or give the shoulder salute.

Then to everyone: "Greetings, my dear Companions!"

Some in the audience cried out in response. The Inner Circle began calling, "Greet-ings, greet-ings!" lifting their arms and clapping in that ¼-meter slap of palms. The ICs would make forays into the crowd to make sure the other Companions kept up the recitation. This rally-esque frenzy set Shaw on edge but he played along and kept a ridiculous smile plastered to his face as he recited the word over and over.

Eventually the clapping and chanting petered out.

"What a gorgeous group you are! Gorgeous!" Eli walked closer to the edge of the stage, which was about six feet high, unnecessarily lofty; though he wasn't tall, he could easily have been seen from the back of the square if the platform had been half as high.

"Welcome to my Discourse. First one. First time's always good, right? You're going to love it. I guarantee you that. All you Novices out there . . . you're going to love it." He looked to several Journeymen near the front of the stage. "Aren't they going to love it?"

The men and women seemed delighted to have been singled out. They nodded and beamed.

"Sure you are. See? I'm telling you."

Clapping. Shaw's hands were already stinging. He'd grow calluses if this kept up. His eyes met John's, and the man gave a faint smile and flapped his hands, as if they stung. Shaw nodded back.

Walter and Sally approached Shaw. He was surprised when Sally said, "Morning, Novice Carter." That she'd retained Shaw's name clearly pleased her husband.

"What'll this be?" Shaw asked, glancing toward the stage.

Walter said, "Introduction to the Foundation and the Process. Meet the master. It's for the newbies but, well, if you didn't guess, Eli likes big audiences. I heard they take note about who doesn't show up."

The infamous *They*.

"It's not a bad idea to sit through it again, though. The Process can be a little . . . ungraspable at first. If that's a word."

"Ought to be, if it isn't."

Eli walked slowly left to right, every eye following him, then he returned to center stage. He wasn't in the sun, yet his face and white tunic glowed. There were no obvious stage lights but looking back Shaw saw several large halogens half-hidden in trees. There was no sound or light booth; it appeared that the beams were operated by a computerized system that followed him automatically wherever he moved onstage.

Eli began speaking in a soothing baritone. "The Today that we live in is so brief. In the whole scheme of the Universe, it's fleeting. A blink. You know what I mean?" He snapped his fingers. "There. Uh-oh. Missed it. Here, then gone. That's why we can't waste a second, not one single second, on regret, unhappiness, sorrow, anxiety, depression, mourning. Not one damn second. All those bad things that plague us. Can't waste time."

Murmurs of agreement.

"Nobody's immune. They've plagued *me*, troubles have, I'll tell you that." He repeated slowly, "Bad things. Oh, the stories I could tell you about my past, my youth. Everything I've been through. Nobody's been through harder times than I have. I know you've checked me out some. I know you've Googled me, right? Of course you have!"

Which wouldn't have done much good, since your minions acid-washed your presence right off the web.

Eli pointed to the crowd. "You're smart, you're the smartest! You're gorgeous!"

"We love you, Master Eli!"

Applause and cheers. He calmed them with a smile and a palm-down gesture, the way you'd still a jumping dog.

"'Googled'! How's that for a word? In my day, we didn't say, 'I encyclopediaed somebody.' Or 'I libraried them.'"

The crowd laughed and Colter Shaw, who had grown up in a tech-free home, decided that at last he and Eli agreed on something.

"So. Fellow Companions, for those who don't know what Google is, I'm going to tell you a little bit about Master Eli. My parents passed when I was young and I endured a series of foster homes. It was a difficult time for me, terrible. Abuse, deprivation. Living on the streets. I was beaten, I was robbed."

The hushed pedal tones of sympathy rose from the grounds.

"Some of you may not believe it, looking at me now, but I was in bad shape. And—you're my friends so I'll share with you—I have no trouble sharing. So I'll share with you that there were some bad people who took advantage of me. Some very bad people. The worst. They forced me to try drinking, try drugs. Oh, I stopped that. I knew that wasn't good for me. I could do that, I could stop. It took strength but that's one thing I have. Oh, I've got strengths you wouldn't believe.

"I can tell strong people. I can tell by looking who's strong and who isn't. I can see you're strong too, aren't you? I can see it. So I stopped all that bad behavior. I woke up one morning and said, 'This isn't right.' And I kicked all the bad things out, the bad people. Nobody was going to get anything over on me ever again. I used my willpower and, bang, kicked all the bad stuff and bad people out.

"I turned my life around. I graduated from high school in three years, valedictorian. I was captain of all sorts of clubs and teams. Football. You like football? I see the men out there, I'm looking at some players, aren't I? I can spot you. And I'll bet you ladies like to go to a game too now and then, right? Sure you do. That was my sport, football. Quarterback. Track and field too. I have a hundred trophies.

"I got a business degree from one of the best colleges in the country, graduated at the top of my class. Summa cum laude. I started companies, a dozen of them. They all did great. I made a ton of money, hired a ton of employees. Successful! All my companies. They were perfect, they were gorgeous! I made money hand over fist!"

Shaw scanned the crowd. Mostly adoring faces. But some perplexed expressions too, among the Novices. Shaw finally spotted Victoria, in the back. Like everyone else, her notebook was tucked under her arm, freeing her hands for the clapping. Her face gazed at Eli with adoration.

"But all the time I was leading the team to championships, a dozen championships, two dozen, all the time I was running my companies, the loneliness and depression were always there.

"My life was loneliness, sadness. Missing my parents, missing my fellow foster brothers and sisters—I'd bond with them and then I'd be taken away from them. You know what that's like, don't you? Losing someone? Sure you do. You know how that stays with you, like a headache that just won't quit. Like that splinter in your finger you just can't get out.

"And it wasn't just me in pain. It was everywhere: people being discontented. In business, in their marriages. I didn't know what to do about it. I tried that therapy stuff. You ever try that?"

Bobbing heads.

"Doesn't work so great, does it?"

Mutterings of agreement.

"Like everybody else, I muddled along. I did the best I could. I made money. And I kept thinking, I'll just have to live with it. But I felt so helpless, right? You know that, don't you? Of course you do.

"But then . . ." Eli eased closer to the edge of the stage. He looked his parishioners over, catching one Companion's eye, pausing, then another's. His next words were whispered. "But then something happened. Something big. It was a day in June. Very much like today. I can picture it now. I can see it perfectly. I was with some business associates driving to a meeting at one of my factories in the countryside." He held his right hand up, palm out. "And in a flash . . ."

Of the hundred people in the Square, not a soul made a single decibel of sound.

"In a flash . . . an oncoming car crossed the centerline and rammed us. Head-on."

Gasps. Cries of "No!"

"Three people died." He shook his head. "Three people . . . and I was one of them."

29.

"You've heard of near-death experiences, right? Sure you have. You read about them all the time. See them on TV. Don't you?"

More nods, whispers of "Yes."

"The doctors told me later that what I experienced wasn't near-death. It was death itself. I actually died."

This stirred up hushed buzzing from the crowd.

"They'd never seen anything like it before. Well, naturally." A broad smile. "I've *got* to do things different. Anybody can get near death. But I was the real deal. That's me. I don't fool around. The docs, they'd given up on me. Then what happened?"

A Companion near Shaw whispered, "I came back."

Eli: "I came back."

The man beside Shaw, a Journeyman, knew Eli's Discourse so well he could recite it. He wasn't alone. The audience contained a dozen other lip-synchers.

"Those doctors, they told me later they'd never seen anyone fight so hard to come back to life. I was one for the textbooks, they said. Some of them wrote about me. I'm in famous medical journals. Oh, they changed my name, of course, so I wouldn't be mobbed, but I'm there.

"And do you know why I fought so hard?"

"Tell us!"

"Why, Master Eli?"

Many of these responses seemed to be coming from the Inner Circle Companions. Premeditated, of course, though they gave the impression of spontaneity.

"Why did I fight so hard?" A whisper once more: "Why did I come back?" Pointing now to the Companions in a slow sweep. "For you. Because I had learned something in that terrible experience. I had learned how to bring an end to your unhappiness.

"Right then, coming out of the anesthetic, staring at the light above the operating table"—he lifted his hands high above his head—"I knew what I had to do. I had to give up pursuing money and success. I would use all my talents from school, from sports, from business, and turn them to a new life goal. To eliminating the sorrow and mourning and the loneliness that I saw all around me. And it doesn't matter how successful you are. In Hollywood. On Wall Street."

Eli fired a smile toward Shaw.

"In the forestry business."

Slick . . .

"So I sold my companies—at huge profits, by the way. I got every last penny, so I could fund this place. I traveled the world to study philosophy . . ."

Another voice near Shaw was speaking simultaneously

with Eli: ". . . religion and science and medicine. I worked day and night . . ."

"I once worked twenty-six hours in one day! How did I do that? Can you imagine how I did that?"

Whispers, "The time zone."

Eli laughed. "The time zone. I gained two hours flying east to west. I studied all the time. Study, study, study. Some of the beliefs I rejected, some I liked. Everywhere I went I looked for people who were happy and those who weren't. And finally . . . finally I learned the secret to overcoming depression and anxiety and that feeling of loss. And I created the Osiris Foundation."

A wave of clapping, begun by the well-oiled Inner Circle, as coordinated as the Rockettes at Rockefeller Center.

Lifting both his arms, quieting the audience. "Do you know why I've named our group after Osiris?"

"Tell us!" came a shout.

"We love you, Master Eli!"

"Ancient Egypt, 2500 B.C., Osiris was a god, murdered by his brother, who cut the body into pieces and scattered them over Egypt."

Shaw half-expected the audience to start booing Osiris's evil brother but they remained silent.

"Now, get this. Are you ready? Osiris's wife and her sister traveled the country, found the pieces and bound them in cloth—that's where the practice of mummification came from, by the way. So Osiris . . . after the parts were put back together, he became even more powerful. He became god of fertility and of the underworld. He controlled birth and death. What a gorgeous man!

"That's why I named our family the Osiris Foundation—because Osiris was dismantled and then reassembled into someone new. Someone stronger, more content, happier. I mean, hey, the god of *fertility*? He'd have to be pretty happy with *that* job, wouldn't you think? Sign *me* up for that one!"

Eli was eating up the laughter.

"Well, that's what I'm going to do for you. I've created a way to take you apart and reassemble you into the person you should be. Happy, content, productive, loving and loved. And how do I do that? Somebody tell me. I want to hear it!"

A chorus shouted, "The Process!"

Fierce clapping, not in rhythm to Beethoven or any other piece of music. Just feverish applause.

"And what does the Process help us do? What does it help us get back to? Somebody knows the answer! Somebody out there. The Process helps us get back to our . . ."

"True Core!"

"See, I said you were the best! I knew it! Our True Core. Some people call it your soul, some people call it your spirit . . . But those words carry a lot of baggage. Let's get rid of that and call it your True Core. It's who you really are, who you were born as. You can look at it like a beautiful garden that over the years has been built on. Now there's an ugly concrete building, dirty clapboard walls, covered with a rusty tin roof. Graffiti. There's trash in the yard.

"But the garden's still there, the roots living under the ground. The Process tears down the clapboard, cuts up the roof, jackhammers the foundation, carts it all away. It opens up the garden once more.

"Through the Process you 'true up.' That's what I call it, tearing down that ugly building and starting over. Like Osiris."

A chant: "True up, true up, true up!"

The whisper beside Shaw: "From the Yesterday, a better Today . . ."

Eli called out, "From the Yesterday, a better Today . . . From the Today, a perfect Tomorrow."

"You're our Guiding Beacon!"

"We love you!"

Eli raised his arms over his head again, shouting, "The best . . . is yet to come. The best . . . is yet to come!"

The ICs whipped up the frenzy: "The best . . ."

The crowd responded, ". . . is yet to come!"

Eli strode off the stage, to his two awaiting bodyguards. Then he vanished. Anja and Steve rose and followed.

The call-and-response chanting filled the valley and, somehow, Shaw felt the words resonating in his chest.

"The best . . . is yet to come!"

30.

Never be obvious.

In other words: keep a low profile. This is how Colter Shaw was presently following Victoria through the camp.

At the end of the Discourse, he'd noted her eyes wide with adulation, staring at Eli. When he walked from the stage, she turned and clutched her notebook to her chest, then headed to the woods bordering the eastern side of the camp.

Shaw had followed. He watched her in the reflection of windows. Watched her in his periphery. Watched her shadow when he couldn't watch her actual form.

She now entered the woods and started up the hill, on the top of which was the bluff overlooking fifty miles of majestic panorama, anchored by soaring peaks. Victoria's head was down, framed by ringlets of hair.

She was climbing steadily to the bluff. The steep incline didn't slow her. Shaw followed with sufficient distance so that if he happened to step on one of the branches or crisp leaves he was trying to avoid, she probably wouldn't hear.

Shaw himself now heard a snap; the sound was from behind him. He stopped quickly, crouched and looked back. Though the foliage was thick—sage, holly and serviceberry—it wasn't so dense that it would obscure the pale blue tops or gray tunics of a Companion or an AU following. Still, he saw nothing. He waited a moment longer. No more noise, no motion. If anyone had been following him, he or she had vanished . . . or had gone silent.

Should he double back and see? No, he decided.

He glanced up the hill. Victoria was no longer in sight.

He continued east, climbing toward the grassy bluff on the other side of the woods. When he got to the top he spotted her on one of the benches overlooking the view. Her notebook was open, though she wasn't jotting in it. She was staring out.

Deciding not to walk onto the bluff from the same trail she'd used—she'd think he was following her—he retraced his steps a dozen yards, once again looking for anyone surveilling him. He saw no one. He found another path up to the bluff and hiked up this one, emerging on the bluff well to Victoria's right.

He walked close to the edge himself, surveying the cliff once more. In the full light, he decided, it was still a bad one for climbing, certainly for a descent. You'd have to rappel. He reflected that the surface was similar to that of Echo Ridge, which he had never climbed but had in fact executed a high-speed rappel to get to the base. He never was quite sure why he did. The body that lay, shattered, in the dry creek bed below was long past saving.

Turning, he glanced Victoria's way. Her eyes were on him. Her reaction was curious. She looked down to her notebook quickly. His impression was that she felt guilty, as if she'd been caught daydreaming when she should have been writing in the journal.

Shaw squinted and walked closer. "You . . . from last night."

"Novice . . ."

"Carter. And you're . . ." Frowning at his feigned defective memory.

"Apprentice Victoria." They did the shoulder salute; hers was reluctant. She wasn't pleased at his presence.

He said, "Didn't remember. This whole place is kind of weird. Or maybe I'm not supposed to call it 'place.'" Her gray eyes were mesmerizing.

"What do you mean?" Her voice was abrupt. She wasn't nearly as timid as last night, though Shaw wasn't the dangerous Hugh or all-powerful Eli.

"Somebody called the Foundation something like that last night and got corrected."

"There's no rule about not calling the Foundation the 'place.'" She returned to her journal.

He looked over the distant mountains. "This isn't a coincidence. Me coming up here."

"I know. I saw you looking at me at the Discourse."

"Just wanted to say sorry. I screwed up. Got you in trouble."

Silence bled between them.

t—to Ashton—exciting. Shaw, as Skye, asked,
I mean, they give you a degree for that?"

ria continued without responding, "I was mar-
great guy, had a beautiful son. Everything was
. perfectly."

had already spotted the past tense verbs.

t year I was visiting my mother. She'd had sur-
on and Joey were home. They were watching a
n the den. A superhero movie. So they'd shut the
ut. They think—the police think—that the man
oke in thought the place wasn't occupied. They'd
the movie to get some snacks. He walked into the
He got spooked when he ran into my husband
n. He started shooting. He didn't need to. But
"

voice was as emotion-free as Adelle's when she'd
m about losing her baby.

damn. Sorry. How're you . . ." His voice faded.
en came the drinking. Some painkillers too, but
the bottle."

here Shaw had been joking about bartenders last

said, "I have days, hard ones. Really hard. It all
back to me."

when she saw Adam, lying dead on the rocks
er. He could picture her face.

I'm working on it." She tapped the notebook.
was going to continue the conversation, get to
r better, but he'd lost track of time. The heavenly
unded and the voice gave the hour and echoed:
s, report to your trainers."

Shaw finally said, "That curfew—ten o'clock. Do they really have bears and wolves here, you think?"

"I don't know. You hear howls sometimes."

A moment passed. "Anyway. Screwed up. Sorry. That Hugh—I met him. He's pretty . . . tough. Wouldn't want to get on his bad side."

She didn't stiffen at the mention of his name—which Shaw had dropped to begin to build an alliance between them. But her eyes stopped scanning her notebook for a moment.

Victoria then softened. "There weren't any serious consequences. I was careless. It was my fault." She glanced down at her open notebook, which was filled with dense jottings, a few sketches too. Clumsy ones. Her handwriting was abysmal. "Last night at the table, I had a thought about a Plus. A good one. It felt important and I was concentrating on that."

"A 'Plus'?" And hadn't somebody referred to a "Minus" too?

She was confused for a moment, then nodded. "Oh, that's right. You haven't met with your trainer yet."

"No. That's next."

"You'll find out. I can't say anything. We can't give away any of the Process to a new Companion."

He sat. He wasn't close but her shoulders narrowed.

"This is all pretty strange," he said.

Colter Shaw was taciturn by nature but he found that being talkative was a helpful tool in his reward-seeking efforts. Chatting put people at ease and gave him a chance to gauge reaction to his words, maybe exposing subjects to probe. He continued to ramble. "I've never done, you know, group therapy. And this place seems so . . . I don't know what to call it. Focused, maybe. Intense. I thought it'd be more casual. Free to come and go, maybe play some Frisbee."

"Master Eli feels that to true up you can't be distracted. You need to be contained for the Process to work. He says the genie gets his power from the lamp he's confined in."

"I like that," Shaw said. He fell silent and looked at the distant peaks. The view was similar to the vista as seen from Echo Ridge, though there the mountaintops in the distance were like rotting teeth. Here, they were gentler, their light gray summits rising above skirts of green forest. He pivoted toward her.

"He's something, Master Eli. I get restless usually. Don't like to just stand around. But I could listen to him for hours. And that experience he had, the death experience."

"Oh, Master Eli is the smartest and most generous man in the world."

Which were, Shaw believed, the exact words of blood-spattered Adelle.

"This better work. I don't have a lot of options, you know. I've tried everything. Meds, shrinks. Nothing really works." Shaw lifted a hand and let it rest on his thigh. He sighed.

Don't overact.

Victoria asked, "All your life? Have you had problems all your life, or did something happen?"

He told her about Carter Skye's lifelong issues—wrong side of the tracks, dabbling in drugs, fights, glanc-

ing involvement with gangs wh[...] "Been in jail. Have to tell you.'[...]

She had no reaction to this.[...]

He told her that what cause[...] was the death of his father in a [...] asked, he would have assigned the[...] not the truth: a tumble from ten [...] would be a bit close to home.

Victoria didn't ask.

"I hope this works." He watch[...] "Guy I knew told me about it. Adar[...] him?"

"No."

Shaw couldn't tell if she was telling[...] been the slightest of hesitations befor[...] in fact had not known him, that would [...] hoped to learn more about the young m[...] happened in his stay at the camp.

His death was a question that had to be a[...]

She absently riffled the notebook pages. [...] were pink. "The Process'll help. Just takes[...] grew animated. "Master Eli's Second[...] afternoon. It's so . . . inspiring. You'll[...] be made clear."

"Why're you here?" Shaw suppose[...] Journeyman Quinn had urged them [...] Maybe being candid was part of tru[...]

She answered without hesitation[...] a private library in Portland. I've lo[...] I have a degree in library science. O[...]

One of Shaw's father's hobbie[...]

When he hesitated, she looked slightly alarmed. "You can't be late. That's Rule—"

"Twelve. I've learned *some* of them."

He'd hoped for a smile.

Shaw waited a moment but she'd returned to her notebook once more, and he had ceased to exist.

31.

Walking down the hill, along the path bordered with trees and bushes, Shaw noticed a golf cart pull up to the back of Building 14.

What was inside the structure?

He veered off the path and crouched behind a dense boxwood, which radiated its characteristically tart smell. The three men inside climbed out. He was curious why they were not wearing amulets though their outfits were the regulation blue and black uniforms. That was a breach of the rules.

One looked up and down the grassy area behind this building and the dorms. He nodded. Another unlocked the back door, while the third, donning work gloves, picked up a cardboard carton from the back and carried it inside. They all marched in and the door closed.

He was still curious if there might be weapons inside. The box seemed heavy and was being carried gingerly; ammunition?

From the angle, Shaw hadn't been able to see clearly,

though he believed he caught a glint of metal before the door closed.

He returned to the path and walked across the Square to Building 7, where he would meet with his trainer, Samuel. He entered the building. A whiteboard on an easel reported that his session was in Room 4. He knocked and it opened.

"Hello, hello, hello! So good to see you again, Novice Carter. Come in, come in!"

Round, cheerful Journeyman Samuel gave the shoulder salute—Shaw did the same—and gestured him to an armchair. Samuel sat in a facing chair. There were small tables beside each. Shaw's held a bottle of water and a box of Kleenex. In the back of the room was a desk. No windows. The walls—purple, of course—were barren of decorations. The space was small, confining, the air close.

The genie gets his power from the lamp he's confined in . . .

Samuel sat, crossed his legs and took a pad of paper, which he set on his lap. No electronic tablet here. He picked up a pen.

"How's your time here going?"

"Okay. I guess. I don't know. Just a few hours. But what Mr. Eli—*Master* Eli—said this morning? I kinda liked it."

Is this what Carter Skye, the troubled forestry worker, would say?

Yes, he decided.

"And you've got more in store for you this afternoon."

Shaw stretched back and examined the room. "Kind

of, you know, weird to me. I don't do so good joining things. End up getting in fights and kicked out."

"Of *course* it's weird. At this stage, for you, it's like summer camp. Don't really know the lay of the land. Did you go?"

Shaw's character uttered a scoff.

Samuel nodded broadly. "I never did either! Mum and Dad couldn't scrape together the moola. I had to work. In a soda shop. You?"

Young Colter had worked almost every day of his younger years—around the Compound. Hunting for dinner, dressing game, repairing fences, cutting firewood, and learning how to grapple a man twice his size to the ground and disable him with a knee in the solar plexus.

"Odd jobs," he said.

"A boy who wasn't afraid of getting his hands dirty! We need more of that, don't we? This generation, I tell you." A sour face appeared. "Okay. Let's get started." Samuel looked him over closely. "Now, remember, the Process is how you true up, uncover your True Core. You're probably thinking it's intimidating, overwhelming. Well, it's not, not at all. That's Master Eli's genius. You don't need to study Sanskrit or memorize the Bhagavad Gita or recite passages from the Talmud or hold some bizarre yoga pose for hours. Master Eli has made the Process accessible to everyone. Your work is simple as can be."

"And what is that?"

Samuel stared into Shaw's eyes. "All you have to do is tell me the truth."

32.

'll ask you about your life—personal and professional—and we identify those aspects where you have strong feelings."

Samuel made a fist. "*Really* strong thoughts and feelings. Passionate. About people, places, situations, work. Every interaction and reaction you have. The bad feelings—anger, fear, sorrow—and the good ones—joy, love, comfort. We call them—how clever is this? The Minuses and the Pluses."

So that's what they were.

Samuel said, "The important thing is that you feel them intensely. I *hate* this, I *love* that."

"And then?"

The man lifted his hands, palms up. "Then you meditate on what we've identified."

"And that, like, tears down the clapboard house and lets the garden of our True Core grow."

A crinkle in Samuel's eyes. "A man who pays attention. Some people don't. With all kind respect to them, they fuddle about—is that a word? They fuddle and they listen with half an ear or with one ear, not both. My witty metaphors are escaping me at the moment. But you can see what I'm getting at. You, Novice Carter, are serious about truing up and you've got the intelligence to do it. More important, you've got the grit, the edge. I like that. Master Eli likes that. He was smart to put you on the expedited track."

Interesting. It was Eli himself who had picked him.

"When a Plus or Minus rears its good or bad head, we'll jump on it and dig deeper."

"So just think about things in my life?"

"Simple as that."

"And I'm paying for this?" he muttered.

Samuel gave a hearty laugh. "Oh, I like you, Novice Carter. Oh, there's a bit more to the Process. But Master Eli will share that this afternoon in the Second Discourse. Now, let's take a look at some Minuses, shall we? We always start with those. Run-ins with the law—understand there've been a few of those. Problems with the parents. Those controlled substances, old demon rum."

He nodded at the box of Kleenex. Shaw looked at it quizzically.

"You get a little cry-ey, it's all right. It means the Process is working."

The last time Shaw had teared up was when his fifth metacarpal on his right hand—the little finger—bent in a remarkable and noisy way during a minor climbing mishap.

Skye gave an insulted scoff. Samuel was tickled by the reaction.

Samuel smoothed pages in the open notebook. "Let's find out a little about you." He asked about the darker side of Skye's life: the reclusiveness, the drinking, the drugs, the depression, the restlessness.

He then spent a long time asking about Skye's job in the forestry field, what companies he'd worked for, did he have aspirations to own a business?

"Lot of Minuses in the world of the daily grind," Samuel explained.

Gripping his cover story hard, Shaw tried to appear calm as he fabricated. He was hoping his memory wouldn't fail him. He'd heard about the Method, where a theater or movie actor draws on real events and relationships in his own life as a springboard to shape the character he's playing. But in reality, Shaw's life had no grounding in Carter Skye's. So his palms sweated as he spun a tale of a thirty-something man of some promise, whose emotional glitches had derailed him.

Samuel then asked about his romantic life. He pulled out Margot's avatar and answered the questions as they came flying toward him.

He sipped water. Wiped some sweat.

Without any watch or clock—and unable to hear the voice of the Timekeeping Goddess, Shaw was disoriented. Had it been an hour? He hoped the session was finished.

Samuel flipped through his notes, nodding. Then he took his glasses off and polished them. "Remember I told you what your job was?"

Shaw nodded. "To tell you the truth."

"Exactly." Samuel now slipped the glasses back on and leaned forward. The kindly grandfather vanished. His face was cold: "Let's cut the bullshit. Tell me what you're really doing here."

33.

Hell, how had he been tripped up?

To be a good liar, you need a good memory. Had he contradicted himself?

Had he sounded too sophisticated for a former con and street hustler?

Had the beardless Santa Claus been too disarming? Shaw too unguarded?

But there was nothing to do but keep the show going. He conjured a perplexed look. "What do you mean?"

"Oh, you've had some boo-hoo moments in your jobs." A tap on the notebook. "And Daddy or Mommy passed down a feelin'-sad gene or two. And you got too restless for your girlfriend's liking. But those're mosquito bites. People don't come to the Osiris Foundation and pay this kind of money and undergo all this work for boo-hoo. They come out of desperation. Not a single thing you've told me paints you as desperate." The eyes through the round-lens spectacles bored into his. "I want to know . . . the . . . truth."

Without a moment's hesitation Colter Shaw blurted, "My brother."

And thought: The hell have I just done?

Later, Shaw would wonder if perhaps he mentioned Russell because of the Method.

Or maybe it was simply an improvised survival technique. He instinctively knew he had to maintain his cover—and avoid a beating and, not inconceivably, death—so he'd blurted out a credible answer to the question.

But Colter Shaw also had to admit that maybe what had happened was this: Here in the close room, sitting before a perceptive and smart and sympathetic man, the undercover fiction had been suspended. *Shaw*, not Skye, was here, a Companion at the Foundation, and really was suffering from the tragedy of a missing brother. He really *was* undergoing the first stage of the Process in an effort to true up. He really *did* desire to move up to the Apprentice level, then become a Journeyman and a member of the Inner Circle, earning a coveted silver amulet.

It was perfectly natural for him to blurt out that the main reason he was here was the consuming Minus in his life: the sorrow of his brother's vanishing.

He thought with some bitter irony of Eli's story about Osiris and his brother.

Samuel was jotting. He looked up. "Ah, yes, yes. I see in your face, Novice Carter, that we're onto something. We get many people here about their siblings. See, that's the trifecta of the Process. People are plagued with Minuses from love, from work and from their families. Parents, of course. What a minefield *that* is! My own father and mother were certainly poster parents for the ill-equipped. I am, after all, ensconced here. Master Eli truly saved my bacon when it came to Mom and Dad. But siblings too. Ever a source for joy . . . and consternation. Your brother. His name?"

"Randall." Too close to Russell? No matter. He had spoken; there was no going back.

"Randy?"

"No. Randall."

"Was he named after a relative?"

Ashton Shaw had named his children after pioneers. Russell, for the nineteenth-century explorer Osborne Russell; Colter, for mountain man John Colter; and Dorie, after Marie Aioe Dorion, one of the first mountain women in North America.

"So Randall has brought you here." Samuel's voice was low as he added, "Has he passed away?"

"We don't know."

"We?"

"The family. My mother, my sister."

Okay, watch yourself. Get ahead of the situation.

More water.

"So he left home, and never was in touch?"

"That's it, yeah."

"I see. A question of to be or not to be. Or to shift from the infinitive conjugation to the present tense—is or is not. Look at that narrowing of your eye, Novice Carter. If I had a stethoscope on your chest, I suspect I'd hear a little acceleration of the lubdub, lubdub, wouldn't I?"

"Maybe. I guess."

Then the man's eyes narrowed and the smile vanished. "You understand I joke because we're treading through dangerous territory when we start uncovering the big Minuses. The serious ones. I want you to feel at ease. What we're doing here is vital to truing up, to your becoming a Journeyman, free of the Minuses that have prevented you from reaching the garden of your True Core. You're hurting, you came here to fix that. Master Eli wants to help you, he *lives* to help you. And we *can* help. We *will* help."

Samuel was right about the ticker.

Lubdub . . .

"Tell me about it."

"He was my big brother, my protector. Then he was gone. Just left."

"You hesitated just a wink there once again. Before 'my' protector. You have mettle, Novice Carter, mettle and street smarts. And you know how to use your fists. I don't really think you would need protecting at any age. No, within your family, I suspect someone else would need looking out for. Your mother, maybe. No . . . wait. You're the product of a strong mother too. Your sister. Am I near the mark?"

"That's right."

"And her name?"

"Doris."

Too damn close. Watch it, Shaw told himself sternly, picturing again Hugh's fierce blow to the reporter's face.

"So Randall was protecting her from what? Or whom? Your father? Was he . . . inappropriate?"

"No, no, nothing like that."

Samuel's tone and furrowed brow were that of an attentive and benevolent father—a man very different from Ashton Shaw, later in his life, whose shifting eyes and mouth chewy from the antipsychotics forced Shaw to look away from him. A man whose words, brilliant in his younger days, grew increasingly inane and dark toward the end.

"Go on."

Shaw was thinking: I come here to find out why a man died in my care, and to help out a complete stranger, and I end up in a shrink's session. Colter Shaw was a man who had never been to therapy, resisting even Margot's suggestion. He recalled an incident from several years ago, his lover tossing her light blond curls off her shoulder looking over at him from behind her desk in the university archeological department. She asked him point-blank if they could go see a therapist. He'd demurred. Sometimes he thought this had been a grave mistake; sometimes not.

Restless . . .

"Doris was strong, *is* strong. But Father pushed her too far. He thought he was doing it for her own good. He was putting her in danger."

"At sports?"

Ashton tried to force her, at thirteen, to rock climb a sheer hundred-foot cliff by herself at night. And that was just one of the trials the demented man had in store for his children. To toughen them up. To teach them how to survive.

"Yes. He was pushing her too hard. He put her at risk, physically. Mentally too."

"And Randall put a stop to it?"

"Yes."

"We're near something here, Novice Carter. But hovering only. A troubled, dangerous father . . . an older brother looking out for a little sister. You . . . you haven't mentioned your role in this story. Let's talk about that."

Palms glistened once more.

"Not long after the last incident with Doris, our father died."

"How?" Samuel asked quickly.

Shaw paused. "At first, it looked like an accident."

"'Looked like.' That's a loaded phrase. But it wasn't?"

"No. Murder or manslaughter."

"My. And you thought . . . ?"

Shaw said, "I thought my brother killed him."

"Patricide. Well."

"He didn't. We found out later who really did it. Ru—Randall had nothing to do with it. But he disappeared right after the funeral. Which didn't make sense." Shaw lifted his hands. "And no word since. It's been years."

"And you think he knew you suspected him. And hated you for it."

Shaw nodded.

"And you never had a chance to talk to him. To apologize or explain."

"No. All these years. I've tried to find him and talk to him. No luck."

Samuel leaned back. "What would you say was the greatest Minus regarding your brother? What hurts the most?"

"He'd been my friend." Shaw took a breath. "I was his. And I ruined it."

"Well, Novice Carter, we've made excellent progress on our first session. Best to give it a rest for now. We'll break that Minus down. Grind it up like making gravel from rocks. Don't worry. You're doing fine. We'll leave it there for now. Go and journal about what you told me. But don't go far. You don't want to be late for Master Eli's Second Discourse. No, sir, you'll want to hear every word."

34.

How bad was it?"

Shaw turned.

Victoria stood ten feet behind him.

"I saw you come out of Building Seven. You don't look so good."

Shaw shrugged.

She gave a wan laugh and her high forehead wrinkled slightly with faint, early-thirties lines. "Who's your trainer?"

"Journeyman Samuel."

"He's good. No hardball tactics like some of them. Still, it's tough to be interrogated over every detail of your life. About the library business. What had my late husband done professionally, how did that affect me? What do I feel about my father being a rich bank lawyer? Do I resent him?"

"That's how it went. What do I know about the forestry business and logging companies? I'm a surveyor. Then there was the family stuff."

"That can be hard."

He shrugged as if he didn't want to talk about the session any more. "How long until you're a Journeyman?"

"A few days, I hope. There's still work to do. Some other steps. The Endurances."

Odd she used that word. Ashton Shaw insisted that the children pass survival endurance tests, one of which was Doris's late-night climb that broke the family apart.

He laughed grimly to himself. He'd used the fictional name. He corrected: his sister, *Dorion*.

"Greetings, Companions" came the soft, male voice from behind them.

Shaw recognized it immediately.

They both turned. Approaching was Eli and his entourage: Anja and Steve, along with the two AU minders, Squat and Gray.

Everyone exchanged the salute, except for Anja. She nodded and with a faint smile stepped back slightly.

"Novice Carter and Apprentice Victoria," Eli said. He appeared pleased to see them.

"Master Eli." Victoria's voice quavered and her head dipped, as if she were in the presence of royalty.

Shaw nodded to the man. Up close, he could see that Eli's blue eyes were so light the color had to come from theatrical contact lenses.

"How did your first session go today?" he asked Shaw.

"Okay, I guess. Kind of a kick in the gut, looking at those Minuses."

"Oh, how well I know. But that's the way it should be. The way it *has* to be, for the Process to work. I've planned it out carefully. I spent years fine-tuning the machine."

"You did a good job."

"You think so?"

"I do," Shaw told him.

Eli's face radiated self-satisfaction.

"Apprentice Victoria, you've come a long way. The reports are glowing. I knew you were going to be a good one from the start. I can spot them. I always can."

"Thank you, sir." She grimaced. "I'm sorry. *Master Eli*."

Shaw remembered that she'd gotten into trouble with *sir* and *ma'am* in the past.

"Oh, no harm done, dear." He smiled. "I'm having a meditation session in the Study Room tonight. Would you attend?"

"Me? Oh, of course, Master Eli." Her eyes widened.

"Good. After dinner." The man turned his attention toward Shaw. "And, Novice Carter, since you're expedited, we'll get you to the Study Room too. Soon. Maybe tomorrow or the day after. They're immersive study sessions in the residence. My own brand of transcendental meditation. Came up with it myself. It's patented."

Victoria said to Shaw, "It's an honor to be asked."

"Yeah, well, sure. Sounds like fun."

Eli chuckled and looked at Steve, who smiled in response. He said to his aide, "We'll see how fun he feels it is after all the hard work. It can be . . . There's a word."

Steve supplied one. "Strenuous."

"Yes. Strenuous."

"But," Steve added quickly, "fulfilling."

"Cool," Shaw said, after running the word past Skye. He noticed that Anja was looking his way. The expression on her face was neutral. Did it mask suspicion, or something else?

"A word with you, Novice Carter." Master Eli said this in a conspiratorial tone and walked away, without saying anything to the others. Shaw followed. When they were out of earshot, he looked Shaw up and down with his silken eyes. "I have a proposition for you. Just something to keep in mind."

"Yes, Master Eli?"

"There's a special group of Companions. The most elite."

"Inner Circle?"

"No, beyond them. They're called Selects. Only one percent of Companions are picked. I do that myself, and train them personally. It can take a year or more. But they earn a salary while they undergo the training and afterward. They're like monks, you could say. You've probably seen some around the camp. They have our uniforms but don't wear amulets."

"I wondered about them."

The sullen workers he'd seen in Building 14. Maybe that was the Select training facility.

"They have our symbol, of course. Their heads're shaved and tattooed with the infinity sign on their scalps. Then the hair grows back." Eli gave a soft smile. "I know this is only your first day but you fit the profile. You're single, no children, you like to travel. Journeyman Samuel says you don't mind working hard."

So they'd already communicated about him.

"You know what it's like to have a hard life. That's an important factor for Selects. And they need to be fit, not the sort who're easily intimidated. Sometimes people don't quite appreciate our worldview. There've been protests. Even some altercations occasionally."

"I've found, you know, if you speak the truth, that pisses people off."

"You and Novice Todd are this group's best choices for Select."

Shaw recalled Todd from the dinner table. The former military man.

"What exactly would I do?"

"Call it customer relations."

Recruiting, probably. Going to bereavement centers and funerals. Convincing people to sign up.

"Yeah, I'm kind of up for it. Let me think."

"Of course. We'll talk more. Oh, and we'll keep this between ourselves. Only I and a few others are involved in the Select program."

"Sure, Master Eli."

They exchanged the salute and Eli joined the others and walked on.

Shaw and Victoria continued their stroll along the path. She looked at him curiously. "Guess my training's going okay," he said.

She seemed to want to ask more but chose not to.

Shaw asked, "Want to get some lunch?"

Victoria hesitated a moment but said, "I should finish journaling." She held up her notebook, as if she were batting away his invitation.

Shaw studied the appealing, thoughtful face.

Art-house actress . . .

"So the Process's working for you?" he asked.

"Every day here there are fewer and fewer bad moments. When I advance in a few weeks," she said, her face bright, "I know everything'll be fine."

The cult-speak amused Shaw; Companions couldn't say they "graduate" from the training. They had to say "advance."

He said, "I'll see you at the Second Discourse."

"I'll be there."

Which wasn't an acknowledgment that they would in fact meet in the Square.

Without giving the salute they went separate ways, Shaw heading down toward the dining hall for a sandwich and coffee. As he walked he was thinking: The Foundation was odd and unsettling, no question about that, the regimentation, the frenzied political rally tone in the dining hall last night and in the Square this morning, Eli's ego and need for control. Shaw decided it was safe in labeling the Osiris Foundation a cult.

A dangerous one, though? It was hard to dismiss the murder of the journalist in San Francisco and the beating of the reporter Shaw had witnessed. Those incidents, however, now seemed like outliers, committed by isolated negatives: Harvey Edwards, in San Francisco, and Hugh, the dangerous, renegade head of the Assistance Unit. Edwards's background suggested he was unhinged. And Hugh? Like rent-a-cops everywhere, he would enjoy flexing his authority—and his muscles, putting his little-used karate moves into practice and bullying and coming on to women.

Eli himself was clearly narcissistic but in an almost comical way. Shaw hadn't seen a truly dark side. He clearly was devoted to his altruistic mission to help people in pain.

As the deprogrammer had said, Eli might not even know about Hugh's attack or Edwards's murdering the journalist.

And the Process itself?

A benign bowl of self-help homilies and off-the-shelf therapy. Shaw had no evidence to blame the Foundation for Adam's death—the reason he was here. The young man was just plagued with an emotional grid gone astray.

Nor was there any particular risk to Victoria or anyone else that he could see. She seemed buoyed by the Process, coming out of what had to be unfathomable depression at her loss.

Beethoven's notes hummed through the camp. The woman's voice then announced, "Master Eli's Second Discourse is about to begin." She reiterated that the lecture was mandatory for the Novices and voluntary for the other Companions.

Shaw cleaned away his lunch dishes and soon he was walking along the path to the Square, a dozen others nearby, heading in the same direction.

Shaw was tempted to privately criticize them all as lemmings. But that was unfair; these Companions were like everyone else—just trying to make their way through an often unnavigable world in the truest way they could. Colter Shaw found that route in an itinerant lifestyle, tracking down felons and missing persons, climbing sheer cliffs, catching air on his motorbike—testing limits.

Who had a lock on the right answers?

And who couldn't use a bit of truing up?

The crowd assembled—trainees in the middle, ringed by ICs, like the morning's session. Across the Square he saw Walter and Sally. He joined them. Her eyes focused on him and she smiled but cautiously. The men did the shoulder salute. Sally watched, mystified. "Oh, you boys . . ."

Shaw said to Walter, "What's this Second Act?" Nodded at the stage.

The man chuckled and said, "All I'll tell you is, it's a doozy."

35.

The ICs began clapping and the longer version of the "Ode to Joy" reverberated throughout the valley, just as it had that morning before the First Discourse.

Beyond the stage and Eli's residence, the mountains and trees stood in sharp contrast, black and brown and green, to an afternoon sky of stunning clarity. The rich scent of loam and pine, tinged with eucalyptus, wafted on a lazy breeze.

The regular clapping broke into frenzied applause as Eli walked onto the stage. His white tunic glowed once again.

He held his hands up and quiet descended.

It was brief, as someone soon cried, "We love you, Master Eli!"

Sparking more applause.

Finally, he silenced the crowd.

"Did you Novices have good sessions today?" He scanned those wearing the blue amulets. He looked directly at Shaw.

Shouts of "Yes!"

One male voice, "You betcha!"

Eli pointed. "I like him!"

The man beamed.

"You're working on discovering your . . . what?"

"Minuses!" "Pluses!" The shouted words collided.

He turned to no one in particular, like a late-night talk show host remarking to his sidekick. "I knew this group was good. They're stars! They're gorgeous!"

Eli's reward was yet more frenzied applause.

"You'll tear down that bad construction in no time and start planting the Pluses in the garden of your True Core. I know you will. I know exactly how you're doing. And you'll do fine. I'm never wrong."

He fell silent.

The crowd too.

"This morning I told you about Osiris. What a man he was! A god. God of the underworld. God of fertility."

Three or four ICs held up tablets, filming.

"Osiris. What a great guy he was. Great! Gorgeous. You know what I like about him? He came back from the dead, remember? He's immortal." Eli walked closer to the edge of the stage. Was it Shaw's imagination or was the spotlight a little brighter?

The master pointed a finger over the sea of upturned faces.

"Just like all of us. Just . . . like . . . you." He pointed. "Immortal."

Many of the long-timers were smiling. The Novices, for the most part, looked toward Eli with rapt attention but varying shades of confusion on their faces.

"Now I'm going to reveal the secret of the Process. This is what it's all about. Immortality. Our slogan: *Yesterday, Today, Tomorrow*. Yesterday, as in your past lives. Today, as in"—he raised his hands, palms up—"today. And tomorrow, as in your future lives." He let this settle. "The Process will teach you how to live"—he pointed to the gold infinity symbol on the backdrop—"forever."

36.

A woman beside Shaw—an Apprentice—whispered, "Death is a fallacy."

Eli called out: "Death is a fallacy! Death is a fiction perpetuated by those in power, by politicians, by religions, by the medical community, by corporations, by the media. Death is a lie!

"They convince you that today is your only shot at existence. They do it to control you. To sell you their bill of goods. Buy this insurance policy, take this medicine, elect that politician, buy this house. Pay a hundred thousand dollars on medical treatment. Live now, you only have one chance. Don't waste it. Give us your money and we'll make sure there'll be some left for your children. After, of course, we take a little bit for ourselves."

On the word *little* he held his hands out wide, as if exaggerating the size of a fish he'd caught.

Which brought laughter and applause.

"*They're* the ones selling you the ugly, rotten concrete

and clapboard houses with rusting roofs to bury your True Core."

Nods and a few affirmative murmurs.

"Immortality . . ." Eli spoke in a soft voice, which had the effect of drawing the attention of the Companions even more. "Remember I told you this morning that today is brief, it's fleeting; it's a blink. And that's true. But today is only a small portion of the entire life your True Core lives, which extends from the beginning of time to the end.

"Oh, I know, I know . . . This is a lot for some of you to take in. How well do I know that? I've been there. I've been where you are. I've been uncertain, I've been cynical. So, just listen to me. Hear me out. That's all I'm asking. Will you listen?"

"We'll listen!"

"We love you!"

He said, "Immortality. Every society, every civilization, every religion, primitive or advanced, has their own version of it. You remember my old friend Osiris, right? We love him, don't we? Isn't he great? Isn't he gorgeous?"

Applause.

Shaw wondered where on earth this was going. He glanced toward Walter, who looked back and nodded.

A doozy . . .

"The Egyptians knew that the soul was immortal. Just ask Osiris and his wife. The Greeks? There were thousands of accounts about resurrection from the dead. Souls and bodies reunited and living in Elysium. Read your Plato, one of my favorites. Have you read him?

You've *got* to read him. He's a genius, he's a gorgeous writer. He writes about the immortal soul all the time. He's the greatest philosopher the world has ever seen. I read him every night.

"The Buddhists. Don't you love Buddhism? I do. They say that when people die they transform from a physical body into an immortal body of light—the Rainbow body, it's called—and they live forever. I love that! Don't you?

"Christians? Believers will go to heaven for eternity. Sinners to hell. Jesus himself, well, look at him. Died, resurrected, then went up to heaven to live with his dad forever. You read the Nicene Creed? You have to read it. It says that every dead person will be resurrected during the Second Coming.

"Hinduism? They've got reincarnation. You live a good life, karma will make sure you come back in a higher place. A bad life, uh-oh. How about the Jewish people? I love people of the Jewish faith. The Pharisees believed the soul was immortal, and people would be reincarnated and, I'm quoting, 'pass into bodies' in future lives.

"Islam? The Qur'an says death is the same as sleep. You awake from sleeping. You will awake from death. I could go on and on. Billions and billions of people have been convinced from the beginning of civilization that we've lived before this life and we'll live again, after it. So how can it *not* be true?

"But with all respect to the religions I just mentioned. They believe in immortality, granted. But there's a problem."

Whispers from the ground: "If you're Christian . . ."

After a dramatic pause, Eli said, "If you're Christian, what awaits you is a Christian heaven. If you're Jewish, a Jewish one. If you're Hindu, you will be reincarnated. If you watch TV, you'll come back as the Walking Dead."

Laughs and applause.

Someone shouted, "Zombies!"

Eli chuckled then grew serious. "The rules for immortality have to be the same for everyone, of whatever religion or no religion. True for atheists, as well as the Pope. But each one of those religions I mentioned excludes the others. That means they all have to be wrong. I'm sorry to be blunt but that's the way I am. I'm a blunt talker. You know that by now, right? I tell it like it is."

Nods.

"Now, I have nothing against religion. Not at all. I hope you all find comfort in whatever church, synagogue, mosque or house of worship you prefer. But when it comes to immortality, all the priests and holy men and rabbis and gurus . . . they should leave the subject to somebody who knows the truth.

"They should leave it to me."

37.

Eli looked over the crowd, most of them mesmerized. After a long moment: "What do I—humble me—know about the subject? Oh, quite a bit. I told you about my death experience—not *near* death but actual death."

"We remember!"

"We love you!"

"When I was dead, I saw things. Images. When the doctors brought me back I couldn't stop thinking about what I'd seen. They were images of people, places that were familiar but that I'd never seen in my present life or in a movie or read about in a book. Where had those images come from? I had no idea. All I knew was that they moved me deeply. Some made me deliriously happy, some made me afraid, some made me angry. But what I felt when I thought about them, I felt intensely.

"So I began to focus on people and places in the present—people and places that gave me the same kind of intensity. I began to meditate on them. When I did that, the images from the time I was dead came back. They were from a hundred years ago, two hundred, a thousand . . ." His voice dropped. "Imagine that! I was witnessing my past lives!"

Gasps of astonishment, joyful murmurs.

So this was what the Process was supposed to do. Samuel had told him to meditate on intense feelings he had in his life. Doing that, according to Eli's mythology, would open the door to his past lives.

Eli continued, "I told you I was orphaned when I was young. It was terrible. Devastating. I missed my parents so much. My father, Tobias. My mother, Rachel. How I missed them. When I was meditating, trying to bring those intense feelings back, suddenly I saw them again. We were together in the 1800s. And I knew then that I'd see them once more—in the future."

Whispers from the Companions as they turned to one another. Most, Shaw could see, were buying what he was saying.

Eli walked to the edge of the stage and looked down at Henry, the balding man who'd been inducted at the same time as Shaw. He was the medical researcher so devastated by losing his wife to cancer eight months earlier. Eli spoke directly to him. "You can never lose anybody. Not permanently. You'll be together again. You'll be with them in the Tomorrow."

Shaw felt the same way he did when listening to Pentecostal preachers explain Bible passages to their flocks. The words didn't follow any logic but it was clear the Companions, like parishioners, were under his spell and took the arguments as, well, gospel.

Looking past Henry, Shaw noted another tall man, a Journeyman, looking Shaw's way. He thought again about Frederick—the man with the orange sunglasses, who might have seen him above the cliff where Adam had died. Was this the same man? The physique was the same but, with the absence of the eyewear, he couldn't tell.

When Shaw glanced again, the man was focusing once more on Eli.

"If thousands of years of religion and spirituality get the path to immortality wrong, how can I say I get it right?" A chuckle. "What do my Jewish friends say? Chutzpah! What kind of chutzpah do I have? I mean, getting one up on everybody's God? That's a pretty big claim. But I'll tell you the answer. Why do *I* have the key to open the door to immortality? And no one else does? Do you want to hear?"

"Tell us!"

"We love you!"

"Because I—and only I—know that immortality isn't based on superstition or belief or faith or hope. It's based on . . ." He looked over the crowd.

"Science," five or six ICs cried simultaneously. Shaw wondered how long the rehearsals had been.

"Ex-actly!

"Science. Cold, hard science. In my travels after my death experience, I spoke to doctors, physicists, engineers and neuroscientists. They all agree that our consciousness and awareness—our True Core—is a unique combination of energy impulses.

"When your body ceases to exist, the energy that is your True Core remains. This is because of the First Law of Thermodynamics. I've written papers about it. Published all over the world. The First Law of Thermodynamics. And what does it say? That energy is neither created nor destroyed.

"So our True Core is energy and energy exists forever! Immortal! And it doesn't matter if you're good or bad or a saint or a sinner or a primitive tribesman . . . or a politician in Washington." He gave a sigh.

Earning the laughter his delivery deserved.

"After you pass, your True Core will end up again in another body." A frown. "How does that happen? I'll be honest. I don't know yet. It's like when I was in school. I could always get the answer. I scored great on my tests. Top of my class. But I couldn't always explain *why* I got the answer.

"Someday we'll be able to know how your True Core travels and ends up in another body. Just like flight. We never knew why for thousands of years birds could fly but eventually we learned about the shape of their wings. For now the *how* doesn't matter. What *does* matter is that your True Core will go on. You'll be reunited with loved ones. Oh, in different forms, but the connection and love will be the same. You won't have the addictions, the sorrows, the illnesses you have now."

His eyes dipped to Walter and Sally, then to Abby. Several others.

"This is what the Process does. You start with meditating on intense feelings from the Today and doing that will raise memories from past lives—in the Yesterday. You'll recognize the bad habits and bad people from your prior lives and eliminate them in the Today. You'll embrace the good people, engage in the activities that are positive for you. That's why we say . . ."

The ICs: "From the Yesterday, a better Today!"

"And the Process will condition your True Core for the next life. You'll avoid the Minuses and embrace the Pluses in the future."

His Greek chorus: "From the Today, a perfect Tomorrow!"

"The best is yet to come!" Eli shouted.

Clapping and chanting ensued.

Now Samuel's comment at Intake made sense:

As you'll see, a guarantee wouldn't really be practical . . .

You never knew if the Process worked until you were in the grave.

"Now, do you see why I can take away all our pain, your depression, anxieties, mourning? Because you'll always know that happiness, a gorgeous happiness, awaits you in the Tomorrow."

Eli's voice rose in volume and resonance. "There's no death; there's no separation from your loved ones. Everyone's True Core moves from life to life, forever."

He smiled reassuringly over his rapt audience. "When the time comes for us to leave the Today, we give the Foundation's traditional farewell." He placed each hand on the opposite shoulder, crossing over his chest. "And we say, 'Goodbye, until Tomorrow.'"

That's what Adam had muttered before he jumped to his death.

Eli continued in a soft, droning tone: "The Tomorrow— when you and your loved ones will meet again, when you'll begin a new life and find the happiness and comfort you deserve. Say it with me. Goodbye . . ."

Collective joyous shouts: "Until Tomorrow."

"Remember, death doesn't exist. We never say we 'die.' What we say is that we 'advance.' We advance from this life into a better one." As he walked off the stage, he cried, "The best . . ."

". . . is yet to come." The crowd erupted in applause and kept the chant going at full volume.

But Colter Shaw didn't hear the driving words. All that was in his head was the line Victoria had said to him just an hour ago.

When I advance in a few weeks, I know everything'll be fine . . .

She didn't mean graduating from the Process; she meant that like Adam Harper she was going to kill herself.

38.

He had his answers.

Shaw had come here to find out why Adam Harper had leapt from the cliff and learn if Victoria or anyone else—like the wounded deer that Adam had been—was at risk.

Eli—David Ellis, the former real estate developer and stockbroker from Florida—was no simple huckster; he was killing people.

The Osiris Foundation was a suicide cult.

He'd wondered why Adam had offered that eerily calm smile just before he plunged to his death. Now he understood. The young man was going to be reunited with his mother. The last three seconds of his life had not been filled with anguish, as the sniper Dodd had speculated, but joy at what lay ahead in the Tomorrow.

Shaw glanced at the Companions wandering from the Square, some talking excitedly, some pensive. He guessed that the majority of them would consider the immortality angle suspect or purely bogus, resigning themselves to having wasted a chunk of their kids' tuition signing up for the Process.

But there were also plenty of true believers. Shaw could see it in their eyes. Like Adam, like Victoria, they were convinced there was a better world in the Tomorrow, and they'd take their lives when confronted by too much pain. Or maybe just minor setbacks.

What could Shaw do?

As for law enforcement, he didn't think a fraud charge would hold up, any more than you could claim you'd been defrauded by donating to a born-again church promising eternal life in heaven. He'd seen Hugh and several AUs beat someone but witnessing the crime wasn't enough for a prosecution, and it was likely Klein would take to heart Hugh's threats and stay mum. In any event, Hugh and the AUs would never implicate Eli, who might not even know about the reporter's assault.

He knew that Harvey Edwards had murdered the San Francisco journalist but could he tie that to Eli? SFPD Detective Etoile might be pursuing the case, though investigations like this would take a long time.

If Shaw could get cell phone records, notes, memos . . . something to connect the homicide to the cult leader. A witness who'd overheard Eli give the command would be perfect but if there were such a person, he or she would be an Inner Circle; they'd never admit to any such orders.

Shaw's meditation about strategy for Eli's downfall was postponed for the moment, however. He heard angry shouting from not far away.

Eli, Hugh and the two bodyguards were on the tree-lined path from the stage back to his residence. They had turned and were facing curly-haired John, the Novice from Southern California, whose friend had died in the car crash. He was leaning forward toward Eli and he was angry. Gray and Squat were cautious but seemed to sense that the young man was not a major threat; either could have dropped him with a single blow. Shaw moved off the trail, remaining in the brush, and got within twenty feet of the altercation.

Several other Companions had heard and turned, walking toward the sound. Two AUs appeared and ushered them away with stern faces.

John said harshly, "You took her to the Study Room. She told me what happened there."

"Novice John," Eli said, "this isn't any of your business."

"It's a breach of the rules. No relations with staff or Companions."

"That's not what the rule is for. In the Study Room we can delve into certain elements of past lives that can be critical in uncovering the True Core."

"Uncovering," John said, scoffing at the word. "Let me ask you a question: Is it only the pretty girls you *delve* into?"

So that was what the Study Room was for, not meditation at all.

Strenuous . . .

Hugh: "You're out of line, Novice John."

"I'm not out of line at all. Abby's sixteen, for God's sake."

So, the Guiding Beacon had committed statutory rape.

Eli's reaction was in fact no reaction at all. His face was momentarily blank, then he looked briefly to Hugh. No reaction from the head of the AUs but Steve frowned slightly then wiped the expression away. Eli said, "I wasn't aware of that."

Steve said, "On her application she stated she was eighteen."

"Well, maybe you should've checked that out, don't you think? Maybe take a look at her, and think, oh, let's see some ID. Hm? You could've found her high school yearbook. They have those online, you know. Or did you just think, she's hot, and decide not to find out her real age?"

In a bland monotone, Eli said, "Thank you for bringing this to our attention, Novice John. I will apologize to her myself. And we'll take measures to make sure this never happens again. I'll speak to our admissions people."

John had apparently expected more pushback. He didn't know where to go from here.

Eli said to him, "To be honest, after this, I don't think you're really the right candidate for the Process. I think it's best for you to withdraw from the Foundation."

"Hell, yes, I'm quitting. And that immortality babble? How the fuck can you get anybody to buy that?"

Eli said, "We'll send you a refund."

Hugh said, "Novice John arrived on one of the shuttles. We have a car to take him back to Snoqualmie Gap."

"What about Abby?" John asked.

Eli said, "She'll have to leave too, of course. We'll have her parents pick her up. I'm truly sorry this happened. But I appreciate your bringing it up."

"Sorry doesn't really fix the problem now, does it?"

No! Let it go, Shaw thought.

However, it was too late. In fact the young man's fate had been sealed the instant he'd brought up the subject of Abby's visit to the Study Room.

Hugh looked around and made certain no Companions were nearby. In one of his slick martial arts moves, he slammed a fist into the young man's chest. John gasped and went down hard, breath knocked from his lungs. Hugh reached into his pocket and extracted several zip ties. He bound John's hands and feet. The man pulled his walkie-talkie off his belt and spoke into the unit. In no more than a minute, a golf cart appeared, driven by an AU. He hefted the young man and dumped him into the back of the cart then covered him with a tarp. Shaw crouched farther into the bushes and the vehicle drove into the woods, turning left onto the hidden path and heading for the main gate.

Eli gave another nod to Hugh, who followed the cart. Eli and his bodyguards returned to the residence.

Shaw had yet another answer: Hugh was no isolated negative. Eli was just as dangerous as his head of the Assistance Unit, and had surely been responsible for ordering Harvey Edwards to murder the journalist in San Francisco.

Shaw turned toward the front gate too. He knew what was going to happen.

The only question: Would he be able to stop it?

39.

Shaw dogged the golf cart as it drove slowly over the bumpy forest path. He kept off the walkway and used trees and foliage for cover.

The cart and Hugh arrived at the YESTERDAY, TODAY, TOMORROW gate. Shaw noted that no Companions were present, only some Assistance Unit men. Hugh's walkie-talkie call had probably been to alert them to keep others away.

At the gate, which was open, the cart stopped. The driver climbed out and looked around, flung the tarp back. He easily pulled John from the bed of the vehicle. The young man was barely conscious. He'd vomited and was groggily protesting, though he had no strength to offer even minor resistance. He was dragged through the parking lot and dumped into the backseat of an old, idling Ford, in which another Companion, a young man, sat behind the wheel. He was a Select—wearing the uniform but no amulet.

A burly AU carried a large backpack—John's luggage,

Shaw guessed—to the Taurus and placed it in the trunk. The driver and Hugh shared some words.

This wasn't like the journo, who hadn't actually discovered anything incriminating on the Foundation. A beating would suffice with him. No, John could report Eli's sexual assault of a minor. The young man would have to die. The supervisor would be giving instructions on how best to murder John and hide the body. Maybe in one of the lakes. Maybe in a deep ravine, where the animals would make the body vanish in days.

So, plan it out.

Shaw couldn't get to the car here, in the camp itself. Too many AUs.

No phone to call the local police.

So he'd try to stop the Ford while it was still near camp.

He closed his eyes and pictured the map. Heading down the mountain near the camp, Harbinger twisted through a series of switchbacks for several miles. The Ford would have to take those tight turns slowly, giving Shaw a chance to catch it. Once the switchbacks ended, though, Harbinger became a straightaway where the car would accelerate to fifty or so miles per hour.

How to intercept the car?

Only one idea occurred.

He'd run.

As the Ford pulled from the parking lot and through the chain-link gate and the gap in the tall granite cliff, Shaw sprinted east to the path he'd found yesterday evening before dinner, his escape route. Instead of continuing in that direction, though, he turned north, running to the top of the rocky ridge and looking down. He could see the Ford driving perpendicular to him along the first of the switchbacks.

Shaw surveyed the ground before him: a fifteen-degree downward slope through greenery and trees and occasional swamp. The surface was loam and rock, some grass.

Well, get to it.

Shaw plunged down the hillside, heading north toward the switchbacks.

Inhaling hard, and wishing he'd had time to stretch, Shaw picked his way around the dense shrubs and over the uneven ground. No time to pace himself. He was dashing flat out—or at least with as much velocity as he could muster, given the surfaces and obstacles. Occasionally he'd have to choose: slowing to duck under overhangs or angled tree trunks or keeping the speed up while negotiating slippery or gravel-covered rock formations. And always keeping an eye out for spiny plants whose thorns could shred skin.

Running was no alien activity to Colter Shaw.

In the Compound, Ashton taught the children to run as a survival skill—sprinting toward prey and away from predators and disasters like floods and avalanches.

Ashton had told them about the famous Native American runners: the Tarahumara in Mexico and the Sierra Madres. Their name for themselves is Raramuri, which means "fast runners." They would regularly course long distances—sometimes two hundred miles—for communication and hunting.

In college, Shaw's wrestling coach—observing the

boy's speed in workouts—suggested he try out for track and field too, but Colter wasn't interested. He ran for himself only. It was a comfort, not a competitive activity. Whether long distances or short, he often had the sense that he was flying, an ecstatic sensation. He alone among the siblings enjoyed running. Not surprisingly—he was, after all, the Restless One.

Though zigzagging some to avoid spills and collisions, he largely let gravity and the direction of the slope keep him true to a downward course—like the vertical line in a dollar symbol, bisecting the S-shaped switchbacks of Harbinger Road.

Shaw broke from the woods and crossed the first switchback, observing that the sedan had just been along here; dust was still lingering. On the other side, he plunged into the forest and flew downward once more.

Then . . . oh, hell! His momentum took him onto a flat-topped boulder that he realized too late jutted into space.

No stopping.

But the eight-foot drop ended on—thank you, Mother Nature—a thick bed of loam and crunchy leaves. He hit, rolled and righted himself. Continued on.

Sudden motion in brush to his right. Deer or wolf?

Please, not a bear cub. Shaw could outrun many species. A pissed-off mama black bear was probably not one of them.

One problem: the ridiculous slipper shoes the cult had issued him. If he'd had time, he would have returned to his dormitory and ripped apart a shirt to bind over his feet, like the Tarahumara's foot covering: they would use *huaraches*, a skimpy cloth sandal that helped them maintain their speed and distance. Modern-day runners and doctors had studied the footgear in an effort to figure out why they were so conducive to running.

Downward, downward.

At the second switchback, he missed the car again but he was closer to his target this time. The dust was thicker, and he caught a glimpse of a taillight flare as the Select braked for the turn and descent.

There was one more switchback before the straightaway. Shaw inhaled deeply and continued the race. Here, the incline was steeper and occasionally he would lose his footing and stumble before catching himself. His wrestling and grappling training helped; he didn't fight the tumbling but used it to increase his speed.

And as he ran he thought: What to do when he caught up with the car?

He decided he'd use a rock to spider the windshield, directly in front of the Select. It would startle him into braking instinctively. Then another rock through the driver's side window—the front windshield glass was tough, the side ones much less so. He'd pop open the Select's belt and drag the man out onto the road, then jump behind the wheel himself.

Shaw would drive to the authorities in Snoqualmie Gap. He would have preferred to wait and find hard evidence linking Eli and Hugh to the various crimes but he had no choice; he had to save John's life.

Once at the police station or sheriff's department, he'd explain to the cops what he'd seen, tell them about Eli's assault of Abby. Shaw would tell them about the

Foundation's connection with the death of the journal-ist, Gary Yang. He'd explain too about the beating of the other reporter he'd witnessed in the camp.

The crimes sounded circumstantial, and some of them absurd. But he'd pitch the case as best he could.

He was now at the third switchback, the last one. Good. He'd beaten the Ford here. There was no dust hovering on this portion of Harbinger and he could see much of the straightaway. No cars. He rested briefly, head down, panting hard, ignoring the stitch in his side. He collected two rocks from the shoulder, both about the size of grapefruits. Kneading one in his right hand, he slipped into the cover of tall grass by the side of the road.

Waiting, ready to pitch the rock toward the driver's side windshield.

Going over the maneuvers in his mind.

But then—no car.

Another sixty seconds passed.

Then he heard, from uphill, the sound of a collision. Crunching metal, the car's horn sounding. It blared for a moment, then went silent.

Shaw turned and, drawing yet another deep breath, he slogged up the hill.

When he broke from the woods this time, he saw in front of him the Ford, which had veered off the U-shaped curve from the second switchback to the third. It had slammed into a ten-foot-high rock face just off the shoul-der. The front of the car was caved in and the airbags had deployed. The vehicle had been doing no more than forty or so; why had it crashed?

Inside the car was movement. The driver was looking

calmly at John, who still sat in the backseat. He'd been tossed around and was groggy and stunned—probably more from Hugh's earlier blow than the collision. He was slowly shaking his head.

Shaw had to get John out before the Select tried to kill him another way. He'd engage Hugh's hitman, take him down and bind his feet. Then he'd help John hike into town. A long way but their only option.

Shaw sprinted toward the car, gripping one of the rocks tightly in his right hand.

He was still fifty feet away when the Select emptied the gasoline container throughout the interior of the vehicle. The Select looked out the window and happened to see Shaw. If he was surprised at Shaw's presence he didn't reveal it. He gave a faint smile, gave the two-armed farewell salute, then flicked a cigarette lighter, turning the interior of the car into an inferno.

40.

Cars generally don't blow up spectacularly in real life the way screenwriters and directors would have it.

There's not enough air in the gas tank for explosive combustion. But when a fire starts elsewhere, fuel lines and gaskets melt and the aromatic and deadly liquid flows out to add to the conflagration. This happened now. A small field of orange flames flickered near the rear of the car, and soon not only was the interior engulfed but the outside too, flames boiling, black smoke spiraling skyward.

Colter Shaw tried once more to get close. He was driven back by searing heat and turbulent black smoke. The glimpses he caught of the occupants revealed that the thrashing had ceased.

Goddamn . . .

Eli had created the perfect weapon. The Selects were not "monks" at all. They were the Praetorian Guard, protectors to the death. They were a secular version of the fundamentalist suicide bomber. Convinced of a better life ahead, they didn't care about escaping after they murdered, always the most challenging aspect of the crime.

Shaw understood now that Harvey Edwards had been a Select and that he'd engineered the shootout with the cops so he himself would die—to *advance*—after killing the journalist, Gary Yang.

Shaw realized too why he had been fast-tracked for the position himself: the fictional violent crimes he'd committed, his edgy attitude. Eli didn't want to cure him of those demons. He wanted to exploit them.

Anyone whom the rabidly narcissistic Eli saw as a threat was at risk: heretical Companions within the Foundation, rival cult leaders, police and prosecutors, Shaw supposed. The deaths would be apparent accidents or murder-suicides—homicide investigators' favorite death cases. Minimal investigation, some paperwork, and on to other matters.

He cocked his head. A noise could be heard over the flames.

Sirens in the distance, getting closer. He walked to a rocky ridge and looked down the mountain. Flashing lights. Police, a fire truck, an ambulance. The vehicles had TOWN OF SNOQUALMIE GAP painted on the sides.

How could they be here so quickly?

Then he realized the answer. *Of course.*

Shaw got under cover just in time. Easing down the switchbacks was the black Osiris Foundation van— maybe the same one that had transported Victoria and the others to the site where Adam had died.

The van parked about a hundred feet from the flaming wreck. Shaw climbed higher on the hill, where he had a good view of the road below and could still stay out of sight.

The emergency vehicles arrived. The law enforcers and the firemen and firewomen, six of them, exited. Not a soul made any effort to extinguish the burning car, though they ran lines and soaked the brush nearby. That was their only concern: a wildfire. Shaw knew that even if the rescue workers had gotten here before the flames killed the two men, they would have done nothing to save those inside.

This was made clear when Hugh and one of the other Selects climbed from the van and walked up to the sheriff and fire chief, handing out envelopes.

The white rectangles disappeared into pockets.

Shaw had no doubt that the vast majority of law enforcers in the state were upright—like Chad Johnson, at the Pierce County Public Safety Office. But in the space of just a few days he'd crossed paths with two sets of bad apples: Welles and the Hammond County protectors of the church, and here, in Snoqualmie Gap, a bunch of cops who were simply on the take.

These men and woman now lounged back, leaning against their vehicles and examining the roiling smoke and flames as the Ford burned to its chassis. The stench was unbearable—some of it from the rubber, some from the occupants.

Shaw began his hike to the camp. He couldn't afford to be missed. He glanced back once and looked over the scene, so similar to the one where Adam had committed suicide, in that it was a crime the law enforcers had no interest in preventing, and about which they had no desire to find the truth.

There was one difference, however. Here, only one cop took a selfie with the burning car and the bodies inside. The rest were too busy making calls and telling jokes to go to the trouble to play paparazzi.

41.

Shaw had taken care of his father's commandment about finding an escape route.

For the moment he had no intention of escaping, though. He would stay as long as it took to find proof of Eli's guilt.

But now that the battle lines were clear, he turned to satisfying his father's second fundamental rule:

In unfamiliar and potentially hostile territory . . .

Never be without an escape route.

Never be without access to a weapon.

If he were found out in his hunt for incriminating evidence against Eli and Hugh, it would come to a fight. There was no doubt about that. And he wouldn't simply be roughed up and told to leave. He'd be hunted down and killed.

So, a weapon.

A firearm would be ideal; it was a deterrent and, in his skilled hands, could wound, taking an enemy out of commission.

He supposed there were guns in the Assistance Unit but getting inside would be next to impossible. And any weapons would probably be locked away in a gun safe.

Though it seemed unlikely, the mysterious Building 14 might contain weapons.

He might steal a knife from the kitchen but bladed weapons were problematic. The only practical way for someone armed with a knife to stop an opponent was to kill him. Nonlethal stabbing or slashing didn't traumatize the body sufficiently to debilitate; to do so, significant blood loss was required and that usually was a short step away from death.

Having just borrowed from indigenous culture in his chase to save John, he turned to the source again. In his father's survival training, the children had made tools from wood and stone. They'd also made weapons.

Warrior tribes of the North American continent in the nineteenth century were skilled marksmen and bowmen but it was braver and more prestigious to "count coup" in battle: getting close enough to the enemy to strike them with hand or a ceremonial coup stick—it was like a whip. Often warriors didn't even kill their enemy; they humiliated them with a simple, harmless touch. A warrior kept a record of his coup count all his life and indicated it in carvings and on clothing.

One of the favorite ways to both count coup and wound or kill the enemy was to use a war club.

At the battle of the Little Big Horn, General George Custer and more than two hundred soldiers were killed. Most of those lives were lost by bullets, followed by arrows, but many soldiers were killed with clubs.

The weapon could be lethal or just debilitating, used in close-quarters fighting and also thrown. It would be perfect for his needs here.

Shaw had no tools so he searched the ground for shale or other brittle rock with a sharp edge. This wasn't difficult; hundreds of rock fragments littered the forest floor. This had been glacial land eons ago. He found a piece, about three pounds in weight, with a reasonably good edge on it. This would not be the head of a club but an improvised axe to prepare the handles. He would make two weapons, he decided. It never hurt to have backup.

The handles would be fresh, green wood, about an inch and a half in diameter. Fallen branches were tempting but they would be too brittle to use, so he needed to cut a sapling. His father had taught him that willow was best but there was none here, so he settled on another good choice: a privet stem, a species that's often used in decorative gardens. It took only five minutes, using his shale axe, to strip a suitable trunk and chop two pieces, eighteen inches or so in length. He split the ends.

For the head of a traditional club, smooth river rock is the best, but you need time and a hearty hammer to notch the surface for a steady fit in the handle. This wouldn't work so he collected two pieces that had rough faces, which would allow for a fair grip within the privet.

The head was traditionally bound into the handle with leather cord. He'd have to improvise this too. He found a growth of dogbane, which is related to milkwood. Selecting two four-foot brown stalks, he snapped them off at the base and then stripped them of their seed pods. He then cracked them open with a rock and dug out the inner core. The resulting fibrous strips were as strong as cotton rope.

Shaw now jammed the rocks into the split at the end of the handles, and used the dogbane strips to bind the wood above and below the heads. He tested them. The rocks were held tight. The clubs felt good in his hands, the weight and balance just right. Good for fighting and good for throwing. The rock heads were five pounds each.

But no. Not "rock." His father would have corrected him: "It's 'rock' in the wild," Ashton said. "When it serves a human purpose—a Michelangelo sculpture or a spear tip—it becomes 'stone.'"

Young Colter had once asked what difference it made.

"Never be imprecise," his father had replied.

Shaw now circled to the back of the eastern dormitories and hid the clubs in a pile of leaves directly behind Building C. From his room he could get to them via the back door or the window in seconds. By rights, they should dry off the ground but they'd be good enough for the next day or so. His investigation would have to move fast. He wouldn't let anyone else die at the hands of the cult.

The echoing tones of Beethoven filled the valley, then: "The time is six forty-five p.m."

Just enough time for one more errand. Colter Shaw disappeared back into the forest.

42.

As he stood in the queue for dinner, Colter Shaw once again scanned around him to see if he could spot the orange-sunglasses man, Frederick.

Was he the Companion who'd been looking at him at the immortality discourse?

He recalled too that while he was following Victoria, he'd believed that he had been the subject of surveillance himself.

However, if so, wouldn't this Frederick have turned Shaw in?

Rule 11. If you see any suspicious behavior, tell someone in the Inner Circle or with the Assistance Unit immediately. Remember: we are all responsible for the security and the Sanctity of the Osiris Foundation.

The snitch rule . . .

The doors opened and the cattle trod forward—now that he knew the true nature of the Foundation, Shaw's cynicism was back. It was hard to look at those in the room and not wonder how many, like Victoria, were finding comfort in the thought of ending their lives and starting over in a perfect Tomorrow, never mind how their friends and family would be devastated by the unforgivably narcissistic act.

The image came into his mind of the Select's look as he poured the gasoline and set it aflame. He steadied his breathing and forced the memory away.

Tonight, he was assigned to Table 5. He noted that John's name was nowhere to be seen on the seating chart. There'd be a story concocted about his absence. What would it be?

Abby and Henry were at his table too, as last night, though Walter and Sally were not. He noted them across the room. She appeared to be having a memory lapse; her face exhibited bewilderment.

Shaw sat and struck up a conversation with the woman beside him. Novice Kate was mid-twenties, exotic looking, with long raven hair and a pale complexion. She tried to keep up her end of the conversation but Shaw could sense her depression. She'd found out about the Foundation at a grief counseling session. There was a reference to the military. A combat widow, Shaw guessed.

When would this woman be asked to the Study Room, like Victoria, Abby and any number of the others? He realized now that most of the unaccompanied women were young and attractive.

He glanced at Victoria, two tables away, looking down at her open notebook.

The voice from on high announced the Journeymen could serve themselves, and the Inner Circle Companions walked to their assigned tables. Journeyman Marion was the host at Shaw's table. She was in her forties, lean, with short gray hair and slender features. Pleasant enough but terse, eyeing the Companions at her table even more closely than Journeyman Quinn had on the first night.

"Novice Carter?" Samuel had come up behind Shaw and was leaning down. "A word?"

Shaw rose and followed him. Marion glanced their way. Shaw's impression was that private conversation between trainers and Companions was, if not against the rules, unusual. She returned to her conversation with Abby, whom she was sitting next to.

The pudgy man cleaned his glasses and replaced them. "We can discuss this more in our next session but I wanted to say one thing now. You can meditate on it. Your situation with your brother? After all you told me, I have a thought."

Shaw nodded for him to continue.

"I think he didn't *want* to leave. He felt he had no choice. If you pursue him now, and find him, he's just going to keep running. But, given some time, he will come back."

"Why do you say that?"

"A protector sometimes protects best by leaving those who're in his care. The way birds lead predators away from their young." He gave his grandfather smile. "You were *largely* honest but not completely honest. You'll need to fill me in a bit more."

Shaw gave a laugh too, both because the script called for it, and because it was true.

"Thank you, Journeyman Samuel."

They gave the shoulder salute and then returned to their respective tables.

The meal continued, as choreographed as before.

With one exception: a napkin caught fire from one of the Sterno cans under a chafing dish. Shaw, having returned to his table with his plate of food, played the hero by grabbing a pitcher of water and dousing the minor blaze. He was greeted with a round of real applause, not the metronomical clapping of the ICs.

When the voice announced the time as eight o'clock, Shaw was preparing to bus away the dishes, when over the dining hall loudspeaker came: "Companions, please remain in your seats."

Like last night, a murmuring flowed through the room as Eli, Anja, Steve and the two bodyguards entered. The ICs started the clapping and Eli smiled and raised his hands. He gave the shoulder salute.

Accompanied by Steve, Eli walked to the back of the room where a low stage had been placed, a waist-high table sitting in the middle. Steve ducked into the kitchen and returned with a wine bottle and some glasses, which he placed on the table.

An IC handed Eli a microphone and the master stepped onto the stage. Since everyone else was sitting, the stage was probably unnecessary but Shaw knew Eli would have ordered it because of his height.

The clapping died. "I'd like to ask Apprentices Taylor, Margery, Ben and Marcus to come forward."

The foursome did and one of the two women, a stunning fashion-model blonde, fired an adoring gaze toward him.

Eli nodded and Steve poured wine and distributed glasses. Eli lifted his. "These four Companions have completed the second phase of the Process. I'm proud of the hard work they have put into their reflections and meditations. They are an honor to the Osiris Foundation. And tonight they are advancing to the level of Journeyman. Please recite with me: From the Yesterday, a better Today. From the Today, a perfect Tomorrow."

Everyone did this.

The ICs clapped and chanted, "Journey-man, journey-man." Over and over.

Shaw realized he wasn't clapping—and that Journeyman Marion was eyeing him. He joined the crowd, hoping he hid the disgust he felt.

The four new Journeymen drank their wine. Steve then handed out purple infinity amulets, and took back the red ones. Eli then addressed the room.

"My dear Companions. You must never forget your responsibility to be vigilant. Remember that we face threats. People say we're nonsense. They'll try to stop us. They don't like what I'm saying. They don't like the truth.

"There are the religious who hate me because what I know invalidates their superstition. There are those in the medical world who hate me because I've proved that this one body of ours is *not* all there is to life. There are self-help gurus who hate me because I expose them as charlatans. And then there are just those who hate anyone who's ahead of his time. What do we call these haters?"

A number of people shouted: "Toxics."

"Anyone who would question me, threaten me . . . betray me from outside, or within, is a Toxic. And we have to be on guard constantly. They want to stop me from helping you. They want to deprive you of what my

Process can do. They want to make sure you never see the Tomorrow."

Angry murmuring.

Shaw scanned the room. Just as during Eli's bizarre Second Discourse, the one on immortality, some Companions were taking the message under advisement—but again there were plenty of troubled faces, evidence that they bought into what he was saying: that there's an enemy out there that threatens the Foundation, the Process and Eli himself. And that therefore threatens them.

Then, the call-and-response chant: "The best . . . is yet to come!" After the voices grew quiet, the dinner was over.

The four walked off the stage and headed for their seats, though the blond inductee—she was Taylor—hung back, smiling toward Eli. He walked past her, directly to Victoria. Taylor took the snub like a slap to the face. Apparently she'd been thinking that the ceremony would continue privately in the Study Room.

She returned to her place at the table and kept up appearances by chatting with all those who congratulated her, but her eyes cut frequently to the conversation Victoria and Eli were having.

Eli whispered into Victoria's ear. She smiled and rose. Shaw looked past them and noted someone else observing them. Anja. Her arms were crossed, her face an emotionless mask. The entourage started from the hall, Victoria with them, the guards at the rear, en route to the Study Room.

When they were almost to the door, Victoria swayed and reached out for a table to steady herself. Frowning, Eli turned toward her. She dropped to her knees. Those left in the hall—about half the Companions—murmured or gasped.

Eli said, "Apprentice Victoria . . ."

Shaw heard her say, "I, something's wrong. I—" She winced, gripping her belly. Then, supporting herself with one arm, she vomited violently.

Two women ICs stepped forward quickly and helped Victoria to a chair. She blurted, "I'm fine."

"You're not fine," one of the women said. "Here." She dampened a napkin and gave it to Victoria, who wiped her face.

Her face darkened with a burst of anger Shaw hadn't expected. Her hands were clenched. "I really am okay."

Eli turned to Steve and whispered, "Clean this up."

"I'll call maintenan—"

"I didn't say to call anyone," Eli raged. "I said clean it up." The first instance of temper Shaw had seen in the man. The display was unsettling.

"Yes, Master Eli." Steve quickly walked into the kitchen.

Victoria was breathing deeply. "I don't know what happened. Something just hit me." She looked down. "I'm sorry, sir . . . Master Eli. I really am okay."

Eli said, "Oh, my dear, don't worry. We'll get you to the infirmary tonight." He was still livid—his "study session" for the evening had been ruined—but didn't want to melt down in front of his flock.

Victoria said, "The Study Room, tomorrow?"

"We'll see." Eli put his hand on her head. "You get some rest tonight."

Her face still bore the blush of dismay. Her head was down.

The IC who'd handed her the napkin took her hand and helped her up and toward the side door, after—of course—Victoria had grabbed her precious notebook.

Eli's attention was back on the dining hall. His eyes settled on Taylor, the blonde he'd rebuffed earlier. Her face was somber initially but then it softened, as if *she* were apologizing to *him*.

But the debate ended quickly. His face twisted into what might pass for a sneer and he turned away. Tears glistened in the woman's eyes.

Shaw noted Anja, watching, with no more emotion than when Eli had picked his Study Room partner earlier.

Then the reconstituted entourage glided out the side door, as Steve returned with mop and pail and set to work.

43.

Verbena is a flowering plant that has quite the history in spiritualism.

Ironically, given the official name of Eli's Foundation, in ancient Egypt the plant was called Tears of Isis—after Osiris's wife, the woman who, literally, put her husband back together.

One variety of verbena was used on Jesus's wounds after he was taken down from the cross, which earned it the name Holy Herb. In indigenous American culture, some tribes use it for dream divination.

Colter Shaw was aware of verbena in its secular role: it can be used to induce regurgitation in case one ingests poison in the field. A tincture of verbena acts just like ipecac and does the job nicely—if, as always, unpleasantly.

After he'd learned what the Study Room "special studies" were, Shaw had decided: Victoria was not going to participate. Obviously one could argue it wasn't his business. And it was decidedly condescending of him to make the decision. But he didn't care. He didn't see the situation as much different from Eli's preying on Abby. One was underage; the other suicidal and vulnerable—and both under the malignant sway of a dangerous sociopath.

But how to stop the assault and not give away his investigative mission?

He remembered seeing verbena flowers in the forest behind the dormitories when he'd made the war clubs. After hiding the weapons he returned to the woods and picked enough of the plant to make a proper dose. In his room he dried the herbs in the microwave then rubbed them between his palms to make tiny flakes. He didn't think they would be particularly detectable; verbena is slightly sweet—not bitter like most emetic herbs—but has no real flavor. He wrapped the powder in a page torn from his notebook.

Then he headed to the dining hall. He knew the correct concentration of the drug. It would do nothing worse than induce vomiting. Provided Victoria wasn't allergic, of course.

The odds of that?

He didn't play the percentage game. He wasn't going to let a sexual assault happen and, since she was going to the clinic, the doctors would recognize an allergic reaction and respond accordingly.

As far as administering the verbena to her, that was easy.

Shaw set fire to the buffet table.

When he'd gotten his plate, he'd slid a napkin near the Sterno can. As he returned to his seat, it flared up. With everyone's eyes on the flames, he'd stepped to Victoria's table and—reaching across it for a water pitcher to play fireman—he opened his palm, releasing the verbena onto her plate of lasagna. He could see she never noticed.

The effects of that dosage, he knew, wouldn't last long. She'd be feeling better already, physically. But he was sure she was still dismayed that she'd missed the chance to give herself to the man who was teaching her how to reunite with her lost family.

As he now stepped from the dining hall into the cool, clear evening, Shaw knew she'd be hoping for another chance to visit Eli in the Study Room.

But that wouldn't happen.

For her or anyone else.

Colter Shaw would make certain of that.

Just give me one document about an offshore bank account in Nevis or Saint Thomas, Shaw thought. Maybe a video Eli filmed of liaisons in the Study Room, revealing a sexual assault. A memo hinting at tax evasion.

What Shaw hoped for most was something linking Eli to the murder of journalist Yang in San Francisco. A phone bill, emails.

He also wanted a list of the other Selects and where they were located. These men were, of course, time bombs.

Shaw would ideally find something, then hike out of the camp east to the highway and get the evidence to federal or state police, not the corrupt Snoqualmie Gap cops.

Where would be the best places to find something incriminating?

Administration, of course.

Building 14? He was looking at it now. Still two AUs

in chairs in the front. Why the guards? And what was the purpose of the earlier furtive visit by the Selects?

Eli's residence too. It would probably be the source for the most damning evidence, if there were any. Eli would keep it close to home.

He'd start with Building 14. He slipped into the strip of grass on the eastern edge of the camp and made his way to the back of the structure.

Shaw noted no security cameras. The AUs in front were talking, which meant they were distracted. Would they patrol back here? Not likely at this time of night, but even if so, on a windless evening he'd hear them coming.

The back door was a solid piece of wood, no windows. He examined the jamb carefully—no evidence of an alarm but, nowadays, there were so many subtle security systems, there could easily be one. The odds? He'd already been told there'd never been a theft here. Why go to the expense of an alarm? He recalled too that when the golf cart of Selects had entered the building the other day, they didn't seem to have to shut off any security systems.

Shaw placed the risk of alarm at twenty percent.

Low enough to take the chance.

As for the entry itself? Not a problem. His father had drummed into the children that there might be occasions when they would have to break the law—to escape from threats, to steal food and weapons, to survive.

"Survival," he liked to say, "bends the ethics."

And so Ashton taught Dorion, Colter and Russell the basics of lock picking. This door was as simple as they came. No deadbolt. The locking mechanism was in the knob: a tumbler for the key, a face plate, a striking plate. A pro would go in through the keyhole with a motorized lock pick. Bang, open in ten seconds. Shaw didn't have that luxury, though he did have an alternative tool: a dinner knife, which he'd just copped from the table in the dining hall. He supposed there might be an inventory but sometimes you just had to take a chance or two.

It was a simple if tedious job. The technique was to insert the blade, use it to slide the bolt away from the hole where it was seated in the strike plate. Then you pulled on the door hard to grip the bolt, which was spring-loaded, keeping it from popping back into the locked position. Shaw did this a dozen times, moving the bolt a millimeter each instance. Two dozen. Three.

Finally with a last tug, he pulled the door open. No lights, no blaring alarms.

He examined the ceiling and walls. No cameras.

He stepped inside and eased the door shut. The place was dim but illuminated by light bleeding in from under the front door and, faintly, through the painted windows.

Shaw looked around him. If he wasn't so conscious of trying to remain absolutely quiet, he would have sighed angrily.

What was the secret that the AUs were guarding and that the zombie-like Selects had carted in?

Gardening supplies.

That was all: bags of carrot, wheat, corn, green bean seeds and fertilizer, containers of rodent and pest killer, rakes and hoes, some gas-powered tillers.

No firearms.

No file cabinets.

Discouraged, Shaw left the building and eased the door quietly closed. He listened for a moment but sensed no variation in the guards' monotonous conversation at the front of the building. They hadn't heard his intrusion.

He walked to the Administration building next. There was a back door here too—the one through which Hugh's boys had dragged that poor reporter, Klein. Through the windows he could see workers, walking up and down the corridors. Three offices were illuminated and a half-dozen people came and went. Shaw guessed selling immortality was a booming business. He'd have to try a different time.

It was then he heard a snap and rustle in the brush. He dropped to his knees and turned toward the woods, irritated at his ridiculous light blue costume, which even in the negligible moonlight made him stand out in contrast to the black-green grass and foliage. He closed his eyes briefly—to help focus his hearing—and listened. Yes. Another, similar sound. Not steps so much as a settling, as if a spy were crouching the same way he was, to make a smaller target of himself. He thought again of Frederick.

Or was someone else following him?

A killer Select?

He remained absolutely silent.

Nothing more.

Get on with the task.

The third source for incriminating evidence—the residence.

He eased up to it, staying in the bushes. The large structure would be occupied too, of course. The two bodyguards, Squat and Gray. Steve would be somewhere in the building by now. The dressing-down in the dining hall would mean little to him. Puppies like that didn't go very far from their masters, even after their leashes were jerked.

Gazing at the octagon atop the building, Shaw saw Anja staring out the window over the camp, which to her was probably just a pattern of yellow lights. She was brushing her long hair absently. He didn't see Eli.

The fifteen notes reverberated on the cool air. "The time is now ten p.m. All Companions will return to their dormitories. The curfew is now in effect."

He couldn't afford to be caught. He'd storm the castle tomorrow.

Besides, according to the rules, the wild animals were descending on the camp, impatient and eager for their entrees.

44.

With the absence of clocks and watches, Colter Shaw didn't know the exact time when they came for him.

The sky was still dark and he felt as if he'd slept for only an hour; he guessed it was around midnight when his door crashed open and two burly AUs seized him by the arms and dragged him out of bed.

"The hell's this?" he snapped. Whether he was playing a role or not, this is exactly what anybody would have said.

"Quiet. You're coming with us."

"No. I'm not going any—"

"Shut up."

One of the AUs flung his uniform and shoes toward Shaw. "Get dressed."

"What did I do? What's—"

"Get dressed. Or we'll drag you through the camp the way you are."

Shaw got dressed.

Five minutes later he was being escorted through the

back door of the Assistance Unit. Gripping his arms near the threshold of pain, the men led him up a corridor and into a small interrogation room, like one of those in police departments the world over. It contained only a table and two functional gray metal chairs. These walls were not purple and did not exhibit Egyptian artifacts or paintings. They were white. It was warm inside and the smell was of pine cleanser.

Claustro *is Latin for "bolt," as in bolting the door. And who doesn't know what* phobia *is?*

Shaw was positive that one of these AUs had been present at Hugh's beating of the reporter.

They turned and closed the door behind them.

Leaving Shaw to reflect on the list of offenses that had been committed by Novice Carter. The knife theft, the break-in at the gardening supply building, the verbena seasoning of Victoria's dinner, the sprinting attempt to save John from a horrific death. It occurred to him that they didn't really need cameras, since Eli had turned his followers into snitches to dime out any Toxics.

Now he was sure he'd been right about being tailed. Twice: on the way to speak with Victoria, and just a few hours ago after the break-in at Building 14.

Who was the spy? Frederick or someone else?

The door opened and Hugh walked inside, accompanied by the AU who'd held the journalist's mouth to stifle any cries when Hugh dislocated his shoulder. This man stood in the corner. Hugh sat and scrolled through a tablet. Glancing up at Shaw, he gestured toward the other chair.

"So?" Carter Skye would be understandably uneasy

under these circumstances. On the other hand, like Adam Harper, he'd done time, had a troubled childhood, had been a scrapper when younger. He was in rock-solid shape. The play Shaw had written did not call for the main character to be intimidated easily.

"Sit."

He did, after a tang of defiance.

Of course, there was always the possibility they had learned that Mr. Skye was a character of fiction, and that Colter Shaw was the one they'd invited into this soundproofed, windowless chamber. No one had used a name in addressing him. Which of the two alter egos did they think he was?

If they knew he was a spy, then acting was irrelevant. It would be a fight. He was thinking of potential combat solutions to the situation when he noticed that the AU in the corner was holding a stun gun.

Hugh looked up from the tablet; Shaw could not see what was on the screen. The supervisor said in a gravelly voice, "What's Rule Fourteen?"

"Don't do anything to dis . . ." He stumbled on the word. ". . . to mess with the integrity of Master Eli, other staff, the Foundation or the Process."

If Hugh was impressed by his memorization skills, the AU didn't indicate it.

"That word, 'integrity.' It has two meanings, you know."

Shaw blinked. "I don't know . . . It means honesty or something, right? The hell's going on here?"

Hugh continued, "And it means structurally sound. Like the integrity of a ship's hull."

"Does it?" He eyed Hugh closely.

"Both of those apply to your behavior."

Damn it, use a name. Let me know who you're talking to. Carter or Colter. Would it come to a fight? Him against the three here?

Hugh flipped through his tablet. "What you've done is a crime against both types of integrity. You've betrayed Master Eli and you've jeopardized the Foundation itself."

"Still don't know what you're talking about."

"We have evidence. Witnesses."

"Bullshit."

Hugh blinked.

Shaw leaned close and snarled, "You got it, let me see it, asshole."

"What?" Hugh whispered, aghast. The other AU regarded Shaw warily.

"Now! The evidence. And the witnesses. Bring them in here."

"You don't talk to us that way, Novice Carter."

So it seemed they didn't have the complete dirt on him. Hugh could, however, still order him Tased and beaten for the sins committed by Carter Skye.

Rule 14 . . .

"Master Eli does good work here. Hundreds of people lead better lives thanks to him. And you'd endanger all that by being disloyal?" Hugh nodded to the AU, who now brandished the stun gun.

"We want to know what your motive is, who's the Toxic you're working for? Or are you here on your own?"

The AU muttered, "Maybe he's in it for the money. He's here to steal the Process. It's happened before."

"We'll find out." Hugh glanced at the Taser.

The AU hit a button and a faint red light glowed like a snake's eye caught in a flashlight beam.

45.

"Whatever you think I did, it's a mistake," Shaw said in a firm voice.

Hugh held up his hand. The armed AU paused.

"I came here because my life is messed up. All the issues I told Journeyman Samuel about. And when I saw what Master Eli's done for the Companions, when I heard how he can change our lives forever, I knew I'd come to the right place. This is . . . What you're saying is crap. You've got me mixed up with somebody else. I haven't been disloyal. I never would. Master Eli is one of the most brilliant, generous people on earth."

Shaw rose and turned to Hugh. "I swear I haven't done anything." Sounding unnerved, supplicating.

The two captors seemed to relent a bit at this.

Which is when he spun to the right, knocked the Taser man's hand aside and in a simple wrestling takedown, upended his opponent and slammed him to the floor.

A curious noise came from the throat. Maybe trying to form words. Maybe just trying to breathe.

Shaw paid no attention. In an instant he ripped the Taser from the gasping man's grip and turned it on the other two. He eyed them calmly, as if searching for the optimal target. Equally unemotional, Hugh watched him carefully.

Shaw muttered, "Your information is wrong. Don't you or anybody else threaten me again. We clear on that?" He tossed the Taser to the floor near the hurting AU.

Then behind Shaw, the clapping started—that infectious, staccato clapping, beating out the time to the "Ode to Joy." He turned.

The sound was coming from Eli, who stood in the doorway, his head cocked, his generous lips in a slight smile. He lowered his hands and nodded at Hugh and the gasping AU, who struggled to his feet, looking with more trepidation at Hugh than at the man who'd just decked him. He collected the Taser. Hugh was clearly not pleased that his man had been bested. But he glanced at Shaw and nodded with grudging respect. Hugh stepped from the room, his minion scurrying after, holding his chest.

Before the door closed, Shaw glimpsed one of the bodyguards, Gray, whose lined face gave off no emotion whatsoever. Then he noted Squat and Steve appear, the latter with his ever-present notebook.

The lock clicked and Eli and Shaw were alone.

"Well done, Novice Carter. You passed with flying colors."

Colter Shaw had in fact decided, about halfway through the kidnapping, that the incident had all the earmarks of a test. Hugh hadn't been specific, citing only "disloyalty," not any particular transgressions. Generic "evidence" and "witnesses." And there'd been a stiffness about his delivery. He'd also decided that if he were to move up in the organization, and get access to the evidence he sought, he'd need to act the part of a Select.

"This is a rite of passage, a test of loyalty. You'd be surprised by the reactions. Some break down and say, yes, yes, forgive me, father, I have impure thoughts about Journeyman Allegra or Journeyman Bill, or yes, I quote 'borrowed' one of the AU's phones to call my wife because she was having a baby.

"And some people have admitted they'd contacted other organizations to give them details on the Process. Or journalists who snuck in to write exposés."

Shaw wondered what their fates were. He didn't ask.

He pulled out his friend Carter Skye to help. "I wouldn't do anything to screw up the Process. After my session with Journeyman Samuel and your Second Discourse? Never. That was amazing."

Shaw had almost said, "Gorgeous," but decided it might be taken for mockery.

"Oh, it is, isn't it? Did you really like it? I'm so thrilled. I knew from the beginning that you were special. I have a good eye for people. I can size people up like nobody else. It's a skill I was born with."

Raging narcissist . . .

He opened the door and asked Steve to join them. Eli shared a look with his gofer and then turned to Shaw. He said solemnly, "It's my pleasure to raise you to the rank of Apprentice." He nodded to Steve, who withdrew a necklace at the end of which was a red infinity sign amulet. Eli lifted Shaw's blue one off his neck and replaced it with the new one.

Eli said, "I like to reward good behavior."

As true cults do, he recalled.

A system of rewards and punishments . . .

"I think you deserve a trip to the Study Room."

Shaw immediately saw it as an opportunity to do some espionage work.

Eli walked closer to Shaw. "You have a choice. Anja, or me."

Shaw returned his gaze. "Anja."

"Ah. Of course." There was no disappointment in the man's face. He had plenty of other Companions for his own diversions.

"Steve, take him there."

"Yes, Master Eli."

Steve gestured toward the door. "Apprentice Carter."

Shaw turned to follow. Eli stepped closer, laid a hand on his shoulder and squeezed. "Enjoy your studies."

46.

The opportunity for surveillance, however, didn't materialize.

Shaw had hoped that Steve would escort him to the front door of the residence and tell him something like: up the stairs, second door on the left. Which would have given him time to prowl. But, no, the underling apparently had orders to not let Companions go unattended here.

As he was led through the halls, Shaw noted that the place was opulent, the walls hung with fine paintings, sculpture sat on the tables, the furniture was chrome and ebony and rosewood and supple leather. Nothing Egyptian about the décor here; it had a ritzy, over-the-top, Miami Beach feel. David Ellis had been, after all, a Florida businessman.

Shaw saw no guards or CCTV cameras. This would be good for future incursions. But nor did he see any obvious offices or record storage rooms.

Steve directed him to an unmarked door on the second floor and knocked.

"Come in." A woman's voice.

The Study Room was a love nest dominated by a huge circular bed that could hold four or five souls. It was a chamber that kept true to the Egyptian theme, hangings, murals, ankhs, bas-reliefs of Osiris or some other gods; Shaw didn't know the pantheon of the ancient kingdom. Pungent incense burned.

Love nest . . .

Osiris was, after all, the god of fertility, as well as the underground.

Steve then turned and sat on a bench in the hallway. He began flipping through a notebook that seemed to contain most of Master Eli's life.

A prize Shaw would love to get his hands on.

Walking inside, Shaw closed the door behind him. Wearing a silk robe—purple, of course—Anja nodded from where she sat on the bed.

He gave the shoulder salute. Anja smiled and did not respond but rose and walked to a cabinet. "Do you want a drink?"

"Drink?"

"There're no rules in the Study Room."

"I'm good."

"You don't mind?" she asked, lifting a penciled eyebrow.

"Go right ahead."

Anja made a cocktail. Vodka was involved, it seemed, fruit juice. She hurried with the concoction and didn't bother with ice.

There was a couch, facing the bed, and Shaw sat on it.

"Your name?" he asked. "Russian?"

She seemed surprised that he'd asked about her. The protocols for the "reward" of the Study Room were probably pretty well established and didn't involve much conversation. "Yes. It means 'grace.' She looked at his amulet. "An Apprentice already? My. After two days." A soft laugh. "Are you ready for the storm?"

He frowned.

"It takes some people a week or more. You'll get some scowls."

"I've been scowled at before."

"You're different."

"Am I? I don't know enough about everyone here to figure out what's normal, what isn't."

She sipped. "I'm sure you've got your problems. But you're not needy. Everyone else here is; that's why they come." Now, a deeper sip. "What're we celebrating?"

"He wants me to be a Select."

"Ah, that makes sense. His own private crew. The monks, the Knights of the Round Table. He doesn't even talk about them to me . . . Well, one *more* thing he doesn't talk to me about."

"How long have you known him?"

"Ten years."

"You met on, what? Some kind of spiritual thing?"

A pause. "We met in a different life."

Did she mean the 1800s or five years ago at a stock-broker convention in Fort Lauderdale? This wasn't what she was here for. Anja didn't want to be interviewed about herself and Eli. She didn't like being offered as a prize in a Cracker Jack box. However, Shaw's impression was that she preferred sex to the questions.

She rose and clicked a light off and when she sat once more, the top of her robe fell open slightly.

"You've gone through the Process?" he asked, glancing at the purple amulet.

"Of course."

"So you can see past lives?"

A hesitation.

"I've done the work."

"Why the lotuses?" Shaw asked, looking around the room at several potted plants. He believed he could smell sweat and perfume, in addition to the sandalwood. This was the conquest bed, the one in which Victoria had nearly been a victim.

"It's the symbol of immortality."

Anja lifted a black brush and stroked her hair. He recalled her doing this earlier, as she stood in the gazebo.

She said, "I was pretty when I was younger. I was a model and a hostess at some posh clubs. That's the world where I met . . . Master Eli."

Had the man's real name, David, been about to trip into the scented atmosphere around them?

"You're pretty now." This was true. "You two married?"

"There was a ritual. Maybe it's not official, technically. But I like to think it is. I kind of wanted the white dress thing. I still have my mother's."

"Maybe in the Tomorrow."

"Maybe."

He couldn't tell if she believed Eli's Process. Maybe

she did. You could convince yourself of almost anything if you wanted to. He himself believed that his brother, Russell, would emerge and they would resume their relationship from years ago.

Which, curiously, Samuel had predicted earlier that evening.

Sometimes the protector protects best by leaving those who're in his care . . .

She drained her drink, set the glass on a table and tugged her robe open farther. Then lay back on the bed. Her body language signaled: the sooner started, the sooner finished.

Shaw noted an infinity tattoo on the upper arch of her left breast.

She followed his glance.

"Aren't I lucky? Only the Selects and a few others are inked with the sign. He's had me marked twice. Nobody else ever got more than one."

Shaw rose and sat on the bed. He reached for the robe and she arched her back, eyes closed, face lifted to the ceiling. He tugged her gown back together. She looked at him, frowning, appearing mystified. And perhaps concerned— that someone had defied Eli by not taking the present he'd offered.

"Are you more interested in Steve? He'd be available."

"No. I'd be interested in you. Under different circumstances."

She tightened the belt around the gown. "I'm such a fool." Tears welled in the corners of her eyes.

Shaw sometimes wondered if foolishness didn't follow from love the way a shadow precedes us when the sun is behind. Sometimes hazy, sometimes sharp, but always present.

Again, an image of Margot Keller's long face appeared. Twice now, in the camp, he'd thought of the woman, who was around his age and willowy and had soft dark-blond curls. He reflected now that he'd always thought of her face as that of a Greek goddess. Ironic that he was here in a room dominated with art from the ancient world.

"It's late." He rose.

"Wait." She gave a faint wince.

He lifted an eyebrow.

"He'd expect you to stay longer. He might think I . . . I didn't do enough. Steve'll tell him. He'd have words with me. Maybe more." She took a tissue and wiped her cheek. The makeup had covered up a bruise. She wanted Shaw to see.

"Sure. Say forty-five minutes?"

"Thank you. Really, thank you." Leaving the robe on, she climbed under the blankets. "I took a pill. I'm tired. I might just sleep."

"Go right ahead."

Anja lay back. She lifted a hand his way, an ambiguous gesture that perhaps meant thank you.

Or: please don't pity me.

Shaw decided it probably meant both.

47.

June 17

The next morning, forgoing breakfast, Shaw resumed his mission to invade the residence. He paused, though, on the porch of his dorm. He'd recognized the noise, so very faint at first, then louder and louder, insistent.

A chest-pounding thud.

Looking over the sky, he finally spotted the sleek helicopter, speeding toward the camp from the southwest.

The craft was a large one, the cabin white, the tail dark blue. On the side were the letters CHP.

California Highway Patrol.

The sound took the attention of all the Companions on the grounds. Those walking stopped in their tracks. Those sitting looked up from their notebooks.

The bird made its elegant touchdown in a clearing on the north side of the camp, toward the wooden fence and the YESTERDAY, TODAY, TOMORROW gate. As the engines shut down, two men climbed out, both wearing suits. One was African American, quite large, with a shiny bald head. The man with him was white, slender. Both had gold badges on their belts.

They oriented themselves and walked to the nearest gravel path. The men approached a woman around forty, her blond hair pinned up in a bun. Shaw didn't recall her name but he'd met her and her husband, who was not present at the moment. The black detective displayed an ID badge and spoke to her. She appeared confused, looking around. She said a few words and pointed south, to the residence. The two officers started in that direction, looking around them. Shaw's impression was that they weren't sure what to make of the place.

Shaw approached the woman, who was frowning, as she looked after the officers. He nodded and gave the shoulder salute. She absently returned it.

"Apprentice Carter. What's your name again?"

"Apprentice Carole." Her face was troubled, her eyes on the residence.

"Were those San Francisco police?"

"Yes."

The SFPD no longer had an air patrol unit; it relied on the Highway Patrol's choppers for air transport. He noted that the pilot, a petite woman with black hair, wore a light green uniform blouse, with gray slacks. CHP colors.

"Was one of them Detective Etoile?"

She appeared lost in thought.

"Apprentice Carole?"

"I think so. Yes."

Shaw expected her to ask how he knew, though she didn't. She was clearly shaken—and, spotting her husband, Carole joined him. They began speaking.

When he arrived in the Square, Shaw saw the Companions were talking among themselves. The ICs were clustered together. Four Selects stood, silent, looking over the crowd. Three had arms crossed over their chests. Their faces were stone.

Behind the stage, Shaw could see Etoile, the other detective and Eli disappearing into the residence.

So the detective wasn't treating Yang's death as used chewing gum at all.

Would this be the end of the Foundation right here and now? But no, not yet, Shaw realized. If Etoile had marshalled enough evidence to directly link Yang's killer—Harvey Edwards—to Eli, he would have brought a full complement of tactical law enforcers, Washington State Patrol officers included. This was merely an interview. A fact-gathering mission.

Twenty minutes later, the two detectives left the residence and walked back to the helicopter. Shaw wished he could talk to the cops but of course that wouldn't work. He wasn't Colter Shaw; he was Carter Skye.

The engines of the craft fired up and, with the rotor noise changing pitch, dropping in tone, the chopper rose skyward and vanished back in the direction of Northern California.

What had the officers learned? And what was Eli's reaction?

A short time later the Beethoven notes rang from the loudspeakers and the voice said, "All Companions are to report to the Square."

No *please* this time.

The command was repeated.

Soon, with nearly everyone present, Eli and his entourage left the residence. The bodyguards remained at the foot of the stairs with Eli. Anja and Steve took their seats at the far end of the stage.

The "Ode to Joy" played twice. Then Eli climbed the stairs and strode to the front of the stage.

The ICs didn't get a chance to lead the metric applause. The crowd just burst into frenetic clapping.

Eli raised his arms.

Cries from the ground: "We love you!" "Our Guiding Beacon!" "Master Eli!"

Finally the noise diminished.

"Good friends and Companions. My *dear* friends and Companions . . . Did you see that? Did you see what just happened? Some Toxics planted fake reports about me. Fake news!"

There were boos.

"Fake . . . Fake . . ." The simple chant lasted for a full sixty seconds.

"A sad attempt by the Toxics to bring me down. That's what they'd like. To bring me down. And bring you down too!"

"No!"

"Hell with them!"

"We have a lot of enemies, you and me. Remember what I told you last night: the medical community hates us. Religion hates us. Politicians hate us. Because I tell the truth."

This started a chant of "True up! True up!"

"And it scares them! But it's the Toxics who should be afraid! I told them. I told those officers and now they understand. I'm being persecuted for my vision. I told them to arrest the Toxics who called them in the first place. It's a crime, misuse of judicial process. And I'm suing. I have the best legal team in the country. They're gorgeous! Nobody's going to get away with trying to hurt you, my family!"

Then, from somewhere in the back of the sea of Companions, a disturbance. Shouts. It seemed to Shaw that someone pushed another.

The bodyguards grew alert. Steve rose. Eli walked to the edge of the stage, irritated that the spotlight had figuratively been turned away from him. He called angrily, "What's that? What's going on?"

More confused words. It was hard to hear.

Then a shout from the back of the crowd. ". . . questioning you! Master Eli!"

Eli held up his hands for silence and peered into the crowd.

A skinny male Apprentice, with a sallow face, was pointing at a woman near him. It was Carole, whom the detectives from San Francisco had approached upon landing. Her husband stood beside her, looking flustered.

"She says you lied to us!"

Turning on the spigot of murmurs.

Eli said, "Hush, everyone!"

Carole, red faced and angry, pulled away from the woman who was gripping her by the shoulder.

Eli said to the slim man who'd called Carole out, "Tell me."

"She said . . ."

Carole stepped forward. "I didn't say you lied, Master Eli. I just . . . Well, those policemen. They asked for David Ellis. They said he was also known as Artie Ellington. And Hiram Lefkowitz. I just wondered, who are you really?"

A collective gasp.

Steve rose and whispered in Eli's ear, then returned to his seat.

In a solemn voice, Eli called, "Apprentice Carole. Come up here in front of me."

"I just . . ."

"Bring her here. Now!" He glanced at two AUs.

One of them stepped in front of Carole's husband and put a hand on his chest to keep him in place. The other gripped Carole's arm and ushered her to a place in front of the stage, directly below the cold gaze of Master Eli.

48.

Arms crossed, Eli looked down at the woman with an expression both bewildered and contemptuous. "Apprentice Carole. Did you think 'Eli' was my birth name?"

"I didn't know. It was just . . . odd. The police asking about different names you had. I was just wondering why."

"Oh, I do? I have more names?" Appearing deeply perplexed, he looked out over the audience, then returned his searing gaze to her. "Do I?"

"That's what that man said. The detective."

"So you know him."

"Know him? No. He just came up to me and asked where you were and he mentioned the other names."

Shaw glanced back at Thomas, her husband, who was arguing with the AU. The security man motioned to a Select, who uncrossed his arms and, in a slow lope, joined them. He whispered something to Thomas and the man fell silent.

"So you're assuming what he said was true."

"I . . . well . . ."

"You . . . well," Eli mocked. "Not very articulate at the moment, are we, Carole? You, *well*, don't know him but you, *well*, believe it when he says I have different names."

"I didn't say that. I'm just—"

Somebody shouted, "Yes, she did! She doubted you."

"She broke Rule Fourteen!"

"Did it ever occur to you that maybe the Toxic called the police, *claiming* I have other names?"

"I just . . ."

"Ah, we move from 'I *well*' to 'I *just*.' And you believed them. It never occurred to you that some Toxic learned that, yes, my given and family names are David Ellis. That's no secret. That's a matter of public record. Did you think I was born Master Eli? That's not something you see on birth certificates, now, is it?"

"No, I—"

He looked over his rapt audience, enjoying every moment. "Would you see that on birth certificates? I don't think so." Eli leaned down. "I died in the car crash!"

Whispers of sympathy for the poor man rose from the crowd.

"I died! Do you understand that? And when I died, I saw myself in the past, and saw that I was named Eli. And 'master'? A title, of course. One I earned, I like to think. Maybe you don't."

"Shame on her!"

"Toxic!"

"We love you, Master Eli!"

"Our Guiding Beacon!"

A man in the crowd stepped forward and shoved Carole. She barked a fast scream and stumbled back. Eli gave no reaction.

"Leave her alone," her husband shouted.

Another word from the Select shut him up.

"So Carole here is accusing me of something I haven't done. Is that fair? Is that right?"

A gasp from the crowd. It took Shaw a moment to understand the reaction. Eli hadn't used the title "Apprentice." Was she being ostracized?

"Punish her!"

"Didn't I tell you to look out for the Toxics? Look out for their lies? But you believe them, Carole, over me."

"No." Her eyes were wide. "I was just . . ."

Some in the crowd reacted with angry muttering. Someone, a young Journeyman, swatted Carole with his notebook. "Bitch," he muttered.

She was looking panicky now. "I was only . . . I didn't know what to think. Three names, different names. You can understand—"

"What I understand, Carole, is that I'm beginning to think *you're* a Toxic!"

"No. I just—"

"Just, just, just!" His mockery was fierce. "Carole, when you told me about the times your father came to your bedroom, when you were a teenager, I was sure you were innocent. But, seeing you now, taking the Toxics at their lying word over me, it makes me think you weren't so innocent after all."

"What?" Carole looked mortified.

"I'm thinking you're so toxic that your boyfriend had a good reason to put you in the hospital."

"That's not what happened." Gasping. "I didn't do anything! He was drinking. He hit me. He abused me!"

Eli smirked. "But he never went to jail, did he? If you were innocent and he was guilty, wouldn't he have been arrested?"

Red faced, choking back sobs, she looked toward Thomas. His face was a mask; apparently Carole had shared the hard details of her past with Eli but not with her spouse.

Like a lawyer on cross-examination, Eli snapped, "Did your boyfriend go to jail?"

"I was scared."

"So the answer's no. Look at this, Carole." He lifted his arms. "I was speaking to all our dear Companions, reassuring them that I can stand up to the Toxics. And you ruin it. Because you don't believe in me."

She'd lost and she knew it. "Please, Master Eli . . . I was wrong. I just . . ." She froze, afraid to be mocked again. "I wasn't expecting what they asked and said. I didn't think. Of course they were sent by some Toxics. They were Toxics too." Her voice dropped and she wiped tears. "You told my secrets to everybody."

Eli's voice was snide. "Because you broke the rules."

Most of the crowd was glaring at her. Cries of "Toxic!" And then: "Traitor!"

"Throw her out!"

"Judas."

Carole held her hands toward Eli. "Please."

He shook his head. "I never thought I'd have to question your loyalty."

"You don't have to."

"What happens to Toxics, Carol?"

She recited what was probably a lesson from a session with a trainer: "They don't true up. Their True Cores stay covered. They can never see the Yesterday and can never advance to the Tomorrow."

Dozens in the crowd took up a chant of "Toxic!" Hands clapped sharply on the first syllable.

Another man near Carole shoved her hard. An enraged woman slapped her face. Blood spurted from her nose, and she dropped to her knees, covering her head protectively. She was being pummeled and kicked. Someone flung a rock. It glanced off her forehead. She let out a faint scream.

The AUs and the Select were holding back Thomas, her husband. Shaw glanced at Henry, the bald man he'd been inducted with. Eight or ten other Companions too. They nodded.

Time for this to stop.

But before Shaw and the others stepped toward Carole, Eli lifted his hands. Everyone quieted. "All right, friends and Companions, enough. Enough!"

He strode off the stage and, flanked by his bodyguards, walked toward Carole. The crowd dutifully parted but not before one woman gave her a solid kick in the belly.

Eli looked the injured woman over, lying in the dust, curled up, an arm covering her bloody face.

Several Companions reached out and touched Eli's tunic as he passed.

He bent down and helped Carole to her feet, as the bodyguards kept watch. Shaw's impression was that this had happened before; a heretic punished. Two of the women ICs glanced at each other, exchanging sly smiles. They were enjoying the incident.

"I'm sorry, Master Eli." Carole choked on her sobs. "I was wrong."

"My poor friend and Companion. A shame you've been hurt." He looked out over the agitated crowd. "We never want violence." But it was clear Eli didn't mean this for a minute. He was close to smiling.

"Apprentice Carole. Everyone! Do you see the risk that the Toxics present? How they're terrified by my Process? By the truth? Do you see the lengths they'll go to to stop me? To turn us against each other? To bring me down? They know I can revolutionize the world. I'm a threat. They'll stop at nothing."

"Please," Carol sobbed, "can you forgive me?"

Eli studied her silently. Then he looked out over the crowd. "Shall we forgive her?"

Calls of "Toxic." "Punish her!"

Most, though, saw that Eli's retribution had come to an end. Steve began chanting, "Forgive her, forgive her!"

The rest of the crowd joined in. The chant was accompanied by the sharp, insect click of clapping.

Shaw glanced across the Square to Victoria. Who was not chanting or slapping her palms together. Emotionless, she stared at the sobbing woman and the man standing above her, his hand on her head.

Shaw wondered what might have happened if a cry of "Kill her" had spread into a chant. The image of a frenzied mob stoning the woman to death didn't feel at all outrageous just now.

Eli embraced Carole, blood staining his white tunic. This was a man who couldn't say no to a dramatic moment.

"It's all right, Apprentice Carol. All's forgiven." He looked toward Anja and gestured impatiently. The woman climbed down from the stage and put her arm around Carole. They walked toward the infirmary.

The Guiding Beacon returned to the stage.

Brilliant, Shaw thought. Eli had not only deflected attention from the police visit, the aliases and a past he didn't want to come to light; he'd also made clear disloyalty would be punished. Carole had told her trainer of the horrors and indignations of her past, assuming that they'd be kept confidential. Eli, though, had weaponized them. Everyone in the camp now knew that Eli had something on them. Betrayal had been taken off the table.

Eli announced there would be another Discourse today, an unscheduled one. Then he added: "Spend the next few hours on Introspection and journaling. And never forget: The best . . ."

". . . is yet to come!"

The ICs leapt in and kept the responsive chant going, smiling and striding about happily, as Eli and his crew walked off the stage. The Companions dispersed.

Shaw watched Carole's husband walk quickly toward the medical center. Shaw then spotted Walter walking his way. The man appeared to be looking for him.

"Hey, there," Walter said, his face clouded.

Shaw asked, "You see what just happened?"

"No. Something came up."

"What's wrong?"

"Sally's gone missing. She was in the room and I went out to see about that chopper. When I got back, she was gone."

"What is it exactly? Alzheimer's?"

"Yep. She's on meds. Galantamine. Doesn't do much for her."

"I'll help you look."

"You wouldn't mind? I'm more than a little worried."

49.

Did you tell the AUs?" Shaw asked.

"I did, yessir. But there's something going on. They said I had to deal with it myself. Then they scurried off like nervous mice."

A disaster control plan was being worked out, Shaw guessed, after Detective Etoile's unexpected appearance.

Walter's face was contracted with concern, eyes shooting left and right.

Shaw now recalled his earlier thought about the color of the shirts and blouses the Companions were issued. Easier to spot escapees, though also easier to find someone who'd gone missing.

The men started searching the Square, then expanded their orbit. The woman would be confined by the natural and man-made barriers on three sides but to the east was the high cliff—an eighty-foot fall—and the path Shaw had found that would lead eventually to the highway. But stray from the route to the road and you'd descend into thick woods and a labyrinth of canyons and rock formations, hundreds of square miles of wilderness. Falling and exposure were the big risks. Other threats existed too: wolves and mountain lions, coyotes and boar. Rattlers could be anywhere.

"Damn helicopter," Walter muttered. "Took my attention. Next I knew, she was gone. Maybe it spooked her. I don't know."

They tried the dining room. Inside was a table of Inner Circles, huddling and somber. The conversation was muted. Shaw also noticed a middle-aged couple in the corner, sitting over coffee. They were solemn too. He recognized them as two of the people who had stepped forward to save Carole from the mob. Shaw shared a nod with them.

The two men continued to circle the camp.

"Her short-term's shot, a lot of the time." Walter's right hand was clenched. "She'll remember what we had on our honeymoon dinner and what brand the plates were. The shape of the teacup handle. The name of the singer in the lounge. Forty-two years ago." He sighed and squinted as he gazed into the dense woods. "Where are you, honey?" he whispered.

As they asked Companions if anyone had seen Sally—no one had—Shaw observed that an uneasiness had descended over the camp. A division, it seemed, had formed among the Companions between Eli's true believers and those troubled by his treatment of Carole and undoubtedly the bogus philosophy of the Process, with the flames fanned by the appearance of the police. He witnessed arguments, some heated.

The two men walked in expanding circles through the

valley, then took to the woods. "It's like the forest preserve next to our house in Akron. We lived there thirty years ago. Might seem familiar to her. Another thing: she's unsteady too. I got her one of those watches that tells me if she falls. But they took it when we checked in. They said, Master Eli can work miracles. She'll be right as rain. So I gave in."

The path ended in a dead end against a rock face. They turned around. The sky was growing overcast. A wind had come up.

A snap of wood. Shaw held up a hand and Walter stopped. Shaw eyed rocks and branches he could use for weapons in the case of a wolf choosing to hunt in full daylight—a rarity—or a mountain lion.

He believed he saw movement about thirty yards behind them, where they'd just come from.

"Is it Sally?" Walter asked.

"No, either an animal or somebody in the bushes following us."

"Those AUs, they don't skulk. They just walk up and ask what you're about."

Shaw picked up a sharp rock and took a few steps toward the figure.

It seemed to recede. He dropped the weapon, and the men continued deeper into the woods, north toward the wooden wall.

"Where would she go?" Walter muttered.

Shaw gave it eighty-five percent that Sally would instinctively stick to a trail or creek bed. He didn't know much about memory illnesses but it seemed to him that what failed was data on a computer disk. Survival instincts would be like the operating system burned permanently onto the motherboard. A trail meant habitation, a creek bed meant an easier trek and water for drinking.

These became the focus of their search.

They swept for a half mile, moving in a compass arc with Sally and Walter's dormitory as the center point. Shaw stayed true to the course; he hadn't gotten lost in the woods since he was a young boy.

Ten minutes later Shaw heard a faint sound and stopped. Walter too, frowning and looking about.

Snap. Snap.

They turned toward the source. Shaw picked up another rock and together the men moved slowly toward the sound, navigating around a thick growth of blackberry.

Twenty feet away Sally stood on the bank of a shallow stream. She was frowning and, curiously, snapping her fingers.

"Honey!"

She glanced at her husband as if not the least surprised to see him; Shaw, though, was a stranger. He introduced himself and she nodded formally. Then her face darkened into a frown. She snapped her fingers again, in the air. "Bobo's gone. Ran off."

Walter said patiently, "We boarded him, remember? He's at the vet's. So we could come on the trip here."

"Oh, that's right. Silly of me. What was I thinking?"

Undoubtedly a pet they'd owned years ago.

"You're looking tired, love. How about you go for a nap."

"Think I wouldn't mind that."

The three of them walked back to their dorm. Walter took his wife inside and returned to the porch.

"Thank you, sir." He warmly shook Shaw's hand.

The men sat in teak rockers. Shaw eased back; the furniture was more comfortable than it appeared. He gazed out over the camp as several AUs hurried past. Their faces were grim. Also making a speedy transit was Journeyman Adelle, the beautiful Intake specialist.

I lost my baby . . .

"Bad move, this was," Walter said, when she was safely past them.

"Signing on?"

"We just came because there wasn't anything medicine could do for her, not really. Last resort. If this Foundation advertised on Alzheimer's websites, maybe there was something to it. I thought experimental drugs, maybe new techniques, surgery. Imagine when we got into the training and found out it was about getting a second chance the next time around—in a future life." He gave a cynical laugh. "Sally and I'd meet again. Her brain cells wouldn't be so jittery. Maybe I'd look like Brad Pitt and could shoot five under par at St. Andrews."

Lifting his arms, he muttered, "Then I realized it's a crock of horse manure I should've spotted right up front. Pluses, Minuses, past lives, future lives." He looked Shaw over. "You could report me for this."

"We're all good, don't worry."

"I figured." They gazed at more AUs, clutching their tablets and moving from Administration to a building across the Square. Walter continued, "We show up on this lumpy planet, blessed with some talents, and saddled with some busted mainsprings. It's what we do with it that's the trick. Sally and I, we got nice kids, two of 'em better than the third but he's not *bad*. My bride and me, we've had a good run. This"—he waved his arm—"is an insult to that. It's saying we didn't do it right."

He fished a flask from his waistband. He took a sip and handed it to Shaw, who downed some whisky and passed it back. It was plastic, impervious to the metal detector.

"You've got to get out of here, Walter."

"Naw, we'll sit it out. Only ten days left."

"You can't wait. There's going to be trouble."

The old man was looking at Shaw carefully. "You say that like a man who knows."

He explained about the murder of one reporter and the beating of another and the murder-suicide: the Select who burned himself and John to death.

Walter was speechless for a moment. "▉▉▉ That nice fellow at our table? And the police didn't do a thing?"

"Eli's lining the sheriff's pocket. I'm working on getting proof of what he's up to. The chopper? It was San Francisco police looking into the murder. I'm worried about what's going to happen next. You know Jonestown?"

"Sure, that psycho Jim Jones. Was another cult, right? Everybody killed themselves."

"Some journalists and government officials flew down to see what was going on. That set off the suicides and the murders."

"You think Eli's got something like that in mind?"

"I don't know, but look at the AUs, all of them in meetings now. And Eli's called for another Discourse.

Just feels like something's going to happen soon, and it's not going to be good. Would you and Sally be able to hike out? Two miles?"

Walter was considering. "That was some thick forest we were just in. Steep."

"Where I'd take you, it's mostly field and light pine woods. Some rock but nothing to climb, not more than a few feet. I'll get you out safe."

"Where to?"

"A highway. I'm sure there'll be cars or you can get to a gas station another mile north. Maybe a little more."

"You checked that out first, before you came?"

"Did some homework, yes."

Never lose your orientation.

Walter turned and looked Shaw over. "I knew you weren't one of the believers the minute you sat down and looked around for the wine at the dinner table."

"Beer."

"What's your story? You're not law?"

"Like a private eye."

"Getting out? I'm game. But our money, credit cards, phones?"

"Those I think I can get. The luggage building isn't that secure. I've checked it out. But what we need is a couple of hours where you won't be missed. I was thinking: you said Sally liked to garden. What if you told your trainer that you both wanted to spend a couple of hours working there."

"Where?"

"The garden."

"They don't have one. First thing I asked about, for

Sally. But we have a light day today. We could be meditating on our Minuses." He scoffed. "Nobody'll miss us
from eleven to two or three."

"That'll work." Shaw opened his notebook and showed
Walter his map. He pointed east, to the grassy bluff
above the cliff, where he'd met with Victoria yesterday.
"There're some benches."

"I know. We sit there some."

"Meet me at eleven. Don't bring anything else. They
can't guess what you're up to."

"Sure."

"But there is one thing I need you to do."

"What?"

"Take somebody with you."

50.

Colter Shaw wasn't surprised to see a stony-faced Select sitting in a rocker in front of the dormitory he sought. But he didn't think it was a problem. In Shaw's world, windows were made for admitting humans as well as light and air. Dexterous humans, at least.

He made his way through the bushes and peeked carefully into each room before he found the one he sought. He kept searching until he located an empty room, then removed from his pocket the dinner knife and jimmied open the window. Shaw boosted himself up and inside, rolling onto the floor. Not as silently as he would have liked; his heels thunked. He paused, listening for any indication he'd been heard.

Apparently not. Shaw then looked into the hallway and walked to the door he sought. He knocked gently. "It's a friend. Can you open up?"

Silence.

"It's important."

A shuffling sound. The door opened.

Shaw looked down at the diminutive form of sixteen-year-old Abby, who blinked and said, "Oh, you."

She sat on the bed and he on the desk chair. He'd moved it near the door so he could hear anyone approaching.

Her eyes were red, and she kept up the fidgeting he remembered from the dining hall. Her nails were bitten to the quick.

He whispered, "What's wrong, Abby?"

She blinked. He hadn't used her title. After a pause, she said, "This's all so fucked up." She controlled her soft crying.

He waited.

She nodded. "Journeyman Marion was going to be my trainer but Master Eli took over. In the sessions he was great. He listened and listened and helped me find my Pluses. I told him when I was a kid I went to an art museum once and it was the coolest thing ever. He said I was an artist in a former life, so I should meditate on art, and I did and I felt so good.

"Then he told me to come to the Study Room. Everybody was like, Wow, that's a big deal. Anyway, he said it was for special studies but you can guess what it was really about. I didn't care. I'm not really into that anyway, not with anybody, not after some stuff that happened to me at home. So it wasn't a big deal to me and it made him happy. He said he loved me. He said I was different, that me and him knew each other in the past. I was so happy.

"And then . . ." She choked and cried quietly. Shaw rose, found a towel and handed it to her. Angrily she wiped her face. "I was talking to Apprentice Rose, and he told her the same thing. And Apprentice Joan. And there were a lot of the others too. That was okay. Sort of. As long as he spent time with me. As long as he loved *me*.

"But today . . . he dragged me in here and said I was a lying slut. I lied about my age. I'd risked the whole Foundation. He said he'd been wrong: that I wasn't special. That I was stupid and deserved to die in a crack house." She sobbed into the towel for a moment. "He said if I ever said anything, Journeyman Hugh and some of the AUs would kill me. I had to stay here until they arranged for me to leave. And I couldn't talk to anybody."

"Abby, you remember John?"

"Yeah, he got sick and left."

"No. Eli and Hugh killed him."

"What?" She gasped.

"He was a threat to them. He was going to expose them."

No need to suggest that Abby herself was the reason.

"Oh God."

Shaw leaned close. "Listen, I'm not here for the training. I'm like a policeman. I'm investigating Eli. I think he wants to hurt you too."

"I told him I wouldn't say anything."

"He doesn't care. You know Walter and Sally? At our table the other night?"

"The old couple. Yeah. They're nice. She's sick, right?"

"I'm getting them out today. In a half hour. I want you to go with them."

"Go back home?" she muttered sourly. "Right."

"Let's get you out safe first and then worry about that. They've agreed to let you stay with them for a while. Walter can contact some of your relatives."

She sighed, turning the towel over and over in her ruddy, damaged hands.

"I kept sitting here, thinking Master Eli was just upset. He'll change his mind about me. He didn't mean what he said. The times we were together, he was so happy. I made him happy and that made me feel good."

"Abby, we have to go now."

"Okay but the guy at the door. The creepy one."

Shaw asked, "You ever climbed out a window before?"

Earning him a small curve of smile, which said, Are you kidding me?

51.

etting into the luggage building was about as easy as Shaw had originally figured.

Since it was midweek and no new applicants were arriving or graduates leaving, the facility was closed. He was also helped by the absence of AUs. They'd be huddling with Eli and Hugh.

Maybe working out an endgame.

Jim Jones convinced over nine hundred followers in his Peoples Temple to murder hundreds of children and then kill themselves with poisoned fruit punch . . .

On the rear windows was a standard latch. The place-setting knife easily did the trick. There was no alarm.

Inside were no lockers but large, uncovered compartments for the baggage. From the claim checks, Shaw easily found Walter's and Sally's suitcases—four of them. They'd packed for three weeks, never knowing they wouldn't need a single item. He found Abby's backpack too. He rummaged through each and took changes of clothing and shoes for all three. These articles he put into a laundry bag he'd brought from his dorm room. He added the older couple's wallet, purse and cash. Abby had a wallet too, one that she'd connect to a belt loop on a long chain. She had little money, though inside was a prepaid credit card that her "asshole of a stepfather" had grudgingly given her.

Shaw found his own suitcase and removed a couple of hundred cash for her. He also took his own wallet, which he stuffed into his waistband, irritated once again at the absence of pockets, which, he decided, had to be one of the greatest inventions of all time.

He put the bags back exactly where they had been.

One disappointment: Shaw could not get their cell phones. Against the wall was a large container with a big lock on it. Shaw recognized the contraption immediately. The sides were of thick metal-oxide-coated glass. On the floor nearby were strands of pink fiberglass insulation, which, he knew, would be packed inside, around the Companions' phones. Glass was one of the most efficient ways to block cell phone traffic. He was sure all the phones had been shut off and, if possible, the batteries removed. Newer phones would have built-in batteries that couldn't be removed, which meant the units remained semi-powered even when they were off. This box would prevent any incoming and outgoing transmissions altogether.

He slipped out of the building and relatched the window. In ten minutes he was at the bench overlooking the mountainous panorama.

Shaw gazed around. No Inner Circles or AUs. They were still, he was sure, formulating plans with Eli and

Hugh on responding to the homicide detectives' visit and the re-upped investigation.

"This way."

With the laundry bag over his shoulder, Shaw led them north along the high bluff until they were some distance from the camp. He stopped. "Let's change here." He distributed the clothing and other things he'd taken from the luggage building.

Sally's eyes lit up magically when her husband put her engagement and wedding rings on her finger. "My," she said. "I thought I'd lost them. I was afraid to tell you, dear."

Walter kissed her cheek.

Shaw handed Abby her clothes, her wallet and his own cash. She blinked, frowning at the two hundred dollars.

"Take it," Shaw said.

"Like . . ."

"Take it."

Her eyes said thank you.

Walter led Sally off behind a thick growth of holly to change.

Abby simply turned her back to Shaw and stripped; he looked away.

The couple returned. Walter was in a brown and yellow shirt and dark trousers, Sally a navy-blue blouse and dark skirt. Fortunately she'd brought flats.

Abby was in black jeans and a Drake sweatshirt.

He passed around the laundry bag and they placed their uniforms, amulets and slippers inside. Shaw buried it under a pile of sticks, leaves and pine needles.

"Let's go. This way."

The day was hot, the sun yellow as yolk, and insects hummed and strafed. Shaw found some wild lavender and marigold. He broke off stems and petals and passed them out. "Crush it and rub it on your skin. Especially ankles and elbows. That's what they go for, the mosquitos."

The four of them did so.

"Ain't we a dandy-smelling crew?" Sally said, drawing smiles. She then gazed about her, eyes curious. Was she aware of the peril, or did she simply think her husband and some friends, whom she didn't recognize, were spending a pleasant afternoon in the woods behind their Midwestern house?

The uneventful hike was as easy as Shaw had anticipated. They passed through the rusty chain link and over the three-foot-wide path between a rocky rise and the cliff's edge. Funny how you have no worry about falling off a sidewalk even narrower than this but introduce a deadly void on one side and you walk just a bit more breathlessly.

Then the foursome was descending a gentle slope through the fields and quiet, needle-carpeted woods.

Walter, holding his wife's hand, said to Shaw, "How should we handle it, when we're home?"

Shaw said, "You don't go home yet. Get to a hotel or motel nowhere near here. Stay there. Eli knows your home address. Odds that a Select'll come after you? Not high. But you've got to be cautious. Wait until you know it's safe."

"Call the police?"

Shaw said no to that too. "I need more proof. And remember that the local sheriff'll tip off Eli and evidence'll disappear. He will too. And, I'm afraid, witnesses."

Soon they broke from the forest and walked down a gentle, grassy grade toward the highway.

Abby asked, "So, like, what's our cover story for any drivers who'll stop? I mean, we got lost on a hike?"

It was a good question, one he hadn't thought of. "Let's blame it on my bad driving."

Once they hit the state route, it took only five minutes to flag down a car. This quartet of fugitives—an older couple with their son and daughter—presented about as low a threat as could be. A Dodge Caravan stopped. It was driven by a young husband and wife.

Shaw explained that he'd stupidly driven off road to get a closer look at a waterfall and the car cracked an axle. AAA was on the way. He'd stay with the car. But he didn't want his parents and sister to wait here in the heat and sun. Could the couple please take them to a motel somewhere along their route? They gladly agreed. The husband shook his head about the axle—the sort of mishap that even the most talented of automotive Good Samaritans can't help fix, which is why Shaw picked it.

No shoulder salutes now. Shaw hugged them all goodbye.

Abby's grip was especially hard. She whispered, "Thanks, mister. I mean, really."

Once the vehicle was out of sight, Shaw turned around and jogged hard the two miles back to the camp.

When he arrived, he caught his breath and walked from the woods. He stepped into the Square, heading for his dorm. A cluster of men stood in front of it, talking among themselves: Eli, Hugh, the two bodyguards—Squat and Gray—and several other AUs. Steve too. With them was a tall, slim Companion, his back to Shaw.

The man turned and removed his orange-framed sunglasses. It was Frederick, from the site of Adam's death. And, yes, he was the man who'd been looking Shaw over earlier at the Discourse.

His eyes narrowed and he said something to Eli and Hugh. Then pointed a long, lean finger directly Shaw's way.

52.

Shaw recalled the beating of the reporter. Face cracked, dislocated shoulder.

One noisy, one silent. Both excruciating.

He calculated he was a good twenty feet from his only weapons: the war clubs he'd made earlier. And thirty from the cover of the forest.

A glance at the ground underfoot. Gravel. Not good for traction, especially with the slipper-like shoes. He stepped toward the men so he would meet them on a patch of lawn. He kept a look of benign curiosity on his face. To allay suspicions and give himself the chance for a surprise strike.

He'd believed Hugh was not armed, though it was likely Squat and Gray were.

He was walking toward Frederick, the logical course, since he was the one who had pointed to Shaw. This would take Shaw past the guards. His plan: do a wrestling takedown of one of them, and search for and seize his pistol. Squat had a lower center of gravity and would be harder to body slam. Also, Gray's military bearing suggested that if anyone were armed it would be him. So, Gray would be the target.

Shaw would get him down, hard, and then go for a gun. Because a weapon didn't present under his clothing in an obvious way, it would be an automatic, slimmer than a revolver. Shaw would draw the slide to chamber a round, even if it meant ejecting—and losing—one bullet.

He could cover Eli and the others and get away.

If there was a weapon.

If he could rack the slide in time.

If Hugh and Squat weren't armed as well and didn't draw and fire first.

And if there was no gun?

He decided that the only way he could prevail against Hugh in hand-to-hand was surprise, and that would have been lost in his assault on Gray. He'd seen Hugh's expertise in martial arts. He was physically fit and emotionally detached. There had been no feeling in the assault on the reporter the other day. The calm opponent has the upper hand over the excited.

As for technique, Shaw knew no close-combat moves like Hugh's.

Never use your fists; too easy to break your own fingers or wrist. Grapple to the ground, then elbows and knees.

Still he'd do what he could, getting in close and using another wrestling takedown. Lift from low, and drive his opponent onto his back.

His odds? Without the surprise, probably thirty percent.

And adding to the mix: two dozen Foundation members were within fifty feet. Loyalists would rush in to save their Guiding Beacon. Maybe even sacrifice themselves to save their spiritual leader from a Toxic. If they'd trued-up, death would mean nothing to them.

Chances of a successful escape?

Thirty percent.

Shaw kept a smile on his face and casually continued toward Frederick, who gazed back with a knowing expression.

When he was about three feet from Gray, Eli said something to Hugh and both men turned toward Shaw, who lowered his center of gravity and got ready to step into Gray, dip low and sweep his leg out from under him, drop him. The weathered man was right-handed. A gun would be holstered on that hip.

Three steps, two . . .

Shaw tensed, preparing physically—and mentally—to take on five opponents.

53.

Shaw was five feet from Gray when Eli turned and glanced his way. The cult leader smiled broadly and gave the shoulder salute, calling out, "Apprentice Carter, thank you, thank you!" To the other he said, "Is he gorgeous or what? I told you so. Didn't I say he was a star?"

Mystified, Shaw slowed and tipped his head, returning the salute.

Steve said, "Thank you, Apprentice Carter."

Best to keep it short and sweet until he sussed out what was happening. A nod.

Frederick joined them.

Eli looked his way. "Journeyman Frederick here was just telling us what happened. Please. Go on."

The man said, "Apprentice Carter came up to me and said he saw Novices Walter and Sally and Abby breaking out of the luggage building and running into the woods. There were no AUs around, so Apprentice Carter and I went after them ourselves." He looked at Shaw. "We thought they might be working for competitors, stealing secrets. Right?"

Shaw nodded.

"We couldn't tell which direction they went, so we split up. I spotted them in the Henderson Ravine. I ran back and told Journeyman Hugh."

The head AU said, "We put together a team."

Shaw, playing a role in a charade he didn't understand, said to Hugh, "Did you find them?"

"No."

There'd been no search. He knew about the ravine, which you'd hit if you turned north out of the fence, not east toward the road. The gully led to a maze of canyons, falls, no roads to speak of. Not even logging trails. Eli and Hugh were happy to let them die in the woods.

Witnesses . . .

Eli said, "Terrible. Such a shame. What *were* they thinking? And that poor girl." He looked at Shaw. "She's only in college, you know."

You mean, high school. Shaw shook his head sympathetically.

"Send out some men. Have Sheriff Calhoun assign some of his too. We'll hope we can find them."

"I will, Master Eli," Hugh said.

This was spoken for Shaw's benefit. There would be no search party. Things had worked out for the best. The only other complaining witness in the statutory rape would be dead in a day or two.

Eli's eyes went to Hugh. "Such a shame," he repeated.

But the missing persons and their convenient demise seemed to vanish from Eli's mind. He moved on, turning his magnetic blue eyes on Frederick and Shaw. "Thank you for your efforts on behalf of the Foundation." A salute Shaw's way. Then Eli's eyes abruptly narrowed and he said, "Those men? In the helicopter? It's all a pack of lies."

A frown crossed Shaw's face. "Of course. People envy greatness."

"Yes! I like that! 'Envy greatness.'" Eli glanced toward Steve, who wrote in his thick notebook, apparently memorializing the phrase. Shaw wondered if he'd just coined a new chant.

Eli, Hugh and the AU goons returned to the main residence, where presumably a war room had been set up to consider how to confront the investigation into Gary Yang's death.

Leaving Shaw to shoot a glance to Frederick, whose eyes said, Yes, let's talk.

The man waited until no one was within earshot. "I saw you on that hill—above the cliff where Journeyman Adam jumped."

"I thought somebody was there," Shaw told him. "The orange sunglasses."

Frederick said, "Not really part of the Foundation uniform. Eli likes to see people's eyes. But I'm good and obedient. He doesn't mind some harmless nonconformity. That's what he calls it. So. You're wondering why I didn't turn you in to Hugh."

Went without saying.

"Gut feel, I guess. I saw your face after Adam died.

You were upset, man. But I couldn't figure it out when I saw you here a couple of days later. You didn't seem like a cop. Maybe a reporter, investigative reporter, you know, writing about the Foundation. Master Eli warns us about them all the time. The Toxic Media. But Adam hadn't been involved in the Foundation for a while, so you probably didn't know he was a Companion."

Shaw had to add, "No. I didn't know anything about the Foundation then."

Frederick's eyes burned, angry. "A month ago I would've said his death doesn't matter. His True Core would surface in the Tomorrow. But now? Hell, it's all bullshit: everything Eli's trying to sell. Now, I'm awake." Frederick examined Shaw. "What were you doing there?"

"Adam was wanted for a crime near Tacoma."

The man was surprised. "Adam? He was messed up. But he wasn't into anything criminal—not for years."

"A shooting. I think it was self-defense."

Shaw realized now that Adam had been in the cemetery, where he met Erick, to kill himself by his mother's grave. That was why Adam had had the pistol. Now that Shaw knew Eli's poisonous teaching, he realized that was the man's mission. He'd changed his mind—at least temporarily—when he saw he could help Erick get over the loss of his brother.

Shaw explained about the shooting and about the case, that Adam probably would have gotten off.

"That son of a bitch. Eli. He teaches everybody, oh, just go ahead and advance—just kill yourself—and you'll wake up in the Tomorrow. Some little setback? You can start over and everything'll be great. And Adam was just the kind to believe that bullshit. He was depressed, lonely. Those're the ones Eli preys on."

Shaw asked, "Why'd you stay?"

"I was leaving at the end of the season. He pays well. Need the money." Frederick shrugged. "Haven't exactly built up a lot of skills here that translate to the outside."

"You were close to him?" Shaw asked. "Adam?"

The man hesitated. "I wanted to be more than friends, you know, but he wasn't interested. That was fine, once we got it established. Fine with me. I liked, you know, talking to him. It's tough here. It gets lonely.

"We could bitch and moan. I had my problems too. I came out when I was sixteen. My stepfather exploded. He screamed and raged that I was going to hell." Frederick's face was almost amused. "I never really got why he was upset. He never liked me, doesn't like gays. So wouldn't he be *happy* I was going to hell?" Frederick looked over toward Shaw. "You're not 'Carter,' then?"

"No. I'm not."

The rich scent of damp smoke wafted their way on a cool breeze.

"You're an undercover cop?"

"Like a private eye." He added that he'd come here to see why Adam died and if he could help anyone else at risk, like Victoria. He told Frederick about how Hugh bullied and tried to grope her on the cliff.

"I saw that. Hugh's an asshole. He's got a whole system worked out. If you break the rules, or just *seem* to break the rules, he'll give you demerits. That can set your training back. Enough of them and you might not become a Journeyman, and have to start all over again. At the cliff, he was spouting Rule 14 at Victoria. You can't be upset when somebody dies. It means you don't believe in the Process.

"Of course, if you're a woman, and willing, you can come visit him and he'll erase the demerits. That can also accelerate your training." He looked Shaw over. "And then there's the fee arrangements."

"You mean the bequests in the will for lifetime memberships?"

"No." Frederick gave a cynical laugh. "You pay a fixed fee, seventy-five hundred, right? Except not. Remember, you have to send a picture in? Why do you think that is?" He gave a cynical laugh. "Pretty young girls and guys get in for a hundred, two. Sometimes for free."

"The Study Room."

A nod.

Shaw was surprised he hadn't figured that out. Nearly all the women here were under thirty and attractive.

"You saw me helping Walter, Sally and Abby. You've been following me for the past couple of days. It was you, right?"

"Yeah."

"You did a good job. Are you military?"

"No. Just I used to go hunting with my father. My real father. We were close. Lost him a few years ago. That's why I'm here. It was tougher than I thought, him dying."

"I can usually spot tails. You were good."

Frederick said, "I was in camo. There's some outfits for the Selects. So? Walter, Sally and that girl?"

"They're nowhere near here."

"Why'd you get them out?"

"Abby's sixteen."

A look of dismay crossed Frederick's face. "███ Eli took her to the Study Room? He'd go down for statutory rape."

"You hear about the car fire?"

"What fire?"

"John—the Novice—found out about Abby. Eli and Hugh had a Select kill him then himself. Murder-suicide. Eli was going to get rid of Abby too, I was sure. I asked Walter and Sally to get her out." Shaw looked over the slim man's face. "What's going on in the camp? What did Eli say about the helicopter?"

"He told the Inner Circle that some Toxic trumped up charges against him. He told the police that. They believed him and they went away. That's what he said."

"It's not going away." Shaw explained about the death of the journalist in San Francisco.

"And you're worried it could get ugly here, if the police come back. You know, standoffs like at Ruby Ridge, Waco, Jonestown?"

"I've seen the faces of the staff and some of the Companions. They'd fight for him. Some of them would die for him."

Frederick asked, "That's why you didn't leave with the others."

"I'm going to bring him down."

"What're you planning?"

"I need evidence before he destroys it. Business and phone records, emails, memos. Something that shows money laundering, extortion, orders to kill the journalist, other people who're threats."

Two stern AUs passed. The four of them traded shoulder salutes. When the guards were past, Frederick said, "His office is off the Study Room."

"I was there. I didn't see any offices."

"It's hidden. As you face the bed—that circular bed? It's against the right wall, in the mural of Osiris."

Shaw remembered the painting.

Frederick said, "I saw inside one time. There were files on a desk and a computer. Bookshelves. File cabinets."

Computer, Shaw thought. Contact with the outside world.

"Is the door locked?"

"I don't think so."

"You know any side or back entrances to the residence?"

"One in back, I think."

"Security cameras?"

"I don't know. But the residence is never empty. There're always AUs around. And Inner Circles. Eli and Anja and Steve. Those two cold-fish bodyguards."

The loudspeaker musical notes resounded and Shaw and Frederick fell silent.

"All Companions are requested to assemble in the Square."

The no-nonsense directive was repeated.

It was the improvised Discourse.

As the two men walked toward the Square, Shaw asked, "What do you think? Does Eli actually believe what he preaches?"

"I've wondered that." Frederick waved his hand around the camp. "I sometimes think he does, and he's created this whole philosophy to save the world from depression and loss. His temper, his need for control, his anger, his mercenary side, his . . . appetite for the women, and men, that's just who he is. And, look at it one way, if he does believe it, then murder's not really murder. You're just sending a soul into a future life."

Tough argument to make in court.

Frederick continued, "Or he could think it's pure bullshit. But I'll tell you one thing: Whether he's in it for the money or to save souls, he's not giving it up without a fight. No way."

54.

The stage was empty at the moment, and many of the Companions were abuzz.

But not all. Others stood in solemn clusters, expressions of uncertainty on their faces.

Shaw looked for Victoria. Didn't see her.

"What's this about?" Frederick wondered aloud.

Shaw said, "I'm betting diversion, something to take our minds off the helicopter and Carole's heresy."

He heard a cheerful voice behind them. "Apprentice Carter. Journeyman Frederick."

Shaw turned and nodded. "Journeyman Samuel."

"Always that delicious sense of anticipation, times like this. Even in the Inner Circle, we don't always know what our Guiding Beacon is up to."

The greater the suspense, the better the sleight of hand.

And the tighter the control.

The men gazed toward the stage.

Shaw thought of the office off the Study Room. What would he find there?

And there was a computer. If Shaw could get online he'd contact Mack McKenzie, who could alert Tom Pepper. His friend in turn would call colleagues at the Bureau and the Washington State Patrol.

Samuel asked Shaw, "Your journaling is going well?"

"I think so. It's difficult."

"Now that you're an Apprentice, you know we'll be looking for Minuses and Pluses from past lives. Those are always trickier. Is this a real memory, or from a John Wayne movie I saw as a kid? They're more subtle, harder to find. We'll do it, though. I often say the Process is about clearing the fog."

"Your metaphors get better by the hour, Journeyman Samuel."

The man laughed.

Shaw asked, "Were you a counsellor or therapist before you joined the Foundation?"

"Me? No. I was a teacher. Middle school. Master Eli taught me everything I learned about training and the Process."

"I've heard glowing reports about you as a trainer," Frederick told him. His mannerisms were natural, understated, his voice calm. A natural actor.

"Ah, now you're making a fat old man blush."

Shaw said he looked forward to the forthcoming sessions, putting what he saw as the right amount of joyful anticipation into his face, which seemed to please the trainer.

Samuel probably knew nothing of Eli's murderous nature. He would be aware of the cult leader's sexual appetites and blunt, egotistical behavior, of course, but, as Frederick had just suggested, those were typically just part and parcel of a visionary's personality.

Shaw looked over the crowd once more. Still no sign of Victoria.

Frederick said, "I was just thinking, Journeyman Samuel. If enough people go through the Process, after the whole world is trued-up, maybe sadness can be eliminated entirely. Like we did with smallpox."

Samuel looked thoughtful. "We can only hope, Journeyman Frederick. Though that would, of course, put me out of a job." He winked.

The clapping started. Shaw was standing near a speaker and realized that this time someone had placed a microphone near clapping hands; the sound was especially piercing.

"The best . . ." *Clap, clap, clap.* ". . . is yet to come."

"The best . . ."

". . . is yet to come."

The droning words and the slapping of palms rose in volume. Thirty seconds, a minute. Two.

Then the rhythmic clapping degenerated into frenzied applause.

Eli climbed onto the stage, turning to the audience and giving the salute. Once again, he glowed in the beam of artificial light from on high.

He then lifted his hands, smiling and nodding. As before, he pointed to certain people in the audience, blessing them with his attention.

That confident face.

Not the face of a murderer. But then Colter Shaw had seen plenty of killers who looked downright angelic.

"Greetings, Companions. Greetings!"

Slowly the sound faded.

"I'm making an important announcement today. I've got something . . . You're going to like this. You're going to *love* this. I guarantee it!"

"We love you, Master Eli!"

"We're with you, forever!"

"Our Guiding Beacon!"

Eli's hand rose. His right only. The gesture resembled a Nazi salute.

The Companions quieted.

"I've brought us to the most successful year ever, with the most Journeymen graduating from training and moving into the world to live better, happier lives."

Now, cheers and frenzied clapping.

"I know what you want, I know what you need. And I'm giving it to you. I am proving to the Toxics of the world, the lying religions, the selfish politicians, the pernicious charlatans . . . You know 'pernicious'? I love that word. Means evil. But sounds worse than 'evil,' doesn't it? I think so."

Laughter.

"The Process proves that what they're trying to sell you is . . . manure!"

The ICs booed a bit, and the crowd took it up.

No chant with *that*, though Shaw wouldn't have been surprised if Eli had encouraged one.

"I am now going to take our family to a higher level."

Didn't the Manson cult refer to themselves as family?

"I am announcing here the formation of the Osiris Foundation Circle of Representatives. This will be an elite group of Companions who will meet with me on a daily basis and help me in planning our expansion around the country . . . and eventually the world."

Shaw and Frederick shared a look.

"And I am delighted to announce that the Director of the Circle will be one of our most loyal servants, a trainer who's distinguished herself." Eli began to applaud as he looked to the area behind the stage where a middle-aged woman stood.

"Come up here, Journeyman Marion!"

Beaming and blushing, she did so and gave the salute to the frenzied crowd.

"Journeyman Marion is one of the best. Don't we love her? Who's been trained by Journeyman Marion? Let's see it! Look at all those hands. Look at them! I picked her, you know. I saw her, talked to her for three minutes, only three minutes. And I knew she was a born Journeyman and trainer."

The chant stretched the word *Marion* out. The woman, intoxicated with happiness, waved to the crowd.

Eli then recited the names of the other four Companions who would form the group. "Come on up here! Join Journeyman Marion and me!"

They did, two men and two women, all in their forties, as surprised as Marion had been. Apparently caught off guard, all they could think to do was offer the shoulder salute.

Eli called, "Later today, we'll have a formal induction

ceremony, and I'll ask each of you to tell me, in your own words, what the Foundation means to you. And if I've helped your life even in a small way . . . I want to know." He was laughing. "Congratulations, my beloved Companions. Remember, the best . . ."

". . . is yet to come!"

Eli strode off the stage, trailed by Anja and Steve. They joined the bodyguards and the group headed south.

When Shaw was sure no one was in earshot, he said to Frederick, "I'm going to get inside the residence. Can you try to get a phone from the luggage room?"

"Oh, you were in the woods, you don't know. After the police showed up, they moved the phone storage box into the Assistance Unit. It's guarded twenty-four/seven now."

Shaw sighed. "Try the parking lot, see if anyone left one inside a car. I know they were searched but maybe somebody got careless."

"But the AUs in the front."

"Looks like a lot of them've been pulled off their details."

"Well, the cars're locked, aren't they? And the keys are with the AUs too."

Shaw said, "Some of the older ones won't have alarms."

He frowned. Then it dawned on him. "Oh, you mean break in."

Shaw saw the man liked the idea. He explained to Frederick how he could take the path to the eastern edge of the wooden fence and then circle around to get to the parking lot.

Frederick thought for a moment. "You know. It's going to be hard to tell if there's an alarm. What if I got underneath, popped the hood and used something metal to short out the battery?"

"Good. Were you a mechanic before joining the Foundation?"

"I was a Mafia hitman."

A line delivered with such a straight face that Shaw thought for a second it was true.

Frederick smiled at Shaw's reaction. "I managed a chain of frozen yogurt shops. Yo-Grrrrt." He spelled it, as he would have done a thousand times. "Our logo was a happy bear. Where should we meet?"

"Behind my dorm. Building C. Make it an hour."

Frederick nodded and vanished into the woods. Shaw turned east, disappearing into the line of trees that paralleled that edge of the camp. Then south, along the hidden path, toward the residence.

It turned out, though, that he'd have to wait. Eli, Steve and the two bodyguards were standing in a deserted grassy area on the eastern side of the residence. Eli was dictating, and Steve nodded fiercely as he transcribed. From where they stood, they'd be able to see Shaw break from the line of trees, heading for the back door, if any of them happened to glance that way.

Just then a faint scream rose from the far side of the residence, the west. Instantly, Squat and Gray turned. Gray's bony left hand tugged up his tunic and his right was poised to draw his weapon. It was a small Glock, Shaw could see. He'd been right about the gun.

The two bodyguards and Steve hurried in the direction of the scream, Gray motioning Eli to stay back. Eli's attention was focused away from the back of the residence, and Shaw started in that direction. But he stopped. He noticed motion in the woods not far from him. It was furtive and slow, careful. The movement of a stalking hunter—very much how Shaw himself pursued game, hunched over, making a small profile, assessing the quietest place to plant his feet, assessing which foliage would rustle and which would not.

Never be obvious.

Shaw froze, hardly believing what he was looking at.

The hunter was Victoria, hair tied into a severe bun. She eased closer to the clearing where Eli stood, thirty feet away. The leader's back was to her.

In her hand was a knife. It seemed she too had stolen one from the kitchen but unlike his this was a lengthy butcher knife. From the discolored and uneven edge, Shaw knew that she'd spent quite some time honing the edge on a rock to turn the weapon scalpel sharp.

55.

She was moving forward steadily. Her posture and her movement told Shaw she was an experienced stalker.

Victoria was presently twenty feet away from Eli and closing the distance steadily, while keeping absolutely silent.

A voice called to Eli, "Just a fire, small one." It was Steve speaking.

"Anyone hurt?"

"No. Just trash in a waste bin. Somebody sneaking a smoke maybe."

Shaw judged distances. Soon, Victoria would break from cover, charge forward, and slash the Guiding Beacon to death.

The woman held the knife with the sharp edge up. This was proper hand-to-hand combat technique. She would come up behind him, cup his forehead and pull his head back, while simultaneously slashing his throat from ear to ear. It was a simple move and one that required little effort, provided you had surprise, which she certainly would if she could make a silent approach.

Who the hell was she really? Obviously not the vulnerable supplicant Shaw had believed. Whatever her motive, though, he could see that her mission would end in *her* death, not Eli's. From where she was, she couldn't see that Gray and Steve had paused just around the corner of the residence. Now that the "emergency" had turned minor, they were about to return. They'd see Victoria on the move and she'd be shot to death.

No time to formulate a percentage of success for one strategy or another.

Shaw circled behind her—picking out a silent path himself—and when he was ten feet away, he charged. By the time she heard, it was too late to turn and assume a defensive posture. He dropped her to the ground with a serviceable tackle. They tumbled into a pile of leaves.

The collision left her breathless, Shaw too—all the more so when she drove a well-placed elbow into his gut. With lightning-fast reflexes she leapt to her feet and tried to put distance between herself and her attacker—the first rule of meeting a surprise assault. Shaw, though, grabbed her ankle, twisted slightly and she went down, following the pressure rather than resisting and risking a dislocation.

One second later she was on her feet again, and in classic knife-fighting position: left hand out for distraction and gripping her enemy, her right slashing the air between them, back and forth.

Her face tightened and she glanced quickly at Eli and saw Steve round the corner. She was taking a measure of the distance between herself and her target.

"You would've died," Shaw whispered.

"I could've made it."

"No, you wouldn't."

"Yes, I would," she said defiantly.

Shaw whispered, "He's armed. The gray-haired one. Maybe the other one too."

"I know," she growled softly. "I saw the imprint. His partner isn't."

She kept the blade pointed his way and looked again at her prey. It seemed she was still contemplating the attack.

Then a look of disgust crossed her face and her shoulders slumped. She rose from the fighting position. She wrapped the blade in a napkin and slipped it into her back waistband.

She watched the men continue their conversation as they resumed their walk to the residence. The guards joined them. Apparently the fire was out.

Shaw walked closer to Victoria.

When she slapped him, with all her strength, it seemed, her palm was slightly cupped and the blow gave a sharp snap, which was every bit as loud and staccato as the rhythmic clapping that accompanied the Inner Circle's chants.

56.

get it now. It was you."

"Me?" Shaw asked.

"You ██████ drugged me to keep me out of the Study Room. To save my honor. ████████ Where are we? Back in the 1950s?" Her voice was a furious rasp.

He looked around. "Not here. We're too exposed."

She calmed enough to consider his words. She asked, "Dormitories?"

"Could be bugged."

"The cliff where you were stalking me," she said pointedly.

Ten minutes later they had hiked up the hill to the bench overlooking the vast panorama and the mountains in the distance. One peak was particularly noble in the glass-clear air. No one else was present on the bluff.

"What was it?" Victoria asked.

"The drug? Verbena."

"I thought I tasted something. Damn it. I've used

pokeweed berries for the same thing. They have a better flavor but—"

"They're deep purple. Telltale."

How did she know this? The number of people in the country who needed to use emetic herbs in the field was extremely limited, Shaw assumed.

"I think we've established you're not a librarian."

Victoria dismissed his flippant comment with a wave of her hand. "I do security consulting. And something tells me you know what a security consultant does."

"The blade. You honed it on a rock, not a whetstone. Where'd you learn that, the Army?"

"YouTube." Her voice was mocking.

"And you kept calling Eli 'sir.'"

She shrugged in concession. "True. Screwed up there."

Victoria's eyes were scanning for threats around them, head tilting slightly at sounds, dismissing them as natural and nonthreatening. This woman knew her skills.

Shaw supposed he'd had a clue that Victoria wasn't quite who she seemed to be. After she'd been sick in the dining hall, he'd noted the wave of fury that appeared briefly on her face. Suggesting she was someone a bit different from the vulnerable, submissive woman she'd been presenting to the world.

"So. What're you doing here?" Shaw lifted his palms.

Her internal debate concluded. "Somebody I was close to, she graduated from this bullshit place. She took the 'goodbye until tomorrow' thing seriously."

"I'm sorry."

She dismissed the sentiment with a scoff. "She was at a low time. She would've come out of it. Just a little more work, a little more help. But she chose different. So I signed on, got myself a blue uniform and started looking for the chance to kill him." Her voice was ice. "I needed to get him alone, away from his guards and that little hobbit, Steve."

"The Study Room. Just you and your knife."

"No knife there. I can use my hands. It just takes a little longer." Her shrewd gray eyes swiveled his way. "Not necessarily a bad thing."

"You're taking a big risk for revenge."

"You can minimize risk by planning ahead."

That, he agreed with.

"Okay," she said, "that's my story. What's yours?"

Shaw had to laugh. "I came here to save *you*."

Shaw told her he had been on the cliff when Adam Harper had killed himself.

Victoria was nodding. "I told you I didn't know him. That was true, though I knew *about* him. He was coming back for one of those rejuvenation sessions. And bringing a recruit. I went along to pick them up. It was a cover to help me figure out an escape route after I killed Eli. I hadn't planned on giving up car keys and cell phone when I checked in."

"I saw you and Hugh. Bullying you. Little free with the hands too. I heard about his demerit system."

"He's a pig. Adam had just died and he wanted me to go down on him when we got back to camp, you can believe it. He gave me five demerits when I said no. Took all my willpower to keep from crushing his windpipe or throwing him over the cliff myself."

She then frowned. "But we only saw Adam, or his body. What happened to the person with him?"

"I took him back to Tacoma."

"So who am I to you?"

"Somebody who shouldn't be mixed up in something like this. Or so I thought. Adam died. From what I learned about cults, I thought maybe he'd been brainwashed or bullied. I didn't want anybody else to end up like him. Then the more I learned, the more I decided Eli had to go." He explained about the horrific murder of John.

"Jesus, burned to death."

He also described Hugh's beating of the reporter and the murder of the journalist in San Francisco. "The helicopter? It was SFPD. But guess you didn't see it. You were busy."

Honing her murder weapon, prepping a diversionary fire.

"They've reopened the investigation into the reporter's murder in San Francisco. Eli and his crew have been meeting about something. I'm worried that evidence'll start to disappear. Witnesses too. I want to get into the residence and find something I can hand over to the FBI."

"So we ruined each other's plans." She gave a cool laugh. "You want to bring down Eli too . . . Just for the record, my way's faster."

"Your way comes with a lethal injection."

She snickered, meaning: if they catch you. "You mentioned the Bureau."

"I have contacts there."

The woman scanned the surroundings once more, head cocked, listening for approaching threats.

Never lose situational awareness.

He supposed Victoria had a set of her own Never rules.

"You're not Carter?"

"No. Colter."

She frowned. "I'll tell you about it later. You?"

"Victoria. No need for you to know the last. Where do we go from here?"

"We've got at least one other person on our side."

He told her about his ally, Frederick.

She nodded. "He was in the van with us, at Adam's death. After Hugh read me the riot act, he was good. Trying to make me feel better about Adam and Hugh's behavior."

"I'm going to try to break into the residence," Shaw told her. "Frederick's looking for a phone. Can you help him? He's in the parking lot."

"Why would he believe me?"

"Tell him I told you I got Walter, Sally and Abby out. He'll know we talked."

"The older couple and that girl, right?"

"She's sixteen."

Her face revealed her disgust. "And Eli took her to the Study Room?"

Shaw nodded. "That's why they killed John. He knew about it."

"Son of a bitch."

"Meet behind Building C in forty-five minutes."

Victoria's eyes had gone into hunt mode, scanning the grounds, the woods around them. She reached around to her back to make sure the knife was secure.

Shaw said, "You're not going to . . ."

"Kill him?" Victoria asked. "Not at this point in time." She wasn't smiling when she said the words.

58.

Wouldn't you know it? The only obvious video camera Shaw had seen in the entire camp sat directly above the one door he now needed to get through. The residence's back entrance.

Next steps?

Growing up in the wilderness, Shaw and his siblings rarely watched films, and they saw virtually no TV shows.

Ashton and Mary Dove didn't object to watching big screens or small per se; it was simply a pain to have to trek thirty miles to the nearest theater to see an action-adventure or romantic comedy—literary cinema not being an option at that particular theater.

As for TV, Ashton's thinking was that a device that beamed information into your home could also beam information out.

In recognizing this the man was ahead of his time.

Shaw did recall that several years ago, he and Margot had seen a caper movie. He'd been amused at the elaborate means the hero used to defeat the security camera: the guy built a set that looked just like the back of the bad guy's building. He recorded the empty alleyway, then hacked into the power grid, creating a ten-second black-out in the neighborhood, during which he set up a min-iature projection screen in front of the security cam and began playing the tape of the empty "alleyway."

He couldn't remember if the heist was a success but he never forgot the utterly improbable plan to defeat the camera.

At the moment, he was looking at a similar one be-hind Eli's residence, above the back door.

Next steps?

What the hell?

He seized a rock and flung it into the device, snapping it off the armature. He'd decided that there was a ten percent chance that somebody was continually watching the monitor—Hugh simply didn't have that large an AU staff. Eli was legitimately concerned for his safety, it seemed, but at most the monitor would be watched at night, when the man would be the most vulnerable.

Of course, odds are simply odds and Shaw now leaned against a tree and waited to see if any armed guards charged from the castle to stop the invasion.

Nothing for five minutes. Good enough.

Shaw went for the unsubtle approach once more and kicked the door in.

No alarm.

He stepped in fast and pushed the door closed. The room he found himself in was a storage area, filled with cartons and racks of musty clothing. Dominating one corner were full-sized fiberglass figures of Snow White and the dwarves, though only six, not the full complement. Shaw didn't bother to speculate about the missing figure or, for that matter, the presence of Disney characters in the basement of a psychotic cult leader's home.

The door might not have been used regularly, though Shaw learned that it did have one potential function: an escape route. On the floor were three suitcases and a backpack, the latter of which turned out to be Eli's go-bag. Inside was several hundred thousand in cash, credit cards in three different names and three passports in those same identities, all with Eli's picture.

No phone. No weapons. To Shaw's irritation.

He climbed the stairs and eased the door open slowly, revealing a dim, lengthy corridor. He oriented himself and headed in the general direction of the Study Room, whose location he remembered clearly from his time with Anja. He paused to listen every fifteen or twenty feet but heard nothing, other than the taps and creaks of a house growing accustomed to its surroundings—wood settling and walls protesting the pull of gravity.

Shaw finally found one advantage of the ugly slippers on his feet: his passage was silent.

He climbed to the second floor and turned left.

A noise startled him. A tap. Metal on metal.

Then footsteps coming his way.

He tested two knobs before he found an unlocked door and stepped into what was a small guest bedroom. He left the door ajar and peered out. He could see only a shadow approaching. A latch up the hall clicked. He heard a grunt. The door slammed shut.

The clinking of metal once more. A weapon? Had somebody spotted his entry point in the cellar?

Another door opened and closed, nearer. The grunt was louder.

The shadow approached. Shaw looked around for something to defend himself with. Break the decorative water bowl and pitcher and hope for a long, sharp shard. His preference to avoid using cutting and stabbing weapons would have to go out the window.

Slipping the bowl under a blanket, Shaw struck it fast with the pitcher. This resulted in a functional porcelain shiv about eight inches long. He improvised a handle from the doily on the dresser and slid the remaining broken pieces under the bed.

He eased the door open a bit farther so he could see into the hallway.

This grunt was very close.

Shaw gripped the shiv, inhaled deeply and held his breath.

The stocky middle-aged cleaning woman waddled past, limping, carting a heavy bucket filled with bottles and rags. Her opposite shoulder slumped under a big vacuum on a leather sling, reminding him of a machine gun or rocket launcher. It was the source of the clinking. She also held a metal mop. She was sweating fiercely and her face was anything but happy.

Shaw slipped the shiv into his waistband and stepped away from the door. The woman, a Journeyman, shuffled past. The grunting and clanking faded.

Back into the hallway, Shaw continued on to the Study Room.

He wasn't surprised that the chamber was empty. The helicopter's arrival and what Shaw guessed was Eli's planning sessions—whatever they were—meant there'd be no time for intimacy today, however lustful the man was feeling.

He found the door in the mural. It was unlocked and he stepped into Eli's office, which contained a modern glass desk and a leather swivel rocker, several matching armchairs and tables. A bathroom was off to one side— the door slightly ajar—and unoccupied.

With disgust, Shaw noted the battery-powered video camera pointed into the Study Room.

A search revealed no phone. The computer was, of course, password protected.

He noted stacks of documents in neat rows on the desk and he began reading. Nothing incriminating. Typical memos and notes on business plans, real estate prospectuses, notes on new Discourses, files on the Companions, bills.

Shaw opened one of the four file cabinets against a wall. It would take days to get through them all. But he started on the first, digging through the folders, skimming quickly. He could find no videos of Eli in bed with Companions, though even if he had, this probably wouldn't be a crime, unless Eli posted them without permission or, of course, they depicted someone underage.

Something. Just give me *something*.

He found no references to the slain reporter Gary

Yang or his killer, Harvey Edwards. Or any other obviously criminal activities Eli had engaged in.

Keep at it.

Shaw pulled another stack of files out and was halfway through them when he became aware that he wasn't alone in the room.

59.

He'd sensed the presence thanks to what his father described as a radar that tells us when sound waves reverberate around us due to someone's presence.

Reaching for the pottery stiletto, he turned.

Anja stood in the doorway.

Shaw lowered his hand.

She asked, "It was you, wasn't it? The helicopter?"

A nod. "I found out that Harvey Edwards was a Companion. He killed the reporter in San Francisco just after his article about the Foundation ran. Edwards was a Select, wasn't he?"

Anja frowned. "I think so. Are you a policeman too?"

"No. I have a personal investment in the place."

"I knew you weren't like the others. He's too blind to see. Everybody's a mirror to him. He looks at them and he sees himself."

"Did Etoile—the detective. Did he interview you?"

"Yes."

"What did he ask?"

"He found out that before Yang was killed somebody broke into his apartment and stole files. His editor said he was doing a follow-up on a cult story. One of them he was researching was the Foundation; there were copies of memos he'd sent to his editor about us. He wondered if Eli or anyone else from the Foundation had been in touch with Edwards recently."

"Had they?"

"I have no idea. We were all relieved when that reporter died. It was a tragedy, but we didn't want to be in some trashy exposé. I swear I didn't know that David, that Eli was behind it."

"The Selects are muscle, you know. Like hitmen. Suicidal hitmen. That makes them very effective."

"He doesn't tell me anything."

"Being told and knowing're two different things."

She looked down to the floor. "Okay. I suspected."

"How many Selects are there?"

"I don't know. A dozen around the country. A half dozen or so here."

Though one less than yesterday.

"What's Eli's plan? To escape somewhere?"

"I don't know. He doesn't tell me what he's going to do until he does it."

"I need your help."

Her head sagged. She looked very tired. In a whisper: "He's all I have."

Shaw's reply was, "I count five deaths since I've become aware of the Foundation."

She said nothing.

"This has to end." Shaw pointed to the computer. "I need to get into that."

Tears flowed. "Carter . . . That's not your name, is it?"

"The computer."

Sobbing now. "He's all I have! What'm I going to do? Go back to . . . *hostessing*?"

"Better than wearing orange for the rest of your life."

She sniffed. "You don't understand. He has this . . . spell. You'd rather die than betray him."

Shaw looked her way. "That's exactly what's going to happen. Now. What's the passcode?"

Wiping her eyes with the sleeve of her purple silk robe, Anja took a deep breath and whispered, "It's impossible to guess."

Shaw met Victoria and Frederick behind his dorm.

Together, the two of them had broken into about twenty cars and trucks without alarms—security was minimal, with most of the AUs absent from the lot—but they found no mobiles in glove compartments or side pockets.

"Did *you* find anything?" Victoria asked, looking at the documents in Shaw's hand.

He handed them copies. They read in shocked silence.

Frederick shook his head in dismay. He asked, "How'd you get them?"

"Anja."

In the Study Room, it had amused Shaw to learn that Anja was cooperating, not being obstructive. Eli's passcode was in fact: "ImpossibleToGuess."

This gave Shaw access to much information, though he wasn't able to go online; the router had a separate passcode that Anja didn't know, and Shaw didn't have the time to track it down or try a hack.

Victoria asked, "Next steps?"

"You two hike out, call the numbers I'm going to give you and hand those over." He gave Victoria one set of documents he'd printed out.

"Not you?" she asked.

"I can't." He showed them another piece of paper.

Victoria and Frederick pored over it. Her face crinkled with faint, lovely crows'-feet in the ruddy skin around her eyes. She was an outdoorswoman. Her nails were of medium length, so she didn't rock-climb. He wondered if she skied or biked.

Frederick looked up, whispering, "Jesus."

Victoria grimaced as she read the words. "You sure you want to do this? It could go south in a really bad way."

"You see any other choice?"

Looking over the document again, she said, "No, I don't. But how're you going to pull it off?"

Shaw said, "I was thinking we'll find something in the kitchen."

She thought for a moment. Her frown vanished. "Oh. That's good."

60.

A half hour later, after the kitchen run and several other errands, Shaw, Frederick and Victoria were in the woods behind Shaw's dorm once again. He pushed aside leaves and uncovered his war clubs, handed Victoria one. She eyed it with admiration. She slapped the head into her left palm.

Frederick, the frozen yogurt guru, simply stared at the weapons.

Shaw opened his notebook and showed them his map, indicating the gate in the east. "You can be at the highway in forty-five minutes."

"Thirty," she said.

So Victoria was a runner.

She glanced at Frederick.

He said, "I'll try." He looked into the woods. He said, "Northeast. Do we . . . I mean, do we look for moss?"

"Moss?" Shaw asked.

"You know—for directions. So we don't get lost."

Shaw and Victoria both frowned his way. She said, "The sun."

"Oh. You can do that?"

A trekker too.

Shaw said, "Stop a driver. Tell him there's been a crime—assault or something—and ask to use his phone." Shaw wrote Mack's and Tom Pepper's phone numbers on another sheet from the notebook and gave it to Victoria.

Frederick asked, "Why not just nine-one-one?"

Victoria said, "No. That'll be routed to the closest LEA. That's Snoqualmie Gap. Can't let them know; they're being paid off by Eli and Hugh."

Shaw continued, "If nobody stops or there're no cars, go north. There's a truck stop." He handed her the credit card he'd taken from his luggage during the break-in earlier. "Now, get going."

"Oh. One thing." Frederick looked at Shaw. He withdrew a notebook from his waistband. "It's one of Adam's. I thought you might want it."

Shaw nodded with gratitude and slipped it into his own waistband.

Then Frederick and Victoria began jogging into the woods, the club handle tucked into her waistband, beside the knife. Frederick wasn't at her level of conditioning but now—at the beginning, at least—he was keeping pace.

The musical tones rang out from the loudspeakers throughout the camp, followed by instructions to assemble in the Square. This would be the ceremony Eli had announced earlier.

Shaw folded the papers he'd gotten from Eli's office

and tucked them in his notebook. He was reaching for his war club when he heard a voice from the front of his dorm.

"Hello, Novice Carter."

A trim man of thirty-five or so approached from the front of the dorm, arms at his side. Shaw couldn't see his rank; he wore a blue sweater. But as he gave the salute he said, "Journeyman Timothy."

Shaw rose, leaving the club on the ground and, returning the gesture, he approached quickly so the man wouldn't notice the weapon. "It's Apprentice now."

"Really! So soon. Good for you! That's right, you were expedited." Timothy was fit and athletic and his blond hair was moussed up in a rooster's crown. He had pinched features, a wrinkle on the bridge of his upturned nose. His skin was pocked. An illness or bad acne when young.

"We should get to the Summons, *Apprentice* Carter."

"I'll be along in a minute."

The man said insistently, "No, no, no! I don't want you to get in trouble. You know the Rules. A Summons, you have to get there immediately. They mark down things like that, and it delays your training if you get too many demerits. I know you'll want to be a Journeyman as soon as you can."

The club was just feet away. He absolutely needed it for what was coming next.

But he saw no way out of this dilemma. He sighed and joined the man.

"You have your notebook with you. Good for you. Always jot things down. That's important."

"Rule Nine," Shaw recited.

"Yes, yes. I hear you're quite the mapmaker too."

So someone had noticed it and reported him. No surprise.

"Didn't want to get lost on the grounds. And I'm not that talented."

"Oh, modest man."

"Do you draw too?"

"Me? Oh, brother, no. I drew something, you'd look at it and say, 'What the dickens's that?'" He seemed to blush. "But I have one talent. I can hum like an opera singer."

"Hum?"

"I don't do good with words but I can hum like Paverelli."

"Pavarotti?"

The man nodded. "Off season, I'm going to try out for some choirs or choruses in Omaha. Off season, I mean the fall and winter, when the camp here's closed. You know Master Eli travels to the Far East, meditates, studies, hones his skills? He's the smartest and most generous man in the world. Don't you think?"

"He is."

Timothy looked around at the people moving toward the Square. "A Summons takes priority over everything." He lowered his voice. "I knew a Companion here once who had an accident in his pants because that was better than showing up late for a Summons. I myself probably would've made a stop in the head. But I respect what he did. How's your training going?"

"Good."

Timothy did the shoulder salute to an AU. "Master

Eli's training me himself. We've found a lot of Minuses from my Yesterdays. I was on the wrong path all of my life. I'd built a *city* of Minuses. I told that to Master Eli and he liked it. He used it in a Discourse. A 'City of Minuses.' And he pointed me out." Timothy beamed.

Shaw and the man passed Building 14, whose front door was open. There was movement inside, three or four AUs. A Select as well.

Timothy said wistfully, "I miss TV."

"Sorry?" Shaw asked.

"Be our secret, right?" Timothy whispered, looking around. In anyone else, reluctance to admit that he liked television would be insignificant, or even played as a joke.

"Sure."

"I wouldn't mind watching a TV program here from time to time. When I was married we watched all sorts of fun shows. Not the news, of course. Master Eli wouldn't allow that. But maybe sitcoms. *Big Bang Theory*. That was a hoot. The new *Star Trek*. And Kelsey Grammer. *Frasier*. Oh, that man made us laugh. My wife and me. When we were . . . Well, it was funny."

"Did you talk to Master Eli about getting TVs?"

"Oh, I'm not one to make waves. He says we can't be distracted from the Process."

They arrived at the Square. Shaw stood at the outskirts of the crowd, gripping his notebook. He wondered if he could slip out, unseen, and retrieve the war club. No. A number of AUs and Inner Circles were herding everyone into the Square, as if guarding the perimeter. The crowd was the full complement, about a hundred people, the Novices, Apprentices and Journeymen in the middle, as usual. At stage right an AU was mounting a camera. The previous Discourses had been filmed on the ICs' tablets; this was the first time a camera, on a tripod, had been set up since Shaw had been here.

On the stage was a table, and on it sat a bottle of red wine, the cork sitting loosely in the neck.

Eli was off the stage, talking to Journeyman Marion. She was having trouble keeping from smiling in pride. Pinned to her blouse was a small bunch of dried lavender. Maybe the herb was supposed to be the symbol of the new group. Beside them stood Steve.

Eli nodded and he and Journeyman Marion climbed the stairs, followed by the chosen Companions and unsmiling Anja. As they took their places behind the table, the applause began, shouts too, instigated, of course, by the ICs. The two men and two women—the new Circle—seemed of mixed emotions. Some were embarrassed by the attention, some were smiling proudly. They sat behind the table. Marion took her place in the center. Eli stood behind her. It was a modified Last Supper tableau.

At Eli's gesture, Steve set down his bulging notebook, then stepped forward and filled the glasses sitting in front of each place. One for Eli too.

When the glasses were topped off, Eli stepped forward and looked over the crowd.

"Friends and Companions, it is my honor to welcome these individuals to our new group. The Circle of Representatives. There will be much work ahead of us, as we expand the Foundation throughout the country. And throughout the world. But we won't be stopped from spreading the word that the best . . ."

". . . is yet to come!"

Wild applause.

Eli raised his glass. "Here's to the Process. To the Foundation . . . To the Tomorrow!"

The Circle downed the wine. As Eli lifted the glass to his lips, there came a cry from the ground. "Stop!" It was Hugh, running onto the stage. He slapped the wineglass from Eli's hand. It crashed to the planks and shattered.

Gasps from the audience.

"It's been poisoned! The wine! You're going to die!"

61.

Cries rose from the Companions in the Square. The inductees leapt to their feet, dropping their glasses, horror on their faces. Everyone but Eli had drunk the wine.

"He got rat poison from Building Fourteen!" Hugh shouted. "Call the doctor! Get him here now!"

An AU pulled a walkie-talkie off his hip and radioed for help.

Eli called, "What is this? What's going on?"

Hugh brandished a sheet of paper. "We found this. A business plan he's drawn up. He wants to destroy the Foundation. Start his own. He's killing those you picked for the new group, Master Eli! And trying to kill you too."

Gasps and screams from the crowd. Several of the people onstage were gagging themselves to induce vomiting. They were disturbingly successful.

"He? Who?" Eli demanded. "Who are you talking about?"

"Him!" Hugh said, spinning around. His face was contorted with anger. He stabbed a finger at Steve.

The young man blustered, "I . . ." He looked to Eli, then back to Hugh. "No. I didn't do anything. I wouldn't. You *know* I wouldn't."

"Two Companions saw him in the gardening shed with the wine bottle."

"No, I swear." Steve's face was crimson. "I *never* . . . I love you, Master Eli."

Hugh said, "He was overheard saying he'd lived in your shadow for too long. You didn't treat him right."

"Treat him right?" Eli whispered. "He was like my son."

"Toxic!" somebody cried.

"He's a Toxic!"

"Judas!"

"Cast him out!"

"Kill *him*!"

"The doctor? Where's the doctor?"

Colter Shaw glanced at the agitated crowd, the fury in their faces.

Frenzy and panic too.

Better get to it.

He walked toward the stairs leading up to the stage. He disliked hurting anyone. He did, however, need to even the odds, given Hugh's martial arts skills and the fact he was vastly outnumbered. He walked casually past Eli's two bodyguards. Since the attention was wholly on the stage, Gray was concentrating on the drama, and Shaw thrust a fist into his gut. The man gasped, paralyzed. Shaw executed a fast wrestling takedown. The man landed flat on his back, moaning and gasping, the air blasted from his lungs.

"Uhn, uhn, uhn . . ."

Shaw knew the feeling. It wasn't pleasant.

In two seconds, the man's gun was plucked from the holster and racked. It was a Glock 26, nicknamed a "Baby Glock," for its small size. It had, though, a double-stack magazine; assuming it was fully loaded, Shaw would now have ten rounds to play with. He trained the weapon on Squat, who stared with wide eyes. Shaw motioned him to the ground and patted his hips. As Victoria had said, he was unarmed. "Ties. Now."

He extracted zip ties.

"Him, then you. Fast."

Squat complied.

Shaw searched and found he had no weapon.

A woman standing nearby glanced over and gasped. "What're you doing?" Her voice was incredulous.

Shaw said matter-of-factly, "Be quiet."

The woman, wearing a purple amulet, said, "You can't tell me what to do."

Shaw leaned toward her and growled, "Sit. Down. And be quiet."

"Okay. Yessir. I will. I will." She dropped onto the grass.

He climbed to the stage, the gun held at his side, away from the crowd. Eli and Hugh glanced at him once, briefly, then again. This time they noted the weapon. Eli's face grew astonished—then red with rage. Hugh cocked his head, noted the bodyguards and remained motionless, waiting.

Two of the AUs standing at ground level gathered that something was wrong. They glanced to Hugh, who gestured them to stand down. He'd observed that Shaw knew weapons and appeared prepared to use them.

Shaw strode up to Eli and held out his hand for the lavalier microphone, pinned to his white tunic, and the transmittal.

The furious man pulled it off and slapped it hard into Shaw's hand. The resulting thud was resounding.

Shaw returned to the center stage, scanned about him for threats. And saw none. Holding the mike to his mouth, Shaw said, "Listen to me! There wasn't any poison. It was sugar."

Murmurs from the Square rose like the sound of swelling waves.

"I replaced it myself." Shaw looked at the inductees, staring at him frantically. "You're fine." He added, "And it wasn't Steve." His eyes took in the audience and returned to the stage. "It was your Guiding Beacon who tried to murder you."

62.

Shaw couldn't join Victoria and Frederick because of what he had found on Eli's computer—the last document he'd given them to read behind the dorm. It revealed that at least five people were going to die onstage during the induction session: Journeyman Marion and the four Companions picked for the Circle of Representatives.

Shaw decided he should have been more suspicious of the mysterious Building 14—filled with gardening equipment and supplies . . . when there were no gardens, as Walter had told him.

He'd concluded earlier that the AUs on the porch were only there to keep an eye on the Square. However, what if his original theory was true? That they were there to protect what was inside?

What might that be?

Several pounds of rat and mice poison: arsenic trioxide.

Eli was going to take a lesson from Jim Jones of the

Peoples Temple in Guyana. The leader, of course, had no intention of "advancing" to the Tomorrow. He was setting up a fall guy. His fiction was that Steve had been behind the killings of the journalist Yang and John and was trying to shift the blame to Eli, in an attempt to derail the Foundation and create a cult of his own.

Shaw, Victoria and Frederick had broken into Building 14 and swapped out the poison for sugar.

I was thinking we'll find something in the kitchen.

Oh. That's good . . .

But Shaw couldn't just leave with Victoria and Frederick after the swap. Eli would simply find another way to set Steve up as a murderer.

Shaw had to expose the king and bring him down.

Somebody now shouted, "He's got a gun!"

Screams. Companions started to turn.

Shaw called, "It's all right. I'm working with the authorities." This was somewhat true: in the sense he would be working with the authorities when they arrived. Soon, he hoped. Pretty *damn* soon.

Eli started to turn but Shaw said harshly, "No. Stand there." Nodding to a place slightly before him on the stage. He wanted Eli where he could see him.

The man glanced toward the gun in Shaw's hand and complied, glaring.

Shaw's treatment of the Guiding Beacon generated a wave of murmuring and protest and gasps but the bulk of the Companions watched the stage, taking Shaw's words under advisement.

"Let me tell you about Master Eli. Whose real name *is* David Aaron Ellis. And Apprentice Carole was right:

fake names he's used in the past are Artie Ellington, Hiram Lefkowitz, Donald Elroy. He's a failed stockbroker and real estate developer. And now he's a scam artist. He's robbed you. And . . . he's ordered murders."

Gasps. And angry murmurs.

"He tried to kill these people onstage tonight and blame Steve because the police are investigating him for a murder in San Francisco."

"Lie!" was the unearthly bellow from Eli. "Toxic!"

"That's what the police helicopter was about. It wasn't a plot to discredit him, and it wasn't a mistake. Eli ordered the killing of a reporter writing about the Foundation. Did any of you know Harvey Edwards?"

The Companions, most of whom had been here for three weeks or less, wouldn't know of the man. But two or three of the Inner Circle glanced toward one another, shadows of recognition on their faces. They'd suspected something about their noble leader.

"Eli told Edwards to kill the reporter and then advance. He committed suicide by shooting it out with the police."

"Lies! He's one of them." Eli snapped his fingers and glanced again furiously at two tunicked AUs. Hugh gestured to them to remain where they were.

Some ICs began a chant: "Tox-ic, Tox-ic!"

The sound was anemic and soon petered out.

Shaw noted Samuel looking his way, his expression stunned. The Journeyman who had accompanied Shaw here, Timothy, also gaped.

"Kill him!" somebody yelled.

"Let him talk!"

Shaw pulled the sheaf of papers from his waistband. "This is from Master Eli's computer."

In disgust, Eli looked toward Anja, who couldn't hold his gaze.

"Eli wrote this earlier today. *After* the police helicopter was here. But *before* the ceremony just now."

Reading, he said, "'Statement to the police. After the terrible poisoning at the Osiris Foundation camp this afternoon, my employees searched the room of Steve Rindle and found that he had planned to kill me and key members of the Foundation. Someone stopped me from drinking the poisoned wine. Others were not so lucky. Our medical staff wasn't able to save them. From the documents we found it was clear he intended to steal my self-help techniques and start his own organization.'"

Steve was crying, shaking his head.

Eli raged, "Lies! I've been set up by the Toxics! Tox-ic, Tox-ic . . ."

Now, no one joined in.

Shaw continued, "'We found files indicating Steve planned to incorporate in California. Steve also was responsible for having Harvey Edwards kill journalist Gary Yang in San Francisco. He was going to blame me for Yang's death.'"

Shaw looked at the crowd, now silent. "You see? Eli knew about the poisoning ahead of time because he planned it. And the ones who poisoned the wine were Journeyman Hugh and some AUs. Not Steve. Steve was his scapegoat."

Eli muttered something to Anja. His rage was gone. Now his face revealed icy contempt.

Someone started a chant. "Lie . . . lie . . . lie."

"Kill him!"

The vast majority of the Companions remained silent. Somebody yelled, "Go on, Apprentice Carter."

Shaw said, "His trips to the Far East in the winter? Not so far, really. 'East' is Florida, where he has two homes, worth millions, and five sports cars—thanks to all of you."

"Stop him!" Eli was calling to two other AUs. They looked at each other uneasily and began jogging toward the stage. Shaw stopped them in their tracks simply by shifting the pistol slightly to the right. He didn't even aim toward them.

One held his hands up, comically high. Hugh grimaced, and the stocky man lowered his arms.

Before Shaw could continue, however, a dozen Companions began whispering among themselves, mostly men. Their faces were dour, shaded with anger. They would be loyalists. They divided up and moved toward the stairs at the opposite ends of the stage, a flanking maneuver.

"Before you do anything," Shaw shouted, "let me finish."

Eli cried, "Stop him! Get him! If the Toxics he's working for win, everything I've done for you will be wasted! The Process dies."

The threat was enough. Ignoring the gun, the two groups rushed the stage from either side. Shaw fired one round into the ground—you never shoot into the air. That sent some Companions scurrying but the mob was undeterred. Maybe they knew he wasn't really going to shoot any of them, or maybe they figured: I'm immortal; what's the problem?

They plowed into Shaw from both sides.

The gun flew from his hand, and he went down hard on the stage, pinned under a ton and a half of frantic believers.

63.

Gray limped on the stage, followed by Squat. Their restraints had been cut off.

Hugh glanced at Gray. "What good are you?" he whispered viciously.

Gray looked frantically for his Glock.

Eli called to the crowd. "He snuck in, a spy, a Toxic. I told you they'll do anything to stop me."

His gut and shoulder in agony from the piling on, Shaw struggled for breath.

"Kill him!" shouted someone.

Hugh and an AU pulled Shaw to his feet. Hugh said, "Get him to the Assistance Unit."

A zombie-eyed young man standing on the sidelines—a Select—nodded.

There'd be another auto accident tonight. Hugh had just signed the young man's death warrant but the assassin greeted the news as if he'd been listening to a weather report.

"Traitor!"

"Toxic!"

"Kill him!"

One woman, her eyes glazed with hatred, spat in Shaw's face.

Others milled about, aimless, confused.

The AU and the Select who were gripping Shaw's arms ushered him quickly off the stage.

When they got to the ground Shaw, gasping and breathless from the crush, called in a raspy voice: "United Technical Development. Triangle Pharmaceuticals. Talbot Manufacturing."

He and his captors got five feet toward the path when a voice called, "Wait!" It was that of an Apprentice, a man in his forties with a trim haircut, wearing expensive wire-rimmed glasses. "That's my company. UTD."

A woman said, "And Talbot. I'm the financial officer."

Shaw called out another company name, "Halifax Energy," before another blow from the AU silenced him.

"Get him out of here," Eli raged. "To the Assistance Unit."

"Triangle Pharma?" a man asked in a loud voice. It was Henry, the balding Companion at Intake the same time as Shaw, the man who'd lost his wife.

He and a dozen other Companions stepped in front of the men leading Shaw away. The two captors stopped, looking back toward Eli, who shouted, "Go, go!"

"No," the CFO of Talbot Manufacturing said. The slim woman with graying hair pulled back looked sternly toward Eli, then to Shaw. "Let him finish."

The crowd was growing quiet.

Hugh was unsure how to handle the situation without a full-fledged battle beginning. He gestured the AUs to wait.

Shaw called, "Do you know why the trainers ask about your businesses?"

"Get him out of here," Eli called.

"No, we want to know," said a tall man in his forties. It was Thomas, the husband of Carole—the heretic assaulted by Eli and the mob earlier. He was the one who'd recovered the Glock that flew from Shaw's hand—and he clearly knew what he was doing with the weapon.

Henry called, "I want to know too."

"Let him talk!" From the back of the crowd. Murmurs of agreement.

Eli said, "Don't listen to his lies. It's all fake, what he's telling you. He's trying to take the Tomorrow away from you. I'm the only one who can give you what you want."

"Shut up, Eli," Henry shouted.

This caused a murmur from the ICs and the loyalists but no one moved.

Thomas stepped forward, Carole behind him. He looked over the AU and the Select, then nodded toward Shaw. "Let him go." And raised the pistol to the Select gripping Shaw.

Henry growled, "Do it."

Hugh nodded.

The strong hands released their grips and the AUs and the Select stepped back. A few loyalists stepped toward

Shaw; Henry turned to face them, his fists balled up. Two other insurgents did the same.

Thomas said, "Go ahead."

Flanked by Henry, Thomas and his allies, Shaw climbed back to the stage and picked up the microphone. He repeated what he'd started to say a moment ago: "Did you ever wonder why your trainers spent so much time asking about your businesses?" Curiously, seeing the rapt attention focused his way, Colter Shaw had an inkling of the power Eli felt during his Discourses.

"Your clients, contracts, deals? Looking for all the Minuses and Pluses? Because what Eli really wanted was insider information. He recorded your sessions and sent the tapes to his business partner in Miami. He uses one of their shell companies to buy stock and real estate."

Some gasps. Companions were regarding one another, dismayed.

But then a voice, "You lie!"

A rock flew Shaw's way; he easily dodged.

"Lies, lies, lies!" Eli's voice, though, was by now white noise.

Shaw calmly continued, "Five years ago he went bankrupt. He decided to start a self-help outfit. He researched what would be the most profitable." From the stage where they'd fallen, Shaw lifted the papers he'd printed from Eli's computer.

"Here." He scattered them to the crowd. "Spreadsheets, projecting income from different types of organizations. One was getting rich in the stock market, one was getting rich in real estate. One was self-assertiveness, one was about sex training. And one was about selling immortality. The projected return on investment for *that* one was ten times higher than any of the others. It also won in the focus groups he held."

More of the loyalists had fallen silent.

"No, lies, lies!"

Shaw shook his head slowly and when he spoke next, he meant his words sincerely: "I'm sorry to tell you this. I know you wish the Process works. I wish it did too. But it doesn't. It's just a lie to get your money. Are any of you lifetime Companions?"

No one raised a hand but Shaw could see several faces glance at one another.

"It ever bother you that you had to bequeath part of your estate to the Foundation in your will—when he's encouraging you to kill yourself? There's an entry in his accounting ledger. Last year the Foundation made one and a half million dollars in income from bequests."

This drew a collective gasp from the grounds.

Shaw didn't feel the need to add that Eli's scheme was also about getting Companions into the Study Room. He saw in the faces of many of the younger women and some of the men dismay and anger. They understood they were victims of Eli's abuse.

Shaw did, however, have to add another bit of information he'd learned from Anja. "He's not an orphan and he never lived in foster homes. His parents are alive. They live in Fort Lauderdale."

Shaw scanned the crowd. Like many budding fights, the battle between loyalists and insurgents dissipated like steam. Some of the Companions were confused, some were thoughtful, some hurt, some mad. Individually or as couples or in groups, they turned and headed back toward their dorms or the Administration building.

Shaw's heart tightened when his eyes settled on Journeyman Samuel. The older man was staring from Shaw to Eli. There were tears in his eyes.

64.

ehind Shaw, on the stage, Hugh walked to Eli.

"It's over," the security man whispered.

Mouth open and looking like a lost child, Eli said nothing.

"David. It's over. Are you listening?"

Eli was staring toward Anja, who was walking down the far stairs, Steve beside her. The young gofer gazed at Eli with pure contempt. The two vanished behind the stage.

Hugh continued, "Now. We have to get out of here. We've got options, places that're safe."

"I . . ." Eli sputtered. "They want me to stay. My people want me to stay." Gesturing at the Square.

Shaw realized now that, no, the cult leader didn't believe in the Process at all. He'd created this fiction solely for the purpose of making a fortune. But he believed fervently in the power he derived from preaching to his flock. He was addicted to it. He'd bought into his own mythology. He was Osiris, the god of the underworld, the god of fertility.

Hugh muttered, "They're going to turn on you. We have to get the files, computers, hard drives. And leave. Now!"

Eli blinked, his face revealing devastation at the loss of an empire in a matter of minutes.

Hugh turned to Squat and Gray. "Go to the residence. You know the files to get. And the computer in the Study Room. The videos."

"Yessir," Gray wheezed, still not recovered from Shaw's love tap. He and Squat turned and hurried south.

Hugh noted his boss's dismay. He touched Eli's arm and repeated softly, "We'll find something else, David."

"Something good," the cult leader muttered absently. He was still numb.

"Yes. It'll be good. Overseas. Somewhere. Just as good as this."

His eyes wet with tears, Eli glanced at Shaw once more. His bewildered gaze was perhaps more chilling than the livid hatred of moments earlier.

Eli gestured to Timothy, the Journeyman who had accompanied Shaw to the Square, who stepped close. They had a brief conversation. The man nodded. Eli and Hugh walked into the woods to the hidden path to go to the Administration building and collect any incriminating evidence and either destroy it or escape with it and dump it later.

Shaw turned toward Thomas, still holding the gun. "I need that weapon."

"What you need doesn't matter to us." He put his arm around Carole's shoulders. He gestured at the gun. "Don't try to take it."

Shaw didn't try to take it.

He jogged into the forest and turned up the trail after Eli and Hugh. In a few minutes they would pass Building C, behind which his war club was hidden. That—and the element of surprise—would give him some advantage.

"David!" a woman's voice behind him called. Shaw glanced back. It was Anja. "Please, David. Let me explain!"

Eli stopped. His face was emotionless as he looked back, seeing both Shaw and, about thirty feet behind, Anja. Eli's eyes cut to the other side of a row of brush—where Timothy had been walking parallel. He was about even with Anja.

It was at that moment that Shaw noted that Timothy had removed his sweater. He was not wearing an amulet.

He was a Select, a suicide killer.

Master Eli's training me himself . . .

The man nodded to his boss, pulled a box cutter from beneath his tunic and charged into the brush.

"Anja!" Shaw sprinted toward her too.

Before he got close, Timothy was on her, grabbing the woman by the hair.

She gasped, "No . . . Please, Timothy."

Without hesitating, he drew the knife across the pale flesh of her throat. Blood cascaded and the woman dropped to her knees, then onto her side, her voice keening in horror.

Timothy glanced toward Shaw. Then the man who laughed at sitcoms and who loved to hum and was perhaps hoping for a spot on a choir in Omaha come the advent of autumn took a deep breath and gave the farewell salute—the double-arm cross. He called, "Good-bye . . . until tomorrow." And slashed his own jugular.

With a perfunctory look back at the woman who had been his longtime lover, Eli turned and hurried north, accompanied by Hugh.

Shaw sprinted to Anja. He'd been trained in the procedure for combat neck trauma. The classic treatment formula of "ABC"—airway, breathing, circulation— went out the window. There's no point in clearing an airway if there's no blood getting to the brain because it's flowing onto the sidewalk. *This* procedure was HABC. *Hemorrhage*, airway, breathing, circulation. The only way to save a victim of a wound like this is pressure, a lot of pressure, which was what Shaw dropped to his knees and applied now.

"Please," she gasped.

"Shhhh, I've seen worse. You'll be okay."

He hadn't, and she probably wouldn't.

She grew more ashen yet beneath her carefully painted-on makeup.

Shaw glanced up the trail and saw Eli and Hugh disappear toward the Administration building. He could only watch them hurry away.

████damn.

A voice called, "I'll do it. You go after him."

It was Steve.

"Get down here," Shaw instructed.

The man crouched.

"No. You need to be on your knees or sitting. This could be a while."

The slim young man did as instructed.

Shaw said, "Follow my fingers."

This he did too, tentatively, as the blood coursed rich and red over his skin. Then with more confidence.

"He . . ." Steve was whispering. "Master Eli. He . . ."

"I know. It's tough. But you need to concentrate."

"Okay."

"Feel the flaps of skin?"

"There? Yes."

Anja started to speak, then fell silent. Her eyes closed.

Shaw said to Steve, "It's not severed all the way. We can keep her alive. Clamp the slash. It'll be slippery but you'll have to do it. Use your nails for a grip. As hard as you can."

"All right."

"There."

"I've got it."

Shaw looked over the wound. "Good."

He rose, wiping blood from his hands, and saw movement nearby, a couple. Apprentices. Shaw called them over.

"We need help," he said.

"My God, what happened?" the man asked, as they joined him.

"Get somebody from the clinic here. Now."

"We will," the woman said. They turned and jogged away quickly.

To Shaw, Steve said, "Go. Stop him."

65.

S printing.

Shaw couldn't see Eli and Hugh ahead, though the two couldn't be far. If he was lucky he'd catch up to the men near Shaw's dorm, where the war club still lay.

Then: a flash of white. Yes, up ahead, there they were, Hugh and Eli, still alone, moving north toward the Administration building. Shaw slipped off the path into the forest to the east, where he could use trees and brush for cover as he closed the distance to his targets.

Hugh was right. The Foundation was over. Even if some still desired to believe, the precarious fantasy Eli had spun was shattered. That Eli had a go-bag in his basement meant he had an escape plan. He and Hugh would get away, leaving the remaining AUs to barricade the camp. When the police arrived, they would buy time for their boss by telling the tactical forces and negotiators that he was still here. Maybe one would pretend to be him. This would keep the authorities tied up for hours, days maybe, while the cult leader fled the country. With his resources, Eli surely had access to a private jet.

Shaw was sticking to the thickets of brush along the hidden path. He realized he'd intercept them just before they made it to the Assistance Unit. Eli and Hugh were looking back occasionally and, not seeing Shaw, would assume he was still with Anja, trying to keep her alive. Eli had probably ordered Timothy to attack the woman partially to keep Shaw occupied while they made their escape.

Shaw decided he would have to forgo the club; he couldn't afford the time it would take to grab it. He'd continue after the two men, come up quietly, then attack. Hugh would have to go down first, of course; a hard tackle, a paralyzing knee to the solar plexus, then a frisk for a gun. He guessed that wouldn't stop Eli, who would, in an instant, leave his friend behind and run. Shaw would have to pursue on foot and disable him too. Hugh would have zip ties; Shaw would use those to bind both men and drag them in the woods until he could get a phone.

He gave the plan a seventy percent chance of working. He hurried through the brush until he was only about thirty feet from the men, who seemed wholly unaware of his presence.

He felt confident he could take them by surprise. Make it eighty percent.

And those odds held right up to the instant two AUs from the front and two from behind rushed him.

Shaw understood why the foursome had gotten so close without his seeing. He'd been looking for gray tunics; these men were in the camo that Frederick had mentioned. Those from the rear slammed into Shaw hard. He went down, flat, breath kicked from his lungs. Before he could struggle upright, his hands were zip-tied behind him and he was being pulled to his feet.

"███ What's with the blood? Is he dying?"

"Listen to me," Shaw said, gasping. "It's over. The police're—"

"Shut up!"

"If you want to—"

The blow to the gut was delivered by the apparent leader of the band, a broad, freckle-faced man with fiery red hair. Shaw struggled to keep from vomiting.

"What now?" one asked.

Red told him, "Journeyman Hugh said make it look like an accident. Like he fell and broke his leg and the animals got him. Great Bear Notch is the closest. Let's go. He gives you any shit, hit him again."

66.

Shaw, hands zip-tied, and his four captors were now about a hundred yards from the camp. Not far from the escape route to the state highway where—he hoped—Victoria and Frederick had scored a phone and were presently giving tactical information to the FBI and the state police.

Red pointed. "There. I think it's that way."

Shaw could see the trees ending about fifty yards ahead, the forest yielding to rocky outcroppings.

"What's the Notch?" somebody asked.

Red said, "It's like a cave. Wolves go there. Mountain lions."

"Why's it called Bear Notch?" a broad-chested man, balding, and with a prominent scar on his neck and ear, asked.

Red rolled his eyes. "They got ▮▮▮▮▮ bear there too. Happy?"

"Just asking."

"Weird place. Lot of bones. Stinks. We get him down there, f——. him up and leave him. Like he fell and broke a leg. Couldn't get out."

So, Shaw decided, he'd run. When they neared the Notch, the AUs would grow distracted, looking for the best place to lead him into the gully. As soon as they paused, he would stop suddenly and pull away from the one that seemed the weakest—a slim blond man. The assailant would react by tugging him back. Shaw would then launch himself in the young man's direction, with a headbutt and knee to the crotch. He'd then run flat out into the deepest part of the woods. They'd follow for a time but would grow uneasy, afraid they'd get lost, especially if they split up, which would be the most logical way to pursue him.

Woods like these? In the summer? He'd have a ninety-five percent chance of survival. He'd have to saw off the zip tie but given the amount of rock in the vicinity that shouldn't take long.

He gave a cynical laugh to himself. Yes, ninety-five percent chance of surviving in the wood. But there was the caveat: *if* he escaped from four fit men, presumably armed with knives, as Timothy had been. Maybe a Taser. A firearm was another possibility. The chance of him getting away from *them*? Make it thirty-five percent.

Then again, thirty-five was as good as a hundred, if you had no other options.

Red, in the lead, held up a hand, signaling them to stop. He was former military, the gesture told Shaw. Discouraging. He'd have some hand-to-hand combat skills.

He looked to the right, where fifty feet away Shaw could see the cliff edge. "Over there, I think. That's it. Brad, with me."

Leaving only the two guards on Shaw. Good.

As Red and Brad started through the woods, Shaw braced, preparing to tug, lunge, break his prey's nose and then run.

Red, though, looked back. He squinted and returned. He crouched behind Shaw, who could only sigh as he felt a zip tie ratcheting into place on his ankles.

Hog-tied.

No sprint.

67.

Brad and Red returned from the cliff's edge to Shaw, Blond and Scar.

"It's there," Red told the others. "Like a pit, ten feet deep maybe. Stinks like a butcher shop."

"Made me dizzy," Brad said.

Shaw said, "You saw the helicopter. California Highway Patrol and detectives from San Francisco. They're investigating Eli for murder. You're accomplices."

"Quiet down," Red said.

"You cooperate, I talk to the prosecutor. He'll cut a deal."

"We didn't do shit," Red told him. "We're just rent-a-cops, wearing these stupid uniforms."

"Well, you're doing shit now," Shaw said. "It's already kidnapping. And pretty soon, it's going to be murder."

Red muttered, "You don't know Hugh. He's not somebody you want to f—— over."

"All right, well, let me tell you this. If he wants an accident, then the zip ties have to come off. When the

FBI finds my body, they'll find the ties. Even after the animals get to me."

The men were silent, Brad and Blond glancing toward Red.

"FBI?" Blond asked.

Red: "Shut up."

"They already have your fingerprints and DNA all over them. So they have to go. And I'll tell you this, whoever cuts them off . . . you're going to die." Shaw kept his eye on Blond. His voice was calm as the breeze around them. "I will crush your throat the instant my hands are free."

Scar said, "Maybe he knows some shit like Hugh. That karate."

"He doesn't know anything."

"He could sure handle that gun."

Red sighed. "Let me ask you: Does it look like he has a gun now?"

Shaw looked from Scar to Blond. "One of you is going to die. And there's nothing you can do to stop me."

This was not remotely true. What they could do was simply bash him over the head here, cut the ties and throw him into the Notch. He was about fifty percent sure, though, that given the urgency of the situation none of them would think of this possibility.

Red said, "We'll just beat you to ████ death here with a rock, cut the ties off and drag you down the hill." He gave an *obviously* shrug.

Shaw said, "Leaving your hair, DNA and fingerprints all over more evidence. They'll have you in a week."

"We don't have time for this," Red muttered. "Get him down there. Now. Break *both* his legs."

Blond and Brad dragged him forward.

They got ten feet before a high-pitched scream sounded from behind them.

The two men gripping Shaw turned fast.

Wincing, on his knees, his face as ruddy as his hair, Red was gripping his right shoulder with his left hand, a mocking version of the shoulder salute.

Standing over him, Victoria swung the war club once more. With a glancing blow to his head, Red went down hard.

68.

Brad and Blond released Shaw, who rolled to the ground.

Scar muttered, "B——h."

All three men pulled locking blade knives from their pockets and flicked them open.

The closest to her, Brad, charged. The woman easily sidestepped, crouched and simply held the club up. Basically, he shattered his own knee. The pitch of this scream was even higher than Red's.

Shaw scooted to a tree and rolled upright. Blond was calling on his walkie-talkie. "We're being attacked!" He sounded incredulous. "We're near Bear Notch. We need help."

A clattering response: "We're sending people."

Blond moved toward Victoria and nearly lost his jaw to the club before leaping back. He nodded to Scar, meaning flank her, which is something Shaw was surprised they hadn't done earlier.

Brandishing the club and keeping her eye on them, Victoria jogged to Shaw. "Roll over."

He did.

Blond called to his partner, "No, stop her!"

Scar moved in but a swipe of the club sent him scurrying back.

Victoria drew her butcher knife and sawed through the hand zips. She handed the blade to Shaw to cut the ankle ties. She rose fast, advancing with the club, standing low and well balanced. She never presented her back to either of them for more than one second.

Her eyes were as serene as could be.

Cold too. Ice cold.

Both men backed away.

Blond said to his partner, "You should've taken her. Afraid of a little pussy?"

"F— you."

Shaw climbed to his feet, with the knife held firmly, ready to slash.

They faced off, the foursome. Shaw could see they were inclined to run but were probably terrified of what Hugh would do to them if they let these two insurgents get away.

Victoria said, "Let's swap."

They exchanged club for knife. She held the blade expertly, as he knew she would, and her face seemed to glow with anticipation of a good fight.

Shaw was filled with an exhilaration too. In these dense woods on a cool clear day. A primitive setting, a primitive fight, even odds . . .

The men moved forward. The AUs backed away and went through theatrical but absurd gestures with their blades, like little kids mimicking martial arts moves.

"Got to the highway okay?" Shaw asked.

"Flagged down a truck, then I headed back. Frederick was on the phone when I left."

So the feds or state would be on the way.

Blond stepped in. Shaw sent him retreating quickly with some swings of the club. He thought about Hugh and Eli destroying or packing up evidence. "Better speed things up."

While Victoria proceeded against an increasingly uncertain Scar, Shaw feinted forward then retreated fast from Blond, who snickered. "Go on, run, asshole."

Shaw had gotten the distance he needed and launched the club underhanded—less lethal power that way. Its head clocked the AU in the center of the face, and he went down, groaning, blood pouring from his nose, hands covering the agonizing injury.

This left Scar advancing on Victoria. His confidence had returned, now that Shaw was unarmed. He eased closer yet to Victoria.

She too seemed to be impatient. "Okay." Spoken as casually as a waitress might address a customer. Taking the knife by the blade, she threw it into the ground about six feet from Scar. It landed handle up in the soft earth.

Scar eyed it cautiously, maybe wondering why, with such apparent control over the weapon, she'd missed him by a wide margin.

Victoria explained to Shaw, "Just in case I need it."

She wasn't in a defensive position as she walked toward Scar. Posture upright, hands at her sides. Strolling, actually. When she was about seven or so feet away, he lunged. She slid to the left and gripped his knife hand in both of hers, stepped forward to make sure he couldn't pull away, then twisted leisurely. With this maneuver, Shaw knew, you can control someone's entire body with minimal effort, and drive them to their knees or belly.

Or you can shatter the wrist.

Victoria went for the second option.

Shaw could hear the pop from twenty feet away.

"Ah . . ." Scar went white and passed out.

Victoria plucked her knife from the ground and said, "Sometimes you just don't feel like stabbing people. You have those days too, Colter?"

Resourceful, pretty *and* a sense of humor.

He said, "We have to go. Now. Eli and Hugh're in Administration. Evidence is going to disappear."

Quickly they zip-tied the men's arms behind their backs and pulled Red's knife from his pants pocket. Shaw slipped it into his sock. They flung the other blades deep into the forest. Shaw collected his bloody war club. Victoria pulled the walkie-talkie off Blond's belt.

As they started north along a narrow path, toward the front gate, Shaw nodded his thanks.

"You weren't in much danger," she said.

He glanced toward the four thugs and beyond them, Bear Notch.

Break both *his legs* . . .

"I'd decided to come back as soon as we found a car or truck. You weren't ready to advance." Victoria was smiling.

The walkie-talkie kept clattering, with demands for updates about the attack. It was Hugh's voice, growing increasingly angry at receiving no response. The good news was that he and, presumably, Eli were still in the camp.

Shaw collected his war club and gestured north, where Hugh and Eli were. She then touched Shaw's arm. "Hostiles coming." They sank into a dense huckleberry stand. Ahead were a half-dozen AUs, fanning out, moving in their direction. The reinforcements Blond had requested. "Weapons," she whispered, nodding forward.

Two of them held pistols.

Shaw and Victoria hurried back to the four men they'd just fought. Shaw bent down and whispered to Red, "You don't believe in the Process, right? You think this life is it." Shaw glanced at Victoria, who knelt and put her knife against his throat.

Gasping, he said, "I'm a ▇▇▇▇▇ bouncer is all."

She said, "What's your name, and if you give me a fake one, you're dead."

"Bullshit. That's murder."

"No, it's retroactive self-defense." The blade pressed harder. Victoria's eyes were dark pits.

Red gasped, "All right, all right. Andy."

"Do you go by 'Journeyman' or any title?"

"No, none of that crap. Just Andy."

Shaw flicked TRANSMIT on the radio. "This is Andy. Carter got away. We followed him to the residence. He's inside. We need more men!"

The response: "▇▇▇▇▇ hell. There were four of you."

A moment later was a transmission ordering everyone to the residence.

The group of AUs approaching them apparently heard the transmissions as well. They turned south and jogged down the path.

Victoria and Shaw turned in the opposite direction and hurried toward the front of the camp. In a few minutes they were crouching, in the tree line, behind Administration and the Assistance Unit building. Shaw pointed.

There'd be firearms inside.

She nodded.

They both surveyed the grounds, which were much as you'd expect after the chaotic events that had just occurred. Clusters of Companions were standing together. Some sat despondently by themselves in the Square or on benches. A woman wept openly. An argument was going on between two ICs.

An SUV sat beside Administration, packed with computers and files. Gray and Squat hurried up to it and shoved in boxes of documents. They then turned back toward the residence.

"You want a club?" he asked.

"Probably."

Shaw walked to his dorm and collected the second club still sitting in the nest of leaves behind the building. He returned, handing it to her. She wrapped the knife in the napkin and slipped it away in her back waistband.

She said, "They'll have a gun safe inside. Diversion in the front?"

He shook his head. "Too many AUs."

"Okay, we'll just move in fast—the back door."

It was ajar. Shaw looked. The back room—filled with office supplies and unmarked cartons—was unoccupied. And, yes, against one wall was a gun safe.

They shared a nod and, gripping the clubs, stepped inside fast. She pointed to herself and the door that led to the front part of the Assistance Unit, meaning she'd guard that. He went to the safe.

Damn. Locked tight.

He gestured to it and shook his head. Victoria scowled. He joined her and they peered through the crack into the corridor that led to the front office. Four doors lined the corridor, two on each side—one was where he'd been interrogated the other night. They slipped into the hallway and moved forward, testing the knobs. All the doors were locked. When they got close, Victoria lifted a hand and they both stopped.

Through the partially open door to the front office, they could see movement.

Yes, Eli and Hugh were here. Troubling. This meant that it was likely they'd finished destroying and packing up files and wiping the computers.

The two men were facing away. The men were speaking to someone Shaw and Victoria could not see. The conversation was amiable. There was laughter.

They were completely unsuspecting.

Shaw pointed to Hugh and formed a gun with his finger and thumb, meaning it was most likely that he was the armed one.

She nodded, understanding: Shaw would take Hugh. She would get Eli and the other person in the room.

There was a chance that Eli was armed but that seemed unlikely. In any event, he would know the least about firearms and would be the easiest to disarm.

Shaw held up three fingers and began tucking them away.

When the last digit curled tight, making a fist, he swung the door open and Shaw and Victoria stepped inside fast, clubs ready.

They stopped just as quickly.

Hearing them enter, Eli and Hugh turned, startled.

Shaw and Victoria stopped in the doorway. They both stared at the men's wrists. They were handcuffed.

The person they'd been speaking with blinked in surprise and glanced from Shaw's and Victoria's faces to the war clubs and back again.

It was the sheriff from Snoqualmie Gap, the man who was deep in Eli's pocket and who, Shaw understood, had just arrested the two men for the sole purpose of helping them escape before the real authorities arrived.

69.

Two gurneys rolled along the gravel path, powered and piloted by med techs from the Snoqualmie Gap Fire Department.

One of the complicated yellow contraptions sped along, the techs sprinting. The other moved more leisurely.

Anja was in the first. She was unconscious and ashen. Her neck was swathed in an occlusive—airtight—dressing. Shaw had once used Saran wrap for this very purpose; it was to avoid an air embolism. An IV dangled. It would contain not whole blood but a resuscitative fluid, like saline. Anja was alive because of the man who strode quickly alongside her, Steve. His hands and clothing were covered with blood.

The trailing gurney held the body of the man responsible for Anja's condition, the man who had advanced, Timothy.

Shaw and Victoria stood outside of the Assistance Unit. They had retrieved their luggage, which sat at their feet, though cell phones and car keys were still locked up.

This was reportedly a matter of finding keys to the lock-boxes; Shaw was sure, though, the keys wouldn't be "found" until the cult leader and his associate were long gone.

Another couple was present—Thomas and Carole. He was the one who had retrieved the Glock when Shaw had been mobbed, and refused to hand it over afterward.

Shaw understood what had happened. Thomas would have forced his way into the Administration building with the stubby little weapon and insisted on a landline or one of the staff's mobiles. He would have called 911.

Dispatch had dutifully referred the emergency call to the Snoqualmie Gap sheriff's office. The same law enforcers Shaw had seen at the site of John's death had arrived at the camp. The sheriff—his name badge identified him as Calhoun—knew that a pile of cash awaited him if he "arrested" Eli and Hugh and got them out of the camp before legitimate law enforcers showed up.

A deputy now led Hugh and Eli to Calhoun's own SUV and the men were helped into the back. Their hands were cuffed in front of their bodies, a procedural violation in every law enforcement agency in the world. Hugh cast a lascivious glance toward Victoria. She parried with a look of pure ice.

The AU, also in cuffs, was led by another deputy out to the parking lot. The two men chatted like they were buddies on their way to a hunt on the first day of deer season. Arresting him and any other AUs was simply for show. They'd be released as soon as they were at the Snoqualmie Gap Sheriff's Department, if not on the way there.

"Look," Victoria said, nodding toward the path that led here from Eli's residence.

Two deputies were carting luggage and go-bags.

"Bellboys," Shaw muttered.

"Bet the tip's going to be pretty nice."

The men set the items in the back of the sheriff's SUV and returned in the direction they'd come. Getting another load, Shaw thought cynically. The Guiding Beacon had to travel in comfort.

Shaw said to Victoria in a soft voice, "They'll have to take a statement. Stretch it out for as long as you can. They don't know Frederick's got the feds and state police on their way."

"Mine'll take as much time as reading *Moby-Dick*. That's a book I never finished; did you?"

"Never started it."

The sheriff whispered to some of his deputies, who nodded, taking in the instructions. When he returned, heading toward his vehicle, Shaw stopped him. "Sheriff Calhoun."

"Yes?"

"I've been a witness to several crimes on the premises here and I'd—"

"'Premises here.' Hey, you sound like a lawyer. Are you a lawyer?"

"No."

"Hey, gotta say, you got yourself some pretty fancy souvenirs." A nod at the war clubs. "Sell them at the general store downtown. Fetch a pretty penny."

Victoria said, "We'd like to make statements."

The sheriff looked over Shaw's bloody uniform shirt. "You sure you're not hurt, sir?"

"No, I was saving the woman who was just wheeled out. The one that Eli ordered murdered."

Eli, your friend. Or benefactor, at least.

Without reaction, the sheriff fished keys from his pocket and loped toward the SUV. He made a call on his radio. "Tony, you got the rest of Mr. Ellis's stuff?"

"On its way, Sheriff."

"'K. We gotta leave." He walked to the driver's side door.

"Sheriff," Shaw called.

The man lifted an eyebrow. His expression was one of boredom.

"Statements? We're ready to make them."

"You're quite the cooperative pair, aren't you, now? The prosecutor'll be in touch."

"You don't have our names."

"We'll figure it out." Calhoun dropped into the seat and fired up the engine.

Shaw crouched and opened up his backpack. He dug inside. A moment later he was jotting something on a page in one of his notebooks. He tore it out and walked to Calhoun, handed it to him.

"My name and number. Just to make it easy for the prosecutor."

"Thank you now. World needs more concerned citizens like yourself, sir."

Shaw returned to Victoria and they watched the deputies load the last of Eli's baggage into the back of the

4Runner. One of them closed the liftgate and tapped the side of the vehicle twice.

Calhoun accelerated fast through the YESTERDAY, TO- DAY, TOMORROW gate and into the gravel parking lot, leaving a trail of gray haze behind. Accompanying it was the SUV they'd seen earlier, the one filled with files and computers and hard drives.

Victoria tapped Shaw's shoulder and pointed. On the ground near where the SUV had been was a small white object. It was the sheet of paper, now wadded into a ball, containing his name and number, which he'd handed to the sheriff not two minutes before.

70.

Finally, the feds arrived.

Frederick's call to Tom Pepper had worked.

Special Agent Robert Slay from the Tacoma field office of the FBI had been accompanied by two dozen tactical, forensic and hostage negotiation agents.

"You're Shaw?" The strongly built, handsome man, wearing a navy blue windbreaker with the letters of his employer on the back, extended his hand and they shook. His hair was jet black.

"This is Victoria . . ." Shaw lifted an eyebrow her way.

She said, "Lesston." Her eyes swung to Shaw; apparently they were on a last-name basis now.

Hands on hips, Slay looked over the camp, the clusters of people in the Foundation uniforms. He said nothing but his eyes were taking in the Assistance Unit and the security men in the gray tunics. Most, Shaw observed, had changed to street clothes.

Slay took a call, listened. His expression was grave. "'K. Keep me posted." He signed off and turned his attention back to Shaw and Victoria. "Appreciate your thoughts on tracking 'em down, Mr. Shaw. I've got people on it. But"—he nodded toward the phone—"nothing yet."

As soon as Shaw had retrieved his phone, he'd called Tom Pepper, who gave him Slay's number. They'd spoken, as the agent and his teams sped to the camp. Shaw had warned that Sheriff Calhoun was almost certainly going to let Eli and Hugh go. He'd shared with the agent some thoughts on finding the two men. It had been unsuccessful so far—as he'd just learned from Slay.

Shaw asked, "How'd Calhoun do it? An escape?"

"Just let 'em go. Said there was no probable cause. Released all the evidence too."

Victoria scoffed.

Shaw pointed into the woods, east, near Great Bear Notch. "There're four perps tied up there. They'll need some medical attention."

Victoria: "Oh. Forgot about them."

"They might stonewall but they're not members of the cult. They're hired help. I think they'll turn, you give 'em the right deal."

"Charges?"

"Assault. Attempted murder."

"Who's the victim?"

"I'm the complaining witness."

Slay frowned at this. "And you took down four of them?"

Shaw said, "Had some help."

"What the hell is this place? David Ellis isn't in ViCAP or any of our files. Neither's the Osiris Foundation."

Shaw explained briefly.

"Immortality," the agent mused. Once again he scanned the Companions, most of whom were standing about aimlessly, wrestling with the death of the dream of living forever. And with the idea that they'd just been swindled. Slay said, "I guess if you're going to do stupid, why not do stupid big?"

Slay pulled out a digital recorder and pen and pad. He lifted a *you ready?* eyebrow.

Shaw and Victoria gave nods.

They got down to the debriefing. Both gave detailed explanations of their experiences. While not as long as a bloated nineteenth-century novel, their words contained plenty of information to form the basis of multiple counts to lodge against Eli and other Companions—sex trafficking, underage sexual assault, insider trading, possible money laundering, assault, battery, murder, kidnapping.

"How many people you think've gone through here?" Slay asked.

"Been going on for four years," Shaw told him. "There'll be a lot of members. Eli got away with plenty of files but there might be a list in Administration. Or in Eli's residence."

"We'll check them out. Some of them must've seen something indictable."

Shaw told him too about the Selects.

At this news Slay paused. "They're like suicide bombers. We'll have to track them down too. After this"—waving his hand, meaning the destruction of the Foundation—"they might be, I don't know, programmed to eliminate witnesses."

"And we have this." Shaw handed over the video camera that they'd hidden in Building 14, when he and Victoria broke in to swap out the poison for sugar. Shaw had lifted it from the office beside the Study Room. It caught AUs doctoring the wine.

One of them was Hugh. On the tape he could be heard barking to a colleague, "████, *get the mask on. This shit'll kill you.*"

"*It's poison. It's supposed to.*"

"*Looks like sugar to me.*"

"*Try some. Let me know how sweet it is.*"

Slay called over an evidence technician, who bagged the camera and took Shaw's name for the chain of custody documents.

The agent slipped away his digital recorder. "Just curious, what the hell're you two doing here? You don't seem like cult fodder to me."

Shaw said, "Just something . . ."

Victoria finished it: "Personal."

"Well, there's a story behind that," Slay said, in a tone that meant he didn't really need to hear it.

Steve approached. He had scrubbed most of the blood off his hands, though the shirt was ruined. Shaw noted that the red of the blood and the blue of the cloth combined to make purple.

"Anja?" Shaw asked.

"They can't say."

Shaw introduced the assistant to the agent. The young man, eyes red and swollen from recent tears, explained his job. Shaw told Slay about the notebook, which contained all things Eli.

"I hid it behind the residence. I'll get it for you."

Shaw had told Slay that SFPD Detective Etoile had reopened the investigation into Yang's death, which had undoubtedly been ordered by Eli because the reporter was looking into improprieties at the Foundation.

The agent now asked, "That notebook? Is there anything in it about a meeting between Eli and Edwards?"

"Yessir. He wanted me to arrange it."

Shaw asked, "When?"

"About two months ago."

Shaw told the agent, "Right around the time Edwards killed Yang."

Steve sighed. "Master Eli." He was staring out over the camp. There seemed to be no words he could find to express what he was feeling. "I did everything for him. Anything he needed. Anytime. Ever." Staring at his cuticles, still stained black from Anja's blood, he licked the corner of his mouth and said, "I'll get that notebook for you, Agent Slay." He walked toward the residence.

A stocky woman in a skirt and bulky sweater approached Shaw. She was in her fifties, maybe, her gray hair pulled back in a ponytail. Like a number of the Companions, she'd discarded her uniform. She still wore her amulet. It was red.

"I'm Sue Bascomb."

Not "Apprentice Bascomb." The spell had been broken.

Shaw and Victoria introduced themselves.

"Are you all right?" she asked, frowning.

The blood.

"I'm good."

"I wanted to say thank you. I was having doubts after the first few days but I couldn't quite figure out what didn't seem right. You in law enforcement, either of you?"

They told her no.

"Well, he would've gotten away with it if you hadn't stepped up. Those people onstage would've died." Bascomb shook her head. "I thought I was pretty savvy. But when I lost Peter, I went a bit crazy." She glanced around the camp. "I said, just give it a shot. See what this place can do. Stupid of me. Should've just muscled through the grief with friends and family. You lose someone, there's no easy fix. Anyway, appreciate what you did."

A nod. Colter Shaw did not wear gratitude well.

"I want to propose something to you," the woman said. "I was thinking about writing about my experience, about the Foundation and Master Eli . . . I mean about David Ellis, the con man. If I did, could I interview you?"

"Unnamed source, sure."

Her eyes on the residence, Bascomb said, "Preying on the lonely, the depressed . . . I think the world needs to know about Eli."

"Of course."

"Thank you. I don't want this to happen to anybody else."

Bascomb walked off, removing her amulet and tossing it into the wastebasket by the Assistance Unit. Shaw watched her pause and jot a few words in her notebook—using it now to record the story of her life in a cult, not nonsense about past-life memories.

Looking away from Bascomb, Shaw happened to notice another woman, sitting on the bench outside the Administration building.

It was Journeyman Adelle, his Intake specialist. She was slumped and her palms were placed flat beside her. Her eyeliner had run from tears. She'd be confronting what Shaw had told the Companions. She didn't want to believe him, though she was surely realizing that it was true: the Process was a sham. Her baby was gone. There would be no reuniting in the Tomorrow. It was hard to see her like this.

He turned to Victoria and waved toward his Foundation uniform. "I'm losing the costume too."

71.

oth wearing blue jeans and shirts—his gray, hers black—Shaw and Victoria sat on the bench where they'd met the day of Eli's Discourses.

She had kept the blue quilted vest provided by the Foundation. Shaw's jacket remained in the gym bag. He didn't mind the fractional chill in the pungent air. His Eccos were on his feet; his soles still ached from the sprint to try to save John, while wearing those flimsy slippers, and he decided against the boots he'd worn here. Victoria, however, was in boots, stylish, low-topped, brown, with two-inch wooden heels.

They were subdued. The view was stunning but, after all that had happened, Shaw wasn't able at the moment to appreciate the aesthetics. They had both gotten their phones from the AU unit and Shaw now called the local hospital. He got through to a doctor in the emergency room and asked about Anja's condition.

"She's stable. She'll survive. Your relationship, sir?"

"An acquaintance."

"There's no next of kin in her personal belongings."

"I can't help you there." Then Shaw had a thought. He gave the doctor Steve's name and told him that he'd have the man call. "They work together."

He relayed this news of her condition to Victoria. Then: "I don't know legally how involved she was in his scams," he continued. "She knew a fair amount about the operation. Didn't report it. That won't go well for her." His head swiveled slowly. "I should have made sure she stayed in the residence. After she helped me break into the computer I should've known that he'd turn on her like that."

"If she wasn't onstage, it might've looked suspicious. Eli could have guessed something was going on."

Still, Shaw said, "She didn't deserve what happened to her."

Victoria was quiet: she disagreed, he could tell. She would be a woman to whom very little happened if she didn't *want* it to happen.

She asked, "Do you think . . . when she thought she was dying, do you think she believed she was going to advance to the Tomorrow?"

"Maybe." It was possible. Though Shaw was also thinking: whatever comfort would be vastly overshadowed by the agony she felt realizing that the man she loved had just ordered her death.

"Oh, look." Victoria touched his arm. Her eyes were skyward.

A golden eagle soared. Most likely it was the same one he'd seen earlier. They were territorial animals; they ruled over an area that might extend to sixty or seventy square miles, and woe to any plumed creatures that encroached. Golden eagles are the second-fastest bird on earth, diving on prey at two hundred miles an hour. Only the peregrine falcon is faster.

This one, however, was in leisurely transit through the clear azure sky.

After a moment Victoria said, "Not revenge."

"Hmm?"

Scooting slightly away, she turned to him. "You said I was taking a big risk for revenge, coming here to kill Eli. It wasn't that. It was public service."

Shaw waited.

"I was stationed overseas. I had a mentor there. You ever serve?"

"No."

"Then you don't know. There're two enemies. There's the *enemy* enemy, and then there's the one you work with—and for. I'm not going to go where some women do and say that because you're a man you don't get it. There are lots of reasons people don't get things and being a man might or might not be one of them. I don't know. I'll just tell you: we have to fight on both fronts. Women do. Gretta was my protector and friend. We took on the Taliban, and we took on Staff Sergeant George Watts and Chief Petty Officer Wayne DeVonne and Lieutenant Colonel Bradley J. Gibbons, who'd have a tantrum if you didn't include the 'J' in his name when you introduced him.

"It wasn't every day and it wasn't full-on. Never attempted rape. It was flirting. Brushing up against you. Put-downs and bullying. It kept up until they felt you finally had the balls to do the job. Funny, that's how everybody put it. Male genitalia. Women and men. Nobody ever said, you have the ovaries to do the job."

She offered a mild smile. Shaw too.

"Gretta taught me to stand up . . . no, I should say, she taught me *how* to stand up. When to say, yes, sir, or ma'am. When to say no. When to ask why. When to call bullshit. When to know that you're going to put up with bullshit because bullshit's part of everybody's job. This's all pretty ▆▆▆ abstract, isn't it?"

"I get it."

She eyed him carefully.

"Then, yeah, the IED. That's a—"

His nod told her he was familiar with the unfortunately sanitized name for *bomb*. Improvised explosive device. In fact one of his reward assignments had been to find one that had gone missing.

"What's the difference between a cannon in World War One and a B-17 dropping a five-hundred-pound bomb in Germany? Probably none. But an IED? No cannon you hear on the horizon lobbing things at you. No air raid sirens. Just a stretch of asphalt, a trash can, a phone card kiosk, children playing, goats. Those ▆▆▆ IEDs could be anywhere. A baby buggy missing a wheel. That's what got Gretta and her team. Three dead. She survived. She said it was like God punched her. Everything moved, the whole world moved. I'm getting boring now."

"No."

"Gretta came back. VA, private docs, therapy. The treatment did what it could. One of the things she tried was the Foundation. I was discharged and moved to where she was living.

"I had dinner with her maybe two months ago. She was in a great mood. She said everything was going to be fine. She'd be forgiven for fucking up, or getting careless, or whatever the hell she thought she'd done over there. Maybe looked away, missed the buggy, maybe texting. Who knows? I guarantee there's nothing to be forgiven for. There's no ████████ handbook. There is only how to kill and not *get* killed, how to get intel, how to refuel vehicles, how to boil drinking water. But not on how to live that kind of life.

"At the end of the dinner, she hugged me and said, 'Goodbye, until tomorrow' and did that salute."

Victoria's eyes swung slowly from Shaw to the sky. Maybe looking for the eagle.

"She went home and shot herself. So happy, so content one minute. Then dead an hour later. I had to figure out what'd happened." She looked his way. "Like you had to with Adam."

She continued, "I helped her brother clean out her apartment and I found her notebooks from the Foundation. All her writing about the Minuses, Pluses. The regrets. The notes about how in the next life she'd be fine. She'd 'advance.' She'd be with her buddies who'd died. Her mother, her nephew. And me."

Victoria was silent for a moment, the breeze hissing through the leaves, clicking branches. She pulled the vest closer around her.

"Annual suicides among civilian women are about five per hundred thousand. For women in active duty or veterans, it's twenty-nine. You're a mother and you go to the Whole Foods after soccer practice in Omaha and the newsstand next to the door blows up, killing four. You're a businesswoman just shooting the shit with your buddy, having crabs at a restaurant in Baltimore, and your friend gets hit by a sniper shot you don't even hear until he's a pile of clothes on the ground.

"If that happens to you, you're never the same again. Ever. But we put on a uniform and so people think we must be different, we must be immune. We're not. It's just as bad for us. And the worst thing that somebody can say to you is, oh, let it go. The next life, you'll be fine. Eli had to be stopped."

After a moment, she put the darkness away. Smiling, she said, "Do me a favor?"

"Sure."

She handed him her phone. "Get a picture of me here."

Victoria walked out onto the grassy field and turned to face him. He lifted the phone. He took several shots. The lighting was good and with the resplendent mountains as a backdrop, he thought she'd be pleased.

Turning away, Victoria gazed skyward. "You see the eagle? I'd love to get him in the shot too."

Shaw was scanning the sky. "No bird."

"Call his agent," she said, laughing. "Have him set it up."

As he aimed the lens once more, Shaw heard the sound of brush rustling. He turned to see someone sprinting quickly through the woods toward the clearing. A heavyset man in a Foundation uniform burst from the foliage, red faced, sweating. He was gasping from the exertion. The climb up here from the camp was steep.

It was Journeyman Samuel. He glanced from Shaw to Victoria, who was closest to him. He sprinted toward her.

"Victoria!" Shaw shouted. "To your right!"

She turned.

It was too late. She had no time to strike a defensive posture. The big man's bulk and speed slammed her flat to the ground. She lay stunned and breathless.

Shaw dropped the phone and started running. "No, Samuel! No!"

The man gripped Victoria by the sweater, dragged her to the edge of the cliff and without a moment's hesitation pushed her over. Shaw heard her piercing cry as she fell the hundred or so feet.

Samuel rose and looked at Shaw, his tear-filled eyes revealing both sorrow and anger. He whispered, "Goodbye . . . until tomorrow," and leapt after her into the emptiness.

THREE:

ECHO RIDGE

72.

June 20

This time the rattlesnake was real, unlike the imaginary serpent Dalton Crowe had used as an excuse to shoot a hole in his rental car's Michelin a week or so ago.

Colter Shaw was hiking up a narrow trail of rock and dirt and gravel in a remote corner of his family's property in eastern California. The snake, a big one, was smack in his route, in its coiled state, lazy, probably full of a tasty rodent lunch. Still it was ready for a defensive strike, which would be fast and accurate. They are, after all, pure muscle.

Shaw had spotted it and paused at the same time as the urgent rattle from the tail began. Amazing how creatures come to be, he was thinking. It would have taken hundreds of thousands of years to develop this curious feature, which said, in effect, *Stop or I'll shoot.*

Shaw was not alone on his trek. He was accompanied by a solidly built black-and-brown Rottweiler. Another canine might have instinctively charged—not having learned from YouTube or 1960 TV Western reruns what the rattle meant. Chase tensed but Shaw's command, "Wait," froze him in position.

There aren't many defenses against a rattlesnake, other than gaiters—leg guards. Pepper spray is useless. Their eyes are protected with an impervious shield, and the capsicum that blinds us is like water to them. And, as many a person who's ever tried to Mace a snake can attest, if you're close enough to hit them, they're probably close enough to hit you.

As for Chase, the dog, a canine's physiology is less susceptible to snake toxins than a human's. But as an added precaution for this outing, Shaw had administered snake-bite vaccine. He recalled, from years ago, his father's question to the youngest of the Shaw children: "So, Button, the odds of a vaccinated dog surviving a rattler strike are what?"

Nine-year-old Dorion had squinted, considering. "Depending on size—of the dog *and* the snake—and where it strikes, maybe around eighty percent."

"Yep, good. And the odds of a vaccinated dog surviving a *dead* rattler?"

"Pretty much a hundred."

"You've got.it."

"But I don't want to shoot a snake, Daddy."

"Who does? But sometimes it's a question of you or them, Button. And the answer is always: you."

Shaw was wearing a hip holster in which sat his Colt .357 Magnum revolver (a model ironically named after another snake, a Python). But he didn't want to shoot a snake either. His thinking was that he and Chase were in *its* backyard, not their own—and, truth be told, the creature wasn't behaving badly at all; it was simply being a snake.

So he chose another option. Detour.

Shaw found a fairly straight branch, about four feet long, and trimmed it with his Ka-Bar knife.

Never go into snake brush without a trekking stick. You can push plants aside ahead of you, and if there's a strike, the snake will likely go for the stick.

"Heel," Shaw commanded and together he and Chase turned left and struck out through the dense woods. The rottie hewed close to Shaw's left thigh as they circumvented the rattler and continued on their mission, the human probing thickets before they trod through them.

That mission was the second of the two he'd been thinking of for the past several weeks, the one he'd put aside to pursue Erick and Adam . . . and, as it turned out, that little trip to the Osiris Foundation.

He was looking for what his father had hidden here in this mountainous part of the family property years ago.

In some University of California archives, Colter had found a clue that told him that the mysterious message was here, in an area roughly the size of a suburban neighborhood. A daunting search to many, but even if Shaw did not know the exact location, he knew *how* to find it.

The path now led them to the crest of Echo Ridge— where, years ago, the woman who'd been hunting his father, Braxton, had sent one of her hired guns to follow Ashton and torture him to give up his secret. Ashton had tricked the man and come up behind him. In the ensuing struggle, though, Ashton had slipped and fallen to his death. Teenage Colter had discovered the body—that was the motivation for his mad, and pointless, high-speed rappel down the face of Echo Ridge to the creek bed where his father's body lay.

Shaw reflected that he'd thought of Adam as the man on the cliff. Now, he realized that he was, as well—and so was Ashton.

Shaw had learned recently that Braxton had dealt harsh justice to her thug; the man was no longer among the living. The woman, apparently, had little tolerance for incompetence.

The hired muscle, Ebbitt Droon, had taken over his job.

Ironically, Braxton and Droon never guessed that Ashton had hidden the secret here. If they had, they would have returned to search and they never did. There was no other access to Echo Ridge except past the cabin and its security system, which Mary Dove had installed just after her husband's death. Braxton would assume the secret was hidden in San Francisco, where Ashton's efforts had been focused. To them, Echo Ridge was a conveniently deserted place in which to waylay Shaw's father and force him to tell what he knew.

The dog now tensed and looked to the left, through a tall line of sycamore, black walnut and gray pine. Brush too: bladderpod, creosote, lupine and snowberry.

A sound? Not a rattle—a crackling of dry leaves. Maybe deer? Bear? Detour was not often an option with the latter, and Shaw's hand dropped to the Colt. But whatever it was meandered away, as ninety-nine percent of forest inhabitants will do when they hear, see or smell you. The two continued on. He kept his eye on the trail and checked his phone for GPS directions.

Shaw felt the urgent anticipation that comes with closing in on your prey. What had his father found, and why were some people willing to kill—and others die—for it?

At the direction of the electronic navigator, he and Chase now turned away from the cliff and headed into the woods. They climbed onto a limestone shelf. Shaw checked his phone once more. They were on the eastern edge of the hunting ground. His father's coordinates defined an entire square mile, one filled with dense forest, thickets, brush and brambles, rock formations, streams and ponds.

He surveyed the expanse now.

"Let's get to it."

This was not an official dog command but Chase caught the gist, and they started down to the forest floor.

73.

Rottweilers fall into the American Kennel Club's "Working" group, a category of large dogs bred to guard, to pull small wagons and sleds and to perform search and rescue. The latter meant they were skilled trackers.

Shaw dug into his backpack and withdrew a plastic bag. Inside was a piece of what appeared to be wood, but was actually recycled plastic.

One of the survival skills taught by Ashton Shaw to his children was the art of hiding objects that could be found only by your allies. He never would use anything electronic, of course, but stuck with the basics. A popular technique among survivalists is to wrap the object you'll hide in something that has a distinctive odor detectable only by tracking dogs. If you need it to be hidden for only a few days, the dog will track the hider's scent. Ashton, however, chose something that off-gassed scent molecules for far longer than that: plastic, specifically recycled plastic, which has a strong and distinctive scent.

There were field scentometers—including the wonderfully named Nose Ranger—that might have detected the smell. But nothing located aromas better than a dog, and when circumstance provided one, he leapt at the opportunity.

Whatever was hidden here, Shaw knew, it would be in or beside something that was still, after all these years, radiating its unique smell. Shaw held it down to Chase's nose, and he sniffed enthusiastically. Shaw hooked a long lead to the rottie's collar and gave a true command: "Find."

The dog didn't race forward but moved fast in a zigzag from rock to rock, tree to bush. Shaw kept up, hurrying behind, his hand near the grip of the Colt. Detours weren't possible now, and if it came to a confrontation, a rattler would lose.

The rottie's nose was up, as he was air tracking. The buried treasure would be stashed in a cave somewhere, Shaw assumed, protected from the elements.

As the minutes turned to hours, Shaw began thinking that maybe this was folly. Was he here on the basis of false information? It was possible that Ashton, in one of his foggier moments, had *thought* he'd left the package yet in fact he had not.

However, this proved not to be the case.

Chase braked to a stop. He did what all search dogs do upon finding the target. They don't point, they don't bark. They sit down.

He was in front of a small cavern. A rock slide had covered most of the opening but there was a six-inch slit toward the top. Shaw gave the rottie a piece of venison jerky and crouched down, firing a beam from his tactical halogen light into the cave. No snakes. Just dust and rocks and—about eight feet past the rubble—what seemed to be a white box, about 9-by-12 inches and an inch thick, made, of course, from recycled materials. The seams were glued with thick adhesive, probably of the industrial-strength waterproof variety.

He started to pull away rocks but there was another mini-slide; he'd need a shovel and pickaxe and some timber to shore the cave entrance properly. He wasn't going to end his quest for his father's secret by being buried alive with it for all eternity. He'd return with the proper tools and lumber for shoring. He noted the exact location via landmarks and he and Chase began the hour-plus trek back to the cabin. They took their time on the descent—it was steep and gravelly in parts. Also, you never knew when you might come across a visitor in the middle of the path, coiled and cautious and just not in the mood to slither out of your way.

74.

Your boy did a good job," Shaw said to the couple sitting on the front porch of his family's cabin, which nestled in the expansive valley.

He rubbed Chase's head.

"'Course he did. I trained him." Teddy gave the dog an ear scratch too.

Velma laughed, nodded toward her husband. "Trained him to lie at your feet while you dish up a big helping of Netflix." Her voice was low and as smooth as her husband's was rough.

Teddy scoffed. "It'll come in useful someday: That dog'll never twitch a *muscle* when a superhero lands in front of him with a crash and does that down-on-one-knee thing. Why *do* they do that?"

Shaw had no clue what the man was talking about.

Velma and Teddy Bruin were visiting from Florida, where they were Shaw's neighbors. Both of their properties—each several acres in size—fronted a large and picturesque body of water in the north central part of the state. It was reportedly gator free.

Never believe it when somebody selling you lakefront property tells you there are no gators.

In fact Shaw had never seen any of the reptiles but he was inclined to accept that rule.

Teddy, early sixties, was round and rosy and—as his names, both family and nick, implied—had a bear-like quality, enhanced by a lengthy beard of the sort favored by Civil War generals. The man wore a brown hat, a slouch—the Australian military one. The right brim was pinned up to the crown, so a slung rifle wouldn't bump it. Not all that helpful if you weren't on the parade grounds, as the uneven tan on Teddy's face proved.

Slim Velma, about the same age, wore her gray-blond hair up in a do that dated to the 1960s, sprayed into the shape of a beehive, which Shaw believed was the style's actual name. Like her husband, she was in trekking khakis.

While they were indeed Shaw's neighbors, the couple was much more than that. They ran the business side of Shaw's operation, scanning the media for reward offers and supervising a bot that did the same online. They also took care of the finances and accounting, tasks that utterly bored Colter Shaw and at which he therefore was inept.

He had yet to tell Velma that he'd given away the Ecumenical Council's entire $50,000. Shaw was forever discounting rewards, if the offerors were in tough straits, or giving them extended payment plans. Velma didn't approve of his generosity and was quite vocal about championing his financial well-being.

The couple and Chase were making a cross-country trip in their camper (Shaw had bought his own Winnebago largely because of the test-drive he'd taken in theirs). A visit to California, of course, meant a side trip to the Compound to visit Shaw and his mother.

Shaw examined something protruding from Teddy's pocket.

"Is that an air horn?" Shaw asked.

"For bears," was the raspy reply.

The black bear population in California hovered around forty thousand, which was a lot of bears. There'd been attacks over the years, though to Shaw's knowledge the only black-bear-related fatality in the entire state in recent history involved a bear's killing a mountain lion that was attacking a hiker, saving the human. The unharmed bear wandered off, leaving the man with a sense of breathless relief and more than a little regret that he'd neglected to get a video.

The creatures were generally docile and timid. And, yes, they did not like loud noises. If Shaw was concerned about bears, though, especially during cub season, he carried pepper spray.

Velma chided her husband: "Air horn versus a bear. Isn't that like bringing a knife . . ." She paused.

Shaw knew the expression: bringing a knife to a gun-fight.

However, she finished with: ". . . to a fight where the other guy has a bigger knife?"

Teddy and Shaw laughed.

Velma said, "We didn't see any. Bears. I was hoping." She frowned as a thought arose. "Hey, Colt. I got the check for the thousand sixty dollars—the reward Erick Young's family offered. But I haven't heard a stitch about the big one. The fifty K. Should I call somebody about it?"

Busted . . .

"Well. About that, Velma."

There was nothing to do but tell her the truth.

The woman sighed. "Let me get this straight. You gave away a fifty-thousand-dollar reward, and then, for no money whatsoever, you spent the last few days nearly getting killed by Charles Manson and family."

He sought grounds for dispute but found none. "Pretty accurate."

"Lord, Colter, you're not made of money."

"You got a Barkley stuffed dog out of the situation." Shaw nodded at the toy he'd bought for her on the drive here.

"Be still my heart." She grunted, which given her melodious voice was a pleasant tone nonetheless. "Set a spell, Colt."

"The boondocks're growing on you, bride." Teddy chuckled. "'Set a spell'? You've never used that expression in your entire life."

She opened her arms. "Look around you. You gotta talk Western."

Shaw said, "Got some things to take care of right now. I'll see you at dinner."

Shaw walked into the kitchen, where his mother was chopping vegetables.

Mary Dove resembled a lean frontierswoman, her gray hair in a braid. Her present appearance wasn't very different from that of years ago, when she was a star medical professor, grant director and psychiatrist/general practitioner in the Bay Area. Her quiet yet unyielding demeanor also was largely unchanged. After Ashton's death, most in the family assumed she'd resume her life in San Francisco. Colter had known she wouldn't, though. Here she'd remain, practicing general medicine and physical therapy, hosting retreats on topics like women's health and psychopathology, and delivering the occasional baby.

"Well?" She gestured vaguely in the direction of Echo Ridge, miles away and not visible from the cabin.

"Found it." He told her where the package was, that he'd get it in the morning.

Mary Dove was incapable of registering surprise but her son thought that maybe, just maybe, her eyes widened a millimeter or two.

"We'll talk when you do. Decisions'll have to be made." Mary Dove's voice was firm. After all, what Shaw had found at Echo Ridge was this secret that had led to her husband's and others' deaths. She was not a vindictive woman by any means—revenge, as Victoria had suggested, is a waste of time at best and leads to misfortune at worst. But self-preservation and survival of the family? That was paramount. Shaw had seen his mother calmly lift a .30-30 to her shoulder and squeeze off a round to drop a rabid wolf. To learn Ash's secret meant to understand a lethal threat. And once you comprehended a risk, you could minimize it.

Or, better, eliminate it.

Mary Dove now poured two cups of coffee, added

some milk to each. Shaw took them from her and walked into the living room of the cabin and looked out the window. He said, "Always liked this view."

"Beautiful," said Victoria Lesston, who was sitting on the couch. He handed over a steaming mug and sat down beside her.

75.

When she'd fallen, she'd fallen into water, not upon rock.

In anger or dismay, Samuel hadn't planned his assault; he'd simply picked the target he could succeed with. He knew he'd never beat Colter Shaw. So he'd flung Victoria over the cliff, assuming that a rocky shore lay below. Or perhaps not assuming anything at all.

In fact her landing bed was the deep lake that stretched to the foothills below the soaring peaks in the distance.

Shaw had run to the cliff's edge. And peered down to the place where Victoria floated faceup, bobbing, bobbing.

Samuel too floated but his back was skyward.

Shaw had called Special Agent Slay's number, gave his location and said, "Now. EMTs." Then he assessed. Eighty feet. Not an impossible dive but one whose trajectory would have to be planned perfectly, and practiced.

No time for that. He pulled off his shirt, shoes and

socks. Then he'd climbed down to a narrow ledge about twenty-five feet below the crest.

Shaw gazed down. The shade of the water suggested it was deep.

No time for percentages. Victoria was going under.

He leapt, windmilling his arms to stay vertical, which never worked as well as you'd hope, he'd learned. Jumping from this height he hit the water at twenty-five miles per hour. He reflected in the three-second descent that one can still float with two broken ankles.

Then the jarring impact, compressing bones and muscles and organs. Shaw managed to fill his lungs an instant before hitting the surface. The stinging cold, though, had the effect of pushing out all of that air.

His soles stung like hell but the complex architecture of the ankles remained intact; water had not shattered bone, and the lake bottom was far beneath.

He kicked hard to Victoria and, in a lifeguard's grip, got her to the shore.

Shaw had looked back. Samuel might have been alive when he hit. Probably wasn't now. In any event, survival involves triage, the decision-making process about assessing who is likely to live and who is not. Shaw had removed Inner Circle Journeyman Samuel from his thoughts.

Soon, fire and rescue had deposited them both on the top of the cliff. The medics examined Victoria, ran their tests and determined that nothing was broken; her spine and legs were fine. She had, however, walloped her shoulder. Maybe dislocation, rotator cuff issue. They affixed her arm to her body with flesh-colored bandages to keep it from gritty movement and she was offered painkillers, which she declined.

She also vetoed a trip to the local hospital.

"Been hurt worse. This's nothing."

With her good arm hooked through his, Victoria and Shaw, in fresh clothing, walked back to the staging area in front of the YESTERDAY, TODAY, TOMORROW gate. The place still bubbled with chaos. FBI and state police crime scene evidence technicians were doing their meticulous job, as busy and efficient as accountants on April 14. Other investigators were under tents, which had appeared miraculously, vacuuming up details from the Companions and staff.

Shaw had noted that many of the law enforcers used tablets just like those the Foundation staff carried around.

Victoria released him and snagged her backpack with her good arm.

Shaw asked, "You drove, didn't you?"

"My pickup. There. The black one. It's got a manual, so I'm not driving anywhere soon. I'll bus it to wherever they drop us off. Call my parents or brother or a friend."

"Where's home?"

"My parents're in Glendale."

Not really an answer to the question. He assumed a woman of her age who is a security consultant/former soldier doesn't live with Mom and Dad. However, no need for her to be completely forthcoming. Shaw, after all, was not unspooling his own pertinent data to her particularly quickly.

Victoria had continued, "It'll be an adventure. I

haven't stayed in a hotel across from a bus station since that post-college junket to Europe. I'll bet there's even a Jack-in-the-Box on the corner."

Shaw fished his truck keys from his pocket. "Let me throw an idea out there."

She glanced his way, her eyes tinted with cautious reception.

He pitched his thought, and, after some mental juggling, she said, "Sure."

An hour later they were on their way to Tacoma, where he would return the Silverado and pick up the Winnebago.

On the way, Shaw negotiated the switchbacks and Victoria handled the phone, trying to get details of the pursuit of David Ellis and Hugh, whose last name turned out to be Garner.

Special Agent Slay and the state police, though, were still not having any luck in tracing them.

Once in the Winnebago, they hit the road, south. They made good time. The first rest break was well past Oregon's southern border, in the small town of Barkley Heights, California. The burg's WELCOME TO sign sported a cartoon dog, its open mouth raised skyward, tongue dangling.

"A barking dog? Not the friendliest of logos," Shaw said.

"Why not a seal? Seals bark," Victoria pointed out.

"Don't imagine there's a seal within four hundred miles."

"Logic and town planning," she said, "don't always go hand in glove."

They looked around them for a restaurant or bar.

"Not much of a town," Shaw observed.

"But I'll bet you can buy plenty of Barkley the dog toy souvenirs and T-shirts."

They parked and walked into the only diner on the main drag.

Victoria won the bet.

76.

Now, in the Compound, they sat on the old couch, which was covered with a Native American blanket. Shaw sipped from the coffee mug and asked, "You okay?"

"The worst movie line ever written," Victoria replied.

"Hm?"

"Movies. Big gunfight. Car crash. Tornado. Sharks. Aliens. There's a lull in the action. Hero A—that's you—says to Hero B, me, 'You okay?' Cliché. The scriptwriter's asleep at the switch."

"That may be. But it's a valid question. You fell off a cliff."

"Was thrown."

"And the answer is?"

Victoria said, "Better every day. She's good, your mother. I've had PT, time to time, and I know a pro when I'm worked on."

They were facing east, and the lowering sun behind them was igniting mountaintops in a most impressive way. Even in this gentle month, defiant snow embraced the staunch peaks.

Shaw had originally thought, believing Victoria to be beset by the loss of spouse and child, that he might arrange for her to see Mary Dove for psychological help. That plan had been negated by the facts: she was *homicidal*, not suicidal. But, after Samuel's attack, it had then occurred to Shaw that Victoria might benefit from some time in the Compound where his mother's physical therapy skills might be of some help.

"What's her plan?" Victoria asked. She was referring to Anne DeStefano, the deprogrammer. Shaw had spoken to the woman at length about the Osiris Foundation.

DeStefano had said, "A lot of cults talk about immortality. Not a lot of them encourage you to see if their theory holds up. And people seemed to buy it?"

"Enough did." Shaw had given her the relevant details.

"I'm going to get on top of it now. Since most of the members were in for the short-term—just three weeks' indoctrination—it shouldn't be hard to reverse most of the damage. The ones who came back for the follow-up sessions will take a bit more work."

Shaw told Victoria that DeStefano would be in touch with the authorities interviewing the Companions and give them her name and the names of psychologists and deprogrammers in the areas where they lived.

Shaw had also heard from Walter and Sally, who had returned home safely to Chicago. Abby was staying with them for the time being but would soon be released to child protective services in her hometown. Frederick and

Shaw had spoken several times. He was working with the police to build the case against Eli and Hugh.

Movement from their left. Chase plodded close, moving with purpose. Like an airplane easing into the airport gate, he turned and slowed to a stop between them. Then flopped down, his chin on Victoria's sneakered foot.

She looked into the sky. "Hey, there. Is that a . . . another golden eagle?"

Shaw squinted. "Believe so."

Their mascot. A thought Shaw kept to himself.

The dark brown form was winging muscularly back toward the forest and cliffs. "That's a male. It's mating season now and the mother will be with the eggs for about a month. They don't make nests. They build platforms."

"So Dad's been grocery shopping." She then asked, "What's the latest on the Guiding Beacon and his sidekick?"

Shaw shook his head. "Not good. According to that agent, Slay, they were spotted getting into Canada, but then disappeared."

The authorities had contacted the Royal Canadian Mounted Police, who were sympathetic, but the area of southern British Columbia was huge and the Canadians simply didn't have the manpower for the kind of search necessary to track down Eli and Hugh.

His phone hummed with a number that was only slightly familiar, like that of a cousin you've met only once, at a wedding a few months ago.

"Hello?"

"Mr. Shaw, Bob Tanner."

Erick Young's attorney in Tacoma, Washington.

"Just wanted to let you know that the charges've been dropped. The police tracked down a couple of kids in a neo-Nazi cell east of Tacoma. Forensics on the graffiti on the church matched cans of paint in their possession. They pled. And when the detectives interviewed the lay preacher? It was like you said: the janitor started shooting at Erick and Adam, and Adam only returned fire. After the boys fled, he gave the gun to the preacher and told him to hide it. He didn't have a license."

Shaw thanked the attorney and disconnected. Victoria knew something about the reward for Erick and Adam and he explained how the job had been resolved.

Shaw and Victoria sat in silence for a moment.

"Just for the record, I'm no longer murderous."

"So my mother can get the sharp knives out?"

She clicked her tongue. "Sometimes normal gets bushwhacked."

How well Colter Shaw knew this—the man who traveled the country, picking through the bones of mysteries that some people hadn't been able to solve, and others simply didn't care about and still more decidedly did not *want* to be solved.

Shaw received a text. He read it twice and rose. "Have an errand to attend to."

Victoria said, "See you at dinner?"

"Probably not."

77.

Shaw preferred his Winnebago and motorcycle for transportation. However, he picked the vehicle to suit the need.

Presently he was fourteen thousand feet in the air, aboard the Learjet, an older model, a bit battered but dependable. The trip was expensive, as all private aviation flights are. Yet he had no option. Time was critical, and commercial wouldn't get him to the town he sought quickly enough.

As they flew, he thought of the box hidden at Echo Ridge. What would it contain?

Whatever that might be, it was worth killing for. Torturing too. He pictured Ebbitt Droon's face, determined to get the treasure, as he pointed a gun at Shaw's knee.

A voice from the cockpit. "We're landing, Mr. Shaw."

The plane swooped down toward the runway, the craft skewing sideways at an acute angle—it was called crabbing and would be alarming if Shaw had not experienced small aircraft landings several dozen times. The

Lear straightened at the last minute, flared and touched down smoothly. They taxied to the fixed base flight operation and cut the engines.

Shaw rose and stretched—to the extent he could in the low-ceilinged interior—and walked to the door.

"This won't be long."

"What should I do about the flight plan?"

"One option is I'll be going back home. The other?" He shrugged. "I'll let you know as soon as I can."

"Sure, Mr. Shaw. Good luck."

The spread was pretty much as Shaw expected: a rambling one-story house with two garages and a workshop attached. A shed behind the home that could've inspired the set designer for *Texas Chainsaw Massacre*. As he drove the rental up the dirt drive, he passed a messy shooting range, in which were mounted dozens of black iron targets. They'd ring like gongs when hit. The ground was littered with fun targets: exploded milk jugs and glass soda bottles blown to dusty smithereens.

The Montana hills were in the background, and ridges of trim forests surrounded the place. The grounds here, though, were mostly scruffy and overgrown. Dead stumps and fallen branches protruded from thick, mustard-colored swamp. The smell was what you'd expect.

On the other hand, there were some pleasing aesthetic elements: an elaborate koi pond was filled with a dozen sleek, elegant inhabitants, in sharp black and white and stark orange. There was, of all things, an easel set up beside a rusting V-block engine; the canvas was a well-done oil of a mountain peak and circling bird. It was not an eagle.

He was thirty feet from the porch when the screen door opened. Before he saw anything other than a beefy hand and tree-trunk arm, a voice called, "Well, if it ain't my good old buddy."

Grinning, Dalton Crowe stepped out and trooped over the planks, which sagged under his weight. He seemed to be wearing the same outfit as when he'd shot out the tire of Shaw's rental Kia last week: camo overalls and lumberjack shirt. A .45 autoloader was in a holster, riding high on his broad hip.

"So nice of you to come for a visit, Shaw." Crowe looked him up and down. His smile was less welcoming than gloating. Shaw's trip here had been both expensive and inconvenient, and Crowe knew it.

"Here." Shaw pulled out his wallet, extracted a check and handed it to the big man.

Crowe pulled out his cell phone and took a picture of the draft. Odd to see a biker/mountain man taking advantage of a camera-phone deposit. But the truth was, Crowe's embrace of high technology was why Shaw was here.

"'K." He handed Shaw a piece of paper. "That's the name of the app you download. And the user name and passcode."

The name was: *TroubleMan666*.

Shaw pocketed the slip and walked away.

The man grumbled, "I'm doing this as a favor, Shaw. You still owe me for the reward, the whole fifty K. I woulda got them boys, you hadn't ████████ cheated. I'm going to remember that."

Without pausing, or turning, Shaw nodded at the easel. "Like the painting, Crowe."

An hour later, he was in yet another rental, many miles
away. The Land Cruiser SUV was rocking over an
unlit dirt road. He was taking his time.

He checked the GPS. Drove another mile and then
noted a haze of illumination ahead of him. It was a small
town in the hills. The name of the place was Moody.
There was a lake nearby, and the burg was dedicated, it
seemed, to the art and business of fishing. You could buy
bait everywhere except for the ice cream parlor, a used
bookshop and an off-brand cell phone store, according
to window signs.

At the one traffic light in town he turned right and proceeded to Lake View Motor Inn. When he was nearly there,
he pulled onto a service road. He killed the engine.

The motel was in a good location for what he had in
mind. Behind the place was a dirt road that bypassed the
town and led south, good for an escape. He'd checked it
out on Google Earth and some better topographic maps
and he knew that the SUV could handle the terrain and
keep ahead of pursuit.

Shaw slipped from the car and closed the door, leaving the vehicle unlocked. He picked up the empty plastic
grocery bag—a thick one—and slipped it into his jacket
pocket. No sport coat now. He was dressed in black jeans
and matching tactical assault jacket. Gloves too, made of
thin leather.

Through the bushes he made his way to the dimly lit

motel. He smelled lake and trash, scents that might or might not have been related. He came to a dilapidated fence and, when he pushed open the gate, it fell to the ground.

The motel was composed of individual cabins for guests and Shaw now oriented himself. Keeping to the shadows, he slipped close to Number 7. The clapboard structure was one of the larger units and it featured a private path down to a dock jutting into the dark lake. He detoured briefly and looked over the pier. A covered rowboat was the only vessel along this stretch of weedy, placid shore.

He returned to the cabin and eased into the space between the outer wall and a row of shrubbery, placing his feet carefully. At the window, which exuded soft, yellow light, he paused and looked inside. The unit was a suite, and Shaw could see into both lit bedrooms.

Unoccupied.

On the floor were luggage, backpacks and cardboard cartons. The TV was on but silent. Local news.

Let's get to it, he told himself.

From his pocket he extracted a tool with a flat blade. A window lock opener. Similar to the dinner knife he'd used to break into the various buildings at the Osiris Foundation, though this was made for that purpose and was therefore much more efficient. Thin and forged of titanium. In a few seconds, the lock was breached and he slid the window up. Just as at Abby's dorm, Shaw went through the awkward maneuver of boosting himself up to the sill, sticking his head in and tumbling to the floor inside. He rose and looked around him.

He supposed the occupants were out to dinner and would return soon.

Shaw unfurled the grocery bag and walked around the room, filling the sack.

Five minutes later, he paused and listened. Then walked to the front door, undid the chain and deadbolt and opened it fast, stepping outside.

He nearly collided with the room's two occupants, who, just like him, had parked their car some distance from the cabin and walked here.

David Ellis—Master Eli—gasped and dropped the carry-out bag of restaurant leftovers he held.

The man with him, Hugh Garner, didn't waste a moment. Instinctively he went into a combat stance and launched a knuckly fist directly toward Shaw's solar plexus.

78.

Shaw didn't move, intentionally not lowering his center of gravity into a defensive posture.

The result was that Hugh's solid fist slammed directly into the bulletproof plate that was part of Shaw's tactical jacket. At the *thonk*, the man blinked in surprise and winced in pain.

Hugh's hand drew back, invisibly fast, for a second blow—aimed at the head—and now Shaw prepared to fight. He flung the filled grocery bag into the weeds outside the door, far from the reach of the two men. He braced and when Hugh's knotty fist streaked toward him again Shaw danced aside and the hand glanced off his shoulder.

The blow didn't hurt much and merely knocked him into the doorjamb.

Behind Hugh, Eli had drawn a pistol. "I've got him . . . Get back."

This was the opposite of what Shaw had anticipated; he'd thought Hugh would be armed and was planning on getting the gun away from him. Eli aimed, and Shaw did the only thing he could do: he dropped low and launched himself into Hugh, his shoulder connecting with the man's belly and driving him back. He drew on his wrestling training and the grappling skills Ashton had taught the children when they were young. He gripped the man's leg and tilted and they went down together.

"You f——r." Hugh grunted.

"Get out of the way!" Eli was calling. Shaw held tight, knowing Eli wouldn't fire as long as the two men were intertwined.

Hugh pounded hard on Shaw's back and shoulder and head, chopping; the blows were painful, though not debilitating. Shaw managed to land a strike of his own—a lucky one—on Hugh's ear and the man cried out in pain.

Shaw hoped the eardrum had ruptured but it probably hadn't.

They rolled into the dirt, as Eli walked close, holding the weapon unsteadily. "Move, get away!"

"No, no shots!" Hugh whispered. "The noise."

Shaw took advantage of Eli's uncertainty. He broke away, lowered his stance and held his hands out, circling. Shaw assumed some generic kung-fu position—something he'd seen in a movie. It was meaningless. Hugh recognized it as such and smiled.

Eli said, "Hugh, let me—"

"No. I want to take him," the big man muttered.

And that was undoubtedly true; Shaw had destroyed Hugh's very lucrative and enjoyable life. But this fight would not be an opportunity for the former head of the Assistance Unit to take anything.

Shaw feinted to the right, then veered the opposite

way and sprinted fast, tackling Eli. He went down hard. The man's eyes turned from expressions of fury to fear. Shaw realized that his thoughts earlier were right. The otherworldly color of his pupils came from contact lenses. The shade now was everyday blue.

"Oh, ⬛⬛⬛⬛⬛⬛! Lose the gun. Toss it." Hugh's voice was thick with disgust. Maybe he was upset that Shaw wasn't playing fair and participating in a mano-a-mano battle to the death.

Eli tried to pitch the Glock but Shaw ripped it from his hand and rolled away. He racked the slide, making sure a round was chambered, and he aimed between the two men.

Hugh held up his hands, palms out. "Look. We can get you a lot of money. I mean, a lot." He nodded toward the grocery bag. "Just leave the documents, the evidence, whatever you stole. We can give you cash right now. Fifty thousand. A hundred."

Involuntarily, into Shaw's mind came some images: Samuel's face of sorrow as he threw himself off the cliff.

Master Eli truly saved my bacon when it came to Mom and Dad . . .

Adelle's expression as she sat, slumped on the bench.

I lost my baby two years ago . . .

And he heard Victoria's voice as she told him of Gretta's suicide.

The muzzle of the Glock strayed toward Eli, who cringed and held up a palm. "No, please . . . no."

Shaw reflected on another of his father's rules.

Never point a firearm at anyone unless you intend to pull the trigger.

Colter Shaw pulled the trigger.

79.

As he bounded over the dirt road in his rental SUV, Colter Shaw learned a fact.

The men had another gun.

As they pursued him in an SUV of their own, Eli behind the wheel of the dark gray vehicle, Hugh would fire in Shaw's direction.

This was because of the gunshot back at the motel. As tempted as Shaw was to kill Eli on the spot, he hadn't in fact aimed for the cult leader. Instead, he'd shot Hugh in the calf, flung the gun into the lake and, snagging the grocery bag, sprinted back to his vehicle. Eli had apparently ducked into the motel cabin and got the second gun, and together they'd sped after Shaw.

Another crack of gunshot.

Handguns are relatively inaccurate under the best of conditions and the combination of the unpaved surface and Shaw's evasive driving meant that none of the slugs fired his way hit the Land Cruiser.

As he barreled down the dark road, Shaw clocked the

miles from the cabin: two, three, four . . . The vehicles were hitting sixty and seventy miles per hour, and Hugh and Eli's—piloted by the desperate cult leader—was slowly gaining.

A glance at the GPS map. Ahead, a mile or so, was a sharp bend in the road. He wondered at what speed he should take it.

He ducked as, finally, a bullet hit the rear of his rental. No injury, no damage—other than a hole, of course. He began to swerve even more severely, though.

Which is when he came to the jog.

It was more pronounced than the Google map had suggested, and with a solid crack of something within the vehicle breaking, his SUV crashed into and through a low berm of dirt and brush and sandy mulch. It plowed into a field on the far side, the front wheels trapped in a bed of sand and loose earth. The airbag exploded. It was an impressive experience.

Shaw heard Eli's vehicle squeal to a stop and, grabbing the grocery bag, he leapt out, taking cover under a rise topped with a stand of forsythia and holly.

"Carter . . . whatever your name is, listen to us." Eli was standing at the roadside, while Hugh leaned against the hood, sweaty, wincing.

"Drop the bag. We'll let you go. Just throw it here. That's all you need to do. It'll all be good."

Shaw hefted the bag by the handle and swung it into the clearing. It flashed as it flew through the headlights of the SUV at the top of the hill.

With the gun now in his hand, Eli made his way over the berm and down into the field, looking about carefully. Peering, of course, for his target. His intent was to murder Shaw the minute he spotted him.

Shaw dug his phone out and sent a text.

No more than five seconds later, the entire field lit up like a football stadium on game night.

A voice over the loudspeaker: "David Ellis, Hugh Garner! This is the FBI. Drop any weapons, lie down on the ground! Do it now, or you will be fired upon."

The speaker was Special Agent Robert Slay.

"Drop your weapons. Down! Now, now! Or we will fire."

Eli hesitated only a moment and dropped the gun. However, he remained standing. "You don't have jurisdiction here! This is illegal. You can't . . ." His voice faded, as his eyes followed Hugh's. The security man was looking back along the road and did as ordered.

"No," Hugh whispered in disgust.

Eli muttered, "Oh, ⬛⬛⬛⬛⬛ . . ." Shaw couldn't help note the irony: those words came from the man who made his living selling resurrection.

A hundred feet behind them was a small stone marker, delineating the Canada/U.S. border. Eli and Hugh had been concentrating so hard on catching Shaw that they'd failed to stop before entering the United States.

Agents ran forward and cuffed them, easing Hugh to the ground carefully because of his gunshot.

An ambulance sped up and the technicians tended to the wounded leg. Both men were read their rights.

Shaw climbed to the road and, pulling off the gloves and pocketing them, joined Slay. Another law enforcer was present too: Detective Laurent Etoile from the San

Francisco Police Department, the man with the resonant baritone. Shaw was surprised he hadn't given the loud-speaker commands; maybe it was a federal vs. state juris-diction thing.

Eli raged, "This is entrapment!"

Slay, searching the men's SUV, looked up. "What?" he asked, distracted.

"This is entrapment."

"No, it's not," the agent said, blasé, and continued with his search.

Eli and Hugh had entered Canada illegally so they had no right to any protections in that country. Anyway, they'd recrossed the border of their own volition and were once again subject to U.S. criminal jurisdiction.

That Shaw had shot an unarmed man in the leg added a wrinkle but he'd had no choice. He needed to get both Eli and Hugh back to the States and if he'd merely fled with the bag it might have been only Hugh who pursued him. The gunshot in the AU's leg guaranteed that Eli himself would have to man the pursuit vehicle.

Eli muttered, "Well, you can't use that as evidence. It's stolen. Illegal!"

Shaw looked him over, thinking of a rule of his own, one hardly up to the level of Ashton, who was, after all, the King of Never. Shaw's was:

Never be dramatic.

But sometimes you needed to indulge yourself. Shaw made a grand show of upending the bag and pouring the contents on the ground. In the light of the headlamps, Eli stared at the newspapers, menus and promotional fly-ers from the motel room: *The Canadian Pacific Railway*

Museum. Visit the Hogworth Maple Syrup Company! The Untold Story of Moody, British Columbia.

Not a single piece of paper that the men had carted away from the Osiris Foundation camp with them—presumably what remained of the incriminating evidence; the rest would have been dumped. It would in fact have been illegal for Shaw to steal the documents.

"We don't need anything more for the prosecution," Detective Etoile said.

From Slay: "All we needed was your asses back in the U. S. of A."

"Oh, ████," Hugh snarled.

The case might have gone a bit easier if they had some of the evidence, but in fact the authorities had plenty to put Hugh and Eli away for a long, long time. Witnesses like Anja, betrayed Inner Circle personnel, Assistance Unit men willing to spill. Steve's notebook was a bombshell.

"How did you find us?" Eli asked Slay.

The agent nodded toward Shaw. "Him."

Shaw shrugged, saying nothing, though thinking it really was a team effort. Shaw's partner had, improbably, been Dalton Crowe.

The search for Eli had started before the cult leader and Hugh had left the Osiris Foundation camp. While the men waited for their luggage in Sheriff Calhoun's SUV, Shaw had dug into his backpack for a notebook to write his name and number on a sheet for the sheriff. But that was just a cover. What he'd actually done was find the GPS tracker that Crowe had hidden on Shaw's Kia, during the pursuit of Erick and Adam. He'd turned it on and stuck the unit in the bottom of Eli's go-bag, sitting in the back of the SUV.

He'd told Slay about it, and the agent had called Crowe to find the log-in details of the unit. But the reward seeker was still pissed off about losing the Erick/Adam rewards and hung up on him. The agent tried to get a warrant to present to the tracking company but no magistrate was willing to issue one, since Crowe had no connection to Eli.

So Shaw had texted Crowe himself and, after some negotiation, he said he'd rent out the tracker codes for ten K—his text agreeing to the final terms was the one Shaw had received while sitting beside Victoria in the Compound earlier.

See you at dinner?

Probably not . . .

The big man would only do the deal, however, if Shaw showed up with the check in person. (To make sure he got the money, of course, though Shaw was sure there was that element of gloat in the demand too, about which Shaw could not have cared less.)

The tracking app had located the men across the border in Moody, British Columbia, where they were undoubtedly staging for a more sophisticated getaway to a location both farther away and far more exotic.

Shaw and Slay were concerned that going through the proper channels with the Royal Canadian Mounted Police would have taken too long, giving the two fugitives a chance to vanish. So they'd hacked together this plan, to lure the men back across the border, as they chased Shaw.

Shaw himself had entered Canada legally at a crossing a few miles away and a man in a U.S. Customs and Border Protection uniform now approached. "Colter Shaw?"

"That's right."

"I'll stamp your passport. Unless you'd want to spend the night back up at the inn in Moody. I hear it's pretty nice."

"No, I'll find someplace here." Handing over the blue booklet to the CBP officer.

The odds were probably ninety percent that no one had seen him shoot Hugh, though if the ten percent came to pass, the consequences would be inconvenient, if not dire. Better to stay stateside.

Which was a shame.

Shaw had never toured a maple syrup factory before.

80.

June 21

After his improvised mining operation in Echo Ridge, Colter Shaw returned with his father's package to the cabin.

Accompanied by Chase only, he walked into the room that had been his father's office, so many years ago.

He glanced at the dozens of framed photos. A particularly good one—crisply focused and in vibrant colors—was of the three siblings, arms about one another. Dorion, Colter and Russell were all smiling.

Shaw cleared a place at the desk and set down the box. He hesitated for a moment. What on earth would he find? People had died for what he was about to see. Was it really as important as the facts surrounding it suggested? Or was it nonsense, the product of his father's dissipating mind? A collection of long-expired grocery store coupons? Or could it even be empty?

The glue at the seams was thick and hard, unbreakable. He used his locking blade knife to cut open the top. He extracted a waterproof pouch, which he also cut open, more carefully than the exterior container.

A large envelope was inside. He tore the top open and removed a half-dozen sheets of paper filled with Ashton's handwritten notes, printouts of articles, and a map of the San Francisco Bay Area, as well as two keys on a ring; they appeared to be for a structure, a house or office. On top was a letter, also written by his father. Shaw smoothed the crackly sheet and leaned forward.

Hello:

My name is Ashton Shaw, former professor, amateur historian and student of political science. Over the course of my years in academia and doing my own research and writing, I grew to distrust most large corporations, institutions and individuals, as well as many politicians and lobbyists—those who thrive in the netherworld between legality and illegality, democracy and dictatorship. I've published numerous articles and organized and attended protests exposing those wrongs.

Of course I received threats from some of the organizations I challenged. For safety's sake I moved my family from the Bay Area to a place where I could better protect them, while continuing my campaign underground. I know this was hard for them. But I saw no other choice.

Working with a few colleagues, I like to think we made some headway in smoothing some of society's rough edges: exposing graft and corruption in the government or corporate world.

And then, a few years ago, I came across BlackBridge Corporate Solutions.

While I was doing research into the dangers posed by big drug companies, I learned that the incidence of addiction in certain lower-middle-class neighborhoods that had little history of drug problems increased suddenly and dramatically, almost overnight. As a result, crime would soar, property values would plummet. The neighborhoods became unlivable.

I learned, to my shock, that this trend was not the natural outgrowth typically facing challenged neighborhoods. The entire drug infestation was engineered by BlackBridge. It's a highly secretive corporate espionage firm, based in Los Angeles. Originally small but now international, it's made up of former corporate executives, intelligence community members, military, mercenary soldiers and even criminals. Its clients are some of the most powerful companies around the world.

Several of those clients hired BlackBridge to engineer a massive decrease in property value of certain target neighborhoods, so their clients could move in and buy up the property at fire-sale prices. BlackBridge did this by creating an artificial drug problem. BlackBridge operatives would flood the neighborhoods with drugs, supplying them virtually for free to gangs. Sometimes they would simply scatter opioids, fentanyl and meth on the streets for anyone— including children—to take. The plan resulted in hundreds of deaths from drugs and crime, and thousands of residents dislocated, many of them becoming homeless.

This real estate scheme, by the way, is simply one of dozens of such dirty-trick projects BlackBridge performs for clients around the world.

I suppose such firms are not uncommon, and you may wonder why BlackBridge became my colleagues' and my—if I may—White Whale.

The answer is simple. A brilliant graduate student in my and several of my colleagues' classes graduated and went on to law school and then was elected a city councilman in San Francisco. We were in touch frequently. Todd became a friend. He was the one who told me about the curious influx of drugs in the district he represented.

He had just begun looking into the matter when he and his wife were murdered. The crime appeared to be a robbery but little was taken and the police found forensic evidence linking the killer to the new drugs found on the street.

My belief is that BlackBridge killed Todd to shut him up. At the very least, they are responsible because of the drugs they seeded into his district.

Nearly all BlackBridge employees refused to talk to us—terrified of the consequences—but I found several who were disgusted with the operations and agreed to meet with me. They wouldn't give me any evidence themselves but they did refer to a former employee, Amos Gahl, who had stolen some documents from the company, something the company was desperate to recover; they believed it was evidence that could bring down BlackBridge and, in doing so, their corrupt clients as well.

Gahl hid these documents somewhere in the San Francisco area, they told me . . . but before he could contact the authorities about them, he was killed in a car crash that did not appear to be accidental.

It became my obsession to find what Gahl had hidden.

Then BlackBridge discovered us.

One by one, under overt or subtle threats, my colleagues backed out of our crusade. Two others died from apparently natural causes that seemed far too coincidental.

The BlackBridge operative in charge of finding us and stopping our search for the evidence—or stealing it from us if we did—is a woman named Irena Braxton. She may look like somebody's grandmother but she's utterly ruthless and does not hesitate to order physical assaults as part of her planning. We had thought she was dead, at the hand of a former assistant of hers no less, but—unfortunately—that report proved to be false. Her search for us continues.

Now, we get around to you.

You've clearly followed the breadcrumbs I've left leading you to Echo Ridge, and now know the whole story.

I can hardly in good conscience ask you to take on this perilous job. No reasonable person would. But if you are so inclined, I will say that in picking up where my search has ended, you'll be fighting to secure justice for those who have perished or had their lives upended by BlackBridge and its clients, and you'll be guaranteeing that thousands in the future will not suffer similar fates.

The map included here indicates the locations in the city that might contain—or lead to—the evidence

Gahl hid. After leaving this letter and accompanying documents, I will be returning to San Francisco and I hope I will have found more leads. They can be found at 618 Alvarez Street in San Francisco.

Finally, let me say this:

Never assume you're safe.

A.S.

81.

An exception to the usual west-to-east rule of the transit of weather in the United States occurs when the bristling Santa Ana winds flow from Southern California and embroil parts north, including the valley in which the Compound sits.

Through the open window of his father's office, Colter Shaw felt the hot breeze now, a leisurely whirlpool throughout the valley where the cabin sat. Today's was a rare wind, the month being June; the crisp Santa Anas are generally an October-to-April phenomenon. But lately they had been appearing earlier, and leaving later. Hotter and stronger too, as anyone who had lost a house to the frequent fires in the state could tragically confirm.

Outside, Mary Dove was walking through a large field, one Colter Shaw knew well. It was where his father's memorial service had been. A sign that the man's mind had not collapsed completely even near the end was his wry funeral instructions:

It's my wish that Ash's ashes be scattered over Crescent Lake.

This ten-acre patch was where the family had raised vegetables, and his mother still did. It was where they had hunted, taking wild turkey and pheasant and more than a few deer, an animal in which evolutionary genetic warnings—this isn't the safest place in the world for you—didn't seem to filter down to subsequent generations.

His mother in fact was on the trail of this evening's dinner at the moment.

Mary Dove was the best hunter in the Shaw family. He could picture her aiming the well-tended Winchester at her prey, sighting through a scuffed Nikon scope, both eyes open. The rifle would be on a steady perch of branch or rock or fencepost.

Never fire a long gun freehand, except in emergencies.

Mary Dove wouldn't squeeze the trigger until she was absolutely certain she had a clean and lethal shot. In all the years of hunting with her, Shaw had never seen her miss, nor use more than one bullet to take game.

Shaw wondered what would be on tonight's menu. At another time, he might have deduced this from the type of firearm she carried—shotgun for pheasant or duck, rifle for boar or venison. But today she wasn't armed. All she wielded now was a pen to sign the truck driver's delivery receipt for the box of groceries. The vehicle sat beside the mailbox at the end of the drive.

Mary Dove tipped the man—it was a twenty-five-mile drive from White Sulfur Springs. She picked up the sizable box effortlessly, as if it held feathers and air, and returned to the cabin.

Shaw's phone hummed. The caller was Sue Bascomb, the woman who was thinking of writing a book about her experience at the Osiris Foundation.

I don't want this to happen to anyone else . . .

"Mr. Shaw." Her voice was animated. "Eli got arrested, he and that horrible man, Hugh. Did you know?"

"Heard something about it, I think."

"I'm working on that book now. I've got the names of two dozen former Companions willing to talk to me. If you're still up for it, I'd really like to interview you."

Shaw said he was, with the caveat he'd mentioned: his name wouldn't appear.

This was fine with her. She explained that as a journalist she frequently used unnamed sources. It was completely ethical as long as there was corroboration when it came to controversial statements.

They picked a place to meet: her home, she said, was in Seattle, and they agreed on Tacoma, where Shaw had some follow-up business.

Shaw rose and joined his mother, as she unpacked steaks and chicken and an elaborate pie.

Mary Dove lifted an eyebrow.

He showed her the contents of Ashton's hidden treasure. She read the letter carefully, then skimmed the rest. She poked her glasses higher and reviewed the map of San Francisco. Shook her head and looked at her son.

"BlackBridge. Never heard of it." She sighed. "But I remember when Todd and Cathy Foster died. It was terrible. Ash was very close to him. That explains a lot." She tapped the letter. "This is real, what he's worried about. This isn't from his illness."

Shaw agreed. His father's paranoia and breaks with reality had resulted in plenty of bizarre scribblings. These notes, however, were articulate and based on actual events; his concern was genuine.

Besides, there was that run-in Shaw himself had had with the BlackBridge hitman, Ebbitt Droon, a few weeks ago, which assured him these documents were legitimate.

Shaw's glance was to the outside, watching the hot breeze tilt needlegrass and graceful pink Muhlenbergia. The wind raised timid eddies of dust on the edge of the green. He was thinking of Droon's shark eyes, the expert way he'd held his weapon. The ruthlessness of his mission.

I like hurting people. And I hurt in ways that change them. Forever.

"Did Ashton ever mention the house on Alvarez?"

"No."

Upon learning that their spouse had a secret hideaway, some women would immediately think: love nest. He's cheating. But not Mary Dove; no one was more faithful to his wife than Ashton Shaw.

Lifting his phone, Shaw showed his mother a text he'd just received from his private eye.

618 Alvarez is a single-family dwelling, three stories, 1200 square feet, owned by a corporation established under California law years ago. DCR Holdings. Tax and upkeep paid for by investments. Sufficient assets and income to keep the property going in perpetuity. Conducted brief interviews with neighboring businesses. They report that

they have seen a man in his thirties entering the house
from time to time recently. Possible a home sitting
service. No further information.

She smiled. "DCR Holdings."

Dorion, Colter, Russell.

So. His father had a safe house, where he had met with
his colleagues as they planned the demise of BlackBridge.
And the house was still operative.

He told his mother, "These people—Braxton and
Droon—probably know about you and Dorie. I'll call
Tom Pepper. He'll pull strings and get a couple of
watchers—here and outside Dorie's."

"I won't object to that. But . . ." Mary Dove lifted
the tail of her blouse and revealed the grip of a Glock,
the .45, sitting in a hip holster. "We're good for now."
She let the cloth drop and turned to a cutting board,
saying, as if she didn't have a care in the world, "Dinner
in a few hours. Alert the crew."

82.

olter Shaw and Victoria Lesston sat on the porch in the Compound. The hour was nearly midnight and a stately crescent of moon sat high in the inky sky.

The Santa Anas were relaxed at the moment and the residual breeze was merely warm and comforting. The soundtrack was the rustle of stalky plants, owls and distant coyotes, the occasional wolf.

He had a beer, she a glass of wine. Chase sat at their feet. His ears would prick up occasionally, maybe hearing or smelling a potential intruder. But nothing drove him to his feet or rose hackles. Shaw could settle him with a soft, "Okay, boy." There was a collar around his neck connected to a leash looped around Shaw's chair leg. Night was predator time, and Shaw wanted to make sure the rottie didn't go off to defend the kingdom in the face of insurmountable odds.

The cabin was dim and quiet; everyone else had gone to bed.

The two of them talked and talked, sharing stories.

Shaw spoke of the Never rules of his father's making, and the survival skills he'd taught the children, which paralleled much of Victoria's training in the military.

"What branch?" he asked.

"Delta Force."

The special ops branch of the Army.

Victoria explained that 1st Special Forces Operational Detachment-Delta, known more commonly as "the Unit," had been recruiting women soldiers for the field, not desk assignments, for thirty years.

They compared notes on incidents that had occurred on his reward jobs and her security work. Immersion in ice water. Making a weapon—and a particularly insidious one—out of a rosebush. Various sustaining, if disgusting, improvised meals in the field.

He told her about the time he and his fourteen-year-old sister had rappelled down a three-hundred-foot cliff to avoid a pack of wolves at the summit.

"They only hunt at night," was her reply.

"That's a fact."

"Well," was her response. "That means you did a descent in the dark. You have moonlight?"

He said no and asked if she'd had any unusual descents.

"A few." Spoken in a deflecting way.

"Okay. How far was the longest?"

"I don't know, about four hundred."

"Not bad."

A moment of debate apparently. "Okay, actually, it was yards."

A quarter mile straight down.

Shaw said, "You get the trophy."

They sat in silence for a moment, until Victoria stretched and winced, as the shoulder took some unexpected stress.

"Think I'm feeling tired," she said.

He was too.

Shaw walked her to the bedroom that had been Dorie's. The decorations were mostly prints of Native Americans, wild animals, dogs and, for some reason, old-time locomotives, which his sister had been obsessed with as a girl.

When they stopped, Victoria turned to face Shaw. Her maneuver was of a certain caliber, sure and unmistakable. She lifted her hair away from her face. Colter Shaw put his hand on her good shoulder, leaned slightly down, and kissed her firmly. She pressed fully into him. Chase was gazing at them with that look of blended understanding and confusion that only dogs can muster. After a too-brief quarter minute, Victoria eased away.

"'Night," she whispered and walked into her room.

83.

June 22

The weather in Gig Harbor had changed considerably from the last time he'd been here.

The sun was brilliant, not a wisp of fog or cloud to be seen. The green swath of pine was radiant, the water blue as sapphire.

Shaw steered the Winnebago through the entrance gate. The two pillars holding the cast-iron panels were crowned with angels made of concrete. The poor creatures were grimy and their wings weather-smoothed.

He braked to a stop and scanned the grounds. The battered, green pickup truck he sought was not far away. He steered toward it and parked behind. Taking an 8-by-10 envelope from the seat beside him, he climbed out of the camper and walked up to the man who stood over a new grave.

"Mr. Harper."

The broad-shouldered man appeared startled, apparently not having heard the camper arrive and park. He frowned, thought a moment. "Shaw."

Adam's was a simple tombstone. Name and the dates of birth and death. No angels, no bas-reliefs like in the Study Room in the Foundation's camp.

The name on the neighboring tombstone was Kelly Mae Harper.

Shaw said, "There's something I want to tell you."

A shrug of the man's big shoulders.

"When Adam was away for those three weeks, after your wife died?"

Stan Harper's response was a tip of his head.

"You said when he came back his moods were better."

"Was like when he was a kid, when he was happy. His troubles didn't hit until he was a teenager. What's any of this matter, Shaw?" A glance toward the grave at his feet. A ragged: "He's gone."

"Those three weeks he was away? He was in a cult."

"Cult?"

"It's been in the news. Osiris Foundation."

Looking blankly at the ground, Stan muttered, "And?"

"What the cult taught was that after we die we come back."

"Like . . . reincarnation?"

Shaw said, "Something like that."

· "And Adam believed it?"

"Yes, he did. It gave him comfort. Before he died he was convinced he'd be with his family again. In another life. His mother, you."

Harper grunted a laugh. Shaw couldn't tell what his reaction to this odd news might really be.

"That's all bullshit. All of it. The church too. Heaven, hell. Way *I* feel anyway. After Kelly."

"It meant something to Adam."

Stan was silent.

"Here." Shaw handed him the envelope. Harper looked inside and extracted Adam's Osiris Foundation notebook, the one Frederick had given him.

Harper glanced at the cover. *The Process.*

"It was Adam's. Like a diary. He wrote down his thoughts and memories. What he liked about his life, what he didn't."

The bad feelings—anger, fear, sorrow—and the good ones—joy, love, comfort. We call them—how clever is this? The Minuses and the Pluses . . .

Shaw had skimmed it. The passages weren't very grammatical, they rambled and ranted. There were irrelevant doodles. But some of the Pluses included memories of times spent with his father.

"I don't want it. Why would I want it?" He stuffed the notebook in the envelope and handed it back, then glanced down to the grave. "Don't know why I came. Thought I'd feel something. Thought I'd think something."

"Goodbye, Mr. Harper."

The man didn't reply.

Shaw started back to the Winnebago. He was halfway there when he heard. "Hold on."

Harper was walking up to him. "Maybe I'll hold on to that. Just . . . Well, maybe I will."

Shaw handed the envelope to him.

Harper took it and returned to his pickup, fishing keys from his pocket.

84.

The Winnebago was parked in a Walmart lot near Tacoma.

Wearing a sweatshirt and jeans, Shaw was at the dinette, on which sat a thick file folder he'd labeled *Ashton Shaw Material*. The map of the San Francisco Bay Area that sat on the top was wrinkled and stained. Shaw was looking over the eighteen *X*'s, most of them in the north—Marin County and on up into wine country. Napa, Sonoma.

The map included here indicates the locations in the city that might contain—or lead to—the evidence Gahl hid.

He was sipping a fine Honduran coffee, which was laced with just the right amount of milk. That was always a question: too little was fixable, too much not.

There was a rapping on the door.

"Mr. Shaw? It's Sue Bascomb."

Shaw slipped the map into the file and opened the door. The camper sagged slightly as she climbed in. The stocky woman was wearing a dark green, long-sleeved dress and black cardigan sweater.

He offered her coffee, which she declined, and they sat at the small table. She asked questions she'd prepared. He answered into a recording app on her phone, and she took notes as well. Shaw declined to give any personal information and, of course, said nothing about Victoria.

He did report in detail on the beating of the reporter Klein and the horrific murder of John. He said nothing specific about Abby, though he described sexual assaults in general. These details seemed to interest her the most.

After a half hour, she said, "That's very good, Mr. Shaw."

"'Colter' is fine."

"Helpful. Quite helpful." She then flipped through her notes and seemed about to ask another question, a follow-up perhaps, when they heard a shout from the parking lot.

They both rose to their feet quickly. "There's a fire, a car," she said, peering through the shade. Shaw grabbed one of the extinguishers he kept near the driver's seat and pushed outside.

An SUV nearby was engulfed in flames, smoke spiraling skyward like a black tornado. It took him back immediately to John's horrific death, which he'd just been recounting.

People were running from the store and their own cars to see what was happening.

"There's somebody inside! Look!"

"Call nine-one-one."

"Stand back! It could blow up!"

Shaw hurried to the vehicle and let fly a stream of extinguisher foam. It didn't do much, though it did suppress a portion of the flames long enough to make it clear that the SUV was unoccupied. What someone had taken for a human was just a stack of packages.

There were several loud pops.

"Those're bullets!" a man cried, and people fled.

Shaw didn't bother to tell them that, no, that's not what burning bullets sound like. What they'd heard was probably food jars exploding.

In the distance he heard sirens.

He set the spent canister in the grassy divider and returned to the camper. Stepping inside, he climbed to the floor and stopped. The woman had left.

She wasn't the only thing that was gone.

The file labeled *Ashton Shaw Material* was missing too.

85.

Outside the camper, there was no sign of the car she'd arrived in.

He might have caught a glimpse but her associate had ignited a vehicle that was upwind of the Winnebago, so that the choking smoke obscured the view of the getaway.

Smart.

Shaw returned inside and did a fast inventory. The bedroom was still locked and she wouldn't have had time to pick the elaborate locks. Still, he needed to check.

Yes, everything was accounted for. His own go-bag (called by survivalists GTHO, as in "Get the Hell Out," or in an R-rated version, GTFO). Then weapons: for handguns the .357 Colt Python and a .40 Glock. His favorite long gun too, a Lee Enfield No. 4 Mk2. The British bolt-action rifle was sixty years old and battered and scuffed but reliable as an iron-block V-8 and devilishly accurate. There was plenty of ammunition too, cleaning gear and his best Nikon telescopic sight.

Would he need the firepower? No idea.

Yet he recalled his father's letter.

Never assume you're safe . . .

His phone hummed with a text. It was from Victoria.

A rare smile crossed his lips as he read.

He thought for a moment and then sent a reply.

Then, time for work.

He texted Mack McKenzie, who was ready and waiting in Washington, D.C.

Sending picture via email.

Her reply:

K.

Shaw then went to the kitchen counter and lifted the Sony digital camera from where he'd hidden it behind a stack of coffee bags and cups. He removed the SD card and, on his computer, found a good, full-face image of the woman who had been sitting eight feet from the camera ten minutes ago.

This he sent in an encrypted email to Mack.

A moment later his phone dinged.

Searching now.

Mack's internet expert would use facial recognition to find matches everywhere it could online and begin assembling a dossier on Shaw's visitor.

Who was not Sue Bascomb, an Apprentice at the

Osiris Foundation camp—that name was just a cover. Shaw was sure that the woman was Irena Braxton, the BlackBridge operative who had devoted years to finding the damning evidence that Ashton and his colleagues were looking for—and eliminating them in the process.

He had not originally suspected her. When she'd come up to him at the camp, proposing a book about Eli and the dangers of the Foundation, he'd believed she was legitimate.

But during her phone call to him later she'd alluded to the fact she was a journalist. That certainly would have been a good cover to get close to Shaw. Except for one detail she didn't know: Eli would never let a reporter into the camp as a Companion. She was lying.

He recalled too what his father had written about Braxton:

She may look like somebody's grandmother but she's utterly ruthless . . .

Shaw tried to figure out how they'd orchestrated the theft.

He supposed Braxton and Droon—who was probably the SUV arsonist—could have followed Shaw to the camp or intercepted his phone calls and texts and learned what he had planned. He changed phones frequently and used burners but as his FBI friend, Tom Pepper, said, "If they wanta listen to you they're gonna listen."

From the hills above the camp, the two could have observed what the Foundation was about. After Shaw's speech exposing Eli, which they would have heard, Braxton saw an opportunity to get close to him. When the authorities arrived, she could have just strolled into the chaotic camp, put a discarded amulet around her neck and walked up to Shaw with the story about writing of her experience.

Her goal, of course, was to find out whatever information he had about Ashton's search for Amos Gahl's evidence.

Shaw had to plan countermeasures carefully. At the meeting with her this afternoon, they might try to strong-arm and torture him. He was prepared for that; he now wore body armor under the sweats, and his .380 Glock was in his back waistband. Also, he had an open phone line with Mack, throughout the conversation with "Bascomb." The PI would call the local police if it turned violent.

But why not avoid a fight? Shaw made it easy for them: He left out, in plain sight, the A.S. file.

Which was, of course, fake.

Shaw had photographed the real file and uploaded the material, encrypted, to both his and Mack's secure servers, then hidden it in a secret compartment in the floorboards of the Winnebago.

On the map in the fake file, Shaw had marked areas of the San Francisco region that were in the opposite direction of those of the actual map, which were places where Amos Gahl had hidden the evidence that could bring down BlackBridge and its clients.

The rest of the material in the mock file was meaningless—and misleading—downloads from years ago, at the time when Ashton and his colleagues were actively looking for the incriminating evidence.

The file Braxton had stolen would lead them in dizzying circles.

Shaw fired up the camper's engine, dropped the transmission into gear and pulled out of the parking lot, now filled with rescue vehicles, smoke and excited shoppers taking selfies with the smoldering SUV.

He steered south. In seven or eight hours he'd be at his destination: San Francisco, his specific journey's end. Ashton's safe house on Alvarez Street.

As he piloted the comfortable—and comforting—vehicle along the smooth highways, Colter Shaw was thinking this: it was a possibility, of course, that Ashton had hidden the package for the benefit of his colleagues, who'd decided to forgo the safety of anonymity and take on BlackBridge once again.

But if so, why hide the material on Echo Ridge? He could easily have picked a place in the Bay Area.

No, the more he thought about it, the more convinced he was that the letter was directed not to any colleagues, but to one of his *children*. They alone would know how his mind worked—the scent tracking, for instance—and could find the document, when no one else could.

They alone had the wherewithal to confront the risks posed by BlackBridge. Ashton had, of course, trained them so rigorously throughout their young lives in the fine art of survival.

But which of the siblings did Ashton intend the letter to be read by?

He had an inkling that it was he, Colter the Restless

One, who'd been in his father's thoughts when he set down his plea for help in the letter, jotting in such fine penmanship, better even than Shaw's.

The odds that this was Ashton's intent? Impossible to say. Maybe ninety percent, maybe ten.

In the end, it didn't matter. Colter Shaw had made his decision. The father's quest was now the son's.

Author's Note

Cults and cult-like organizations—of which there are presently tens of thousands active in America—have been the subject of voluminous books, articles and documentaries over the years. Here are a sampling of titles from some of the sources I found helpful in researching *The Goodbye Man*, if you're interested in further reading:

American Messiahs by Adam Morris;

Banished: Surviving My Years in the Westboro Baptist Church by Lauren Drain;

Born into the Children of God: My Life in a Religious Sex Cult and My Struggle for Survival on the Outside by Natacha Tormey;

Cartwheels in a Sari: A Memoir of Growing Up Cult by Jayanti Tamm;

Daughter of the Saints: Growing Up in Polygamy by Dorothy Allred Solomon;

Girl at the End of the World: My Escape from Fundamentalism in Search of Faith with a Future by Elizabeth Esther;

Going Clear: Scientology, Hollywood, and the Prison of Belief by Lawrence Wright;

Heaven's Gate: America's UFO Religion by Benjamin E. Zeller;

In the Shadow of the Moons: My Life in the Reverend Sun Myung Moon's Family by Nansook Hong;

A Journey to Waco: Autobiography of a Branch Davidian by Clive Doyle, with Catherine Wessinger and Matthew D. Wittmer;

Manson: The Life and Times of Charles Manson by Jeff Guinn;

Prophet's Prey: My Seven-Year Investigation into Warren Jeffs and the Fundamentalist Church of Latter-Day Saints by Sam Brower;

Radical: My Journey out of Islamic Extremism by Maajid Nawaz;

The Road to Jonestown: Jim Jones and Peoples Temple by Jeff Guinn;

Ruthless: Scientology, My Son David Miscavige, and Me by Ron Miscavige;

Seductive Poison: A Jonestown Survivor's Story of Life and Death in the People's Temple by Deborah Layton;

Shattered Dreams: My Life as a Polygamist's Wife by Irene Spencer;

The Sound of Gravel: A Memoir by Ruth Wariner;

Stolen Innocence: My Story of Growing Up In a Polygamous Sect, Becoming a Teenage Bride, and Breaking Free of Warren Jeffs by Elissa Wall with Lisa Pulitzer;

Stories from Jonestown by Leigh Fondakowski;

A Thousand Lives: The Untold Story of Jonestown by Julia Scheeres;

Troublemaker: Surviving Hollywood and Scientology by Leah Remini;

Massacre at Waco: The Shocking True Story of Cult Leader David Koresh and the Branch Davidians by Clifford L. Linedecker;

The Unbreakable Miss Lovely: How the Church of Scientology Tried to Destroy Paulette Cooper by Tony Ortega;

Under the Banner of Heaven: A Story of Violent Faith by Jon Krakauer;

Underground: The Tokyo Gas Attack and the Japanese Psyche by
    Haruki Murakami;
*The World in Flames: A Black Boyhood in a White Supremacist
    Doomsday Cult* by Jerald Walker.

Acknowledgments

Writing a novel is, for me at least, never a one-person operation. I'd like to thank the following for their vital assistance in shaping this book into what you have just read: Mark Tavani, Madeline Hopkins, Danielle Dieterich, Julie Reece Deaver, Jane Davis, Francesca Cinelli, Seba Pezzani, Jennifer Dolan and Madelyn Warcholik; and, on the other side of the pond, Julia Wisdom, Finn Cotton, Felicity Blunt and Anne O'Brien. And my deepest gratitude, as always, to the incomparable Deborah Schneider.

Just hours after the harrowing events of *The Never Game* and *The Goodbye Man*, Colter Shaw finds himself in San Francisco, where he has taken on the mission his father began years ago: finding a missing courier bag containing evidence that will bring down a corporate espionage firm responsible for hundreds, perhaps thousands, of deaths. Following the enigmatic clues his father left behind, Shaw plays cat and mouse with the company's sadistic enforcers as he speeds from one gritty neighborhood in the City by the Bay to another. Suddenly, the job takes on a frightening urgency: only by finding the courier bag can he expose the company and stop the murder of an entire family—slated to die in forty-eight hours.

With the help of an unexpected figure from his past and with the enforcers closing the net, Shaw narrows in on the truth—and learns that the courier bag contains something unexpected: a secret that could only be described as catastrophic.

Filled with dozens of twists and reversals, *The Final Twist* is a nonstop race against time to save the family . . . and to keep the devastating secret Shaw has uncovered from falling into the wrong hands.

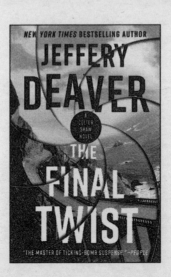

NEW YORK TIMES BESTSELLING AUTHOR

JEFFERY DEAVER

COLTER SHAW NOVEL

THE FINAL TWIST

"THE MASTER OF TICKING-BOMB SUSPENSE." —PEOPLE

The Steelworks

Colter Shaw draws his gun. He starts silently down the stairs, descending into the old building's massive, pungent basement, redolent of mold and heating oil.

Basement, he reflects. Recalling the last time he was in one. And what had happened to him there.

Above him, music pounds, feet dance. The bass is a runner's heartbeat. But up there and down here are separate universes.

At the foot of the stairs he studies where he is. Orientation . . . Always, orientation. The basement is half built out. To the right of the stairs is a large empty space. To the left are rooms off a long corridor—fifty feet or so in length.

Scanning the empty space to the right, he sees no threat nor anything that would help him. He turns left and navigates toward the corridor past the boilers and stores of supplies: large packs of toilet paper, cans of Hormel chili, plastic water bottles, paper towels, Dixie paper plates, plastic utensils. A brick of 9 mm ammunition.

Shaw moves slowly into the corridor. The first room on

the right, the door open, is illuminated by cold overhead light and warmer flickering light. Remaining in shadows, he peers in quickly. An office. File cabinets, computers, a printer.

Two bulky men sit at a table, watching a baseball game on a monitor. One leans back and takes the last beer from the six-pack sitting on a third chair. Shaw knows they're armed because he knows their profession, and such men are always armed.

Shaw is not invisible but the basement is dark, no overheads, and he's in a black jacket, jeans, and—since he's been motorcycling—boots. They're not as quiet as the Eccos he usually wears but the beat bleeding from the dance floor overhead dampens his footsteps. He supposes it would even drown out gunshots.

The men watch the game and talk and joke. There are four empty bottles. This might be helpful. The reaction time issue. The accuracy issue.

If it comes to that.

He thinks: Disarm them now?

No. It could go bad . . . 75 percent chance of success, at best.

He hears his father's voice: Never be blunt when subtle will do.

Besides, he isn't sure what he'll find here. If nothing, he'll slip out the way he came, with them none the wiser.

He eases past the doorway, unseen, then pauses to give his eyes, momentarily dulled by the office lights, a chance to acclimate to the darkness.

Then he moves on, checking each room. Most of the doors are open; most of the rooms are dark.

The music, the pounding of the dancing feet, are a two-edged sword. No one can hear him approach, but he's just as deaf. Someone could be in the empty room, having spotted him, waiting with a weapon.

Thirty feet, forty.

Empty room, empty room. He's approaching the end. Ahead, the corridor turns to the right. There'll be other rooms to search. How many more?

The last room. This door is closed. Locked.

He withdraws his locking-blade knife and uses the edge near the tip to ease the deadbolt back into the tumbler. He pulls on the door to keep the bolt from snapping back into place as he gets a new grip with the blade. After repeating a dozen times, the door is free. Knife away, gun drawn and raised, finger off the trigger.

Inside.

The woman is Black, in her early twenties, hair in a complicated braid. She wears jeans and a dusty gray sweatshirt. She sees the gun and inhales to scream. He holds up a hand and instantly holsters the weapon. "It's okay. You're going to be okay. I'm getting you out of here. What's your name?"

She doesn't speak for a moment. Then, "Nita."

"I'm John. You'll be all right."

The place is filthy. Uneaten chili sits in a flat pile on a paper plate. A bottle of water is half drunk. There's a bucket for a toilet. She's not bound but she is restrained: a bicycle cable is looped around a water or sewage pipe and her ankle is zip-tied to the cable. Shaw shuts the light off. There's enough illumination to see by.

Shaw looks back into the corridor. The flicker from the

screen continues with the ball game. What inning is it? Would be important to know.

"Are you hurt?"

She shakes her head.

He takes his knife out and opens it with a click. He saws through the tie and helps her to her feet. She's unsteady.

"Can you walk?"

A nod. She's shivering and crying. "I want to go home."

Shaw recalls thinking of the game Rock, Paper, Scissors just ten minutes ago. He wishes he'd played harder, much harder.

They step into the corridor. And just then, Shaw thinks: The third chair.

Oh, hell.

The six-pack didn't need its own seat. Someone else was in the office watching the game.

And at that moment the man comes down the stairs. Just as he sets foot on the concrete floor he glances up the corridor and sees Shaw and Nita. The six-pack drops to the ground. At least one bottle shatters. He calls, "Hey!" And reaches for his hip.

In the baseball room, the flickering stops.

PART ONE

June 24

THE MISSION

Time until the family dies: 52 hours.

The safe house.

At last.

Colter Shaw's journey to this cornflower-blue Victorian on scruffy Alvarez Street in the Mission District of San Francisco had taken him weeks. From Silicon Valley to the Sierra Nevadas in Eastern California to Washington State. Or, as he sat on his Yamaha motorcycle, looking up at the structure, he reflected: in a way, it had taken him most of his life.

As is often the case when one arrives at a long-anticipated destination, the structure seemed modest, ordinary, unimposing. Though if it contained what Shaw hoped for, it would prove to be just the opposite: a mine of information that saved hundreds, perhaps thousands, of lives.

But as the son of a survivalist, Shaw had a preliminary question: Just how safe a safe house was it?

From this angle, it appeared deserted, dark. He dropped the transmission in gear and drove to the alley that ran behind the house, where he paused again in front of an overgrown garden encircled by a gothic wrought-iron fence. From here, still no lights, no signs of habitation, no motion. He gunned the engine and returned to the front. He skidded to a stop and low-gear muscled the bike onto the sidewalk.

He snagged his heavy backpack, chained up the bike and helmet, then pushed through a three-foot deep planting bed that bordered the front. Behind a boxwood he found the circuit breakers for the main line. If there were an unlikely bomb inside it would probably be hardwired; whether it was phones or computers or improvised explosive devices, it was always tricky to depend on batteries.

Using the keys he'd been bequeathed, he unlocked and pushed open the door, hand near his weapon. He was greeted only with white noise and the scent of lavender air freshener.

Before he searched for the documents he hoped his father had left, he needed to clear the place.

No evidence of threat isn't synonymous with *No threat*.

He scanned the ground floor. Beyond the living room was a parlor, from which a stairway led upstairs. Past that room was a dining room and, in the back, a kitchen, whose door, reinforced and windowless, led onto the alleyway. Another door in the kitchen led to the cellar, an unusual feature in much of California. The few pieces of furniture were functional and mismatched. The walls were the color of old bone, curtains sun-bleached to inadvertent tie-dye patterns.

He took his time examining every room on this floor and on the second and third stories. No sign of current residents, but he did find bed linens neatly folded on a mattress on the second floor.

Last, the basement.

He clicked on his tactical halogen flashlight, with its piercing beam, to descend and see that the room was largely empty. A few old cans of paint, a broken table. At the far end was a coal bin, in which a small pile of glistening black lumps sat. Shaw smiled to himself.

Ever the survivalist, weren't you, Ashton?

As he stared into the murk, he noted three wires dangling from the rafters. One, near the stairs, ended in a fixture and a small bulb. The wires in the middle and far end had been cut and the ends were wrapped with electrician's tape.

Shaw knew why the two had been operated on: to keep someone from getting a good view of the end of the cellar.

Shining the beam over the back wall, he stepped close.

Got it, Ash.

As with the rest of the basement, this wall was constructed of four-by-eight plywood sheets nailed to studs, floor to ceiling, painted flat black. But an examination of the seams of one panel revealed a difference. It was a hidden door, opening onto a secure room. He took the locking-blade knife from his pocket and flicked it open. After scanning the surface a moment longer, he located a slit near the bottom. He pushed the blade inside and heard a click. The door sprung outward an inch. Replacing the knife and drawing his gun, he crouched, shining the beam inside, holding the flashlight high and to the left to draw fire, if an enemy were present and armed.

He reached inside and felt for trip wires. None.

He slowly drew the door toward him with his foot.

It had moved no more than eighteen inches when the bomb exploded with a searing flash and a stunning roar and a piece of shrapnel took him in the chest.

The risk in detonations is usually not death.

Most victims of an IED are blinded, deafened, or mutilated. Modern bomb materials move at more than 30,000 feet per second; the shock wave could travel from sea level to the top of Mount Everest in the time it takes to clear your throat.

Shaw lay on the floor, unable to see, unable to hear, coughing, in pain. He touched the spot where the shrapnel had slammed into him. Sore. But no wound. For some reason the skin hadn't broken. He did a fast inventory of the rest of his body. His arms, hands and legs still functioned.

Now: Find his weapon. A bomb is often a prelude to an attack.

He could see nothing but, on his knees, he patted the damp concrete in a circular pattern until he located the gun.

Squinting, but still seeing nothing. You can't *will* your vision to work.

No time for panic, no time for thinking of the consequences to his lifestyle if he'd been permanently blinded or deafened. Rock climbing, motorbiking, traveling the country—all endangered, but not something to worry about right now.

But how could he tell where the assault was coming from? In a crouch he moved to where he thought the coal bin was. It would at least provide some cover. He tried to listen but all he could hear was a tinnitus-like ringing in his ears.

After five desperate minutes he was aware of a faint glow coalescing at the far end of the cellar. Light from the kitchen above.

So his vision wasn't gone completely. He'd been temporarily blinded by the brilliance of the explosion. Finally he could make out the beam of his tac light. It was ten feet away. He collected it and shone the bright light throughout the basement and into the room on the other side of the hidden door.

No attackers.

He holstered his weapon and snapped his finger beside each ear. His hearing was returning too.

Then he assessed.

What had just happened?

If the bomber had wanted an intruder dead, that could've easily been arranged. Shaw shone his light on the frame of the hidden door and saw the smoking device, gray metal. It was a large flash bang—designed with combustible materials that, when detonated, emit blinding light and stunning sound but don't fling shrapnel. Its purpose was to serve as a warning.

He looked carefully to see why he'd missed it. Well, interesting. The device was a projectile. It had been launched from a shelf near the door, rigged to explode after a half second or so. This is what had hit him in the chest. The trigger would be a motion or proximity detector. Shaw had never heard of a mechanism like this.

He carefully scanned the room for more traps. He found none.

Who had set it? His father and his colleagues had likely made the secret room, but they probably would not have left the grenade. Ashton Shaw never worked with explosives. Possessing them without a license was illegal, and, for all his father's serious devotion to survivalism and distrust of authority, he didn't break the law.

Never give the authorities that kind of control over you.

Then Shaw confirmed his father could not have created the trap. When he examined the device more closely under the searing white beam, he noted that it was military-issue and bore a date stamp of last year.

Shaw flicked on an overhead light and tucked his gun and flashlight away. He saw a battered utility table in the center of the twenty-by-twenty space, an old wooden chair, shelves that were largely bare but held some papers and clothes. Other stacks of documents sat against the wall. A large olive-drab duffle bag was in the corner.

On the table were scores of papers.

Was this it? The hidden treasure that people—his father among them—had died for?

He walked around the table, so he was facing the doorway and bent forward to find out.